UNTAMED

REDFORD RANCH
BOOK ONE

ARIEL HENDRIX

MJ HENDRIX PUBLISHING LTD.

ABOUT THIS BOOK

She's a Dixon. A good girl. The mayor's daughter.
I'm a Redford. A bull rider with a criminal record.
And if our family rivalry wasn't enough, Rosie Dixon is my
little brother's ex.
Off-limits.
When I'm released early from the prison her father put me in
for shedding Dixon blood, seeing her working on my family's
ranch is the opposite of a welcome home. Her father is
determined to ruin us.
I want her gone almost as much as I want her body.
But I have a strong suspicion that the only reason she's here
is to spy on me, and I've learned to keep my enemies close.
Even so, finding her in my bed in the middle of the night is a
shock.
But when she's beside me, the nightmares don't come. And
there's no better revenge I can extract from Mayor Dixon
than stealing his daughter's heart.

All I have to do is guard mine.

Previously published under the pen name Mj Hendrix.

REDFORD RANCH
WHERE BLOOD IS THICKER THAN WATER

UNTAMED

UNGUARDED

UNRAVELED

UNBRIDLED

PLAYLIST

Listen on Spotify.

Sunrise by Ryan Bingham
Pretty Little Poison by Warren Zeiders
Tourniquet by Zach Bryan
Something's Gonna Kill Me by Corey Kent
Straight and Narrow by Sam Barber
Hate Me by Track45
Weight of Your World by Chris Stapleton
Marfa Lights by Kaitlin Butts
To Hell & Back by Maren Morris
Angel of the Morning by Juice Newton
Cowboy Kind of Love by The Castellows
Steady Heart by Kameron Marlowe
Wish I Never Felt by Nate Smith

For the girls who think a man in Wranglers with no shirt is 10x hotter than a well-tailored suit.

1

ROSIE
THREE AND A HALF YEARS EARLIER

None of the men around here are dumb enough to fuck with the Redford brothers.

But I'm not a man, and I have no sense of self-preservation.

I let out an exasperated sigh as I stomp toward the barn, searching for Dolly, the only girl in the Redford family and my best friend since first grade.

Duke, Dolly's brother, is about to be stripped of his title as my boyfriend if he doesn't stop pissing me off. He's been an ass all day, and I just got done telling him to leave me the hell alone before I go around spreading a rumor that his dick is the size of a baby carrot.

My daddy already hates his entire family with a burning passion. It wouldn't be too hard to get the rest of the town on the anti-Redford brothers train that the mayor is happily joyriding.

"Dolly? Where the hell are you?"

It's midnight on a moonless Saturday night. I can't see shit. My boot catches on something in the dark, pitching me forward and nearly landing me face-first in the dirt. I steady myself, resisting the urge to scream at the top of my lungs in frustration.

My mama says the short temper I have came straight from my grandmother on my father's side, the only other redhead in the family.

"Some *best friend* you are, Doll, abandoning me during a squabble with your stupid brother," I mutter into the night.

I finally reach the big red barn, searching around for the cold metal handle in the pitch-black February night. My fingers finally make contact with the steel. I shove the massive door open, and a dim light from inside spills out to illuminate the scattered hay on the floor of the barn.

"Dolly?" I'm whispering now, trying to avoid waking up any of the horses who might be sleeping. Duke's been training one for a while now that's meaner than a rattlesnake mama with brand-new babies.

My boots don't make a sound as I inch farther inside, peering around in the shadows in search of an ebony head of hair. The Redford matriarch was a full-blooded Tigua Native American, and all her kids have the thick, dark hair from their mother. Dolly was only eight when she died, and we were already best friends. I grieved the deep loss with her, and we grew as close as sisters.

My skin starts to crawl as I step farther in. The barn is lined with high stacks of hay bales, which can be crawling with snakes and rats. They're nocturnal creatures, so this is their ideal playtime.

I was raised in the country, but that doesn't mean I like

things that slither. I reach into the back pocket of my jeans for my phone.

I could try calling her again.

A rustling sound comes from the hay to my left, causing me to jolt in fear and take a step back. I remain frozen in place, listening for more signs of life that would indicate a human's presence instead of an animal.

A soft moan, followed by more rustling, reaches my ears. My taut muscles relax. I wonder who would possibly be in the barn at this time of night, doing ... things. Curiosity gets the best of my virginal mind, causing me to step forward again.

I search the stacks of hay bales for where the sound is coming from, curious to see if it's Dolly and one of the ranch hands. Last I heard, none of them were even cute enough to flirt with, much less fool around in the hay with. Dolly wouldn't do anything like that without telling me first.

I take another step forward, holding my breath so I don't get spotted by whoever it could be.

Finally, I see a head of hair that nearly blends in with the hay. It's blond, so I immediately know it's not my best friend. The head is moving ever so slightly, which ignites even more curiosity in me to see what the hell they're doing and who it's with.

I take another step closer, eliminating the last bale obscuring my vision before screeching to a halt.

The blond head facing away from me is bobbing up and down in front of a rippling set of tanned and toned abs. My eyes travel over his muscular frame and up to the ebony head of hair that's attached to the face of a man I *instantly* recognize.

Holden.

Holden James Redford, the oldest of the Redford brothers.

His pink lips are parted, chiseled jawline as sharp as ever in the dim light from the lantern hanging on the wall a few feet away from him. I notice the shotgun he usually carries on his horse is leaned up against the wall underneath the lantern.

His eyes are closed, and his face is bathed in ecstasy. He reaches his veiny hand forward, gripping the roots of the blonde's hair as he guides her head down over his dick.

I swallow over the lump in my throat, unable to command my limbs to move back before he sees me.

Holden is known for hooking up with girls in the barn. I've heard the stories. Ever since the girls in my class were old enough to care, they've been counting down the days until their eighteenth birthday, all hoping for a chance to spend an evening rolling around in the hay with the oldest Redford brother, like it's some kind of badge of honor. He only hooks up with girls closer to his age, but that doesn't mean the ones in my and Dolly's class haven't tried.

He flexes his ab muscles, thrusting into her mouth with his eyes still closed. She moans around him, clearly enjoying herself just as much as he is.

My mouth dries up as I continue to gawk at the scene. My internal voice is screaming at the top of its lungs, but I can't convince myself to move.

"That's right, just like that," his deep voice encourages her, the erotic sound jolting me back to reality.

I stumble back in a panic, making a scraping noise with my boots against the floor. My eyes dart up, wide and terrified as I make direct eye contact with Holden.

His black-brown eyes bore into mine from about fifteen feet away. His thick eyebrows lower with disapproval as his gaze rakes over me, as if I were the one in a compromising position with my pants around my knees and not him.

His hard stare freezes me in place again, like a damn laser beam holding me captive. My mouth forms an O. I keep expecting him to say something, to tell me to fuck off, or to make her stop and push her off of him, but he doesn't do any of that. Instead, he keeps his eyes locked on to mine for what feels like forever, but is probably only a few seconds.

The girl's head starts moving faster, but his eyes never leave mine. He grips her hair tightly, fisting it so hard that the veins in his forearm pop.

"That's it, baby. Good girl." His hand is still on her, but his eyes are on me.

My breathing grows more shallow while my skin grows hotter, a flush crawling up my neck. I've never seen anything like this. Duke and I haven't done anything sexual at all. We've only made out in his pickup truck and gotten a little handsy. I'm eighteen now, so we probably will cross that line soon since I'm legally an adult and planning to move out soon.

My father already said he'd have Duke cuffed before he could get his pants all the way down if he tried. Duke is only eleven months older than me, but my father has never approved of us dating. Even though the age of consent is seventeen in Texas, he would find something to pin on Duke to get him in trouble or forbid me from seeing him. Mayor Dixon has the county sheriff in his back pocket.

Truthfully, I'm not sure I'm completely ready to take that step with my boyfriend.

Holden, on the other hand, is twenty-six. A full eight years older than me. He's *very* experienced, and he's probably gotten hundreds of blow jobs in the hay, exactly like he is now.

My upper lip is starting to sweat under his steady, carnal gaze.

You will count to three, and then you will turn around and march out of here!

My thundering heart rate is almost as loud as the sloppy sound of the girl's wet mouth around Holden's member, which I really can't see from here. Like a complete and total pervert, I feel the urge to step closer to get a better view.

Holy shit, turn around and leave. You're dating his BROTHER!

My memory and overall common sense finally snap me back to the present.

What the hell am I doing?

With one last stolen glance into his dark, bottomless eyes, I spin around and flee the scene. My lungs are screaming for air as I try not to make a sound, waiting until I'm outside the barn before gulping in oxygen. My body feels like it's on fire, hot coals pressing into my chest and cheeks. The cold air helps minimally. I wish I could jump into an ice bath to shock my system back to reality, hopefully erasing every hint of what just happened from my memory.

What did I just witness?

I don't know if I'll ever be able to wipe away the erotic picture of Holden's gaze, his sensual parted lips, the contraction of his muscles as he was being ... *pleasured* by some nameless, faceless girl.

Who was *that?*

I didn't get a single glance at her face, probably because I was too distracted by him. His hands, his eyes.

Holy shit, his voice ...

The deep, lustful tone of his voice is going to haunt me.

I continue stomping up toward the house, forgetting what I was even doing out there in the barn to begin with as I replay the scene over and over, unable to stop myself. My skin feels like it's sunburned.

"Dolly!" a voice calls from the back porch ahead of me.

My eyes jump to see Duke standing there with Sterling, the brother right above him in age. A new wave of embarrassment and shame washes over me at the sight of my boyfriend after what I saw in the barn.

Duke and I have barely fooled around, but I've never even gotten half this aroused and overheated with him.

What on earth is wrong with me? Am I broken?

I keep walking, shifting my eyes to the dirt in front of me.

"Hey, Rosie. Is Dolly with you?" Sterling asks.

I shake my head. "Nope. Couldn't find her."

My boots finally reach the porch of the stone house. I steal a glance up at Duke's downcast face, quickly shifting my eyes over to Sterling.

"I don't know where she is. I'm getting worried," I say.

Sterling nods, looking down at his phone. Cash walks out on the porch to join us. Of all the brothers, he's the patient, calm one.

"I'm calling Holden," Sterling says.

My throat feels tight, but I cross my arms over my stomach in an attempt to feign indifference at the mention of his name. He's always the brother they call, the one who fixes things and makes it better, usually through violence. Sterling raises his phone up to his ear, a scowl on his face.

"Whose truck is that?" Duke asks.

I turn to see what he's referring to, still avoiding eye contact with him. The truck in question is a single-cab red Dodge, and the sight immediately makes my tongue feel dry.

"That's my uncle Cain's truck ..." My voice trails off.

Duke and Sterling both step off the porch, walking directly toward the vehicle. Cash and I trail behind them. My stomach is in knots.

What is my uncle doing here?

"Holden," I hear Sterling say into the phone, "Dolly is missing."

2

HOLDEN
PRESENT DAY

I reach down to grip the strap wrapped around the bull's chest, squeezing my legs tightly around its back. My thighs are stronger than ever after the last three and a half years of continuous weight lifting, but that kind of strength is different from this. This is work strength. This muscle is all from memory. It's from years of growing up on a Texas ranch and jumping on bulls with nothing but a fucked-up idea of fun and a bet to stay on for eight seconds to avoid a shitty consequence.

I guess that's not any different from what we're doing here, only I'll win a lot more if I can stay on this one.

"You ready, Redford?" a cowboy to my left asks me.

I nod, forcing myself to exhale as they open up the chute. The crowd and the bull go wild in unison. It's been over three years since they've seen me in this arena, but I guess a few of them remember.

The Riders is an underground bull riding organization

run by old, bored, crippled cowboys with a lot of money and not much else to do. Our family ranch supplies the animals for a hefty fee, but we boys come to ride every so often just for the high.

My grip strength doesn't fail me as I hold on for dear life, my body repeatedly being thrown into the air like a rag doll as the animal tries to throw me off with every ounce of strength in its two-thousand-pound body.

I wish I felt afraid of it. I wish something in this life scared me, but all I feel is excitement and adrenaline. The idea of death has never caused me any fear.

That's probably why I killed a man.

Finally, the buzzer sounds in my ears. My raised hand shoots back to join the other one on the leather strap, gripping tightly. A rider comes up beside me to release the flank strap. I grip the back of his saddle, sliding off easily and landing on my feet. Sometimes, that shit works out; other times, it's a fucking nightmare.

"Good to have you back, Redford," the man on the horse calls to me.

I wave a hand up at him as I climb over the steel fence.

I glance over my shoulder, watching my back for potential assailants. Getting jumped regularly in prison made me paranoid because it was the only way to survive.

The Riders is an unofficial, illegal operation. If the Feds were to ever show up, which they wouldn't, we'd have to immediately cease and desist any exchange of currency or bets on rides. Not that they'd believe it was all we were doing, but there's technically nothing illegal about riding a bull in front of a crowd of spectators. The part that's not in line with the law is the betting. Lots of money is exchanged here—a lot of dirty money. Hundreds of thousands of dollars change hands every night we ride, which is only every few weeks.

Mayor Dixon has had a field day, trying to shut it down for the last three years, but my brother Cash told me during his last call to the prison that the good ol' mayor had started singing a different tune recently. Word has it, he's been silently betting on rides through a few goonies to earn some extra cash flow. If that's the case, The Riders might not be in any legal bind whatsoever for the foreseeable future, which means Redford Ranch has a lot of business lined up for bull breeding.

"Holden? Oh my gosh, is that you? I had no idea they released you! I can't believe Cash and Sterling didn't tell me." A grating female voice reaches my ears.

I glance up, seeing a flash of blond hair and pink lips before looking away. "In the flesh."

Madi giggles, inching closer and boldly placing her hand on my forearm. "I thought you were still locked up. I would've thrown you a welcome-home party."

"A party doesn't sound too welcoming to me." I spit in the dirt, hoping she'll get the hint and go bug someone else. Even after a few years in a men's prison, I didn't miss her high-pitched voice one bit.

I was sentenced to fifteen years for manslaughter, but the Texas governor granted me clemency after three and a half years in hell. Just like that, I was suddenly a free man.

"Well, I figured it wouldn't be until the part where you snuck me off to the barn again. Remember that? The night everything happened, you and me in the hay?" she purrs, pressing her breasts into my upper arm.

I've gained muscle, but she's definitely gained something that feels unnatural and plastic. There's nothing wrong with fake tits; I just prefer them soft and pliable.

Fuck, but it's been forever since I've touched a woman ...

"Sure as fuck is hard to forget the night you kill a man." I finally turn, looking her straight in the eye and expecting to see her recoil.

Instead, Madi bats her fake eyelashes and leans farther in, excitement sparkling in her blue eyes. "I sure hope prison didn't make you forget *anything* from that night."

After three and a half years behind bars for manslaughter, she's still into me? What the fuck.

The truth is, I remember every little detail from the last time I saw Madi. It's a story I've had to recount over and over, a thousand times, to law enforcement, lawyers, judges, and other inmates. After my gun ended up blowing out the brains of another human being that night, the details from the entire evening were permanently cemented into my skull.

"I gotta get going," I tell her, stepping past her and striding toward the parking lot, shoulders back.

A few faces turn to stare at me, everyone clearly taking this moment to suddenly pay attention to detail. My skin is heated from all the eyes on me and the stark difference the outside world is from being tucked away in prison. My instincts to stay on high alert and watch my back are still roaring at me.

None of them expected to see me for almost twelve more years.

"Rosie, there you are!" an excited woman's voice calls.

My steps falter at the familiar name. I glance to my right to see a flash of copper-red hair, a shade I'd recognize anywhere on this planet. She's only standing about six feet away. As I turn fully, her long, wavy hair swishes to the side as she stops dead in her tracks at the sight of me. Her black felt cowboy hat contrasts against her skin.

She's staring at me, pale blue-green eyes—the color of pure tropical ocean water—taking me in like I'm a ghost. I guess, technically, I am somewhat of a ghost to these people, considering they all thought I'd be locked up for years. It must be unsettling to see a man who was in prison after murdering their neighbor out and about, roaming the streets freely a few years too early for comfort.

Rosie Lou Dixon's perfect crimson mouth forms a flawless O, much like the last time we saw each other. I let out a deep exhale.

So many memories were made on that fateful winter night. Rosie either remembers it as well as I do or she's terrified and can't move out of pure fear and shock.

The girl who's been calling her name finally reaches her.

"Rosie! Didn't you hear me? He's out. I just heard, he's *out.*"

My eyes slide over to take in the bearer of the clearly shocking news. The girl is taller than Rosie with short brown hair. I don't recognize her, but as soon as she sees me, she sure as hell knows exactly who I am. Her eyes pop open wide, face paling as she gasps.

"Oh shit," she mumbles, reaching for Rosie's hand.

Rosie stays as still as a statue, again tearing my mind to three years back, when she froze in place and gawked at me in the barn, only minutes before I committed that life-altering crime.

Without thinking it through, I let my eyes trail over her grown-up frame. She was an adult woman the last time I saw her, but the years have altered her, all for the better. Her breasts have gotten bigger—quite a lot bigger from what I can see. Her hair is longer, and she's wearing less makeup. She looks a little less innocent and a lot more ... tempting.

I'm sure by now, my brother Duke has fucked her so many times that she's got a rock on her hand and babies on her mind. I don't look at her left hand to see before tipping my black cowboy hat in her direction, touching the brim before turning to strut out into the parking lot.

I guess it's time I go home and tell my family that I was released, my conviction overturned. It certainly wasn't for good behavior, although he admonished me to stay on the right side of the law once I was out.

Now that I am, I have no intention of doing any fucking good at all.

I'm here to raise hell.

"You could have called! You could have given me a warning so I could have at least had the house deep-cleaned and arranged a ride for you! I would have baked you a cake. I'm so pissed off; I'm barely even happy to see you!" Dolly bursts into tears as soon as she's done yelling, running up to me and throwing her arms around my neck. Her long black hair slaps me in the face as she wraps herself fully around me, shaking and sobbing uncontrollably.

Emotion stirs up inside my chest at my little sister's incredible ability to express herself, always wearing her feelings fully on her sleeve. I pat her back, squeezing her tight.

"I'm here now, aren't I? I'm here to stay, and you know I fucking hate parties."

Heavy footsteps are clomping down the hall. I look up into the eyes of Duke and Sterling. They both gawk at me for a moment before grinning from ear to ear.

Sterling walks over first, slapping me on the shoulder. "Well, fucking hello, brother."

Duke walks over next, pulling Dolly back gently to go in for his own hug.

"Looks like you finally started growing some chest hair," I say.

Duke, who's shirtless, chuckles as he pulls back and reaches for the coffeepot. "We've all had to grow up since you left."

Sterling pours himself a cup next. "When did you get out? How the hell did you get out?"

"Yesterday afternoon."

I came home after bull riding, expecting everyone to be up, but I guess they've all started a bedtime routine. I went straight to my old room and lay awake, wondering if it was a dream. The bed felt like I'd never even left, and thankfully, I woke up still here instead of inside a prison cell, realizing it was all in my head. I couldn't sleep. I just kept trying to trick my mind into believing it was real and I was actually home for good.

I had anticipated seeing a few of my brothers at The Riders last night, but they must've sent some ranch hands to manage the bulls.

Dolly sniffles, reaching for her pink coffee cup as she wipes her cheeks with the sleeve of her sweater. Sterling fills up her cup. Duke stretches his arms out, and I notice how much he's grown up, his chest and arms bigger than the last time I saw him at the prison.

After the first year, I told my family not to visit. Cash still came every few months to talk business, but the others finally listened to my request. I wanted them to keep living their lives without me. I didn't want the dangerous connections I was making in prison to catch on to how close-knit my family and I were.

"Where're Dad and Cash?"

"Cash is probably in the barn, saddling up to check the cows. Dad won't be up for hours," Sterling answers.

I take a slow sip of my coffee. In the three and a half years I was locked up, my father only came to see me once. He was drunk and could barely hold a conversation. It doesn't sound like much has changed.

"Guess I'll go see what Cash needs help with then." I pour the rest of my coffee down the sink, turning to exit out the back door.

Dolly pulls me in for one more hug. "Don't think you're getting out of a family celebration tonight and an in-depth story time about how you got out so early. As soon as I get dressed, I'm going to town for fresh strawberries and cream to make ice cream."

"I can't turn down your homemade ice cream, Dolls."

3
ROSIE

If I could afford to call in sick to work, I definitely would. If I was in my right mind, I would just quit.

I stare at myself in the rearview mirror of my Honda minivan, debating what kind of mental problems I must have for showing up here today of *all* days.

They're going to notice you did your hair and makeup. They're going to be able to tell you wore your best bra and booty scrunch leggings.

I exhale, trying to keep myself from turning the car back on and hightailing it out of here, back to the world of logic and reason. Before I can talk myself into leaving, I open the door and march up to the house. I'm ten minutes early.

Before I even reach the front porch, the door swings open, and I make eye contact with Duke. He smiles, leaving the door open as he walks out.

"Hey, Rosie. Did you hear Holden's back? He got out."

"Uh, yeah, I did hear that. It's all over town." I push past him into the house, hoping he doesn't want to engage me any further into conversation about Holden's return or notice my outfit is more flattering than usual.

Working on my ex-boyfriend's family ranch has its ups and downs, but Duke and I were able to part ways amicably and settle into a comfortable friendship. He was my high school sweetheart and my first love, but we agreed that we weren't a good fit as a couple. The breakup was mutual, although I'd initiated it. We don't usually hang out alone or spend much time together.

I'm still best friends with Dolly, so even if I didn't work at the ranch, I'm sure we'd have to see each other quite often. Dolly seems to think we'll get back together after he's grown up a little. I don't have the heart to tell her it's not in the cards for us, no matter how much growing up he does. All my romantic feelings toward Duke dissolved years ago.

"I think Dolly wants to throw a party. You might have your work cut out for you today." Duke chuckles, continuing to walk toward the barn.

I already searched the exterior for any sign of Holden when I drove up. He's probably out in one of the back pastures with Cash and Sterling, rounding up cattle or fixing fences.

I should quit. I shouldn't be here. My father is never going to forgive me.

Working for the Redfords has always been unacceptable to him, but when I first took the job as housekeeper and cook, I promised I would quit long before Holden was released from prison for killing my uncle Cain.

Yet here I am, showing up for work ten minutes early with my hair blown out to scrub his toilet.

Seeing him at the bull ride last night was a shock. I rarely ever go to watch unless Dolly is, but my friend Cheyenne convinced me to join her because she has a crush on one of the guys competing.

I need therapy ... real therapy, not a glass of wine—or three.

He wasn't supposed to get out for over ten years. I thought I'd have more time to process it all.

I adjust my plunging white V-neck, zipping my black hoodie up, hoping Dolly doesn't say anything about the amount of cleavage I'm showing. This top is typically what I wear out when we go to music festivals or the local bar, not to the ranch. My tennis shoes make squeaky noises as I walk through the living room. My stomach is in knots, and I completely forgot to eat breakfast.

The Redford Ranch house looks like a shrine to a fallen cedar forest. The walls used to be decorated with so many mounted buck and elk heads that they ran out of room and had to start hanging them out in the barn. Dolly forced them to remove all of them, except for each brother's prized kill, from the main house, which made it a much cozier environment.

The massive stone fireplace always has a roaring fire in the winter. I've spent many evenings curled up on the leather chair with Dolly, reading fantasy and romance novels and munching on popcorn.

"Rosie! Thank goodness you're early. Holden is free! He's out! The Texas governor granted him clemency! He's pardoned—like it never happened. I can hardly believe it!

I'm leaving now to go get all his favorite things, but I wanted to see if you could start today by deep-cleaning his room. I know no one has slept in there since he left, but I just want to make sure it's perfect for him." Dolly is talking a mile a minute, scurrying around the kitchen with a notebook in hand, scribbling on it as she counts the beer bottles in the oversize fridge before moving over to the pantry. Her black hair is up in a messy bun, and she's still in her pajama pants.

"Yes, I heard. I'm happy for you! No problem. Duke said something about a party?" I set my purse on the kitchen counter before picking at my nail beds.

"YES! Holden has no idea, and I want it to stay that way. He needs to think it's low-key, family only—you get it. I'm just so excited, and I want him to know how much the whole town wants to welcome him home."

Is *the whole town going to welcome him home?*

I nod, reaching for a water bottle in the fridge to keep my hands busy. Dolly is still darting around the kitchen, not even glancing in my direction.

"I guess I'll go get working on that."

"When I get back from the store, we'll start the food!" She flashes a grin at me.

"Okay." I force a smile.

I head down the hallway toward the laundry room, where the cleaning supplies are. After grabbing the bath-room caddy and a pair of green rubber gloves, I make my way down the hall to Holden's room. I inhale a deep breath before knocking loudly. After a few seconds of silence, I push open the heavy solid wood door.

The large room has an enormous king-size bed right in

the center. The rough-hewn wooden posts on the corners are eight inches thick. The frame has a copper-brown-and-white cowhide overlay. The neatly made bed holds four pillows and a bedspread of faded oranges and grays in an Aztec pattern. There are no fancy throw pillows or extra blankets. The wood floor has a black-and-white cowhide rug strewn across it.

I expected to see some kind of luggage or maybe an orange jumpsuit in the corner of the room, but all that's there is the worn leather armchair next to the end table. The only light in the room is from the two lamps—one beside the bed and one by the chair. There're a few streams of sunlight pouring in from the sides of the closed curtains in front of the window.

The whole room smells like raw leather. I always take a deep inhale when I come in here to dust.

I walk up to the en suite bathroom door, knocking loudly. The last thing I want to do is walk in on the oldest Redford brother while he's in the shower.

I've caught Holden in a compromising position before, but once is enough to last me a *lifetime*.

There's no answer, so I push open the door. The bathroom is in the same state it was the last time I cleaned it, which was months ago, just to keep it dust-free, at Dolly's request. I don the rubber gloves and get to work.

After scrubbing down the double sink area and the mirrors, I move over to the toilet room. It's spotless, but I clean it anyway.

Once I finish the bathroom, I move into the bedroom. I

remove the gloves and strip the sheets from the bed. I find a set of clean white ones in the hall closet and begin to make the bed. I'm leaning over to straighten the comforter when I hear the door squeak open. I don't turn to look, expecting Dolly to speak up and tell me she's leaving for the store.

"What are you doing in my room?" a deep voice speaks from behind me.

My spine snaps straight. I slowly stand up, my copper-red hair hanging like a long curtain in front of my face, blocking my view of him. I tuck it back behind my ear, peering up at the tall, built form standing in the door.

Holden.

His arms are folded over his black T-shirt. Mud splatters are covering his clothes and muscled arms. His jaw is set, and I notice he's shaved since last night.

Holy shit, his shoulders have gotten massive.

I didn't have much time to look him over at the bull riding event, but I can't help but do it now. His dark eyes are shadowed by his brows, which are furrowed in clear distaste for me. I bite my bottom lip. His eyes drop down to the movement before meeting mine again. He flexes his jaw, waiting for my response, and I realize too much time has passed since he spoke.

"I, uh ... I was just cleaning up." A flush creeps up my chest.

He steps closer to me, boots scraping across the floor. "You and Madi can keep trying, but flashing those tits in my face and showing up in my room ain't gonna get you anywhere with me."

My skin prickles when I realize that he thinks I'm here to *seduce* him.

And he just threw me in the same category as Madi.

She's only grown more hopelessly obsessed with him in the last three and a half years, telling the story of their rendezvous in the barn over and over, to the point that no one even knows what parts are true and what she's embellished.

Supposedly, he proposed and wrote her love letters from behind bars.

I clench my fists by my sides. "I work for your family now actually. I was told to clean your room this morning. But if you must know, my tits will never be anywhere *near* your face, and the only way I'll ever enter your room *by choice* is when I'm getting paid to clean it."

I bend down to grab the last pillow off the floor, tossing it onto the bed. Holden cracks a smile, taking a step toward his bathroom.

He lifts the hem of his shirt, pulling it off in one motion. I try not to stare, but my mouth waters immediately at the sight of his rippling abs.

He sure didn't miss a day at the gym ...

He starts to unbuckle his belt before slipping the button out of the loop of his jeans.

"Is shower assistance part of your job description too, Dixon?"

I jut my chin out, crossing my arms and spinning on my heel as I march out without bothering to shut his door.

I can't believe him. Seduce him? Ugh, what an entitled jackass.

Ex-convicts aren't my type.

Typical Holden, expecting women to throw themselves at him and worship the ground his filthy boots stomp around on.

"Scrub your own damn toilet next time," I mumble under my breath.

4
HOLDEN

My father was always determined to maintain my grandfather's legacy and life work by building up Redford Ranch. After my mother died, he started seeking comfort in whiskey. I was sixteen, barely old enough by then to take over things, so ever since his gradual slip into oblivion, I ran the ranch. For years, it thrived. Cattle and bull sales were up until they sentenced me to fifteen years in prison. That's right around when our profits went down, but we've stayed afloat well enough.

Our income sources are spread out over breeding steers for slaughter and bulls for rodeo. We train our bulls for the Professional Bull Riders, which means all us boys grew up riding the crazy fuckers since we were old enough to hold on for dear life. The secret, under-the-table side income we make is from "renting" out the bulls who aren't fit for the PBR to The Riders.

While I was locked up, Cash and I stayed in communication. I continued to help run things from behind bars, keeping things moving smoothly. I couldn't have done it without Cash. What my brother failed to mention to me was how badly our father had deteriorated over the last three and a half years.

Pops finally stumbles out of his room and into the kitchen around mid-afternoon, clutching the neck of a glass bottle containing a clear mystery liquid. He stares at me with hazy eyes for a few long seconds before his eyebrows rise in surprise.

"Well, shit. They don't tell me nothin' around here. Thought you were Cash for a minute."

It's undeniable that all of us boys favor each other, especially as we get older, but we're not twins. Telling us apart is simple—for a sober person.

I fold my arms over my chest, debating if I even want to bother chastising him about the hour of day it is.

"Been home since last night."

"Hmph," is all he says as he walks over to the counter, reaching for the plate of poppyseed muffins—my favorite flavor.

"Mr. Redford, do you mind if I strip the sheets off your bed now to wash them?" Rosie chimes as she appears in the kitchen, her arms filled with folded bath towels. She avoids eye contact with me.

"Sure thing, honey. I'm up."

It's about time I find out whose idea it was to hire her in the first place.

Duke's girlfriend prancing around the house and cleaning up after everyone doesn't sit well with me, primarily because of who her father is. I guess none of my family members give a shit that the man is responsible for the last three and a half years I was locked up.

Why does she even need the money? The mayor is sitting on thousands of acres of generational farmland, rental property, and successful businesses.

Why is she really here?

He not only runs the town; he basically owns it. Redford Ranch is his only real rival when it comes to generating income.

"Rosie, take a load off. You've been running around all day." Duke marches into the kitchen, making a beeline for the muffins. He doesn't stop to kiss or hug her.

"Workday isn't over yet," I say, grabbing myself a muffin before the scavengers in this house eat them all.

Rosie's blue-green eyes darken for a moment as she glares at me.

"He's right; the workday is not over, but we have no more time for laundry! It's cooking time, baby!" Dolly skips into the kitchen, a smile plastered on her face. She comes up to me, pulling me into a hug.

"Rosie and I are making your favorite—Frito pie with Mom's venison chili recipe and meat from Duke's latest kill. Whatever you've been eating probably didn't even qualify as food. I used to lay awake and cry, thinking about what they were feeding you in that horrible place."

Rosie doesn't look too happy about the idea of having to cook for me, which gives me a small dose of satisfaction.

"Don't overdo it, Doll," I say, hugging my little sister back.

She's eight years younger than me, and I've always been overprotective of her.

She pulls away from me. "I'm fine! Rosie does all the physical labor stuff now."

My gaze lands on Rosie's neutral expression for a moment before moving back to Dolly's face.

My sister was born with congenital heart defects. Her heart was deformed at birth, causing her to need lifelong medication to treat the problem. She suffers from heart murmurs, fatigue, fainting, low energy, and a range of other symptoms. Sometimes, she doesn't know her own limits. Since she was born, she's received biannual checkups. One of the hardest parts about being in prison was not being able to go with her to her doctor's appointments.

"Can you get the groceries from the truck, Duke?" Dolly asks.

Duke nods, walking out the back door as he shoves a muffin in his mouth. My dad helps himself to another muffin before planting his butt on one of the kitchen island stools. He's getting into his mid-sixties, but he functions like he's at least ten years older.

"Soo, when are you planning on taking Madi out on a fancy date?" Dolly reaches under the cabinet for the cherry-red stand mixer, placing it on the countertop before plugging it in. She has a knowing smile on her face.

I raise a brow. "What are you talking about?"

Rosie pulls a recipe book from the bookshelf, holding all of our mother's old ones. She flips through the pages while Dolly starts to lay out glass jars with flour, sugar, and other baking ingredients.

"She's really looking forward to it, and honestly, she talks about it nonstop. I can't believe she isn't here or at least blowing up my phone about how excited she is."

I look from my sister's face to Rosie's, wondering where the joke is. Rosie's expression gives nothing away. If anything, she looks bored.

"Madi who?"

Dolly tilts her head, her hands stilling. "Madi Wright."

"I haven't spoken to Madi Wright in three and a half years, aside from last night."

A snort and giggle echo through the large kitchen. Rosie covers her mouth while Dolly gapes at me.

"Are you serious? You haven't been sending her letters all this time?"

I shake my head, turning to Rosie, who is trying to contain her laughter. "Is something funny, Dixon?"

Rosie shrugs as she measures out the flour. "You wanna make a double batch?" she asks Dolly.

My sister nods at her question before replying, "That bitch has been lying to me this whole time then! What the actual hell? I will kick her ass!"

"No, you won't," Rosie muses.

"Like hell you will." I speak at the same time Rosie does, both of us shutting down Dolly.

"I'm sure it was just an attention grab. She's had everyone wrapped up in their angsty *Romeo and Juliet* love story all this time, and she thought she'd have more time to say they tragically broke up, and then he was just out," Rosie suggests, waving a hand in my direction.

I take a bite of the muffin. "I don't want her over here. I

don't want a party—and don't think I don't know you're still trying to throw one. I have shit to do on the ranch. I don't have time for clingy women and this bullshit." I head toward the back door, needing to get out of the estrogen-filled space.

Dolly folds her arms. "Fine. I've never felt so used in my life. Our friendship for the entire time you were gone was a lie." She turns to Rosie, pulling her tightly into a hug. "You're literally the only friend I've ever had who wasn't just talking to me to get close to one of my brothers."

What about Duke? She's here because she's boning our brother, not because she's Dolly's friend.

Rosie smiles, hugging my sister back despite the flour that's now coating the front of her leggings, which hug her ass perfectly.

It's been way too long since I got laid ...

Dolly starts murmuring about how they need a girls' night, which jerks me back to the reality that I have no business hanging out in the kitchen with two women when there's work to be done on the ranch.

My father is still sitting at the bar, but he seems to be in his own world and not paying attention to the conversation.

I pause with my hand on the doorknob. "What do you say we go for a walk, Pops? I need to be brought up to speed around here."

Pops nods, reaching for another muffin before standing up with a grunt.

"Careful, Mr. Redford. You need to eat some protein with all those carbs, or you'll get lightheaded. Here, take some of this sausage that's left over from breakfast." Rosie opens the fridge and shuffles through some glass containers. She pulls out one with sausage patties in it; she takes a few out, wraps them in a paper towel, and hands it to my dad.

"Thanks, honey."

He turns and starts walking toward the back door with a half smile on his wrinkled face. I walk out after holding open the door for him, my mind spinning with questions about when the hell Rosie Dixon got so close to my family.

Rosie dating Duke was always an inconvenience, but after my arrest and conviction, things changed. The mayor of La Pradera, Clay Dixon, was a key player in my charges and sentencing. Rosie's father and mine always had a healthy rivalry after my mother chose the Redford last name over becoming a Dixon.

It still amazes me how time doesn't heal all, or even most, wounds. It just makes them fester and seep with infection.

Rosie's part in all of it is unclear, but her presence at the ranch makes me uneasy.

Do her loyalties lie with my brother and sister or with her father?

The Texas chill is in the air as the early November wind sings around us. Pops shuffles through the dirt while taking bites of the breakfast sausage. The horse barn looms ahead of us, a few of the ranch hands milling about. I watch each of their hands, checking for weapons.

You're home. You're safe here.

I try to relax my shoulders, exhaling deeply.

"So, when did the Dixon girl start working here, Pops?"

He shrugs, looking up at the sky. "A few months ago, I guess. She's a great cook."

I have to slow my long strides to match my father's pace. "Whose idea was it to hire her?"

Pops shrugs. "They don't tell me much. Cash runs things now."

I could bring up my concerns with Rosie working here to Cash, but I'm aiming to keep things amicable with my brother. If I start questioning all his decisions two days after I got back, I'm afraid it could cause an unnecessary rift between us. I respect the hell out of the way he stepped up.

"I know Cash is running things. I just figured Duke had something to do with Rosie being here. Does she stay in his room?"

The idea of Clay Dixon's daughter living under my roof makes my skin itch.

I've got to get her out of here.

Pops chuckles. "You seem awfully upset about a girl who's just washing the dishes and baking cookies. What's the big deal?"

I clench my teeth. Pops grabs a rope from a hook on the wall in the barn, looping it around like it's second nature.

"Just trying to catch up with what's all changed."

He nods, leaning against the horse stall. "Well, son, it's been quite a while. More things around here have changed than stayed the same." He sways back and forth with his words, struggling to maintain his balance.

Well, ain't that the damn truth, Pops.

5

ROSIE

When I pull up to my deteriorating apartment complex, I park in my usual spot. I try to avoid the potholes in the parking lot, but my car jostles into one anyway. My teeth chatter as I jog up to the third floor, looking over my shoulder every few steps to see if anyone unseemly has entered the vicinity.

Verbal harassment at this complex isn't unusual, so getting in and out quickly is ideal. When I get closer to my door, I gasp at the sight of a shadow standing nearby.

"Shit, Mom, you scared me."

My mother turns, her auburn hair in a bun on top of her head. She has streaks of makeup down her face.

"Rose, darling, I'm so glad you're finally home. Your father spent the night with another hooker."

I sigh, leaning up against the doorjamb as I insert my key. "Let's go inside to talk."

Once I get the stubborn, rusted lock to twist, I shove open the rickety door. No matter what I do, the inside always smells like leftover cigarette smoke from the previous tenant's nicotine habit. I've tried every deodorizing spray, bleached the walls, and steam-cleaned the carpet. It still hangs around like an unwelcome houseguest.

My mom follows me inside, shutting the door behind her. She doesn't dead bolt it, so I move around her and secure the lock.

"This isn't the Hilltop Heights, Mom."

The gated community my parents live in is extravagant, to say the least. The entry has a twenty-four-hour security guard.

"I am just disgusted with him and his gross need to stick his dick inside every willing girl in La Pradera. It's like he doesn't have a single shred of self-control!"

My mom moves to set her oversize handbag on my small round table. The legs wobble as she pulls out a bottle of vodka, twisting off the top.

I sigh, kicking off my tennis shoes to give my aching feet room to breathe. I worked all day, cleaning and cooking at Redford Ranch. The tension in my shoulders is more stiff than usual, probably because I was under the *watchful* eye of the eldest Redford brother, who seems to have a stark disapproval for my employment at the ranch.

My mom makes herself at home in my little kitchen while I grab the plush throw blanket from the basket and curl up on the corner of my sofa. I might not have the nicest place to live, but I will always splurge on cozy blankets.

After pouring herself some vodka over ice, she sits on the other end of the sofa with a big sigh. I would tell her to leave him, get a divorce and her own place, move on with her life and start healing, but I know it would fall on deaf ears. I've told her the same thing many times. I've realized that she just needs me to listen to her rant. She needs someone to care that she's in pain even though it's becoming increasingly difficult to hear the same story over and over and elicit a compassionate response.

Her eyes pool up with tears. "I know what you're going to say. I know what I need to do. I'm just ... I'm too old now. I'm turning fifty this year, Rose. I can't get a job. I can't date. I can't *start over*. I still love your father."

She exhales before taking a long sip of the pure alcohol.

"You can sleep in my bed tonight. I like the couch better anyway." I scoot closer to her, sharing my blanket with her and wrapping my arm around her slim shoulders. It's all I know to do.

My mother was a pageant queen in her early twenties. Sheri Belle was crowned the most beautiful woman in Kowata County five years in a row and once as Miss Texas in '97. My father proposed to her that night, right after she walked off the stage, while she was still wearing her crown and sash.

"I really don't think I could even get a job if I tried. What would I do? Work at the Walmart in Elmott? Become a night stocker at the gas station?"

She starts shaking and crying silently. I squeeze her shoulders tighter.

Once, when I was fifteen, I called her, ugly-crying, to come pick me up from school because I'd been cut from the cheerleading team. She scolded me at pickup, reprimanding me with a harsh reminder that we only cry when we absolutely have to, in private, and even then, we keep our grief quiet.

I've never heard my mother cry out loud, and I've never been able to cry out loud since.

"It's the second-best day of the year, Rosie! We're making enchiladas."

Dolly's eternal good mood seems to still be with us. She's always been an optimist, but since Holden's release, it's like she's on Prozac. She canceled the welcome-home party at his request. We've been cooking big meals every night.

"What's the second-best day of the year?" I ask.

"Bull testing day! Holden's release is the first best, obviously." She pulls a nine-by-thirteen pan out of the cabinet before gathering up ingredients.

"I've actually never been here for bull testing day."

Dolly's mouth drops open as her eyes grow wide. "Oh, honey, you're going to *love* it. They're flushing out the real competitive, money-making bulls from the duds. They could use weighted dummies to test them, but the ranch hands and my brothers just prefer to risk their lives instead. After we get the food in the oven, we'll go watch with popcorn and mimosas."

I laugh, nodding my agreement. "I can't turn that down."

We work quickly, making homemade chicken and beef enchiladas. I don't mind cooking, but baking is my preference. Dolly loves it all. She was made to be barefoot in a giant ranch kitchen. I've tried to encourage her to write a cookbook because she's always creating new recipes.

"Okay, I'll just set the timer on my phone so we can go out to the arena," Dolly says after we put the big pans of enchiladas into the oven.

I already made us popcorn and filled our tumblers with champagne and orange juice. We put on our boots on the back porch—a very necessary step before venturing out to the muddy arena, our arms filled with our snacks.

"It poured rain last night. I know they're all going to be filthy. Installing the outdoor shower was the best decision I ever made for this place." Dolly leads the way over to the enormous red barn. We walk through it, passing the stacks of hay bales and bags of cow feed piled up.

Every time I'm in here, I inevitably flashback to when I walked in on Holden and Madi in an unseemly position in the hay. I've tried to forget everything that happened that night, but it's forever burned into my memory, like a recurring nightmare I can't escape.

Dolly is speed-walking ahead of me, eager to get to the arena. We're both wearing high-waisted jeans, but I have on a red tank top with an unzipped gray hoodie over it, and she's wearing a pale blue sweater. We're nearly the same size, except my boobs are a few cup sizes bigger than hers. We share whatever clothes we can both fit into.

We hear them before they come into view, hoots and hollers in male voices filtering through the barn doors. I push open the heavy sliding door, the mid-morning light illuminating the scene before us.

Mud is caked on the hide of the animal in the middle of the oval-shaped arena. The cowboy currently riding the bull gets thrown off, flying into the air before he lands on the muddy, trampled ground.

Dolly is still leading me quickly over to the raised platform that overlooks the main area of the bulls and their riders. Cash is up on the platform already with Mr. Redford—Pops. Cash is making marks in a notebook, clearly not having taken his turn on a bull, as his jeans, boots, and button-down shirt are still clean. The tattoo that covers his entire arm and hand is peeking out beneath his sleeve. Pops is smoking a cigarette, but he smiles at me and his daughter when we climb the last iron stair.

"Hey, ladies. Come to see the boys get their asses kicked?"

Dolly hugs her dad's neck before pulling a bench closer to the railing. She pats the seat next to her, and I plant my butt on it.

"Who's up next? Any good bulls this season?" Dolly asks.

"Got a couple winners. Ain't seen many yet," Cash replies, clearly focused on making his notes. He never says much.

I pop a piece of popcorn into my mouth, shading my eyes from the glaring sunlight to see who's riding next.

Cash stands up, leaning against the iron rail. "You sure you're ready for the big boy, brother? Been a while."

My eye catches the broad, toned shoulders of the next rider climbing up onto the copper-colored hide of a massive bull. These animals weigh upward of two thousand pounds, and they're trained and bred to be aggressive and deadly.

The ones they ship off for the PBR are tame compared to the ones they rent out to The Riders.

I glitch for a second when Holden removes his black cowboy hat and gives it to a ranch hand before peeling off his muddy T-shirt and tossing it over the nearest fence railing. He takes the hat back, placing it back on his head. He glances up at the platform, almost black eyes making brief eye contact with me, before his steely gaze flicks over to Cash's. He settles down on the bare back of the bull.

"Wanna bet on it? I'll stay on this fucker for eight seconds, first try."

Cash chuckles, shaking his head. Holden looks back down as he wraps the rope that's tied around the bull around his hand. His shoulder muscles ripple with each movement. My mouth waters involuntarily. The taut planes of his abs are smeared with mud, so it must not be his first ride.

Abs, shoulders, back muscles ...

Holden's body is shockingly chiseled for how big he is. All six foot three inches of him is packaged to perfection, complete with fit Wrangler jeans, mud caked on his upper thighs, and sweat dripping down the center of his chest.

His height and size have always been intimidating, but in the three and a half years since I last saw him, he's noticeably bigger, stronger, and scarier.

Well, he's an ex-prisoner now. You should be scared of him.

Holden dips his cowboy hat, signaling that he's ready to ride. They open the gate, releasing the animal. I hold my breath as I watch him being spun around by the bull. He holds one hand in the air, the other tied to its back, muscles tensed and rippling with each twist of the animal's body that

Holden seems to follow naturally, like he was bred for it the same way the bull was. His ancestry is all cowboy, so I guess he kinda was.

The thrill of watching a bull rider is something I've felt down in my bones since I was a little girl. Growing up in a small Texas town, surrounded by ranches overflowing with cowboys, I've seen my fair share of rides, both in official competitions and the unofficial ones.

Dolly gasps as the buzzer goes off right when Holden loses his balance, half falling, half jumping off into the mud. He lands on his knees, but the bull suddenly spins around, feet kicking up right in his face. His body jerks backward from the force of the blow.

My heart drops into my stomach, which cramps tightly as Dolly screams beside me.

6

HOLDEN

"Rosie did a year of nursing school, so she does all the wound care on the ranch that doesn't require an ambulance. You're *lucky* I didn't call one. You're lucky he didn't snap your neck with that kick." Cash storms out of the bathroom, leaving me alone with a bleeding jawline.

My head is pounding. I shut my eyes to try and ease the dizzy feeling.

I hear quiet footsteps, but I don't open my eyes. The light smell of vanilla reaches my nostrils, and my first instinct is to inhale.

Rosie.

I open my eyes to see her meticulously opening a first aid kit and setting things out on the bathroom countertop. Her aqua eyes meet mine briefly before she looks back down to thread a needle. She reaches for a bottle of saline, pouring it onto some gauze.

"This might sting," she says quietly. She moves her hand up to gently dab the gauze on the slice over my jawline.

I exhale slowly, trying to focus on the pain instead of the way my head is swimming.

I've never been this close to her. For the first time, I'm noticing the pale freckles on her nose. Her full lips are shaped with flawless dips and swells, the perfect shade of rosy pink.

"Any dizziness?" she asks.

I grunt, not wanting her to show any concern for me. "Just stitch it up."

She presses the gauze harder, making the cut sting. I hiss out a foul word, shutting my eyes again.

"If you're dizzy, it could mean you have a concussion. If you pass out, we'll have to take you in to make sure there's no internal bleeding."

She stares into my eyes like she's looking for some sign of a concussion.

"I'm fine. Stitch it up," I grunt.

She has no idea how I had wounds ten times worse than this in prison after getting jumped regularly.

She sprays something on my jaw. "This will numb it."

"I need a drink."

I feel her move away, which gives me the space I need to exhale.

Why am I letting her get in my head? She's probably here for her father, using Duke and Dolly as a decoy reason.

Her uncle's blood is on my hands, so if I'm honest with myself, I can fully understand why she dislikes me. What I can't wrap my head around is why she's still dating my brother and working for my family if it's not for an ulterior motive. Her friendship with Dolly should be on the rocks after what happened, but they seem closer than ever.

She has to be spying on us.

"Here."

I open my eyes to see her hand outstretched, holding a glass of amber liquid. I toss it back, letting the whiskey burn down my throat. It's my first drink since my release.

"Why are you here?" I finally just spit it out. I've never been one to avoid confrontation.

Her ample chest rises and falls as she inhales a deep breath, narrowing her gaze at me and pursing her lips.

"My boss told me to doctor you up. I do what I'm told."

Is that so?

She reaches out a hand toward my face, pausing before her skin meets mine. Her lips part slightly as she tenderly touches the skin near my cut. "Can you feel this?"

"Yes." I finish the whiskey, leaning my head back and settling my back against the chair Cash dragged in here. "Just do it. I need to get back out there."

And I need to get away from my brother's spying little girlfriend.

"It'll be numb in a few minutes."

"Last I checked, you work for me too, and I'm telling you to do it *now*."

She sighs, reaching for the needle she threaded, where it sits on the counter. "Hold still."

I watch her eyes as she leans in, slowly poking my face with the needle and filling my nostrils with her vanilla scent.

"Why'd you drop out of nursing school?"

She stills, lashes fluttering for a moment before she continues to work. It barely stings.

"I had to take care of my mom."

I keep staring at her face, wondering if her skin is as smooth as it looks. "What's wrong with her?"

The last I heard, the Dixon family was still as rich and haughty as they'd ever been, grieving the loss of Clay Dixon's brother as if he were a saint. Cain is better off as worm food, along with all the other pedophiles who prey on teenage girls.

Rosie purses her lips, pulling the thread so tight that I almost wince. "None of your business."

It's a damn shame she's so fucking beautiful and completely off-limits.

She looks exactly like what I need to quench my thirst after three and a half years in a drought.

I lean forward, moving into her personal space. She pauses, blinking slowly before she meets my gaze. Our faces are inches apart.

"What are you really doing here, Dixon?"

THREE AND A HALF YEARS EARLIER

Rosie can't seem to tear her eyes away from my body. The sloppy sound of the girl moving over my dick fills the cold night. The hay is sticking onto the skin of my bare ass.

I keep my eyes locked in on the mayor's daughter, wondering why the hell my little brother's girlfriend is so fascinated by the sight of me getting blown.

I know Duke and she haven't done anything sexual yet because of her father's threats about pressing charges. Now that she's eighteen, I figured they would've jumped into the hay themselves. My little brother seemed agitated and anxious about it a few weeks ago when it was almost her birthday. He was counting down the days.

I don't make a habit of corrupting barely legal females. In fact, I prefer to hook up with women my age or older. Dolly's friends and classmates have a weird fetish for sleeping with as many of her brothers as they can, and it seems the older the brother, the bigger the accomplishment it is to them. I've been fending them off for years now.

Rosie Dixon's mouth is agape as her eyelids droop slightly with what looks an awful lot like ... desire. Her breasts are rising and falling with deep breaths as she stands just a few feet away, gawking. My dick gets harder, and the girl moans around it, gripping the top of my thigh.

I'm about to ask Dixon if she wants to take a picture or maybe sell some damn tickets when she suddenly turns around and bolts.

I chuckle, watching her as she goes. I pull myself out of the girl's mouth, staring down at her face. My phone buzzes in my back pocket.

"It's okay if you forgot a condom. I don't care." Her tits are out, and she doesn't look like she has any intention of redressing herself.

I stare into her eyes as I slowly pull up my Wranglers. My phone buzzes again. I pull it out, looking at the screen to see Sterling's name.

I press the green Answer button. "Yeah?"

"Dolly's missing. Cain Dixon's truck is here."

My blood turns ice cold in my veins as I stand upright. I never took my boots off, so after buttoning and zipping my jeans, I grab my rifle from where it's leaning up against the barn wall. My pistol is on a ledge next to it. I tuck the handgun into my waistband.

"The fuck did you just say?"

"Where are you? Rosie said she can't find her."

So, that's why Rosie was in here. She was looking for Dolly.

I check the safety on my gun. "I'm in the barn. Get your ass in here with a gun."

Madi jumps up and grabs my arms. "What happened?! Where are you going? Aren't we having sex?"

I look down at her, suddenly feeling sorry for her. "Shit's about to get fucked up. You need to leave. Get off the ranch—now."

I know what kind of man Cain Dixon is. I've saved young women from his perverted intentions before.

She claps her hand over her mouth.

I find her shirt stuck to a hay bale, tossing it toward her. "Go now. It's for your safety."

She pulls the shirt over her head before grabbing my face, pulling me down and kissing me on the mouth. "Call me."

She spins around and runs out of the barn just as Sterling, Duke, and Cash walk in. They're each holding different guns, except Duke, who's holding a bow and arrow.

"Where was the last place you saw her? When did Cain get here?"

Sterling's face is grim. "Rosie said Dolly got upset that

she and Duke were fighting and went on a walk. When Rosie went to look for her, she couldn't find her."

"What the fuck does Cain have to do with it?"

Sterling clenches his jaw, looking at our other brothers' faces before answering me. "Duke saw them talking in town the other day."

I turn to face my younger brother, ready to crush his nasal bone if his answer doesn't satisfy me. He juts his chin out in defiance—typical of Duke.

"It wasn't a big deal. I drove Dolly to the store for groceries. When she came out, Cain was helping her carry shit. They were laughing, talking. Nothing was weird about it."

I clench my fist around the butt of my shotgun. "He's fucking twelve years older than her. His brother has it out for the ranch. You didn't think this was relevant to mention?"

Duke is too young to have knowledge of Cain's nefarious activities and habits. I can't fully blame my younger brother for this, but it's his fucking job to protect our sister too.

"We need to focus on finding Dolly," Cash says. "Maybe she invited him over."

My gaze cuts over to his, thoughts spinning. I'm the man of this house now. These decisions weigh on me, but whatever is happening tonight, I know it's not good. My gut has never failed me, and tonight, something fucked up is going down.

7
ROSIE
PRESENT DAY

"What are you really doing here, Dixon?"

His voice is deep and intimidating, but the one thing I learned from my father is not to back down from a bulldog. Staring them down is the best defense.

I level him with half-lidded eyes. "I'm here to fix your ugly-ass face. You gonna let me do that or nah?"

The corner of his mouth twitches up, almost like he's stopping himself from smiling. He leans back against the chair, but doesn't close his eyes.

Trying to stop my hands from trembling, I lean forward with the needle and thread. He stares at my face as I stick the needle into his skin and doesn't react to the pain.

I try to keep my breathing steady as I work on him, doing my best to make each stitch even and close to the cut to reduce the size of the inevitable scar.

"It'll scar. You can use vitamin E oil on it while it's healing to help the skin look smoother."

"Doesn't matter."

Somehow, the imaginary picture I conjure up in my head of Holden Redford's already ruggedly handsome face with a scar on his jawline makes him impossibly—and annoyingly—hotter.

The walls in the bathroom are starting to feel like they're shrinking around us. The temperature is growing warmer, and my tank top is sticking to my lower back. I stand up straight, unzip my hoodie, and shrug it off my shoulders. I toss it on the sink before leaning back down to continue working.

"Still trying to seduce me?"

I roll my eyes. "You wish." I thread the needle through his face, leaning in closer to see. "Now that Madi's whole scheme has come to light, Dolly will never forgive you if y'all hook up again."

"I never had any intention of hooking up with her again."

"Well then, should we alert the media to announce to the females of La Pradera that they're free to start lining up outside your bedroom door?" My voice drips with sarcasm.

"Are you suggesting that I'm a man-whore?"

I snort, meeting his steely gaze for a moment before focusing on the wound again.

Yes.

"I'm suggesting you haven't been with a woman in years, and judging by your habits before you went to prison, you'll most likely be looking for a female companion to warm your bed again soon."

"I've got more important things to do for the ranch. Why don't you find me one? I prefer blondes and brunettes."

I flip my copper-red hair over my shoulder, wishing someone would crank up the AC even though it's in the forties outside.

"That's not in my job description. Sorry for the inconvenience, *sir*."

He pauses for a few beats before responding, "Too bad I love my little brother, or I'd just borrow you every once in a while. The convenience of your employment would be nice. You could strip the bed when we were done and wash my sheets."

I clench my jaw, shoving the needle unnecessarily deeper into his face. He inhales a sharp gulp of oxygen.

So, since I dated Duke, I'm damaged goods now?

Not that I give a shit what Holden thinks either way, but still ... rude.

"I repeat, it's not in my job description." I lean back, searching for the scissors because I'm finally done with the arduous task of sewing up his face. I snip the thread before slowly tying it into a double knot.

"Wouldn't matter either way. I don't dip my pen in the family ink." He stands up and walks out of the bathroom without so much as a thank-you.

"You're welcome, dick," I mumble.

That's two thank-yous he owes me now.

It's not that I want to date Holden or for him to see me as the grown woman I am now, but the fact that he's made it abundantly clear he would never entertain me as a romantic—or even strictly sexual—partner still stings for some mysterious and frustrating reason.

THE DAYS DRAG ON, and out of nowhere, Thanksgiving is coming up. With my family relationships in shambles, I have no intention of going home for the holiday.

My mother hasn't even texted me to ask what my plans are. Sadly, I think she's probably been too in and out of a drunken stupor to even notice the date. I've called her a few times. The last time we spoke, she was in Oklahoma, visiting her sister, so at least I know she hasn't been completely alone.

I haven't talked to my father in months, and I have no desire to see him. I have a few missed calls from him. I have no desire to return them.

When my uncle Cain, my father's brother, was first shot and killed, I stuck by my father's side and grieved with him. After I learned the truth about what had really happened the night Holden killed Cain, I quit nursing school and moved out of the family mansion. My father had been paying for my school, but I decided I'd rather drown in student loans than take another dime of his money.

"Are you in the mood for romance or comedy?" Dolly asks, reaching for the remote.

"Your choice." I pop a piece of popcorn into my mouth.

We call Friday nights *braless Fridays*. We binge guilty-pleasure movies, eat high-calorie food, and drink wine in our pajamas, no bras allowed. Sometimes, Dolly comes over to my apartment when we want a true girls-only night, but in the winter, it's drafty and cold. It's hard to beat the warmth and crackle of a real wood fire, even with the occasional testosterone-filled interruption.

"You remember that night ... when everything happened?"

Dolly's words cause the hair on my arms to stand up. She rarely talks about the night everything changed. It took her months to confess to me what had really transpired in the darkness, all while the trial was still going on and our friendship had gone up in flames. She patched it back together when she told me her side of the story.

"I don't think I'll ever forget that night," I say quietly.

She lays her head back, her face devoid of makeup and her glasses perched on the end of her cute nose. She's mindlessly scrolling through the Romance Movies tab. The fire is glowing orange on her smooth skin, the sun fully set now.

"I thought Cain really liked me. I wanted to ... date him."

I stare at her, trying to keep my expression from revealing the shock coursing through me.

After a few long seconds, I finally speak. "But I thought he—"

She nods. "He did. He did force himself on me, but at first, we were just talking, laughing ... flirting. When he showed up at the ranch that night, that's what I thought it was about. I thought he was going to ask me out on a date or for my number. We'd seen each other at the grocery store that day. He told me how pretty I was, how much he liked my long, dark hair. He was so charming."

My heart is thumping loudly inside my chest as I listen to her tell me a part of the story that I've never heard before.

My uncle Cain was incredibly charming. He was always popular among women.

Holden shot my uncle because he caught him trying to rape Dolly. He had his pants down, dick out, starting to rip her clothes off. She was screaming for help. Holden found them, stopped Cain, and shot him with his pistol. He didn't give him a chance for a trial or conviction. He took matters into his own hands and acted as judge, jury, and executioner. Cain was also carrying a weapon, which Holden testified he'd aimed at him. Dolly confirmed seeing it happen with her own eyes. Holden had told him to lower the gun, but Cain had refused to, cocking it to prepare to fire.

My father did everything he could to get Holden behind bars for killing his brother.

Holden was charged with second-degree manslaughter because it wasn't preplanned. The first-degree murder charges weren't able to stick because Holden's lawyer claimed the gun was fired in self-defense, and the jury agreed due to Dolly's testimony.

My ears are hot as I look over at Dolly again. "Why didn't you tell me?"

She shrugs, chewing on her bottom lip. "I've never told anyone. I was afraid Holden would get a worse sentence if I did."

The way she's casually still scrolling through the movie choices after dropping this on me is confusing me. My world is spinning.

"So then ... how did it end up getting to the point that it did?"

She exhales, taking a slow sip of her wine before answering. "He tried to kiss me. I backed away ... and then his face changed. He got annoyed and tried again. I tried to laugh it off, but my heart was pounding with fear. I told him we should at least go on a date first. I guess it just pissed him off. I don't know." She turns to look at me.

I know she's telling the truth. She wouldn't lie to me. I'm completely blown away, finding out that she left that whole part of the story out. She testified that Cain just showed up, unannounced; they started having a casual conversation, and then he forced himself on her before Holden showed up. I guess it's still the truth, but it certainly wasn't the whole story.

"I'm so sorry, Dolly. I'm so sorry for what he did. I'm sorry that ... you liked him and he treated you that way." I can't imagine how it's affected her mentally. I've seen her struggle emotionally ever since the traumatic day that she was nearly raped and then watched her brother kill a man before her eyes.

But for her to have liked him, trusted him?

I shake my head.

She nods, wiping a tear from her cheek. "Don't tell anyone, okay? I just want to move on from it."

I nod. "Of course not. It's our secret."

My heart swells with emotion with the realization that she trusts me with this huge secret. A secret that could change a lot of things.

I wrap my arms around her slim shoulders, pulling her in for a tight hug. "Have you picked a movie yet?"

"Yes, we're rewatching *Pretty Woman*."

"Perfect."

I lay my head on her shoulder, and she presses play.

8

HOLDEN

I walk into the kitchen to search for more bourbon that Pops hopefully has stored away somewhere. Cash, Sterling, Duke, and I have been poring over the books and having a late-night business meeting of sorts with liquor and cigars in the man cave upstairs.

It feels good to be home with my brothers and doing these things in person instead of through Plexiglas in an orange jumpsuit, sober.

Still, I'm barely sleeping. I can feel the exhaustion deep inside my bones. The calm, quiet stillness of the ranch makes my ears ring. No guards are screaming at me to wake up in the morning. No groups of paid assailants are hunting me down, forcing me to defend myself and fight for my life. The nightmares bring me back to hell, night after night.

It's over. You're out. You're not going back. You were pardoned.

Rosie and Dolly have taken over the living room. There

are opened packs of Oreos, Sour Patch Kids, and popcorn bags, along with wine corks, littering the kitchen counter.

"Women," I mutter.

I'm not used to the sounds and sights of feminine presence, but there's something comforting about it I never noticed before.

I'm reaching up into the cabinet above the fridge when I hear footsteps.

"Ope, didn't see you there, *sir.*"

I turn to see Rosie, covering up a smile with two empty wineglasses as she sways on her feet. She tilts her head to study me for a moment, squinting her eyes like she can't see clearly.

She's wearing a white tank top, the clear outline of her nipples making it obvious that she's not wearing a bra. Her breasts are definitely bigger than a double-D, swaying right along with her. My neck feels hot.

It's been years since I've touched the soft skin of a woman. Rosie Dixon has always been conventionally beautiful, but since I've been back, she's turned mouthwateringly sexy and impossible to ignore.

She sets the glasses down on the granite, nearly dropping one on the floor. She moves around the large kitchen island toward the pantry. She's wearing tiny little pink pajama shorts, exposing her legs and the bottom crease of her ass cheeks. Her long, thick hair is tumbling down past her shoulders toward her lower back.

How the fuck is Duke in the man cave with us and not out here, touching and exploring every inch of her?

She disappears into the pantry, not bothering to turn on the light.

"Hey you, jerkasaurus. Be a dear and fetch me that wine bottle on the top shelf. Pretty, pretty please?" she singsongs from inside the pantry.

I exhale, debating whether or not I should just get in the truck and drive to town in search of some female companionship. If I went down to Old Harry's, the bar I used to frequent, I'm sure there would be a few women I'd been intimate with in the past who might be interested again. For some reason, the thought of sex with a stranger just doesn't hold the appeal it once did. Maybe it's the years I spent behind bars.

Just man the fuck up and get the bourbon.

I walk in behind her, hoping to find the bourbon next to the wine. She's attempting to climb up the shelves, knocking down a can of beans with her foot.

I watch her in the dim lighting, leaning back against the wall with my arms crossed. "What are you doing?"

"I've decided I don't want or need your help." She grunts, taking another step up.

I look up to see the shadowed bottles on the top shelf, doubting she'll make it that high up. At my height of six foot three, I'll need every inch to reach them.

She grunts one more time before yelping loudly, her grip slipping as she falls back toward the ground. I react instinctively, moving forward to catch her with my hands around her waist. Her body thumps into mine, her back against my chest. Immediately, I'm overwhelmed with her scent of vanilla and something that must be pure Rosie.

My basic male instincts kick in. I squeeze her waist tighter, holding her against me for a few moments as my intrusive thoughts win over. Her soft hair tumbles over my arm. My sex-deprived mind imagines flipping her around, picking her up and inhaling a pure dose of her scent, her back pressed right up against the shelf of canned tomatoes and bags of rice with my hand gripping her hair at the scalp.

Her breath is coming in short little bursts, and she remains motionless in my tight grip. The darkest parts of my imagination conjure a thousand different provocative positions I could have her in before she takes even one more inhale.

Before I lose my fucking mind, I let her go and move back a step. A split second later, and my erection would have been pressing right into her ass cheeks.

Great, I just got a hard-on for my little brother's girlfriend.

Instead of acknowledging the elephant in the room, I step around her and reach for the bottles. I grab two, hoping they're what she wants because I need to get away from her and her skin and her smell.

She's as still as a statue, so I turn around and hand her the bottles, trying not to touch her skin again. I grab two more, praying one of them is something strong.

I stalk out of the pantry and into the kitchen, where I can actually read the labels and breathe. My dick is still protruding into the zipper of my Wranglers, and it hurts.

Fuck this. I have to get fucking laid.

"Um, thanks," she mumbles.

I don't respond, lifting the bottles to the light and realizing that one of them, thankfully, is bourbon. I set the other down on the counter before turning and leaving the room with the liquor in my grip. My skin feels tight, and my jeans are caging in my hard length.

Shit, I should tell Duke about this.

I've been planning to talk to him about whether he thinks Rosie is truly here for him and her friendship with Dolly or if her motive could be something more sinister, like spying on our family to help her father. It's no secret he's been getting into the betting rings at The Riders events and that he hates everyone with any Redford blood in their veins. His involvement in one of our main sources of income doesn't sit right with me.

Now that this little incident has occurred, anything I say about Rosie could be misinterpreted. I also don't know if she plans on telling anyone about how I held her waist a few beats too long because that could really fuck up all my plans for the ranch. I can't afford to cause a rift with my siblings or the Dixons right now. I'm trying to keep the peace and work on the business, keeping things low-key.

Technically, nothing happened. I've been deprived of a woman's presence for years, and her scent, her scantily clad body, and her nearness all overwhelmed me. It was instinct, not true desire.

I didn't do anything. I pushed her away.

"Fuck me," I grumble under my breath.

"WHERE'S DUKE?" I ask Sterling as he hops up into the back seat of the Ford F-150 King Ranch pickup.

Cash is driving, and I'm in the passenger seat. It's seven thirty at night, and we're all dressed in our nice Wranglers and long-sleeved button-ups with cowboy hats and snake-skin boots.

We stayed up late drinking, smoking, and bonding as brothers last night. I figured there was no need to talk to Duke while he was shit-faced and accidentally start a fist-fight. I planned to track him down once his hangover cleared up today, but I haven't seen him around. I don't know how I'm going to tell him that his girlfriend got me hard and that I think he should dump her because she could be spying on us, but I'm sure I'll find the words.

Sterling adjusts the steel at his waistband as the tires kick up dust. "Ah, I think he went hunting this morning with some buddies out at Sam's place."

"Sam Seymour?"

"Yeah."

"He doesn't need to be there. Not yet," Cash says.

Duke is old enough to be involved in the business, but I keep my mouth shut.

Cash is also carrying a concealed handgun. If I hadn't been pardoned when I got out, I would've been on parole. Thank fuck I can actually carry a gun again because after the hell I experienced in prison, I'll never walk this earth without the ability to protect myself and my family with a firearm.

"These men, you're sure about them?" Sterling asks.

I look out the window at the passing dry terrain. "As sure as I can be about doing business with ex-cons."

"You're an ex-prisoner, brother," Cash reminds me.

I flex my jaw, wondering why it feels like I somehow don't belong out here with the regular civilians after doing time. The shit I saw, the bonds I had to form for survival, none of that shit could ever make sense on the other side of the bars.

"You trust these guys, Holden?" Sterling isn't one to enjoy bending the law. Of the four of us, he's the straight shooter.

Cash answers for me. "The Riders is an unofficial organization, and with how much they've grown, they're worried it could draw attention from government authorities. Anytime someone is making big money they can't tax, the government sniffs around, looking for a cut."

I add to Cash's explanation. "I heard from several sources on the inside that if they don't start getting a voluntary cut, they'll either shut it down or force it on us. If they force it on us, it means rules and regulations. That's pointless, considering businesses like that already exist with the PBR and so many others. The Riders would most likely merge or crumble. That means the only remaining option is paying off the bulldogs sniffing around. We might not trust them, but we're backed into a corner unless we're prepared to lose half our income."

Sterling grimaces, facing out the window. "I fucking hate the government."

The Redford family has always had a very firm belief in small government. It's partially due to our mother's heritage and the fact that Tigua land was basically stolen from the original settlers of America. Our father agreed and raised us all to believe that the more power and control the government has, the less freedom we the people have. He was a founding member of The Riders, essentially passing it on to us boys as an extremely vital part of maintaining the Redford Ranch's income.

With each tax bracket that we've climbed, the risks have grown. After only a few months behind bars, I learned that my name garnered respect from men I'd never known because my father was so anti big government. On the one hand, I'm very much for laws and lawmakers enforcing them, especially for people who don't have the power or means to take matters into their own hands when it comes to protecting their family.

On the other hand, when it came down to protecting mine, I didn't hesitate for even a moment before blowing the head off the man who tried to rape my sister.

I'm a bad guy, a lawbreaker, a rebel. But that doesn't mean I don't have fucking standards. I don't think murder is okay in most circumstances. But I sure as hell think there are exceptions.

9
ROSIE

This bar is always too crowded, and the smell of cigarette smoke makes it one of my least favorite places to spend a Friday night. There are several reasons why I don't normally frequent this place, but with Dolly's recent confession and Holden's sudden release from prison, I'm in the mood to drink a little too much in a sketchy place. She picked this spot, and tonight, I'd rather be anywhere than the ranch, where there's a high chance of running into Holden like I did last Friday. I haven't seen him since that night, and I hope my luck doesn't run out while I'm inebriated yet again. The tension between us is becoming unbearable. He leaves every room once I enter, like he can't tolerate being near me.

I'm not exactly sure what to make of our little exchange in the pantry or if my imagination was playing tricks on me. It's been running through my head on repeat, which is driving me effectively *mad*. This is the type of thing I would normally confide in Dolly about, but she's made it abundantly clear that she's sick of feeling used by the women who are obsessed with Holden. Madi's betrayal is fresh. I would never hurt my best friend, so the inconvenience of my attraction and contrary strong distaste for her brother are going to have to remain a silent suffering.

There's an abundance of testosterone at Old Harry's. There's maybe one woman for every ten men. I'm wary of drinking too much more, although Duke agreed to stick to water and be our designated driver. I'm glad he's here with us. I look down at my plain white shirt, hoping there are no mystery stains from all the tobacco spit I can smell going around. Thankfully, it's still clean, and everyone seems a little too drunk to notice I'm not wearing a bra underneath.

"I can't believe we're having braless Friday *here* of all places," I lean in to yell into Dolly's ear over the music.

She giggles, shimmying her chest at me. We started the night off at the ranch—our usual spot for the tradition that we had kicked off in tenth grade. After we each drank our own bottle of wine, we were bored and tipsy, begging Duke to drive us to Old Harry's. He only agreed because he was bored too. The rest of the Redford brothers hadn't been around since I'd arrived today. I forced myself not to inquire about their whereabouts.

"Oh shit, it's the third Friday of the month." Dolly's eyes widen. She looks around the bar that's packed with people.

I follow her gaze, trying to see whatever it is she's seeing. The few women in the bar are all wearing white T-shirts, just like me.

I tilt my head to the side. "What's the third Friday?"

She points up to the stage, where a live Texas country band is playing. I look up, still confused.

One of the regular waitresses comes up beside us, ushering me toward the stage, where the other women are congregating.

"Let's go, girls! It's starting!"

I have no idea what the woman is talking about, resisting her efforts to usher me toward the front.

"What's starting? Dolly, what's the third Friday?"

Dolly starts giggling, covering her mouth as she lets go of my hand. "Go on! Maybe you'll win! We could go on a shopping spree."

I gawk at her, my head swimming with rosé and confusion. "Win what?"

The waitress shoves me harder this time, clearly annoyed with my lack of cooperation. I finally relent, shaking her off of me.

"All right, all right, I get it. I'm going."

Maybe it's karaoke night. I'm tipsy enough to shamelessly belt out a George Strait or Dixie Chicks song to this crowd. Who knows? Maybe I will win whatever is up for grabs.

"It'd better be a cash prize," I grumble under my breath.

A blonde in front of me, standing in what appears to be a line forming to walk up the stage, turns around with puffy lips and a big smile. "It is! One thousand dollars to the winner!"

I perk up at that sum. "Oh, damn. Count me in."

I make decent money working for the Redfords, but any extra cash I earn for my nursing-school fund isn't something

I'm in a state to turn down. "It's every third Friday?" I ask her.

She nods, turning back around as she starts walking up the stairs, hips swaying dramatically. I follow her up, nearly tripping on the last one before finally reaching the top of the wooden stage. My scuffed white sneakers are out of place among the other girls, who are all wearing bedazzled leather cowgirl boots with Daisy Dukes or denim miniskirts. I seem to be the only one in black leggings, although strangely enough, we're all wearing a white T-shirt. I'm the only one with a hoodie tied around my waist. It's cold outside, but the bar itself feels like a sauna.

"Look at us, all matching. Ha-ha," I joke.

The blond girl giggles before facing the crowd, pushing her chest out proudly. I face the drunken group as well, getting more confused with each passing moment.

Are we singing in a line? Is it a line dance?

I find Dolly almost instantly, who's laughing and waving her hands supportively.

"Yeah, Rosie! You got this, babe!"

I wave at her, grinning widely as Duke gapes at me from behind her. I'm still not one hundred percent sure what we're doing, but I'm guessing it's either karaoke, a line dance, or some kind of trivia night. Either way, I'm ready to bring my A game and win.

"Woo!" I hoot from the stage. The cheer dies in my throat as the older Redford brothers appear behind my best friend and ex-boyfriend.

Cash's and Sterling's expressions are emotionless until they see me. Their eyebrows rise simultaneously with surprise. They look at each other before facing forward again, a subtle smirk on both their faces.

Before I have time to process the reaction, the oldest Redford is glaring at me, a dark scowl on his ruggedly handsome face. He's *very* displeased. His expression is beyond annoyance, frustration, or even anger.

He's enraged, vibrating with negative energy I can feel from over thirty feet away. He scowls, jaw flexing as he turns to say something to Duke. I force myself to look away. Whatever toxic family drama he's wrapped up in is none of my concern.

"All right, gentlemen, after four long weeks, it's the night you've all been impatiently anticipating! We love bringing you this incredible lineup of young ladies each third Friday of the month here at Old Harry's, and as usual, only looking is permitted!"

I look around for where the voice is coming from, still completely in the dark about what kind of competition this is. A stage light shines in my face, and I raise my hand to block it.

"On the count of three! One, two, three!" the voice booms.

The girls next to me all suck in a breath, seeming to hold it.

"What is he—"

Without warning, a bucket of ice-cold water is dumped on my head, causing me to inhale sharply. My body freezes up as my lungs stop working and my ability to breathe suddenly escapes me, the shock to my system blocking out all my logical thoughts.

"Let the wet T-shirt contest begin!"

My mind is scrambling to make sense of what is happening as I continue to gasp for breath. I grasp the girl's arm next to me, feeling my nipples pucker up and harden as the cold water drenches the front of my shirt.

My chest is freezing cold, but the girls around me don't seem to be fazed one bit.

The blonde grabs for my hand, raising my arm up with a holler into the crowd. "Yeah, baby!"

I glance over at her with my mouth wide open before turning my face toward the crowd, my limbs beginning to tremble.

An abundance of male eyes with leering gazes is focused on us—well, on our chests. I frantically search for Dolly's face in the sea of hungry expressions.

"Dixon." A deep, commanding voice demands my attention from the right, down at the front of the stage.

I look down, meeting the dark, unflinching gaze of Holden. His jaw tics, even as he keeps his line of sight trained on my face, never dipping lower than my eyes.

"Get the fuck off that stage," he growls.

For a brief, fleeting moment, I almost listen to him. I do want off this stage. It's way too damn cold for this, and when it comes to cold water, my feelings are similar to a house cat. *Absolutely not a fan of this.*

"Or what?" The words leave my mouth before I even have a chance to think it through.

I don't want to be up here. I didn't even know what kind of contest this was, but now that I do know, it's certainly not worth the money to me, personally.

But if he would just fucking ask *nicely*.

If anyone else had come to demand I get down from this stage, I would have gladly relented and thanked them for the rescue.

But fuck him. Fuck him for telling me what to do or having the audacity to act like he hates me one hundred percent of the time then suddenly come to the rescue.

He grits his teeth, taking a visible deep breath before speaking again, his dark eyes glinting with rage. "Get the fuck down, or you're done working at the ranch." His hard gaze is unflinching.

"Is that a threat?" I bite back.

I'm sure he'd love to get rid of me. It's clear as day that he hates me for what my father and my uncle did even though his entire family—including Dolly—don't blame me at all.

Holden was locked up in prison while the rest of them gave me a shot at proving I'm not the same as the rest of the Dixons.

He's stuck in the past, stuck where everything first went up in flames.

Then, it hits me.

He blames me.

I can see it etched on his face. He blames me, the daughter of the man who put him behind bars.

His voice is cold. "It's a promise, Dixon."

10

HOLDEN

The struggle to keep my eyes locked on to hers is a battle within what little honorable parts of me are left.

I don't have any right to fire her for this, but I'd say almost anything to get her off this stage and out of the spotlight illuminating her body for every pervert in the vicinity. Duke doesn't seem to give a fuck that she's up there, which pisses me off. It's his job to protect her, not mine. As long as she's with him, she represents our family.

She lifts her chin defiantly, taking a step back from me. I saw the look on her face when they poured the bucket of water over her head, and she had been completely unaware of what was about to happen.

Why the fuck do you care?

Something about the look in her eyes, like she's terrified, reminds me of a mouse caught in a trap. The protective-older-brother instinct in me kicked into overdrive.

That's it. She's Dolly's friend. That's what this is. She's my little brother's pain-in-the-ass girlfriend.

Maybe it's due to the time I spent in prison, listening to how the lowest men in society talked about women. Maybe it's the fact that my brother is acting casual about the compromising position his girlfriend is in when he should be hauling her ass off the stage.

Whatever it is, I'm incapable of standing by and letting it happen.

"All right, girls, let's see you shimmy! Remember, it's a one-thousand-dollar prize!" the announcer's voice booms over the microphone.

I turn to see that it's greasy Old Harry himself, beady eyes leering at the stage. Every man in the room is, like they're helpless to stop themselves.

I look back up at Rosie's face, seeing that same expression—wide, panic-stricken eyes darting around the bar, looking for an escape. She shrinks back, clearly not wanting to participate in the competition that every other girl on the stage is enthusiastically joining in on, shimmying their chests back and forth and gaining hoots and hollers from the onlookers.

"Look at that, fellas. Hot damn, I love women! Don't you?" Harry chuckles into the mic as the crowd presses in closer to the stage.

Before I can stop myself, I place both hands on the stage floor, lifting myself up and standing up as the wood creaks underneath my weight.

"Hey now! I said no touching allowed!" Harry bellows.

I take one step toward Rosie. The other girls around her gasp as they see my face under the brim of my Stetson.

"Holden, you're out! Why haven't you come to see me?" a female voice purrs.

I ignore her, reaching out to grab Rosie around the waist, careful not to touch her swaying breasts. She grips my forearm, digging into it with her fingernails. This is my first time to ever intentionally touch her.

"What are you—" she starts.

I lift her up easily, tossing her body over my shoulder before carrying her right down the stairs on the side of the stage like she's a sack of cow feed. She yelps and kicks against me, which doesn't slow my stride one bit. The crowd parts for me, a few men giving me knowing nods and slapping each other's backs with approval. I keep my eyes trained forward, arm locked tight around my cargo.

We finally get outside, the cold air biting against my heated skin. I debate dropping her, but instead, I carry her all the way to the ranch truck Cash drove us here in. The door is unlocked—*thank fuck*—and I jerk on the handle before throwing her onto the worn leather seat inside.

"Are you out of your fucking mind?" she screams at me, slapping my shoulder.

I grit my teeth, making the mistake of slowly looking up at her, seeing her wet shirt that's effectively sticking to her breasts, nipples puckering under the thin, wet fabric. I can see the outline of her areolas, but the fact that every other man in that bar got the same tantalizing view ignites a rage inside me that simmers underneath my skin. They're perfect, round globes that

I'd need much more time and privacy to properly inspect.

I need to get the fuck away from her.

"You're fired." The words are out before I have time to think. "You're not working for Redford Ranch and acting like this in public. It's unacceptable."

She gapes at me, blue-green eyes wide and unblinking. "You have no right to fire me. I'm not your employee."

"I can do whatever the fuck I want when it comes to *my* family ranch. I'm back, and I'm not going anywhere. There needs to be some changes around here, starting with you, Dixon. You're *gone.*"

She blinks then, and I see a pool of moisture building up in her eyes. An invisible pang hits me in the chest. I ignore the feeling as I lean in closer to her ear, her vanilla scent in my nostrils.

"I don't trust you." My voice is a low growl, and I'm careful not to touch her again. "Who your father is will never change, and you dating my brother doesn't mean a damn thing to me. He'll grow up and see that I'm right. Now that I'm back, I won't keep letting him make *this* mistake."

Her lips part, the cold air visible as she exhales. "You think ..." She blinks, swallowing. "Duke and I aren't together anymore. Did you not know that?" Her voice is growing hoarse as her teeth begin to chatter.

My brow furrows just as Cash, Sterling, Duke, and Dolly all walk up together.

I turn to face my youngest brother. "You broke up?" I need to hear it from him directly.

Duke's brows shoot up. "Uh, yeah, like, over three years

ago. Right after you were locked up." He glances at Rosie with squinted eyes.

Dolly is gaping at me. "What's the issue, Holden? It was just a harmless competition. She was about to win!"

I glance down at my little sister's face. "One you'd better not even *think* about entering."

She snorts. "Right, like I'd ever win. Now, if I had Rosie's set of knockers, then you might have something to worry about." She laughs, skipping around to the other side of the truck.

Now that I know she's not in a relationship with my little brother, I feel even stronger about the need to stay as far away from Rosie Dixon as physically possible. I turn back to her, grabbing her knees and tucking them into the truck before slamming the door.

"Let's go," I bark.

THE COLLAR of my shirt is itching my neck. The muscle I gained from doing prison workouts grew parts of me I didn't even realize. Even now, I'm waking up at all hours of the night to do one-armed push-ups, pull-ups, and planks. It clears my head when I can't sleep, which is most nights.

"I need some hard liquor to get through this shit," Sterling leans over to whisper.

I keep my eyes trained ahead of me, where the mayor stands onstage. Clay Dixon is taking the podium to give a speech that's full of bullshit and lies, as all politicians do when they're approaching an election year. My blood is rushing in my ears as I watch him standing above us, still so powerful. Mayor Dixon waves to the crowd. He's wearing a navy-blue shirt with a bolo tie and a sports coat with a black felt Stetson.

La Pradera is on the outskirts of one of the last remaining Indian reservations in Texas. The proximity to New Mexico and old Mexico has a heavy influence on the local fashion.

"Good morning. Thank you all for rising so early to come hear me give a boring old speech. As mayor of La Pradera, I'm always happy to see so many faces of the hardworking individuals who call Kowata County home. After all, I am only a humble servant to the people, chosen by you to keep our town a place of integrity, safe for your families to live." His eyes skim over the crowd, a practiced smile on his thin lips. His gaze lands on mine, his smile faltering for a millisecond before he moves on.

"I'm sure you all have wondered what the next campaign will look like, but I can tell you now that I have no intention of wasting your time with empty promises. My new proposal for our great city is to not only increase funds to the schools for educating the next generation, but instead of raising the taxes on our good citizens, we'll also be taxing the businesses and landowners who can actually afford it. Anyone who owns a business with an annual gross revenue of over one million dollars in specific sales will now see an increase in taxes. In addition, the local businesses that use cattle in events or shows will pay an additional tax to start finally paving the dirt roads that lead to the arenas—a project that is long overdue."

The crowd roars with applause. I exhale a deep breath as my heart pounds loudly in my ears. Cash shifts in his seat next to me, forever the calm, quiet one.

The Dixon-Redford feud is an age-old bullshit story. It all started before I was born, when my mother ended up dating both Clay Dixon and my father, Wyatt Redford. She chose my father, ran off with him, and married him while pregnant with me.

Clay Dixon has hated every Redford descendant ever since.

I'm about ready to launch the cheap metal chair I'm sitting in at our good mayor's head. To most people, his proposal sounds genuine. It appeals to a larger crowd of citizens who are not cattle ranchers and do not produce all the beef for hundreds of thousands of people. This new tax bill sounds like a promising idea to benefit the school system. Why shouldn't the business owners pay it?

To a businessman who understands how it all really works, it will only hurt the layman and the consumer, and it will heavily pad the pockets of the local government. Increased taxes result in bigger personal bonuses for the politicians, which I'm positive is a detail that Dixon is leaving out.

Increasing taxes on my head of cattle forces ranchers like us to raise the price of it, which the consumer will pay. Just because Redford Ranch grosses over a million dollars a year does not mean we profit that much. We must first buy feed for the cattle, then pay our ranch hands, buy equipment like trailers and ATVs, build new barns to replace old ones, and the list goes on and on. Work on a ranch is never done. Just last year alone, we actually lost money by the end of the year, which means we all technically worked the entire year for free. We won't be making that same mistake again.

"He sure knows how to convince a crowd he's the second coming, doesn't he?" Sterling mumbles under his breath.

11
ROSIE

"I only have thirty minutes for lunch. I have to go meet Dolly after."

My father chews his chicken fried steak, studying me closely. He's a big man with a rounded barrel chest and large hands. The gray in his mustache has become more prominent since the last time we sat down, just the two of us, to talk.

I avoided his calls and texts for as long as I could. Guilt had been gnawing at me, so I finally responded and agreed to Sunday lunch with him at his favorite steak house in town when he said he wanted to discuss the holidays. They sat us at his usual table during the busy hour.

"So, the maid work hasn't lost its luster yet?"

I spear a dry cucumber slice on the edge of my salad bowl. "I'm not a maid. I'm a housekeeper and a cook."

"I certainly would have never guessed that a daughter of mine would stoop to this degree. You have more of your mother in you each day."

The barb doesn't surprise me, as he's always verbally torn down my mom with subtle passive-aggressive words. I sigh internally, glancing at my phone screen to see that I have thirteen minutes left to endure.

"Now that the man who murdered your own flesh and blood has been released from prison, I expect to have you back home, where it's safe."

"I like my job." I don't bother mentioning that the oldest Redford brother *technically* fired me over the weekend. "My best friend is sick and can't keep up with all the housework and cooking alone. It's not like I live there. I have my own apartment." I pop my knuckles, frustrated that I'm even sitting here in this position, being forced to answer these questions.

I'm a grown adult woman. For some reason, cutting off my father despite his many shortcomings hasn't been easy. So far, the only part that has been easy was letting go of the financial assistance. Even that has been difficult, considering my credit card debt grows almost daily.

I poke at the salad.

"If you're going to be fraternizing with an ex-con, you could make it a point to listen in on any important conversations they might have. You heard any talk of The Riders?"

The skin on the back of my neck prickles. I swallow over a lump, reaching for a cold roll in the basket in the center of the table to butter it.

I shrug. "I don't really hang out with the guys when they talk business. Dolly and I are always in the kitchen or around the house. Did you want to discuss Thanksgiving?" I mentally prepare myself to tell him I'll be eating frozen pot pie on my couch, alone.

My father ignores my question. He leans forward, a dark smile curling on his thin lips. "Now, I know I didn't have such a pretty daughter for nothing. You're perfectly capable of getting one of them to spill something valuable to me. What about the one you ran around with during high school?"

I blanch at his words. He *hated* me for dating Duke. He hated it so much that he installed a spying app on my phone that would send him all of our text messages. He used to get the sheriff to pull Duke's truck over anytime he saw it even if Duke wasn't doing anything wrong. My father made our relationship so stressful, and to this day, I haven't been able to forgive him for it even though Duke and I are way over.

I glance at my phone to note the time.

"I have to get going soon. I'm worried about Mom. Have you heard from her?" A subject change seems like the safest response at this point in the conversation.

He shakes his head, signaling to the waiter that he needs another glass of sweet tea. "Your mother is a woman with her own mind and her own life. We're the type of couple who doesn't check in every other hour."

His dismissal is typical, yet the way he avoids eye contact with me while he says it raises a tiny pink flag in my mind.

Does he not know where she is?

"I talked to her yesterday, but she didn't mention when she'd be home," I muse.

He narrows his gaze, studying the floral design of my

glass as condensation drips down it. The waitress returns with a pitcher of tea, smiling at my father as she reaches for his glass. She fills mine up next. I've always loved sweet tea, just like my dad. Every time we come here, he orders us two glasses of sweet tea with extra ice. It's one of the rare tender moments we still share, but it always makes me smile.

"Can I get you anything else, Mayor Dixon?" Her Southern drawl is heavy with a flirtatious undertone, and I resist the urge to roll my eyes as his trail over her curves.

"Not today, Ashley. The food was excellent." He watches her swaying hips as she sashays away.

My appetite has abandoned me, but I nibble on the buttered roll to have something to do with my hands. The ball in the pit of my stomach tightens with his next words, which he speaks as calmly as if he were ordering dessert.

"The man is responsible for spilling my little brother's blood. Three and a half years behind bars doesn't scratch the surface of paying for what he did. As your father, all I'm asking is for you to keep your ears open for any pertinent business-related information. He's a hardened criminal, a murderer. I have it on good authority that he's gotten himself mixed up with the wrong crowd while he was locked up."

He waves at one of the town council members who just walked through the doors, as if he didn't just drop a bomb on me.

As much as I despise him, there's a chance he's telling the truth about Holden.

Is he just trying to watch out for me?

What about what Dolly told me Cain was doing?

"I'm Dolly's best friend. He loves her, and even if it were only for her sake, he wouldn't hurt me."

He scoffs, shaking his head as he pulls out two crisp one-hundred-dollar bills from his wallet and tosses them onto the white tablecloth.

"You'll learn, Rosie. I just hope you find the sense to make the smart decision before it's too late for you too."

THE FOLLOWING MORNING, I arrive at the ranch bright and early. For some strange, mysterious reason, I decided to wear muted pink lipstick and a push-up bra under my white V-neck today.

If Holden Redford expects to fire me, I'm hoping it'll be slightly painful for him.

Is this beneath me?

Obviously.

Does it make me pathetic to use my body to try and keep my job?

Of course.

Am I doing it anyway because I love working here and I really don't want to have to start job-hunting?

Also yes.

I strut through the front door like it's just another Monday. The icky memory of lunch with my father washes over me, along with his comment about spying on the

Redfords for him. The instant physical discomfort nearly makes me trip, but I shake my head, trying to get rid of it.

The kitchen is empty. It's still early, just past seven in the morning. I start brewing a full pot of coffee, knowing it'll be emptied as soon as the guys and Dolly make their way in. I'm sure a few of them are already up, checking on the animals in the barn.

I'm dumping the fresh grounds into the filter basket when I feel a warmth behind me.

"What do you think you're doing here?" A deeply erotic morning voice right by my ear makes me gulp.

I spill the black grounds all over the white marble countertop. My heart is thundering in my ears. I manage to finish up making the pot, brushing the spilled grounds into my hand and dumping them in with the rest.

After pushing the Start button, I slowly turn around, tilting my head back to meet Holden's gaze. The sharp, freshly shaved jawline, with stitches on the side, steals my focus for a split second before his full lips come into view, followed by an angular, strong nose and almost black eyes. His gaze is hard and unflinching.

"Coffee?" I ask, praying that my flushed neck isn't visible to him in the dimly lit kitchen.

He moves forward, crowding me against the cabinetry with one step. My lower back is wedged up against it, but he still leans in close enough until his upper thigh is pressed against my hip bone. I gasp, barely audible, my right hand reaching back to grip the countertop to gain some kind of physical leverage.

"You don't work here anymore," he grits out, his rough, scratchy tone causing goose bumps to rise on my arms.

Is he trying to scare me?

I lift my chin. "I don't take orders from you. You're not my superior."

My chest is rising and falling rapidly as we face off.

My father's words are still fresh in my mind. *"He's a hard-ened criminal, a murderer."*

My pulse is a fluttering flag in the wind, wildly unmanaged.

Why does he have to smell so damn good though?

Like leather and cedar and musky soap. It fills my nostrils, weakening my knees. Holden flexes his jaw, and I catch his eyes as they roam down over my chest briefly before returning to meet my gaze.

Ha, gotcha.

"Are you trying to piss me off, Dixon?"

He leans farther down, reaching his hand up to brace it against the upper cabinets. His lower half is pinned against me, sending a flood of warmth over my already-flushed skin.

I respond in my sweetest, sultriest voice, "You sure you really want me to leave? Who will you mess with when I'm gone?"

I tilt my head to the side, calling his bluff. I hold my breath, willing him to smile, laugh, even just to back away in defeat. The room gets warmer with each second that crawls by.

He finally moves, reaching behind me with his other hand, sending a shock through my nervous system when he grips the back of my neck firmly with his strong fingers, reminding me just how big and dangerous he is. I'm completely at his mercy, powerless to fight him off if he wanted to actually hurt me.

He tilts closer to my ear until his breath sends a shudder down my spine. "I have no interest in my brother's sloppy seconds."

He takes a step back from me, immediately causing my nipples to harden with the cold air that hits me.

What the fuck does that mean?

"I'm sorry, what?" I ask, trying to remain calm.

Is he suggesting that because I dated Duke in high school, *I'm ... used up?*

He lifts his chin, folding his muscular, tanned arms across his chest. He's wearing a soft-looking black T-shirt, stretched across his broad shoulders, the emblem on the front so faded that I can't make it out. His whitewashed Wranglers make it hard to keep my eyes up, but really every part of him is delightful to look at.

Bastard.

"I told you Friday night that you're done working here. If I have to change the locks on the house, I will. I'm sure you'll have no trouble finding similar employment on another ranch after your display at Old Harry's."

I release the oxygen from my lungs, counting to ten slowly in my head before responding.

"Not that. What did you mean by *sloppy seconds?*"

He blinks at me, like my question is somehow confusing. Footsteps interrupt us, and Dolly's voice breaks through the trance we were both in.

"Good morning! How'd you sleep?" She walks up to her

brother, pulling him into a side hug. Her mood since his release is still upbeat, apparently.

Holden hugs her back, but doesn't take his eyes off of me. "Fine."

She seems to sense the tension, her smile dropping as she inspects his face before switching her gaze to mine. "What happened?"

I fold my arms to match his stance. "He fired me."

Dolly gasps, her hand clapping against her chest. "*Who* fired you?"

Holden jerks his gaze from my face, turning his attention to Dolly's clutched chest. "Are you okay?"

She's still looking at me, and I indicate her oldest brother with my eyes, using our best-friends-since-first grade telepathy.

She turns to face him, her mouth rounded into an O-shape. "Holden James Redford. You can't fire her! What were you thinking?"

His jaw is clenched as he observes her carefully, her hands now planted on her hips. He sighs, unfolding his arms and shaking his head.

"I'm not saying she can't be your friend anymore, but we can't take any risks right now with—"

"Do you want me to be hospitalized? To pass out from all the work that needs to be done around here?" she demands.

He surveys his little sister, leaning back from her as she continues.

"I got really sick, Holden. Really, really sick ... six months ago." Her voice softens with what I sense is completely fake emotion.

The demeanor in the room darkens immediately.

He interrupts her. "Why the fuck was I not—"

"We didn't tell you because you couldn't do anything about it anyway ... but it was bad. Rosie showed up for me. She came over daily and made me soup, cleaned up, kept this place going and me company so the guys could work. After a week straight of it, Cash, Sterling, and Duke all insisted on paying her. I got better, but we agreed that hiring Rosie was the best decision for the ranch and for my health. It's also ten times less lonely for me. Does that matter to you at all?"

He sighs, rubbing the back of his neck and looking up at the ceiling.

"You should have told me you were sick. Cash should have told me." The pained sound of concern in his voice squeezes my heart. There's also a hint of anger.

This is the same dick who just tried to intimidate and fire you for no reason.

He also called you sloppy seconds.

Fuck this guy. Fuck this guy so hard.

If he wasn't my best friend's brother and my employer *and* an ex-con, I would seriously consider punching him in his smug face.

He turns to me, taking a step in my direction. I plant my feet firmly on the kitchen floor, daring him to make another stupid, sexist comment, but he doesn't even look at me. He reaches for the cabinet next to my head, extracting two mugs. He grabs the now-full coffeepot and fills the two cups, turning around to hand one to Dolly.

"She can stay. For you, Dolls." He kisses the top of her

head before leaving the room, not even bothering to give me another glance.

Dolly's mouth gapes after him as he retreats through the back door. I turn, reaching for my own coffee mug. My pride stings, but at least I'm still employed.

"Rosie, what did I miss?" Her voice is an intense whisper. "Did he even give you a reason?"

I shrug. I don't want to voice the part about being labeled *sloppy seconds*. It was hurtful enough, and I'm not ready to talk about it.

"He was pissed off about the wet T-shirt contest. He said it was a bad look for the ranch."

Dolly raises a brow as she walks to the fridge to get the maple-flavored creamer—our favorite. "What? A bad look? That's insane. If anything, you brought us *more* business. It must be something else."

I take the creamer when she's done, pouring myself some and stirring it in with a spoon. "I know you love him, but he was kind of a dick to me."

She nods, her face softening. "I'm really sorry. He's always been ... difficult, but I can tell that prison changed him. I don't think he's anywhere near seeing past your last name. While we've all been healing and growing to fully trust you, seeing that you're not at all like your father and uncle, Holden's been rotting in a cell. He's been actively suffering because of what they did ... and the way he dealt with it, obviously. I think he just needs time to see you how I see you, how all of us do."

I nod, taking a deep breath and letting her words caress my bruised ego. As much as I'm reeling from his words and the fact that he's so hell-bent on getting rid of me, I know she's right.

"He hates me. He fucking *hates* me, Dolly." I release a shaky exhale.

She nods, pulling me into a tight hug. "I'm going to talk to him, okay? Maybe you two just need time to talk, to express your hurt and his anger?"

I shake my head, pulling back from her. "I think it would be best if we just kept away from each other. He's adapting back to normal life, and I'm a hindrance."

The dishwasher needs emptying, so I start working on it. "Maybe my presence here just reminds him of everything that happened that night."

My stomach feels queasy at the thought. Holden actively wants to get rid of me and hasn't been subtle about it, but whenever that night comes up in my head, I still picture him in the hay, getting a blow job.

Against my will, the scene appears in my mind every time I use my bullet vibrator. I'm tortured and intensely aroused by it, so much so that I'm disgusted with myself. Feeling what I *thought* was his boner in the pantry when I was drunk last week has only made it worse, and now, the tension between us is making me ache in all the wrong ways.

I've never even experienced sex, but I know with one hundred percent certainty that it would be mind-fucking-shattering with him. I've fantasized about it more times than I can count.

And now, he's back here, so deliciously sexy and fucking mean as hell to me. I'm pathetic, but I can't tell Dolly about it. I'll take these humiliating feelings to my grave.

She rushes to my side, cupping my face tenderly. "You had nothing to do with it. You were an innocent bystander. He just needs to get acclimated to you being here—that's all. We should've warned him that you were working here. Either way, neither of you is going anywhere. You're both too important to me."

12

HOLDEN

Her tits are in my face, nipples wet and puckered, covered only by the damp fabric of her white T-shirt. I grip her hips, pulling her down over my denim-covered erection. I'm so hard that it hurts, straining against the thick fabric.

"Been thinking about me, Redford? You sure are hard and ready for it. I thought you hated me." Her voice is breathy and sensual.

The room is so dark, only lit by the moonlight spilling through the window. I'm not exactly sure where we are. I grit my teeth, not knowing why the hell we're even in this position. I'm way too fucking turned on to push her off of me now even if she has Dixon blood running through her veins and she's fucked my brother a thousand times.

I just need her once, one time. Now.

"Shut that pretty mouth, then open it and wrap it around my dick," I order.

She bites her lip, closing her eyes and tilting her head back. My eyes trail down her delicate neck before focusing on her flaw-

less tits. I move my thumb over the top of one, hardening it with the stimulation.

"I fucking hate you too," she exhales, panting and moaning. "Oh, yes, don't stop."

She's just as turned on as I am. My dick is brushing up against the sensitive spot between her thighs.

"Oh, yeah? You hate me … but right now, you're riding me like a damn cowgirl, angel."

Her eyes snap down to meet mine. I've never called her anything but her cursed last name. She reaches down for the button of my jeans, biting her lip as she undoes it, eyes shining with excitement. We're both silent now, the anticipation too great to break it with words.

We've both been picturing it for so long. What if it doesn't meet our expectations?

I'm so close to busting that as soon as she touches my dick, I almost come. It's been three and a half years since I've felt a woman's hand or mouth on my dick.

Rosie Dixon is the one I begrudgingly pictured in the dark of my cell when I had to rub one out to prevent myself from going insane. I would imagine her blue-green eyes, copper-red hair, and the same lust-filled look she gave me that night in the barn. The big tits are new, but I'm not mad about that development.

She licks her lips before lowering herself down over me, gripping my erection tighter with her hand before she gently licks the sensitive, seeping tip.

I groan with thick pleasure, dropping my head back on the pillow as the hot semen spews out of me, completely uncontrollable.

"Fuck, angel. Fuck."

. . .

I wake with a start, sweat dripping down my bare chest. The room is sweltering. Someone must've turned the heat up to eighty-five degrees. The only sound is my gasp for oxygen.

The wetness inside my boxers is sticking to the skin of my balls and upper thighs. I reach my hand down, discovering that the sticky mess is definitely the result of me having a vivid, dirty dream about Rosie Dixon—my little brother's ex-girlfriend—and coming in my sleep.

Fuck.

I called her sloppy seconds like a complete dickhead yesterday morning.

I didn't mean it like she clearly took it, judging by the look on her face.

I meant that I could never sleep with a woman one of my brothers had been inside. It's a matter of principle. Fucking her would essentially be ... incest, which is sick.

Not to mention, I have no idea how Duke feels about his ex. *How could he not be sick over losing her and desperate to win her back?*

And Dolly, who seems to think the sun rises and sets when Rosie walks into the room, would definitely not be okay with it. On her end, I get the Rosie obsession. She barely remembers our mother, and because of her illness, she couldn't be a fully functioning teenage girl when it was her time. Rosie has never left her side.

I lie awake in the darkness, letting my body temperature return to a normal range as I listen to the noises of the ranch.

An owl hoots somewhere outside my window, followed by a coyote in the distance, signaling his pack.

Why the actual fuck did I just have a wet dream about Rosie Dixon?

The heat of the night starts getting to my head, making me remember what it was like to wake up in prison when the AC was broken and it felt like the Santa Fe desert in July. I throw the covers off, swinging my legs over the side of the bed.

The hallway is dark as I walk to the kitchen from memory. I don't know what time it is, but based on the silence, everyone appears to still be sleeping.

A lamp on the countertop in the large kitchen illuminates the space. A plate of jumbo lemon-poppyseed muffins is in the center of one of the islands.

I reach for a clean glass in one of the cabinets, filling it with water from the refrigerator. The sound of me gulping it down is loud in my ears.

"Oh ... I didn't know anyone was up."

My muscles tense instantly. I lower the cup, turning to face the sultry voice. Rosie is standing in the kitchen, biting her lip, staring at my shirtless torso with wide eyes. Her demeanor is a far cry from the woman who so boldly stood up to me yesterday, refusing to let me fire her. This version of her looks vulnerable and ... shy somehow.

I look down at her hands to see a half-eaten bowl of *my* strawberry ice cream in her hands.

"What are you doing here?" No matter how much Dolly needs her, I can't risk softening toward her, not when my subconscious clearly has other desires.

"Are you going to ask me that every time you see me in this house?" She cocks her head to the side, arching an eyebrow. She slides her spoon into the bowl, lifting the pink dessert up to her full lips. She leisurely tastes the sweetness with her lips.

I set the glass down on the countertop. The memory of what just happened in my head and in my sheets is still too fresh for me to be alone with her. I'm afraid of what I might do. My dick starts to fill with blood again. The physical boundary of the double kitchen islands between us is necessary for me to not consider reenacting the dream. I'm not used to fighting my desires for women. They've always come easily for me ... in more ways than one.

The image of her the night of the wet T-shirt contest clouds my gaze. I clench my fists, flexing my arms as I brace myself against the island.

I should walk away before that melted strawberry ice cream gets in places it shouldn't.

"No, Dixon, I'm not. Just wondering, since it's the middle of the night, if you're really this dedicated of an employee or if there's something else keeping you around."

I keep my gaze on the veins in the marble, refusing to look up at her.

"Um, yeah, no. My car wouldn't start. Duke told me to sleep on the couch."

I scoff. "Duke told you that, did he?" I shake my head, finally meeting her gaze. "Surprised he didn't invite you to share his bed."

Maybe he did, and she turned it down.

"We're not together anymore. Why do you keep bringing

it up? It's getting weird." She hops up onto the countertop, swinging her legs in the air. She slowly licks off another bite of my ice cream. A pale pink drop lingers on her lips, activating my salivary glands and sending more blood into my groin.

Get it together.

"When I left, you were two little lovebirds, and all he talked about was how he couldn't wait to get in your pants. Guess it's hard to imagine y'all in a different dynamic."

"Maybe you're overthinking it. How often do you think about it?"

I force myself to physically relax my stance. She's suspicious of my interest in her. She thinks it has something to do with me wanting her physically.

She's not wrong, but it starts and ends with her sultry, feminine allure and the temptation of those lips tasting like sweet strawberries.

Just because my body wants to fuck hers doesn't mean I don't hate her.

"You seem to think that just because the low-cut tops work on ninety percent of the male population, the sex-kitten act will have the same effect on me. This thing between us is about your last name and the fact that I don't trust you—and I *never* will. I don't trust you with my family, on my ranch. I don't fucking want you here." I lean forward, my body tense as I try to get it through her head exactly where I stand. "You can spread your legs for each and every one of my brothers if you want, but I'd rather rot in prison for another three and a half years than touch you. I'd stay celibate for life if you were the last woman on this fucking planet. So, keep prancing around my house like I'll give in one day and take you to my bed, but you're wasting time and embarrassing yourself."

Her normally tough, impenetrable expression seems to have fallen. Her eyes are blinking rapidly, wild copper-red hair spilling around her shoulders. A fleeting sense of guilt shoots through me, but it vanishes as soon as it appears.

I need her to hate me too.

She slowly slides down from the countertop, walking toward me. I don't risk moving because my erection hasn't fully subsided yet. It's currently hidden by the countertop. She ignores me, taking her bowl to rinse it out in the sink. She carefully loads it into the dishwasher before walking down the hallway toward the bedrooms without another word.

I wait about ten seconds, steadying my breath, but as soon as I turn around, I can't see her anymore in the darkness. A door clicks shut, and I have no idea which sibling's room she's in now, which is somehow more tortuous than having a wet dream about her, alone in my bed.

THREE AND A HALF YEARS EARLIER

"Where have you looked for her? I'm assuming you called her phone?"

"Yes, we called her. We searched the house and the horse

barn," Cash says. He's always the calm one, and now is no exception.

"Do we have her location? I thought she shared it on her phone?"

"Rosie probably has it on Snapchat. I'll ask her." Duke pulls out his phone, tapping the screen and putting it up to his ear.

His little girlfriend has been up to no good tonight. I'm hoping her best friend isn't in the same camp out in the cold, dark night.

"Let's go look at the cabin. She couldn't be far. What about the hilltop? Are any of the mules or four-wheelers missing?"

The four-wheelers and mules are ATVs, used for work and recreational travel across the expansive ranch.

"I'll go check," Sterling says. His big frame stalks off toward the barn we keep them in.

"Hey, baby. We were just wondering if you were able to find Dolly on her Snap Map. Does she have that on?" Duke walks a few steps away as he cradles the phone against his ear.

My little brother's infatuation with the mayor's daughter has been a thorn in my side for a year now. He's painfully obsessed with her. Cash and I have tried taking him to the Strip in Vegas, local bars, parties, anywhere we can think of to distract him from Rosie Lou Dixon, using our old IDs to get him in.

He's consumed with her.

I can't deny that she's fucking hot, but her bloodline

should be enough of a reason to turn the complete opposite direction without a second thought.

"Oh shit. Okay. I'll tell them. Thanks, baby."

I shift my stance, getting restless the longer he takes. "What did she say?"

He turns back to us as he ends the call. He exhales as his gaze shifts from mine to Cash's. "She said her location is pinging somewhere around the creek, the low crossing."

I cock my gun, the sound of the bullet sliding inside the chamber echoing through the hay barn. "Let's go."

If someone has to get hurt tonight, so be it. I'll do anything it takes to protect my little sister.

13
ROSIE
PRESENT DAY

Another week passes without a call from my mom. I'm desperate to hear her voice. I miss her so much that my chest aches. She's texted me back periodically, but nothing substantial enough to ease my anxiety. Her coping mechanisms have never been healthy, but as an adult, I've grown to realize just how toxic they truly are. Drinking heavily every day and taking off with no warning or communication isn't the way most mothers act.

Ever since having lunch with my dad, followed by my confrontation with Holden, I've been more than a little on edge. I finally sat down with my dusty laptop and started looking into nursing school again. School has been on the back burner for a while now, but after coming dangerously close to losing my job and the inescapable tension that remains, I've realized that my days at Redford Ranch are clearly numbered. I sent out a request for my transcripts and a few emails to school financial aid offices, trying to get it sorted out and begin the process.

"What's on your mind? You've been acting weird for days." Dolly sets four plastic boxes of organic strawberries inside the grocery cart.

She's been making homemade strawberry ice cream for Holden every few days since he's been home. She makes a huge batch of it so that he has enough stocked away in the freezer for his nightly bowl, banishing the other guys from touching it.

"You ever think you and Holden are a little too close?" I change the subject, not wanting to dive into anything that's on my mind.

Dolly shrugs. "He killed a man and went to prison to protect me. Homemade ice cream is the least I can do to repay him."

They were always close, but the incident with Cain amplified their bond tenfold.

A bite of guilt gnaws at my side. I've been letting my personal issues with Holden interfere with my friendship with Dolly when I should be happy that she finally has her older brother back.

"I just wish he didn't have it out for me. It's making for a toxic work environment."

Dolly sorts through a pile of bright green limes, meticulously inspecting each one before selecting the ones she wants. We've made our weekly shopping hauls into a ritual, always stopping for a croissant at the bakery and white chocolate lattes with almond milk at the in-store coffee shop. I sip on mine slowly, savoring each taste after the long week I've had.

"He's being protective. I told you, he just needs time to

get used to you being around. He's naturally suspicious, and who knows if he's still mentally operating on a prisoner's social hierarchy? I've been reading this book about helping loved ones adjust back to civilian life. The trauma that ex-cons survived in prison is something they might never talk about. We can't know what he's seen or endured. Have you noticed how enormous his shoulders have gotten? He probably had to fight to protect himself." She shudders.

Yeah, I haven't stopped noticing how big and muscular his shoulders are ... as well as how vascular his hands are and how defined and toned his abs, back muscles—

"You know what I think would help?" She interrupts my corrupt thoughts, causing my cheeks to flush, as if she could hear what was going through my head. She directs a meaningful look at me. "I think you and Duke should really just *try* going out again. If you started dating him again, Holden would have no choice but to—"

I hold a hand up. "We aren't like that anymore. I really don't see Duke that way. Plus, I thought you were done with any friends who hang around just to sleep with your brothers?"

There's an endless list of friends Dolly's lost after they ended up in one or another of her brother's beds. She always feels used, and usually, she's right. The friendships were a farce from the start.

She waves me off, setting the huge bag of limes inside the cart and moving over to the lemons. "I lost friends because they only wanted to talk to me to get close to one of the guys. You're different. You've already dated one. And we've been friends since first grade. You didn't even know I had four older brothers back then. I've decided I want you to be my sister. I've caught Duke looking at you longingly a few times lately. I don't think he's over it at all. What y'all had before was high school; it was immature. You've both grown up a lot."

I push the cart forward as we make our way through the produce. She's romanticized the idea of us in her head so much now that I don't know how she'll ever let it go. She's never liked any other guy I've ever dated, which is hardly anyone. My dating track record is almost as sad as hers.

After changing the subject and chatting about what our recipe plans are for the week, Dolly stops right in her tracks in the middle of the cracker aisle. I nearly run into her with the basket.

"Was it the sex? Is that it?" she says.

I freeze. "Huh?"

She spins around. "I know we've never talked about it because he's my brother and it would be weird as hell, but was he, like, bad in bed? Is that why?"

"Shh," I shush her, looking around. "You are talking so loud right now."

"Well, was that it?" she insists. "You told me you only made out with Trevor, and you let Cody suck on your boobs, right? So, the only guy you've had sex with is Duke."

I open my mouth, shutting it and pursing my lips before finally speaking. "Duke and I never did ... it."

She stares at me, jaw slightly ajar. "All this time, I thought I was the only virgin between us. Why didn't you tell me?"

I bite my lip. After Holden's arrest, Duke and I stayed

together for a while, but I was too shaken up about the entire thing. We finally broke up, and Dolly and I quit speaking. Once she and I finally worked our issues out and became friends again, I only told her about the guys and experiences I'd had since. None of them were memorable.

"I'm sorry." I shrug. "It wasn't exactly a secret or anything. We did fool around, and he took my top off and sucked on my nipples. That's where it stopped."

She nods, turning to select a box of crackers from the shelf. "Well, I'm pretty sure he hooked up with Shayley Brown a few times after the breakup. She said they did anyway. I haven't asked him."

She turns and studies me, gauging my reaction. I laugh, tightening my thick, low ponytail.

"I am not bothered by it, okay? I'm sorry, but there's just nothing there anymore. And if he is bad in bed, I'd have no earthly idea or anything to even compare it to. I'm not exactly saving myself, but you know better than anyone how shallow and smelly the dating pool is around here."

She groans. "Ugh, tell me about it. I haven't even had a crush on anyone in ages. We should see if we can start getting a say in the next ranch hands they hire and only let the hot ones through."

I laugh. "Yes, excellent idea. They're always picking the ones that are missing teeth or have horrible breath."

"Who's missing teeth and has horrible breath?"

We both turn to face the voice, which happens to be Madi, flanked by Ginny and Shayley. They were one grade above me and Dolly.

Ginny and I were acquaintances in high school, but we've

only stayed in contact since then by occasionally replying to each other's stories on social media. Shayley and Madi have always been close, bonded by their mutual obsession with dating and sleeping with the Redford brothers. I guess, now, they've both accomplished it.

I wonder how long they've been standing there, listening to us talk.

Did they hear the details about my lack of sexual experience?

I'm not embarrassed about being a twenty-one-year-old virgin, but I'm also not keen on everyone in our town knowing my business.

"Uh, the guys they always hire to work on the ranch," I offer.

I doubt Dolly will entertain a conversation with Madi after finding out she was faking her entire relationship with Holden. It was a fucked-up thing to do, and as her best friend, I'm definitely on Dolly's side. I've never liked Madi.

"I heard you were planning a welcome-home party for Holden," Ginny says.

An awkward silence follows her words. I grind my teeth for a moment before shaking my head.

"Not really. He doesn't want a bunch of strangers in the house," I offer.

It's the truth. Holden probably wouldn't even show up if we tried to throw him one. He hasn't hung around the house much the past few days, and I have no idea if he's off meeting women in bars, working the ranch, or simply enjoying his freedom in various nefarious ways. My father's words about the criminal relationships he built in prison floats through my thoughts.

"Well, if you change your mind and decide to, we'd love to help host," Ginny says. "I feel like a lot of people really missed him."

"They used to have awesome parties out there." Shayley speaks for the first time.

I stare at her, wondering if that was one of the times she hooked up with Duke. He and Sterling were usually the ones having friends over to drink. Dolly and I were never allowed to join in because we were underage.

The conversation is growing more awkward as Dolly stares down Madi, neither of them speaking. I start to slowly push the cart in the direction of the dairy aisle.

"We got some frozen food that's starting to melt, so ... we'll see y'all later."

Ginny and Shayley both nod, but Madi huffs and spins around on her heel without a word.

BACK ON THE RANCH, I'm working at the kitchen island to chop an onion. My eyes water more with each slice of the knife. It's Friday, but I won't take my bra off until after dinner, when the guys have scattered and Dolly and I have the living room to ourselves, even though the underwire is digging into me. I need to get rid of this bra. It doesn't fit anymore.

"What's cookin', good-lookin'?" Duke struts into the kitchen, followed by Cash, Sterling, and Holden.

My eyes dart up to meet the dark eyes of all of them, one

after the other, skipping over Holden. My breath is temporarily shallow in my lungs as I'm struck by the sheer overall hotness they exude when they're in a pack like this, fresh from working the ranch. It's almost too much for my hormones to cope with.

I must be ovulating.

They're filthy from working bulls and cows all day, slightly smelly but still incredibly attractive. There's something about dirty, hardworking blue-collar men that makes my eggs slide down my tubes like they're riding on a pat of butter.

Duke slides right up behind me, reaching his arms around my waist. It's overly familiar and unlike him, and my body tenses.

"How do I smell?" he asks.

"Ugh, disgusting. Get off me." I try to shrug him off.

He chuckles, leaning closer to whisper in my ear, "Wanna help me wash off?"

I turn to gape at him, wondering if he hit his head when he got bucked off the last time. He winks, and I realize he's playing some kind of game with me. My eyes flick to Holden's for a split second, seeing that they're focused on the place where Duke's arm is around my waist. His jaw is tense, but the rest of him looks relaxed and uninterested in us.

"Um, I have to watch the venison steaks or they'll burn."

He moves closer, his breath on my ear, "Dolls thinks this will get Holden off your ass. Trust me."

He reaches a hand down, gently patting my ass before pecking my cheek with a kiss. If I wasn't leaning up against the cabinets, I'd have fallen over when he moved away from me.

"Damn, do I need a cold beer. You boys want one?" he hollers back as he walks into the hallway, where there's an extra fridge to store cold beverages.

"I'll take one," Cash says.

"I'm gonna shower first," Sterling replies, walking out the back door toward the bunkhouse, where he and Cash sleep. Duke, Dolly, and Holden stay in the main house with Pops.

Holden is the only one who doesn't answer the question. I resist the urge to glance back at him.

"Y'all smell awful! Everyone has to shower before dinner!" Dolly announces when she returns to the kitchen.

I nod in agreement. "Please."

Duke returns with two beers, handing one to Cash before popping his open and leaning up against the counter next to me. He's smirking, bright blue eyes sparkling with mischief.

"So, after your little display at Old Harry's, I've been getting texts and DMs, asking if we're together or if you're up for grabs. I wasn't really sure what I should say."

My hand stills over the cast-iron skillet. I chew on the side of my lip, debating my response in light of our present company. Small-town rumors are rampant, and it seems since my employment here, people aren't sure what to make of my relationship with Duke. I never date anyone.

Would it make Holden more accepting of me if it looked like I was dating Duke again?

"Hmm, what did you want to say?" I say, leaning closer toward him.

Duke tries to hold in a laugh, tipping his beer back over his lips. I lick my thumb before reaching up to wipe off a smudge of dirt from his cheek. A shuffling sound from behind us draws my gaze. Holden disappears into the pantry, returning a moment later with a bottle of Gentleman Jack, pouring himself a generous amount into a glass. He lifts it to his lips, his gaze focused out the window over the kitchen sink.

"You two need to chill with that PDA. I'll have to wash my eyes out with soap," Cash grumbles.

Dolly laughs from the other side of the kitchen, where she's slicing the tops off strawberries. "Are you ditching me on braless Friday, Rosie? For my brother no less?"

I look over at her with wide eyes.

Are they really that committed to this ruse?

I shrug, turning back to the stove. Maybe this will work. Maybe Holden will get over his hell-bent desire to fire me. Maybe he'll drop his accusations that I'm spying on him for my father.

"Nah, she's not ditching you. Not until she's ready for bed, that is," Duke says. He brushes my long copper-red hair out of my face, plants a kiss on my cheek, and stalks out of the kitchen and into the living room.

14

HOLDEN

He's my little brother, the youngest of us boys.

I love him.

I care about his well-being.

I would sucker-punch a motherfucker for having the violent, unhinged thoughts about him that I'm currently having.

Duke and Rosie are a good couple. They make sense. I'm irrational for not being happy that they're rekindling their relationship.

My limbs are tingling the same way they would when a fight broke out in the prison, one I knew I wouldn't be able to avoid. The sensations coursing through my body are similar, but I know the situation is a much more dangerous one.

Why the fuck am I stressed about my little brother fucking his ex-girlfriend?

Three fingers of whiskey aren't enough, so I pour another glass, tossing it back just as quickly as the first. I can feel the heat of Cash's gaze on my face. I turn to meet his eyes. He raises a dark brow, clearly wondering why I'm suddenly drinking like this after three and a half years sober.

"You good, brother?" he says.

I tip my cowboy hat back, raising the glass of amber liquid. "Never better, brother. Never fucking better."

I allow my eyes to travel over to where the treacherous Dixon-blooded woman is currently making my dinner.

I can't fire her.

I can't be around her.

I can't fuck her.

I can't fucking stand looking at her all the damn time and *not* getting to feel her wavy, copper-colored hair and freckled skin underneath my fingers.

Most of all, I can't take watching my brother do it right in front of my eyes.

I slam the glass down on the island, turning to Cash. I clap my hand on his back. "Let's go out tonight."

Cash looks at me like I've lost my damn mind. I need him to drive at the rate I'm going.

He shakes his head with a sigh. "I guess I'd better. Who knows what kind of mess you'll get into on your own?"

AFTER TAKING a hot shower and shaving, I change into a plain blue T-shirt that fits me tighter than it used to and a worn pair of Wranglers. My hair needs cutting. I put on my tan felt Stetson and my snakeskin boots with blue-and-brown-hued scales. I'm ready to lay some good old-fashioned cowboy charm on a woman, preferably a redhead.

We leave as soon as we finish scarfing down dinner.

Once we pull up to Old Harry's and see a few cars and mostly trucks filling the dirt parking lot, I get an uneasy feeling in my gut. The word about my early release has spread far by now—and not just to the women who wrote me letters.

The doors are being manned by two brawny bouncers who look vaguely familiar. One of them has an armful of tattoos with different parts of the female form and anatomy, along with a neck tattoo of a chain. The other one is tall, at least six inches taller than my six-foot-three stature.

"Redfords, boss wants to see you," the one with the neck tattoo says. Instead of opening the main door, he starts leading us around the side of the building.

I glance at Cash and Sterling. They both shrug, clearly not knowing what this is about. Cash briefly rests his hand on the handgun concealed in his waistband. I had assumed once I was free I'd be on probation and not allowed to carry in public, but since my conviction was overturned, the cold press of my pistol on my hip brings me a peace of mind I haven't felt in years. If things go downhill, I know I can trust my brothers to have my back.

"We at least gonna get some bottle service?" I ask, following the bouncer.

Around the corner, there are three identical black Dodge pickups with extended cabs. One of them has bullet holes in the side of the truck bed, but other than that, they're in good condition.

"Boss'll fix you up," he says, reaching up to knock on a metal door that says *Employees Only*.

A few seconds later, the door creaks open. A woman wearing a men's pearl-snap button-down shirt, baggy jeans, and a flat-brimmed cowboy hat stands in the opening, blinking up at the three of us with oversize, calculating brown eyes. Her hair is tied back. She has a hunting knife sheathed on one hip and a nine-millimeter pistol strapped to the other one.

Without a word, she turns around to lead us through. I step over the threshold, followed by my brothers. The sound of male voices and high-pitched laughter reaches my ears. The place smells like an old distillery, musty with the strong odor of spilled alcohol. The walls are lined with old barn-wood, looking like a bad splinter and a tetanus shot waiting to happen.

"Who are you?" I ask.

"Jo," is all she says.

The hall finally ends, opening up to a room with the same cramped barnwood furniture that looks like it came from an estate sale in a retirement home and a crowd of old cowboys. I immediately recognize a handful of them as the organizers of The Riders we sell bulls to.

"Redford, about damn time you showed up here. Heard you were the fucker who abducted one of the girls the night of my wet T-shirt contest! I was worried you were back in jail after I found out who she was." Old Harry stands up from a poker table in the corner, a cigarette stuck to his lips.

A few Stetsons turn my way as hushed murmurs float throughout the smoky room.

A woman in Daisy Dukes with a low-cut blouse approaches us, smiling suggestively. Her blond ponytail sways with her steps.

"What can I get you, gentlemen?" She bats her overly thick eyelashes.

"Whiskey, neat," I say.

Cash doesn't want anything, but Sterling asks for a beer.

Harry gestures for us to sit at the poker table as he lights another cigarette, and the cowboys in three chairs vacate them. I choose one with my back to the wall, keeping my eyes on the exits and occupants. Cash chooses to stand, and Sterling sits beside me, leaning back and exhaling as his dark eyes sweep the room. Of all of us brothers, Cash is the silent one, but he's always on high alert. Our blood runs thicker than water, and I know both of them would take a bullet for me. Duke would too; he's just still in his early twenties, fucking around like life isn't mostly pain with little bursts of pleasure mixed in.

"You're looking robust, Redford. Some guys get out of the clank, all scrawny and lean, but you're fucking big. One of my boys said they ran into you up in Idaho. Slim Tim is what he goes by." Harry cracks a yellow smile, puffing out a cloud of smoke. He has twin silver braids resting on his drooping shoulders.

Slim Tim was bunked three cells down from me. He seemed to know everyone. He was a rare breed who didn't have enemies on either side, just contacts without any clear loyalties or gang affiliation. It doesn't surprise me that he's involved with Old Harry.

"He's in for another ten, right?" I ask.

Harry nods, tapping the ash into a tray. "Yep. He's more useful on the inside anyway. Man knows everyone."

"And seemed to piss off none."

Harry chuckles, his raspy voice on the verge of lung cancer. "So, he tells me you made some powerful friends behind bars. I've always said, if I were to ever get in the clank, I'd make good use of the time."

My eyes stay steady on Harry's. I know he's waiting for my expression to give something away. I made more friends than enemies, but that doesn't mean circumstances won't change on a whim. I've never liked Old Harry, though he's mostly harmless and my father's friend.

"Couldn't get my ice cream fix without making a few buddies, now could I?" I fold my arms over my chest.

The blond server returns with our drinks, leaning over unnecessarily far in front of me, her chest spilling out of her top as she sets the glass down. For a moment, I consider taking her back to the ranch and exploring her body. It's been years, literally, since I've felt a woman's warmth.

"Well, any flavor of ice cream you want is readily available when you have the right connections, Redford. A few things have changed since you were locked up." Harry leans forward, his weathered skin telling the story of years of sun damage and smoke inhalation.

"Cash handled things well. We're operating at full capacity."

Harry presses his elbows into the table. "Yes, but are you making your full income potential? There's always room for improvement."

I don't respond, waiting for my brother to step forward

and give his input. Cash isn't outspoken. He's the silent type, but he gets shit done without needing to be loud. After a few seconds pass, he senses me waiting on him and turns to Harry.

"Your interest in Redford Ranch isn't new. We don't need your dirty money. You wanna buy some bulls, then we'll talk." Cash sounds bored.

He kept me up-to-date on all things business behind bars, but Old Harry's propositions weren't something he felt were worth mentioning. I trust he had a good reason for it.

Harry's eyes shine brighter. "This isn't about my investment in The Riders, although that offer will never be off the table. I'm talking about a product. Something every rancher who wants to be the top producer in the next five years is getting their hands on. Something you can only get if you know someone. I'm offering you boys a deal, the deal of a fucking lifetime. Your generation could be the one to make or break the Redford Ranch name."

"What is it you're so keen on us purchasing? I used up all my patience in prison, so make it quick." I take a swig of the whiskey, the burn feeling good down my throat. I know whatever the hell he says, we're not interested.

Harry leans back, swiftly attempting to get back in control of the conversation. "You're either going to jump on this train while it's moving slow enough down the tracks for new passengers or it's going to fly by you in a flash. You'll miss your chance if you wait."

He's beginning to sound like a door-to-door knife salesman, and I'm getting really fucking tired of it.

"Spit it out, or let us go get fucked up in your bar," Sterling says, annoyance in his tone.

Harry reaches under the table for something. My muscles tense as I take a defensive stance, pushing back from the table. Cash and Sterling both draw their weapons, aiming them straight for the old man. Harry chuckles, waving at us with his hand, lazy cigarette smoke trailing toward the ceiling.

"Gentlemen, I give you M-59." He reveals a small black plastic case. He unsnaps the sides of the case, revealing a massive syringe. It's half an inch thick, filled with red liquid. The needle is far too big to be used on a human.

I release the tension from my shoulders, but I don't reclaim my place closer to the table. Cash and Sterling lower their guns.

"What's M-59?" Cash asks.

Harry's face is giddy with excitement as he rubs his hands together.

"It's a genetically engineered steroid, created to make cattle gain weight at a rapid rate. The calves you're selling at auction next month for feed? They'll gain fifty to one hundred pounds after fourteen days of this. You multiply that by however many thousand heads you're auctioning off, and you boys will make yourself a six-figure Christmas bonus—in the middle of the summer." Harry grins, running his tongue over his straw-colored teeth with excitement.

I toss the rest of my drink back, wiping my mouth with the back of my hand as I stand up. "And if this shit works so fucking perfectly, why the hell wouldn't the FDA approve it? If it was legit, we could get it at the vet."

Harry shakes his head, coming to a stand. "It'll get approved, but by that time, you'll be too far behind to catch up. The government takes years to pass these things through the lab rats. Then, they jack up the price so high and get ninety percent of the profits. If you don't jump on the horse now, boys, you'll be too far behind to catch up." He repeats. "Think about it and take the sample. Test it on one of your runts and see just how damn powerful this shit really is. They ship it up from Mexico, so we need some time to get enough for a herd your size."

He comes around the table, handing Cash the box. He grins, wrapping his arm around the blond server as he leads us toward another door. Country music pours through it as we get closer.

"You boys tell Billy Bob your tab is on mine tonight, okay? Don't get into too much trouble out there."

The girl reaches for the handle, but Cash beats her to it and pulls open the door. Rough cowboys never let women touch door handles.

15
ROSIE

"Oh shit, sorry." I freeze in place. "I, uh ... I didn't know anyone was in here." I word-vomit all over my shoes when I see the knockout blonde standing in Holden's oversize bathroom. She's wrapped in a towel, one of the ones I washed, folded, and put away last week.

Her long hair is wet, spilling over her delicate shoulders, sending buckets of molten lava all over my sense of self-worth and giving me stupid, trivial thoughts, like, *Do I have naturally wavy hair that lies perfectly over my chest like that after a hot shower?*

"Who are you?" she asks. Her tone is more curious than accusatory, but I feel my hackles rise just the same.

The words *the housekeeper* are on the tip of my tongue, but for some reason, they taste like bile, so I shove them back.

"I'm Dolly's best friend, Rosie."

"Hmm," she says, tilting her head to the side. "And who is Dolly?"

I blink at her. "Um, she's Holden's sister."

"Ah, so this is like a family-lives-off-of-him situation." She shakes her head, smirking.

Bitch, what?

"Um, more like a family-business situation."

"But you're not family," she states.

"I don't live here. I'm a friend."

A friend who's about two seconds away from pulling that pretty blond hair right out of your scalp.

Okay, chill. Why are you letting this girl get to your head like this?

She crosses her arms over the towel. "Then, why are you sneaking around Holden's room like a criminal?"

My eyebrows shoot up as I physically take a step back from her. "I think I could very well ask you the same question. Did he actually invite you to stay the night?"

She quickly glances away before squaring her shoulders. "That seems like none of your business."

"I take that as a no."

You're being a bitch for no reason. Why do you care who Holden fucks on his ranch?

She exhales deeply. "I don't have to explain myself to you. Where's Holden?"

I shrug, trying to force my muscles to relax. "Probably out mending a fence or riding a horse, bull, or an ATV. He's a rancher. They get up early and stay out working late."

Thankfully, I'm not currently holding the bathroom caddy full of cleaners, or she'd know I'm in here to clean. I pick at my nail beds, debating the source of the strange sensation of jealousy that's raging inside of me.

Another problem for another day.

"That surprises me with how much he drank last night. I'd be in bed all day after that much whiskey," she muses.

I blink up at her, biting my lip. She seems like a decent person. I'm irrational for being so rattled about finding a girl in his room.

And she's blond, of course. Probably the first of many.

My stomach rolls over at the thought.

"Look," I start, softening my voice as I step closer to her, "Holden isn't the type to get up and cook you breakfast. I get that he's"—I struggle to find the right words—"enticing, and I'm sure last night was one for the books. I would strongly encourage you to leave before he gets back. You should log this away as a fun experience. He doesn't really date. I've known him my whole life, and he's never even had a girlfriend. I don't mean to scare you, but he was released from prison like, barely over a month ago."

She shakes her head. "I know exactly who he is. We had a connection last night. He didn't even try to sleep with me. He told me he's not looking for a hookup. He just wanted me to sleep next to him." Her eyes grow distant. "Isn't that ... romantic?"

My lungs decompress slowly as I process her confession.

Holden didn't fuck her?

I know it couldn't be because he wasn't attracted to her. She's literally flawless, Playboy Bunny perfect.

"Oh, well ... that's something." I shrug, the casual gesture betraying the relief flooding my system like oxygen. "I don't really know him that well." I hesitate, pursing my lips before finally deciding to spit out my next words. "Do you want some coffee?"

As a politician's wife, my mother took pride in raising me to be an immaculate hostess. I'm not the woman of this house, but as the housekeeper, I tend to take on the role of serving guests. Dolly prefers it that way, it seems.

I lead the girl down the hallway after giving her time to dress in her clothes from the night before. From the looks of the skimpy outfit, she's a bartender.

"I don't think I caught your name?" I turn to say to her as we enter the kitchen. It's eleven in the morning, so I was about to start cooking lunch.

"Savannah. And yours was Rosie, right?" she says.

You can be nice to her. You can. You will.

"Right. Dolly should be around here somewhere."

I'm hoping she is, so I can get to work and stop having to make small talk with Holden's latest conquest. The fact that they didn't sleep together makes it a little easier for me to breathe, but I'm still too busy to be entertaining her.

Unless she lied about it ...

"Do you know where Holden is?" she asks.

I shake my head, moving toward the pot of cold coffee that has a little left in it. I pour it into a mug and pop it into the microwave. After it heats, I remove it and set it on the island with the bottle of creamer. She grabs the cup without a thank-you.

I move over to the farmhouse sink, where the beef is thawing out. I planned to make steak sliders with green beans for lunch, and the meat needs tenderizing.

I disinfect the butcher block countertop and lay it out.

The metal mallet for tenderizing weighs in my hand as I get ready to begin.

"What's for lunch, sweet cheeks?" a male voice speaks from behind me.

I spin around with the mallet still in my hand.

"Whoa, what's got that frown line in your forehead so deep?" Duke approaches me, raising a hand to lower the tool.

My eyes flick over to Savannah briefly before returning to his. He tilts his head to the side, peering at me curiously.

"Huh?"

I raise the mallet again, turning back to the meat. "I'm making steak sandwiches. It'll be ready in forty-five."

Duke turns around to face the stranger sitting at the island. "Have we met? You look strangely familiar. Ah! Don't tell me—you're the babe from my dream last night."

She giggles. "I'm Savannah. I didn't see you at Old Harry's last night."

I bring the mallet down with a whack. They continue talking, but I block it out and focus on the task. The bright red meat is from a Redford Ranch cow, rich and thick. It'll taste like heaven once I'm done seasoning it and searing it in the cast-iron skillet.

The mallet comes down again and again, helping to release a bit of tension from my shoulders with each thud.

"Rosie." A soft voice from beside me breaks through my focus. I pause, turning to face a wide-eyed Dolly.

"Are you good?" she asks, eyeing the mutilated meat on the counter.

"Yeah. Just prepping lunch." I turn back, raising the mallet again.

"That cow is already dead, honey, very dead."

I look down, realizing I forgot to put on an apron and now have red splatters on the front of my pale blue tank top. "Oh shit."

She lowers her voice, stepping closer. "Did Holden say something to you again?"

I shake my head. "Nope. I'm really okay." My voice is too high-pitched.

Deep male voices remind me that we're not alone. I turn to see who all is in the kitchen, seeing that it's all the guys, except for Holden. Cash and Sterling are talking among themselves while Duke continues to flirt with Savannah. She looks enraptured by him. I guess if she and Holden didn't actually have sex, she's fair game.

Speak of the devil ...

The back door opens up, and he struts through it, wearing a straw Stetson, a pale gray T-shirt with the sleeves cut off, worn Wranglers, and boots. Saliva immediately pools inside my mouth.

This crush is getting out of hand. Need to figure out how to get rid of it.

MUSCLES.

Holden freezes when he sees Savannah sitting at the island. His eyes narrow as he flexes his jaw. My gaze focuses on the stitches I sewed into him, where he was kicked by a bull. I do the math in my head, realizing it's been too long and I should've already taken them out.

His gaze cuts over to mine, sending heat over my skin instantly. He notices the blood on my shirt, the mallet, and the meat on the counter before turning to walk into the mudroom where the guys wash up before meal time.

I turn back to the meat.

"Holy shit. He really does *hate* you. I'm going to have a talk with him," Dolly whisper-shouts right in my ear.

I generously season the meat on both sides, shaking my head at her. "Don't bother. It'll just make it worse. He's been ignoring me lately, which is better than him firing me, accusing me of spying on him, and hauling me off like a sack of potatoes."

"You call that death glare him *ignoring* you?"

I shrug, move over to the six-burner gas stove, and turn one on high. I slide the fifteen-inch cast-iron skillet over it to let it preheat.

"You want me to get the buns buttered and toasted?" Dolly asks.

"Yes, that would be perfect. I'm going to slice some tomatoes too."

"No tomatoes on mine, sugarplum," Duke says, winking at me.

I narrow my eyes at him, wondering how long we're going to fake flirt with each other. It doesn't seem to be changing much in my opinion. We might have to actually fuck on the kitchen table to get Holden to believe I'm too important to the family for him to get rid of me.

"Okay, love bug." Sarcasm drips from my lips.

Duke chuckles, turning back to Savannah. She's unbelievably pretty, even with her makeup-free face. She glances over at Holden as he walks back into the kitchen.

"You need a ride?" he asks her without smiling.

I continue slicing the thick tomatoes from the garden.

She blinks up at him. "Well, good morning to you too."

"Duke can drive you home," he says.

Duke raises his hands. "Why do I get stuck on taxi service?"

Holden glares at him. "Call her an Uber then."

"Now?" Duke asks.

"No, next week." Holden doesn't wait for a reply or acknowledge Savannah again as he walks over to the dining room, sits down at the table, and waits for his lunch to be served.

I see Savannah's face fall. I'm not sure if it's the inner hostess in me, the irrationally jealous and raging bitch, or the overall fed-up employee, but I can't stop myself.

"Oh, don't be silly. She should eat first. There's plenty to go around! What do you say, Savannah? Would you like tomatoes on your steak sandwich?"

Savannah looks up at me like I just saved her pet from being put down with a miracle surgery. I can feel Holden's angry scowl from across the room, and it fuels my resolve to inconvenience his life as much as he does mine.

"I'll take tomatoes. Thank you!" she says.

I nod, smiling to myself. "Coming right up."

16

HOLDEN

The nightmares are never-ending. Once I lie down to sleep in my too-soft king-size bed, I can't close my eyes without seeing those four white walls closing in on me. The one tiny window with bars was the only link I had to the outside world. The thick stench of urine and grease from the leaking toilet and the gruel they fed me lingers in my nostrils.

I wake in a cold sweat, panting for breath. My bathroom door is ajar, the light still on. I peer around the room, seeing that I'm alone. My heart rate doesn't slow. I swing my legs off the bed and begin doing push-ups. After I count to fifty, I switch to one arm.

Once I reach the point of physical exhaustion, covered in sweat, I collapse on the hardwood floor. It's cool on my skin, providing relief for my screaming muscles.

Another flashback hits me like a train. The only fight I've ever lost was the first day they let me out of solitary confinement. I was in the shower when six guys jumped me. They beat me until my blood ran with the cold water down the drain and bruises covered my body. I had four broken ribs, two almost black eyes, and my fists were raw and bloodied from returning their blows.

The guards found me on the cold tiled floor, lying face down. The prison doctor told me the only way I hadn't suffocated from the broken rib protruding into my left lung was due to the position I was lying in.

Three of my assailants were in the infirmary, recovering with me, and when they tried again, I took them all out, even with the half-healed ribs.

No one fucked with me after that unless they were in groups, and they never won.

I get up off the cold floor, tearing off my boxers as I step inside the shower. The cold spray shocks my overheated system, drawing my scrambled thoughts back down to a slower pace.

You will not succumb to this.

You aren't there anymore.

You're home.

You're not in danger here.

You're not alone.

You're not alone.

You're not alone.

I repeat it to myself over and over again until I'm finally able to make it back into the room, collapsing onto the bed just as the sun begins to filter light through my curtains.

"THE BEAUTY of braless Fridays is that we get to free-boob it without the awkwardness of y'all being around," Dolly explains.

Duke scoffs. "Then, what was with the night we all went to Old Harry's and Rosie got a bucket of ice water dumped on her head while up on the stage?"

Dolly pops the cork off a bottle of red wine, shrugging. "That was a rare exception. We were wine drunk, bored, and we both needed to get laid. With y'all around, that's never going to happen, apparently. Go play with your bow and arrows out in the field and see who can avoid getting shot in the dark, like y'all used to do when you were in high school."

I tighten my hand around the beer I'm holding. My eyes can barely stay open even though it's only eight o'clock.

"I was trying to make some extra money actually. This is my last Friday night for a while." Rosie takes her glass, walking into the living room.

I can make out the soft curve of her breasts as they jiggle with each of her steps. My salivary glands spring to life.

Fuck.

I'd pay to see that contest again any day. Preferably a one-on-one version.

The popularity of the wet T-shirt contest is making more sense the longer I go without sex. Rosie has been ignoring me ever since the firing incident. She thinks I'm doing the same, but I'm hyperaware of her every time she enters a room.

Being aware of the enemy is how you stay one step ahead.

Right, craving a whiff of her scent is just keeping you one step ahead ...

She sets her balloon wineglass down on the coffee table, stepping toward me. She's wearing a heather-gray T-shirt with a scooping neckline with the silky pink shorts. She approaches me slowly, like I might bite.

I might actually.

"I need to remove your stitches," she says quietly, standing a few feet back from me, chewing her lip.

My eyes flick up to meet hers. I turn my head to show her the pink scar along my jawline.

"Oh ... never mind then." She turns back around, finding her seat on the sofa and pulling a plush throw blanket over herself.

I cut the stitches out myself last night because they itched.

"Well, in that case, I guess I'll go make myself scarce in the barn with the animals," Duke grumbles.

I continue sipping on my beer silently as the girls chatter about their week. Dolly scrolls through the movies under the Romantic Comedy tab. They finally select one, and I doze in and out of sleep as the movie plays.

"How many glasses is that for you?" Dolly asks, rousing me with her distant voice.

Rosie shrugs. "It's my last Friday night for a few months at least. This gig has me scheduled every weekend."

"In that case, I hope you know you have to sleep in my

bed. I won't settle for you out on the couch anymore. Unless you'd rather sleep with Duke ..."

Rosie tosses back the last of her wine, leaning forward to pour another glass. "We'll see how I feel after this bottle is gone."

My eyes are drifting shut again when something hits me on the shoulder.

I open them up to see my sister smiling at me. "Go to bed, old man. You've been asleep for the whole thing."

I blink at her. I could tell her that sleeping alone is essentially impossible for me right now and the only way I've been able to drift off in this chair without jolting awake from nightmares in cold, dark places is from hearing her and Rosie's soft voices.

Instead, I stand up and head toward my bedroom. "Night, Doll."

"Good night."

I stumble toward my room, my head swimming with incoherent, sleep-deprived thoughts of the frigid cell, the silence, the nothingness of solitary confinement that nearly drove me mad.

I remove all my clothes, except my boxers, collapsing on top of the covers. There's no point in showering; I'll have to do it in the middle of the night anyway, just like last night.

And nearly every night since I've been home.

I keep the door to my room open so I can still hear the murmur of the girls and their movie. I keep my eyes open, staring up at the dark ceiling and the slowly rotating fan for as long as I can.

It's ice cold in my cell. The guards must have neglected to turn on the heating element in solitary confinement. During the night when the Idaho temperatures drop below freezing, the cold seeps down through the threadbare blanket and into my bones. My movements are slow from the temperature.

Time passes as I drift in and out of a restless sleep. The seconds tick into minutes, and I finally realize that if I don't get up and move my body, I very well could freeze to death—or at least lose some toes.

I force myself to stand, teeth vibrating against each other. I start with laying my blanket on the concrete floor to put a barrier between my hands and the icy surface. When I drop into the push-up position, it takes me a few tries before I manage to get a grip firm enough to lower my body down, then push back up.

I repeat it over and over again until the blood finally starts to flow through my veins faster, becoming its own source of heat.

I will not die in this fucking prison cell.

A RUSTLING NOISE wakes me with a start. I bolt upright, gasping for oxygen. A soft humming and exhale to my right jerks my gaze sideways. My body tenses as I prepare to face whatever intruder is in my cell. I shove my hand under my pillow, gripping the blade I keep hidden, hovering over the shape in my bed.

The outline of a slim body in the moonlight is under a

pile of wavy, distinctly copper-red hair. My blood is still racing, but her steady breathing and her subtle vanilla scent spread a blanket of peace over my nervous system.

Rosie is curled up, sleeping soundly. I reach down, slowly moving a piece of her hair out of her face.

Her sensual, plump lips are parted slightly, long eyelashes resting on the top of her cheeks. She has one of those profiles that are on magazine covers, every feature somehow inexplicably flawless.

The top of the covers is pulled up to her chin. I envy the way she sleeps.

Why isn't she in Duke's bed?

My attraction to her is an inconvenience, one I'm growing weary of fighting. Her father's role in my prosecution and my time in solitary confinement are enough reason for me to hate every Dixon who ever lived.

The fact that she's had sex with my brother doesn't make me hate her, but it does guarantee that I'll never be able to touch her.

The line between hating her and desiring her is growing more blurry with every second I let her work in my house and sleep in my bed.

But, hey, you didn't have to do two hundred push-ups and take a cold shower to stop the panic.

Whether or not allowing the enemy to sleep in my bed is wise or not is a question for the morning, when I've actually gotten enough sleep and I can read her reaction to waking up next to me, no doubt ending up here by mistake after too many glasses of wine. My thoughts are incoherent with lack of sleep. I can't process this.

Instead of waking her and throwing her out, I lie back down on the pillow, positioning my body toward hers so I can watch the gentle rise and fall of her chest as she inhales. I return the knife to its spot under my pillow.

In the moonlight, it's easier to pretend that she's not here to ruin my life and share my weaknesses with the men who want to destroy my ranch. I'd let a grizzly bear sleep in here if it helped me not have flashbacks of waking up in a freezing cell, completely alone in solitary confinement.

A grizzly would be less dangerous than her.

She stirs, shifting slightly toward me and throwing one of her arms out. It latches around her pillow as she shifts over to lie on her stomach, making another sound that goes straight down to my dick.

It was a sleepy moan, a gentle groan of pleasure that I've never heard from her lips. It gives me a desperate need to know what she could possibly be dreaming about.

Probably a memory of fucking your younger brother.

It doesn't stop me from picturing what her eyes look like when she's being touched in a way she likes.

What does she like?

The vivid dream I had that made me come in my sleep after the night of the wet T-shirt contest infiltrates my dark thoughts. I shift farther away before I drift off to sleep, gripping the sheets between us and having selfishly filthy, hedonistic thoughts about my enemy's daughter sleeping right next to me.

17
ROSIE

A warm, heavy arm is wrapped around me. I stir from a deep sleep, not wanting to open my eyes.

I'm so cozy.

Where am I?

I try to recall what happened the night before, drawing the conclusion that there's no way the arm belongs to Dolly. She's way too small.

It could be Duke's ... but it feels bigger.

I sigh, hoping that my ex-boyfriend and I didn't make a stupid decision last night when I finished off the last of the merlot.

My eyes flutter open, bringing into focus the ceiling of the room. The slowly spinning fan is unfamiliar. I tilt my head to the side, sucking in a sharp breath when I see the man sleeping next to me.

He's holding me so tightly, and I'm afraid I'll wake him up if I move at all. I hold my breath, taking a moment to study him. I've never been this close to Holden. I've never been touched like this by him.

His expression is uncharacteristically relaxed. Since he's been out of prison, I have yet to see him without a scowl; even before then, it was rare. I can count on one hand the times I've seen him smile, none of which were directed at me.

His black eyelashes are thick and fanned out over his sharp cheekbones. The naturally tanned skin tone all the Redfords got from their mother is something my pale, freckled self will always be envious of.

I finally release the breath I was holding gradually so that I don't wake him. His bare chest and shoulders aren't quite touching me, but if he pulled me even three inches closer, we'd be in a full-on cuddle position.

I really shouldn't drink so much if I'm going to end up in the den of the fucking viper.

I've seen Holden shirtless before, but being so close now, I'm able to make out the notched brand on his shoulder clearly. The two-inch double R depicts one letter mirroring the other. They use it to brand their cattle, but all the brothers bear the brand on their chest or shoulder. Duke got his at age sixteen, so I'm assuming that's when they all did. I remember it well because he told me it was a rite of passage as a Redford to permanently mark the brand into their flesh, forever swearing family loyalty. They've all always been slightly unhinged.

The deep yearning inside my lower belly is growing stronger with each minute I stay locked in his hold. Holden will never feel the attraction toward me that I've had for him since I was a teenager, and I'm beginning to *loathe* myself for it.

You need to get out before he wakes up and sees you here. Maybe you can replace yourself with a pillow.

I slowly start to inch down. It seems like the best route for escape. I hold my breath again as I go. He's still in a deep sleep, so maybe I'll be able to sneak out without him ever knowing I was here.

One minute, I think I'm going to make it. The next, his eyes slice open, their black depths freezing me in place. He moves so quickly, I don't even have time to react.

A cold blade of metal is pressed to my throat as he straddles me, pressing his lower body over my hips and pinning one of my arms back. His muscles are taut, the veins in his hands and neck popping out.

I gasp at the abrupt change in position, his weight on me, the thick bulge between his legs pressing right against my sensitive groin, and the effortless way he pins me down without me having even a moment to react or escape him.

He blinks at me, almost like he's registering my face after he decided that I was an imminent threat. He slowly releases the pressure of the knife he's holding against my throat. I drag in a sharp inhale, fear still gripping me tightly.

The terror of what he was about to do is replaced by something entirely different in the next moment when I feel his length harden. My lips part, our unexpected proximity drawing all attention to the nerves between my thighs.

Holy shit, he's big.

Not that I'm quite sure what big or small would be,

considering I've never actually felt a dick before. His feels ... too big to fit up *there*.

He flexes his jaw, but doesn't move off of me. His eyes are pinning me down just as much as his hands, studying me intensely. His chest rises and falls steadily as he glares at me.

I'm afraid, so afraid of him ... but also so fucking turned on right now.

"What are you doing in my bed, Dixon?" he finally spits out.

I rush to explain. "I, uh ... I think I ended up here by mistake. I thought this was—"

It's on the tip of my tongue to say *Dolly's room*, but he fills in the blank for me.

"Duke's bed?" he says through gritted teeth.

I nod.

I'm having trouble holding in the moan that's threatening to spill over my lips with every tiny burst of friction between my thighs. He's so ... overwhelming. I'm completely helpless right now, at his mercy to do whatever he wants with me.

Shit, I am the most pathetic twenty-one-year-old virgin who ever lived ...

After another few intense moments of staring, I wiggle my bottom half against him. He immediately shifts, moving back to give me room to escape.

I scramble up, pulling my legs out from underneath him. He sits back on his haunches, palming the small knife. My eyes are drawn down to see the tip of his dick, sticking straight up inside his boxers and creating a tent effect. My mouth drops open. The image draws me back to the night I walked in on him getting blown in the barn. He didn't have any shame then either.

My cheeks flush deeply.

"Get out," he bites.

"What can I get for you?" I approach the table with a fake smile, trying my best to make it seem genuine.

It's been six grueling hours on my feet of taking orders, running trays, and fake laughing at the jokes of flirty old men.

Waitressing might not be for me. After working at the ranch all week long, I'm not sure how many nights per week I'll be able to do this with a smile on my face.

You don't have much of a choice if you want to get into nursing school and pay for it without your father's help.

My goal is to save up enough so that I only have to work minimal hours while in school. I make good money at the ranch, but it's taking too long while having to pay all my own bills.

The customers are looking me up and down, approving smirks and head tilts being thrown back at each other. It's two men in their mid-forties, dirty from a long day of working outside in the Texas heat. They're both eyeing me like I'm the first woman they've seen in days.

"Well, hello there, princess. Didn't know we were getting the special tonight. How long you been working here?"

I blink up at the redheaded man with the bushy beard. "It's my first day." My smile probably looks more like a grimace, but I try to keep it on my face.

"Well, hot dog, it's your lucky one then, sweetheart. Me and Chaz come in here most every night when we get done working on them power lines. You serve us just right, and you'll get a damn good tip, maybe more." He winks at me, leaning forward to rest against his elbows and pop his knuckles. The ring on his left ring finger winks in the overhead light.

My lips peel back with another forced smile. "You should know what you want then, in that case."

The men chuckle. It's almost ten o'clock, which is when the kitchen shuts down and I can't put in any more orders.

They order two porterhouse steaks, rare, with double sides of mashed potatoes. I walk over to the bar after entering their food to grab the pints of draft beer they asked for.

I shift on my feet, the ache in my arches growing worse with each step. I thought I was used to standing for most of the day at my other job, but it turns out, I get more time off my feet than I realized.

This is good for you. This is for your future. You're doing this so that you can break out on your own, be your own woman, and stop depending on unreliable people.

I pull my phone out of my back pocket, checking to see if my mom texted me back. The screen is blank. I push it back in with a sigh.

The bartender finally shoves the beer toward me, clearly annoyed at the customers for coming in five minutes before closing time. I thank her, reaching for the mugs and grabbing them. I trudge back over to the table where the men are chuckling among themselves. My skin crawls at the way their eyes travel over me, taking in every inch from head to toe. The uniforms here aren't especially skimpy, but the manager seemed to intentionally give me an extra-small T-shirt that's definitely too tight. All the girls wear denim cutoff shorts and aprons with the company logo on them.

"Anything else while you wait?" I ask.

The married man with the red beard licks his lips, leaning toward me. "What's your name, honey?"

It's clearly printed on the name tag that's pinned to my shirt, but I answer him anyway.

"It's Rosie."

He reaches forward, fingers moving toward my hands that are clasped in front of me. I'm frozen in place, debating if I should move back from him or let him touch me.

Well, that's an easy choice.

I start to move back, but the decision is made for me by a third party who intervenes. A callous hand grips my elbow, pulling me back a step from the table.

I glance up, shock crossing my features as I see Holden Redford's clenched jawline.

"I was told you're my server, and we haven't ordered yet," he says, his demanding voice and overall menacing presence enough to shut up the other men.

I gape at him, trying to resist the urge to lean closer in desperate gratitude for the rescue from the creeps to my left.

"Of course. I'm so sorry. I'll be right there."

Holden half tugs, half drags me along with him toward

the table in the corner, where Cash is already seated. They must've come in when I was at the bar, getting the beer. They're both wearing their typical jeans, boots, and cowboy hats, looking intimidating and scary as hell with their moody glares and muscular shoulders. I'm somehow still not immune to it, and my lower belly tightens as I look them over.

"You'll have to put your order in now before the kitchen closes," I warn them.

Cash scoots out of the booth, ignoring me as he heads for the bar. I open my mouth to tell him that I can get a beer for him, but I shut it before speaking. More power to the man if it saves me a trip.

"What can I get you?" I ask Holden.

I look down at my notepad, thankful for the opportunity to break the ice of speaking to him in such a neutral environment after his dick was between my thighs and his knife was at my throat.

You're still serving him, still at his beck and call.

Serving him as a waitress at a steak house is ten times less demeaning than being his maid. At least he can't fire me here.

After a few beats of silence, I look up. His jaw tics as he studies me with dark, calculating eyes. My lips part as I inhale a few slow, steady breaths.

"They'll close the bar too if you don't hurry."

"How much have you made in tips tonight?" he asks.

I stare at him, my brow furrowed in confusion. "What?"

He nods his head toward my apron. "How much in tips?"

I sigh, too tired to try and work out in my head why he

would bother asking or to be stubborn and refuse to answer. "Around two ten, not including those guys." I nod toward my other table.

The girl who trained me said Saturdays are the busiest, so I shouldn't expect to break the two-hundred mark on any other night.

Holden's eyes don't leave mine. His tan face is raw and perfect, and I can't help but wonder if he's been thinking about what happened this morning as obsessively as I have.

I'm incapable of stopping myself from replaying the scene in my head over and over again. I didn't expect to have to see him again until Monday morning. I thought I would have time to work on my indifferent, bored expression.

"What if I doubled it? Five hundred dollars a night."

My mouth drops open, forming an O. Holden's eyes flicker down to take it in before returning to lock on to my gaze.

"You ... you want to pay me five hundred dollars a night to ... what?"

My fingers tighten around the pen in my hand. If he's saying what I think he's saying, I might actually stab him in the eye with this pen.

Surely not.

He leans forward, biceps bulging out of his T-shirt. "I want to pay you to sleep with me."

I react without thinking, shoving my hand toward his face with a swift, jerky motion. He dodges the blow effortlessly. I barely miss his right eye, my pen flinging toward the ground behind him.

A barely perceptible smirk touches his lips. "Did you just try to stab me in the eye with that pen?"

I inhale, gritting my teeth and spinning around to stomp away from him. His hand grips my wrist tightly, jerking me back and pinning me in place.

His mouth is right next to my ear as he speaks softly but firmly. "Now, you wouldn't want me going off and asking your new manager what that was, would you?"

I gasp, trying to jerk my arm away from him. He holds it firmly, not hurting me, but not giving me any room to wiggle free.

"I'm not saying you have to sleep *with* me. I'm saying I will pay you to sleep *next* to me four nights out of the week. Five hundred dollars a night, two thousand dollars a week. Just to sleep in my room, like you did last night."

My thundering heart rate begins to slow down. His warm breath on my cheek moves away as he releases my arm. I step back, rubbing the spot on my wrist where he held me—the same one he had this morning while his other hand pressed the knife to my throat.

He's not safe. He spent years in prison with criminals and murderers after killing someone himself.

Cain deserved it, but what does killing do to a person?

"Hey, miss! Can we get a refill over here?" the red-bearded man yells at me from across the restaurant.

Holden's offer is bizarre. Still ... I think about the back exit that I'll have to walk through every night on the way to my car. I think about my car, only starting when it feels like it. I think about my apartment and how I woke up to shouting and sirens blaring a few nights ago due to some kind of dispute, a drug deal gone wrong or who knows what?

I think about how I haven't felt safe in a very, very long time.

Am I safer there?

I crave the stability of feeling like someone has my back. I know Dolly does, but she's not physically capable of protecting me. She doesn't have much decision-making power at the ranch—at least not yet. She lets the guys handle things, and she trusts them to take care of her.

He had a literal knife at your throat this morning. It doesn't get much more dangerous than that.

"What about the other three nights?" I ask.

Holden tips his cowboy hat back, tilting his head to the side. "You'll do as you please. You can sleep in Duke's bed, your shitty apartment, your daddy's BMW. I don't care."

And what will you do? Pick up more bartenders?

I fold my arms across my chest, sticking out my chin. "Why? If it's not about sex, then why do you want me to?"

He stands, his height shrinking me instantly. "Do we have a deal or not, Dixon?"

"What about the knife under your pillow?" I pop my hip out. "Am I going to wake up to it pressed against my throat again?"

"Only if you're a good girl."

My core clenches at his words, but I force out a huff. "I'm not sure I'll feel safe sleeping with you."

"I'll let you sleep with a pen under yours—how 'bout that?" He tilts his head, the muscles ticcing underneath the fresh scar on his jaw. "Deal?"

I stare up at him, internally calculating how much money I could make doing this for three months. I only work part-time as their housekeeper and cook. The hours have never been full-time, so this will be more money.

That's twenty-four thousand dollars, just for sleeping. It would take you a year to earn that here.

I feel myself nodding, my aching feet being the main motivation at the current moment. Also, I could never make two thousand dollars a week at a part-time job anywhere, not in a million years. I don't know why he wants this from me, but I'm in no position to deny him.

Once again, he has all the power.

"On one condition," I say.

Cash rejoins us then, spinning the truck keys around on his fingers.

Holden doesn't ask; he just waits, not looking at me.

"You can't touch me," I state, turning around to walk toward the manager's office to quit.

18

HOLDEN

"It's like these cowboys haven't been riding bulls their entire fucking lives," I grumble. "Jensen! You want me to call your mama out here so she can teach you how to do your damn job?" I holler from my place on the fence, spitting into the dirt.

Jensen slowly rises to his feet, the short cowboy shaking his head. "No, sir. I just went left, and he went right."

"How am I supposed to sell bulls for riding if my men can't even stay the fuck on the babies? That steer ain't even a year old."

Jensen nods before hanging his head in defeat and walking back to where the chutes are being loaded with another rider.

"Do I need to go over there and give them a first-grade lesson?" I look over at Cash, who hasn't said more than three words all morning.

Even the way the wind blows is pissing me off right now, and I know it's because it's been two nights since I've gotten any sleep. My chest and shoulder muscles ache from the push-ups. Last night, I went for a five-mile run at two in the morning, trying to exhaust myself.

I kick at a pile of dried cow shit, debating whether or not to go sit in the truck and try to get a power nap in before all the ranch hands quit on me or I throttle someone. The horses we rode here are tied up to the fence. Maybe I'll take one for a ride out in the pasture to get some air.

"Old Harry stopped by this morning. Asked me if we'd made a decision on the injections," Cash says.

"What'd you tell him?"

"We'd be in touch."

The sun is already high in the sky, nearing noon. It's still hot as shit in Texas, but it should start cooling off in the evenings in the next few weeks. Sweat drips down the center of my back.

"Buddy of mine in Idaho would probably know something about it if we went up there and asked him. He was one of those science geniuses who got locked up for being way too fucking smart for the government's comfort."

Cash squints at me. "Might be worth a visit. Sure you wanna go back there?"

I look out across the ranch at the leaves on the oak trees blowing in the breeze. The idea of walking back into prison, even as a free man, makes my empty stomach churn. I don't know if I could physically do it.

"It's either that or we risk calling him. Don't think this is some shit we should talk about on a recorded line."

Cash nods. We both turn at the sound of an ATV approaching. The girls are pulling up to the pen, a large picnic basket sitting in Rosie's lap. Her eyes find mine imme-diately. She doesn't smile as she climbs out of the ATV as Dolly puts it into park.

We're out in the back pasture, two miles from the house. They're both wearing sundresses that hit mid-thigh on the unseasonably sunny day. Texas weather has no rhyme or reason. Rosie's dress is a pale green with little white flowers on it. Her sun-kissed shoulders are exposed. Copper strands of hair are lying in messy waves around her shoulders, loose pieces drifting in the gentle breeze.

My eyes take in the rest of her as my mouth waters at more than just the thought of the lunch she's carrying.

She's going to be sleeping in my bed tonight, but I can't lay a hand on her.

I'm not used to having self-control with women. I've never had to. I'm not worried that I won't be able to resist touching her. I'd never do that without her consent. I killed a man for doing that to a woman.

I'm worried I'm going to have another wet dream about her with her sleeping so close to me.

Better than the alternative of not sleeping at all.

I hope.

"You ladies sure are a sight for sore eyes! Damn, I'm starving." Jensen hops off the fence, grinning widely as he practically skips toward them.

"Get the table off the back of the mule, Jensen," I order.

He nods, walking toward the back of the ATV to grab the fold-up picnic table. The four other ranch hands start following the girls as they head toward a large tree to serve lunch under the canopy of leaves. The wind picks up, nearly blowing Rosie's dress all the way up and revealing her ass. She reaches down to grab it, but she can't do it well while still holding the basket. I curse under my breath, waiting on edge for her to flash the entire group of men. I quicken my steps to catch up to her.

"The fuck are you wearing?" I grab the basket from her so she can properly hold the hem down.

She throws a glare up at me. "Oh, is my outfit an issue now too? Can't do anything right around here, can I?" Her eyes are bright blue-green in the sunlight. She flips the hem up to reveal tiny white spandex underneath.

"Relax, Rosie. Holden's been barking at us all morning. You're just fresh meat." Cash takes the small ice chest from Dolly.

My sister takes a step toward me. "What's wrong?"

I open the top of the picnic basket to see what it is. "Starving. What's for lunch?"

"Nothing for the grouchy, ungrateful asshole," Rosie snaps.

My eyes slowly rise to meet hers.

Someone needs a good, hard spanking.

Whoa ... the fuck did that thought come from?

"Okay, wow. How about I serve lunch? Rosie, will you please get the plates and cups from the mule?" Dolly asks.

Rosie spins around and marches toward where the ATV is parked. Five pairs of hungry eyes follow her, hoping for another gust of wind to pick up.

The thought of firing each and every single one of them all at once filters through my brain, but I close my eyes instead, exhaling slowly. Rosie returns with the plates and cups, depositing them on the table before opening up one compartment on the veggie tray and extracting a handful of baby carrots. She turns toward the horses and makes her way over to them.

You just need to get some sleep. That's all this is. Your brain can't form coherent thoughts right now.

"What's wrong, really? You have been in a god-awful mood lately." Dolly steps closer to me, her eyebrows pinching together. Her long ebony hair is in a thick braid resting on her bare shoulder.

I sigh, helping her unpack the spread of sandwiches, a fruit salad, individually wrapped brownies, and the veggie tray Rosie already opened.

"Haven't been sleeping," I say quietly.

"Is it the stress? I thought Cash said the ranch was doing fine?"

"It's not that. It's just ... different, being home. I'm not used to it."

I could tell her about the nightmares and the panic attacks, but there's nothing she can do about it. I'm handling it.

"Is there anything I can do?"

I shake my head. "No. I've got it under control. Thanks for bringing lunch out."

Dolly nods, handing me a bag of food and nodding toward the horses that Rosie is now petting. "Why don't you take it somewhere farther away and get a breather this afternoon?"

Cash grabs a sandwich for himself. "We need someone to

check the fence on the edge of that pasture on County Road 1592, where those calves got stuck last week."

Their message is clear. My disposition is shit, and everyone is over it. I nod, grabbing the bag from Dolly.

I watch as Rosie shoves her boot into the stirrup, hauling herself up onto Cash's horse. The gelding whinnies, nuzzling the back of my mare's rear end. Queen Liz ignores him, still feasting on the carrots Rosie gave her. Rosie tries steering her horse toward the pasture, but he won't move.

Neither of us speaks as I mount my horse, looping the handle of the plastic grocery bag around the horn of my saddle before clicking my tongue at the horse.

Cash's gelding, Trooper, follows Queen Liz wherever she goes. I assume Rosie is aware of this as I steer the mare toward the pasture. Rosie doesn't say anything. After a few minutes of silent walking, Rosie's horse steps up closer to mine. She leans down to pet his neck, her hair spilling down past her shoulder and forearm. The copper tones shine brightly in the sunlight, the rich color a shade darker than Queen Liz's coat.

"He's obsessed with her," she notes.

Can't blame him.

"Queen Liz is the prize," I tell her, observing her from the corner of my eye.

She looks good, so damn good, on top of that horse. Her sundress is blowing in the wind, wrapping tightly around her curves.

We ride in silence until reaching a patch of ancient oak trees on the fence line. My hands are beginning to shake from my exhaustion, so I pull back on the reins of my horse.

"I'm going to stop and eat," I tell her.

Rosie nods, not needing to give the command to Trooper, as he follows everything Queen Liz does. She glances back at the group with uncertainty.

I dismount, moving over to Rosie to help her down. She was raised out here as much as Dolly was, so I doubt she needs my help. My Southern roots go too deep not to offer her assistance. My fingers curl around her hip bones, squeezing gently as I guide her safely down to the ground. Her dress rides up slightly, revealing the creamy white skin of her upper thighs.

She turns to look up at me, chewing her bottom lip. "I should get back," she murmurs, looking around as if just noticing that we're alone out here.

"Scared to be alone with me, Dixon?"

She sets her jaw, lifting her chin in defiance. "I'm not afraid of you, Redford." She folds her arms across her chest.

I turn away from her before letting my lips curve into a smile at her words. After grabbing the sack lunch from my saddle, I collapse at the base of a tree, leaning back against the trunk. Rosie stands, aloof, petting Trooper before moving to give Queen Liz some attention.

My fingers reach for the sandwich in my bag. I need protein for energy to get through the rest of this day. I bite into it, chewing mindlessly as my eyes trail over her hips and ass, absently admiring her shape. She turns to approach me, observing the rough ground around me.

"Why can't you sleep?" she asks.

I look up at her through half-lidded eyes, my vision blurred. Telling my family about my issues feels impossible, but Rosie isn't a part of the family. She's strangely easy to talk to.

"Never slept well in prison. It was ice cold. Solitary confinement felt like being on another planet, completely isolated."

I have no idea why I'm opening up to her, except that my guard is down with how physically and emotionally weak I feel. She disarms me somehow.

"Why were you in solitary confinement?" she asks quietly.

I tear the ham sandwich in half, handing her a piece of it.

"Fighting," I murmur, battling the urge to let my heavy eyes close.

Her soft voice and gentle presence draw a blanket of peace over my tingling limbs.

She lounges beside me quietly, the gentle breeze blowing her hair.

Why the fuck are you opening up to her?

I drift in and out of sleep for several minutes. Every time I manage to open my eyes, I force myself to take a bite of the sandwich. Rosie sits quietly beside me, observing the leaves dancing in the breeze. Her even breathing brings a sense of calm over my shattered nerves.

Tonight. I'll get some sleep tonight, with her.

Finally, I slap my thigh to wake myself, rising suddenly. "I need to check the fence. You should get back."

HOLDEN

Be here at 9.

I LOOK AT MY PHONE, watching the message I sent to Rosie shoot through the universe. I'm lying in bed, showered and nearly drifting to sleep as I sit up against the pillows. It's only eight fifteen. The TV mounted on the wall is playing an old John Wayne movie, *McLintock!* I'm so exhausted, my vision is blurry. I can barely make out the scene.

ROSIE

What am I supposed to tell Dolly?

HOLDEN

Tell her you're trying out all the brothers to see which one's the best ride.

ROSIE

Ha-ha. I'm serious. She'll obviously have questions if she realizes I slept over. She might bring it up to Duke.

I tap on the handle of my knife, mentally debating the issue. This is just one of several times I've seriously considered building my own ranch house somewhere else on the property. Even though Rosie and I won't be doing anything other than sleeping, it's past time for me to have my own place. I'm almost thirty years old.

Eventually, I'll be making some girl scream my name, which would be quite disturbing for my family to witness.

Cash and Sterling have been living in the bunkhouse that neighbors the main house for years, since before I was locked up. It's a two-bedroom, two-bath, so there isn't room for me.

It makes more sense for everyone to live on-site while we all work here. We start early, and we end late most days. We work a ton of weekends. No one wants to pay rent on a shitty apartment just to drive back here every day.

Duke was only eighteen when I was locked up. I don't know why he's still living at home, except that he hasn't figured his shit out and doesn't have a clue what he wants in life.

Dolly is sick. Her heart condition is something she can fully function with, but living completely on her own makes us all nervous. I don't think she'd admit it, but she's afraid to be by herself. She never has been.

Before I was charged and sentenced, my plan was to stay here to take care of the ranch, Pops, and Dolly. I was fine with hooking up with women in the barn or in the hunting cabin, which is miles away but still on the property.

HOLDEN

Guess I'm unlocking the window. Did the mayor's sweet little girl ever learn to sneak out?

ROSIE

Wouldn't you like to know? I'm on my way.

I put the knife inside the nightstand drawer. It would be a shame to accidentally slit her pretty throat if I woke up and thought I was back in prison like I had the other morning.

The day was wrought with stress and men tempting me to end up back in prison. Jensen joked with the group of cowboys about an old bet they'd had going around years ago —that whoever took Rosie Dixon's virginity would get her initials branded on his chest as a reward, a forever reminder that he fucked her first.

The temptation to fire him on the spot was so great that Cash had to physically hold me back and remind me that he's our only reliable hand at the moment. The little fucker had been begging for a fist to be planted in his jugular.

My boxers are all I'm sleeping in. She'll just have to deal with it if it bothers her. I move to the window, unlatching it and continuing to wait on her.

After what happened this afternoon at the picnic, I was nervous she wasn't going to come, forcing me to go pick up another woman at the bar to sleep with. For some reason, sex with a stranger doesn't have the same appeal it once did. The blonde I brought home last week was ready and willing, but the way she made it so easy was a turnoff.

Sure, that's why you turned it down.

A tapping sound on the window draws my attention. I move over to it, brushing the curtain back to see Rosie with a black hoodie over her head. The window creaks loudly as I slide it up.

"Did you rob a 7-Eleven on the way here?"

"I didn't want anyone to see me!" she whisper-yells, climbing through the low opening with a backpack on.

"Damn right, you don't. They'd probably shoot you, thinking you're a thief."

Once she's all the way through, I shut and lock the window, brushing the curtains back in place. When I turn around, she's standing in the center of the room, hoodie still on. She looks like a rabbit caught in a trap.

"So, who's sleeping on the floor?" she asks.

I raise a brow. "Not me. Don't know why you would either. Bed is plenty big enough for two."

I fall into it, exhaling as her mere presence draws a sense of calm over my exhausted body. Now that she's here, I know I can sleep. I'll be able to rest without panicking—at least for tonight.

She lingers at the foot of the bed. I watch John Wayne yell at his wife on the screen for another few minutes before turning to her.

"What are you so afraid of, Dixon?"

"I could ask you the same, Redford."

Someone still needs a good spanking—that's for damn sure.

"I put the knife in the drawer. Did you bring your pen?" I hold back a smirk, not wanting to give her the satisfaction of knowing how much I fucking love bantering with her.

My eyes travel back to the TV. After a few beats of me pretending to ignore her, she finally inches closer to the bed.

She exhales decisively. "Listen, I am physically *incapable* of sleeping in a bra. I know that sounds made up, but I'm serious. It itches, and it sticks into my ribs in a bunch of weird places. I have to take it off."

"Who are you talking to?" I turn to her, schooling my expression into mock disinterest.

She rolls her eyes, marching toward the bathroom. "I just didn't want you to take this the wrong way."

As soon as her back is turned to me, I break into a much-needed smile. Dixon is fucking hilarious, and she's not even trying.

Lack of sleep must be making me delirious.

After a few minutes, I hear the water running, the toilet flush, and the door open.

I don't acknowledge her. My eyes are half lidded, and I'm struggling to stay awake. Part of me needs to confirm that she really is going to keep up her end of the bargain and actually sleep in my bed. She could try sneaking out, slithering off to Duke's room for all I know. I force myself to watch the movie until she gets into bed.

"Do you normally sleep with the TV on?" she asks.

I blink, facing her. "No."

She's wearing a loose pink tank top with tiny, silky shorts that look just like the pink ones, but these are white with yellow hearts on them. They are so *fucking* short.

"I can't sleep in pants either," she mumbles, quickly crawling into bed and under the covers.

I try to ignore the way her nipples are clearly outlined under the thin tank top, but, holy *fuck*, it's hard. Blood rushes to my lower half, so I turn to lie on my stomach, stretching my arm around my pillow.

No touching. There's only one rule, and it's no touching allowed.

This is going to be a long night.

19

ROSIE

I debated which pajamas to wear tonight for over an hour. I angrily sorted through my drawers in search of something that I could be comfortable and *modest* in.

At the end of the day, I went with a standard tank top and shorts, covered with black sweats and a hoodie. I planned to remove the hoodie and sweats after Holden fell asleep.

Once I got here, I decided he could go fuck himself. If I'm going to be sleeping here indefinitely for four nights a week, I deserve to be comfortable. Ever since I grew into 32F bras at the age of nineteen, I have been incapable of wearing them to sleep. I physically can't force myself to do it.

I lie awake in the dark of Holden's room, listening to his breathing. It seemed to change and grow steady almost immediately after he turned the TV off and we both settled under his covers. I arranged a line of pillows between us in an attempt to keep the no-touching rule in effect.

We can do this without getting caught. This is totally possible.

I will make it into nursing school. I will not sleep with him. Even if he begs me, I will not do it.

High school Rosie is somewhere in the universe, doing somersaults right now.

We're sleeping in Holden's bed?!

Holden Redford's fine ass is nearly naked right next to us?!

In mental defense of my own sixteen-year-old self, I remember how every girl in my grade wanted to sleep with Holden. Hell, even just having him look in my direction would've felt like an accomplishment.

I cared about Duke for a time. He was truly my first love, my girlhood love. But even when we were together, Holden still had my attention. No matter how hard I tried, my eyes followed him whenever he entered the room.

It wasn't a crush exactly, more like a rapt fascination. Like seeing a natural disaster on the news and being unable to peel my eyes away or stop running imaginary scenarios through my head.

If I had been there, would I have survived it?

If Holden noticed me, would I survive it?

I love Dolly like a sister and always have, but when I met all her brothers in second grade, Holden was an adult man. It wasn't until around sixth grade that I started to really crush on him. I thought I had died and gone to heaven ... no, hell. Of course, he never even glanced in my direction. The first time I ever remember him really *looking* at me was the night when I walked in on him getting a blow job, when he later killed my uncle Cain.

Now, here I am, sleeping next to him in his bed for five hundred dollars.

I roll over, stretching my arm across my pillow and curling it around it.

I hope Dolly doesn't hate me for this if she finds out ...

She knows Holden is somehow tortured from his time in prison. He's been a complete dick to everyone on the ranch. Whatever is going on with him, it would benefit everyone if he could get over it. I don't want to keep secrets from her, but this situation is bizarre.

No one would believe that we're just sleeping in here. Is it actually realistic to think we could be doing this innocently?

I can't risk her freaking out and demanding that I turn down his offer.

At the end of the day, she has her family. Her brothers will always take care of her, no matter what. I'm so grateful that she has that safety net, but the reality is that my situation is not the same.

I'm on my own in this world. And technically, I'm not doing anything wrong.

I wake up to sunlight pouring in on my face. Once again, a heavy arm is draped over me, holding me in place. My eyes flutter open, taking in the room.

Holden.

I look down, seeing that his muscly, tanned arm is firmly caging me in. Not only that, but the covers have also been pulled down, along with my tank top, revealing a substantial amount of my cleavage. My nipples are barely being contained by the thin straps.

My pulse starts to race as I glance over at him. He's still knocked out cold, sleeping like a very muscly corpse. I try wiggling free. He doesn't budge. I try again, moving down the bed as much as I can, but instead of waking up, he pulls me in tighter, like his subconscious knows I'm trying to escape. His body turns to face me more fully, his lower half connecting with mine.

My mind goes black as his hard length comes into contact with my thigh.

Not again ...

Not. Again.

Why me?

I close my eyes, willing myself to move and get out of his grasp, not caring whether he wakes or sleeps at this point. When I place my hands on his chest and physically push, his eyes slide open.

He immediately shifts to a point of aggression, pinning me down to the bed as he straddles me, hands around my throat this time.

"I'm starting to think this is just how you say good morning." I sound winded.

His eyes blink into focus. The pressure around my throat loosens, but the bulge on my upper thigh grows. I whimper internally, resisting the urge to roll my eyes back in my head.

At least he lost the knife.

"I slept all night," he says it almost like there should be a question mark at the end.

His hands release my neck, and he pulls back, dropping

them at his sides with an exhale. His glorious chest and abs are making it hard for me to keep my attention on his face.

"Well, it's morning time, so ... yeah. Do I get a bonus for this part? We said no touching." I try to control my breathing, but I still sound like I've been running.

He's gonna know I'm into this.

His eyes drift down over me. He freezes, and I begin to feel his dick pulse. I follow his gaze, sucking a breath when I see that one of my nipples has escaped the tank top completely.

His pink tongue darts out to lick his lips. His eyes grow hungry, like he could devour me at any moment. Neither of us dares to move.

The way his pupils dilate as he stares at my chest makes my thighs quiver. I'd give *anything* to read his mind right now.

One night in, and we're already here.

Fire, meet gasoline.

His groan is barely audible as he slides off of me and stands up. His dick is sticking straight out proudly inside his boxers, and he doesn't try to hide it. When he turns to walk toward the bathroom, I see that his broad shoulders and back are marked with jagged scars in sporadic placements, like he received them all at different times.

"Trust me, Dixon, if I chose to touch you, that would be bonus enough."

"Monroe Blue is playing at nine thirty. I'm so pumped! It's been so damn long since we've gone anywhere!" Dolly drags me through the crowd of concertgoers, aiming for the front of the stage.

"We're gonna lose Cash and Duke if you don't slow down."

She can't hear me over the noise of the crowd. It's Friday night, and the venue is packed with people. Dolly is wearing a shimmery bodycon white dress with silver cowboy boots. Her hair is curled and pinned into a messy updo. She's a big fan of Monroe Blue, and she loves concerts. We spent the entire afternoon getting ready.

I opted for a dark red dress with a thigh slit and a halter top. My hair is in waves around my shoulders. The black cowboy boots are worn out, but with the dirt floor of the outdoor venue, no one will be able to tell. We somehow get all the way to the very front, resting our forearms on the gate separating the stage from the crowd.

"You look amazing! I bet you'll get asked for your number at least ten times tonight." Dolly smiles as she holds up her frozen peach margarita.

I clink our plastic cups together and sip on mine, the mango flavor bursting on my tongue.

"Mmm, that's so good. You wanna try it?"

We trade cups to try each other's drinks.

Dolly leans close to talk directly in my ear. "We should try to get rid of Cash and Duke. We'll never get to flirt with anyone with them hanging around us."

I glance over at her brothers. Duke is smiling and chatting with two blondes. Cash looks irritated that he even had to come, standing with his feet apart and his arms crossed, as far from other people as possible. He doesn't like people.

I heard Holden say that Dolly and I needed two guys with us if we were going out. They debated who would come with us and who would go to The Riders event tonight, where some of their newer bulls were being ridden for the first time. I guess Cash got stuck with us.

I don't know what he's so worried about. He's always been overprotective of Dolly, but since the night when Holden killed my uncle Cain, they don't let her go out alone. She doesn't fight it. This is the first time I've ever even heard her say she wants to get away from them.

"Well, Duke is plenty distracted. Cash is the only one you're gonna have trouble losing."

Someone is strumming a guitar up onstage as they prepare the equipment for Monroe Blue. Dolly and I have listened to her music for the last six years, but she's gained popularity like crazy in the last two. She's only one year older than us, and her music is a cross between folklore and country. She has a raspy voice, and people say she looks like a country Marilyn Monroe with her short blond hair and sensual, slim figure. She's one of those women with off-the-charts sex appeal and natural beauty.

"Do you want me to go punch Duke in the face for flirting with those girls? Because I will. You should try to make him jealous."

I laugh, shaking my head. Our pretend flirting must be convincing, or Dolly is just giving in to her delusions about me and him giving our relationship a second chance.

"Duke and I have an understanding."

The three nights I've spent in Holden's bed have infiltrated my ability to think logically. I slept there last Friday, then Monday and Wednesday this week. He didn't say a word to me Wednesday night. When I woke up, the pillow barrier was in place, and he was gone. I had to get dressed and ready in his bathroom, sneak back out his window, and walk through the front door.

There's a pinch of giddiness in my stomach for tonight. He hasn't said anything yet, but I'm assuming he wants me to stay over.

Pathetic. That's what you are.

The fact that I'm looking forward to sleeping in Holden's bed is something I'll take to my grave. But for crying out loud, I am *only* human. Any red-blooded female with eyes, ears, a nose, and any sex drive at all would be jumping to take my place. Hell, they'd probably throw me in front of a moving train to take it.

Even though I know he's a dangerous criminal, I still don't have any sense of self-preservation.

"Let's tell Cash to save our place while we go to the bar and get refills before she starts. That one bartender with the tattoos was hot."

"You need to get out of the house more."

She nods emphatically. "Preferably without a male relative trailing after me all the time."

We start making our way back toward the bar area. When we pass by Cash, Dolly whispers in his ear. His eyes narrow in on her. She gestures to the stage. He finally nods, eyeing me before returning to his bored expression.

"We're good." She smiles, grabbing for my hand. "He

hates concerts. Hates the crowds. I asked him to save our spot."

My phone buzzes in my hand. Butterflies sprinkle through my belly as I hope it's from Holden.

HOLDEN

My bed. Tonight. When will you be home?

I can't hold back the smile that forms over my lips. *Doesn't like you. Actively hates your guts. You feel the same! Holy shit, why does that text look like a special invitation?*

ROSIE

Whenever I feel like it.

HOLDEN

Have you always been this big of a brat?

I clap my hand over my mouth. Dolly is walking ahead, and we're almost to the bar. I don't want her to see that I'm texting and smiling like an idiot. She'll catch on to me. She's way too perceptive not to. She'll ask who it is, and I won't have an answer.

ROSIE

Only when someone acts like I'm at their beck and call.

HOLDEN

Four nights a week is hardly at my beck and call.

Your father is at the ride tonight.

Debating whether or not to ask him if he knows where you've been sleeping lately.

My smile fades. Dolly turns around at the perfect moment.

"You want the same mango one?" she asks.

I nod, clicking the button to darken the phone screen. If Holden tells my father that I've been sleeping in his bed, my family life will blow up in my face. I have no earthly idea what my father would do, but it wouldn't be good. I'm not cut off, that I know of, but having sex with Holden Redford would definitely be the end of my inheritance. I don't know if he would ever speak to me again. Our relationship is beyond complicated, but the idea of it ending forever makes my throat feel like it's swelling up.

Dolly turns back around with the drinks, handing me mine.

"Thanks," I mumble.

"What's wrong? Are you okay?" she asks, concern pinching her eyebrows together. She grabs my forearm.

I attempt a smile, but she sees straight through it.

Holden and I will *never* happen. The reality of it just hit me straight between the eyes when his text about telling my father about our arrangement came through. I'd almost thought he was flirting with me before then. I'd almost thought maybe tonight he'd actually look at me like a woman and not the daughter of the man who had pushed for his trial and conviction.

I'd almost thought maybe he'd get over the fact that I'd dated Duke, but it's all too much. The family rivalry, the fact that he ended my uncle's life ... all of it is way too much for us to overcome.

Telling Dolly about my stupid crush is on the tip of my

tongue. A single tear slips out of the corner of my eye. I open my mouth to speak, but a scream tears through the crowd.

We both turn to face the stage, where it came from. A man is on the stage, and he has Monroe Blue on the ground. The scream must've come from her. Dolly and I start to run toward the crowd, but we'll never make it through. She's fighting back, but it looks like he's refusing to let her go.

I look around the edge for where her security should be.

Can no one get to her?

Suddenly, another man from the crowd, wearing a cowboy hat, hops over the fence and jumps onto the stage. He reaches the man, jerks his collar back, and punches him hard in the face. It makes the man lose his grip on Monroe. The cowboy tackles him fully to the ground, straddling the guy and landing blow after blow in his face.

Monroe crawls away, her shirt clearly torn.

"Holy shit, that's Cash!" Dolly screams, running for the stage.

20

HOLDEN

The way Mayor Dixon observes the rides reminds me of a king looking out over his slaves. Haughty and debating how he can squeeze more money out of them.

"What's that fucker doing here, you think?" Sterling latches his helmet on, preparing for his ride.

I shake my head. "Ignore him. Focus on the ride. You're up in two."

The cowboys who run The Riders are similar to us—ranchers who don't care for big government involvement. Redford Ranch supplies the bulls for the event, which we are paid well for. There's nothing illegal about that part of the operation because we report the income. The betting is illegal. If they can't tax our money, they don't want it changing hands.

Sterling walks over to the chute, where he'll get on the bull. Everything we make riding is ours to keep, but who knows if any money will go out for these rides? The Riders are getting more cautious every night. They might wait weeks to pay out after this one, if any bets are even made.

I look down at my phone screen, gritting my teeth when I see that Rosie hasn't replied to my text.

That's what you get for being a dick.

The fact that I'm even waiting for her to text me back sets me on edge. Her existence is becoming too important to me.

You killed her uncle.

She fucked your brother.

I chant my reasons for disliking her to myself.

I push off the fence, walking over toward where Mayor Dixon is talking to the county sheriffs. They're all buddies, the law enforcement officials and the mayor. The night I was arrested, he had them take me out of the jail cell, and he beat me to a pulp. I was left bleeding in the cell for two hours before my lawyer finally got there.

They claimed the injuries were from a fight with another cellmate. I told my lawyer to let it go. We'd never be able to prove it, and I wanted to focus on not going to prison for murder.

After a year of constantly being targeted in prison by groups of violent criminals, I finally found out from making internal connections that the good mayor was paying them to assault me and attempt to take my life. I would defend myself, inevitably ending up in solitary confinement for sixty days at a time for fighting. It never stopped, not for the three and a half years I was there. My muscles are coiled for an attack, even now.

"Came to support the boys, Dixon? You're too good for

this town." I'm a few inches taller than him, but I still stretch out to my full height.

He turns to look up at me, his blue eyes sizing me up coolly. The sheriff takes a step toward me, like I might pull out a gun at any point and shoot the mayor.

How would he hold up in a fight?

Dixon holds up a hand to the sheriff. "It's all right, Jim." His eyes stay on me. "Well, I'd heard there was overcrowding all over. Good for you. I'm sure your family was happy to have you home."

The way he clearly just spews lies sends adrenaline shooting through my veins. It doesn't surprise me that he's not going to acknowledge that I was pardoned. One thing I do miss about prison was being able to find a time and place to clock a guy who'd pissed me off with generally no conse-quences.

"You know, it is good to be home with my family. They hired some damn good help while I was gone. I've always had a weak spot for a woman who knows her way around the kitchen." I smile at him, seeing the invisible smoke rising from his ears. "And redheads," I add.

After a few tense seconds of silence, he chuckles. "My daughter can make anything. She's been telling me all about how much she loves that ranch. We have lunch every Sunday. I've really enjoyed hearing about it."

I clench my fists at my sides.

What has she told him?

The radio strapped to the sheriff's shoulder crackles to life. "Altercation at the Sundance Pavilion. We've got a man in custody. Need you here ASAP, Sheriff."

My head whips in the direction of the sheriff. Before he has a chance to answer the radio, I'm reaching for my phone. When I look down, Duke's name is on the screen with an incoming call. My thumb slides across it to answer as I walk away from the mayor.

"What happened?"

The announcer says Sterling's name and number, so I turn to watch his ride while Duke talks.

"Some guy from the crowd jumped up onstage and attacked Monroe Blue. Her security was apparently held back, gone, I don't know, so Cash got up there, pulled him off of her, and beat the shit out of him. I mean, beat the living shit out of him. An ambulance just hauled the guy off on a stretcher, and ..."

"And what?" I bite out.

The other end of the line is silent.

Sterling held out for four seconds before violently being thrown off into the dirt. He stands up and walks toward the exit gate, clearly not hurt. I stride over to where he is, dusting the dirt off his jeans. He removes his helmet, and I jerk my head toward the parking lot to let him know we're leaving. He slides through the opening in the fence, following me.

Finally, Duke speaks. "And I can't find the girls. They're gone."

My blood runs cold. My little brother sounds scared, but he's not nearly as scared as he's gonna be when I get there.

"*Find them. Now.*"

I ABRUPTLY STOP PACING my bedroom floor, towering over her. I'm still wearing my hat and boots, unable to sit still for long enough to remove them. Adrenaline is pumping through my bloodstream at one hundred miles an hour.

"You and Dolly just ran off to the bar to get a drink, leaving Cash and Duke? Did you realize how fucking dangerous that was?" My voice betrays how deeply pissed off I am, but I can't manage to even out the tone.

Rosie is standing at the foot of my bed, arms crossed and lips sealed. She's wearing a ridiculous dress, her boobs practically spilling out of both sides of it.

And every man there got to see it, got to see her like this. She's an arrest waiting to happen.

I know I'm being irrational. The rage and frustration I'm already feeling with Cash getting arrested is making it difficult for me to process the night. After what Mayor Dixon said about Rosie having lunch with him and talking about the ranch, I'm debating whether or not a random girl from a bar would be a better option for me to get some sleep tonight.

I need to get rid of her, but I can't force myself to do it. I need her here.

She has an effect on me that has become vital for my sanity. Ironically, she also drives me mad.

I slept a solid seven hours when she was here on Wednesday. It would've been longer, but I got up early to check the bulls we had just cut the day before. I only got two hours on Thursday night, sleeping alone before waking up in a cold sweat, and spent the rest of the night trying to hold back the panic and convince myself I wasn't back in prison.

At this rate, I can't afford to *not* go to sleep soon. It's already midnight, and our lawyer, Warner, said we have no choice but to bail Cash out tomorrow. They won't let him go tonight.

I have no doubts about what he's going through right now.

"Cash will be okay, Holden. He had thousands of witnesses tonight. He was saving her." Rosie's voice is soft.

I stop pacing, peering down at her. I'm suddenly overcome with intrusive thoughts of what would happen if I took her to bed, stripped her out of that sinful red dress, and explored her body like I've been craving to do.

What would happen? You'd fucking betray every major conviction you have.

Still, I desperately need a distraction from the fury I'm experiencing.

"What's going on with you and Duke?" I demand.

She blinks up at me innocently. I see the way he is with her. It's not exactly … direct desire. It's flirtatious and forward, but the other day, when he and I went to lunch, he seemed about ready to take the waitress home for the night.

And Rosie is clearly *not* interested in him, although she plays along.

She flicks her hair over her shoulder, looking down. "What do you mean?"

I step closer to my bed, reaching my arm out to rest on the bedpost. "I mean, are you still fucking my brother?"

Why the hell it matters, I don't know. But it does.

Her eyes shoot up to mine. She looks down at my lips for a split second before slowly shaking her head.

I exhale.

"I'll have you know, I'm still a virgin," she says, lifting her chin.

Her words end me and bring me back to life in the same instant.

She's still a virgin. She's never slept with Duke.

An invisible rope around my neck is suddenly loosened and removed. Her words settle inside my bones, their weight bringing a sense of calm over me.

Her tongue darts out to wet her lips as she studies my reaction to her words.

"I'm gonna need you to expand on that statement," I say slowly through calculated exhales.

How far did they go?

My heart pounds.

That doesn't solve any of the issues you have with her father and her spying on the ranch.

That doesn't change things.

But doesn't it?

She slowly sits on the bed, pulling her bare feet up under herself. "It means, I've never had sex before. I've never done anything close to it."

I can't stand here and look at her without touching her, so I start pacing again.

She's a virgin. Inexperienced. Too good and pure for me.

"So, you and Duke dated for over a year and he never fucked you?"

She shakes her head. "I was still sixteen when it started. My father had made threats about charging him for it. He said we had to wait until I was eighteen. Once I was, I just … didn't want to yet, I guess. I wasn't ready."

I stop, facing the wall away from her. "What about after, while I was locked up? There was no one else?"

I find that *impossible* to believe. She's a walking, talking temptation. Every man in her vicinity leers at her like they've never seen a woman before.

"I haven't been in a serious relationship since Duke," she says simply. "I fail to see how this is any of your business."

I flip around, seeing that she's lying back on the bed, staring up at the ceiling.

Even when I thought she was off-limits because Redford blood is thicker than water, I nearly succumbed to all my carnal urges and twisted desires when I was sleeping next to her. I could never be with a woman who was with one of my brothers. But if what she says is true and she and Duke were never together like that … I have no earthly idea how I'll do it now.

If I'm being honest with myself, Rosie Dixon has been my obsession for three and a half years, since the night she walked in on me with Madi in the barn.

And it just got ten times worse.

21
ROSIE

I never had time to go home and get my pajamas for tonight. I had planned to stop at my apartment after the concert, but after Cash got arrested, Holden drove us home at breakneck speed, cursing at all the other drivers.

He's staring at the wall in his bedroom like it's going to speak to him. My eyelids are drooping from exhaustion and overstimulation.

Screw this. I'm going to bed. He can pace all night if he wants.

I slide off his bed, walk over to his dresser, and pull open the top drawer to see the neatly folded underwear that I washed and put away this morning. I select a blue pair of checkered boxers that look comfortable before moving two drawers down to where his T-shirts are. I find the one that feels the softest—a plain white one with a faded Coors Light emblem on the front.

I spin around and head to the bathroom. After washing my face free of makeup and scrubbing my teeth with toothpaste on my finger, I change and walk back into the bedroom, wearing his shirt and boxers.

The weight of his gaze is on me as I tuck myself into his big bed, settling deep down into the mattress. I don't bother with the pillow boundary. It feels like we're past that now, and I'm too exhausted to care if that's wise.

"Cash will be fine tonight. We'll have him back tomorrow morning," I murmur, closing my eyes.

A few minutes later, I feel the other side of the bed shift, and the lamp goes out. Now that he's next to me, I'm wide awake. I can hear his breathing, and I know he's still awake too. He's worried about his brother. Whatever demon it is that makes it hard for him to sleep alone, he's battling it tonight.

I turn over on my side, reaching out in the darkness. My fingers collide with the warm skin of his arm. His shoulder muscle is tense under my touch, and I lightly squeeze. I don't know why I'm trying to comfort him, but it feels like the right thing to do in the moment after causing him extra stress tonight.

"If I touch you now, I won't stop until morning." His voice is a deep growl in the darkness.

My breath catches at his words. I have no idea how to respond, so I don't. I close my eyes, hoping that if I can fall asleep, he will too.

I slowly wake with my arms fully wrapped around Holden's neck. His hand is curled up under me, cupping my ass. I'm basically half straddling him, my face pressed against his neck. His other hand is wrapped around my neck, loosely holding me in place on top of him.

How do we keep ending up here?

It's like our subconscious bodies can't stay away from each other.

His deep breathing tells me that he's still asleep. The sun is beginning to peek through the curtains.

I feel his dick harden before I sense his breathing pattern changing.

What is it with him and boners in the morning?

My inflated ego wants to pretend it's me, but even with my limited knowledge of men and sex, I've heard of morning wood. I just didn't realize it happened *every* morning.

His fingers curl tighter around me, cupping my ass. Wetness pools between my legs. I'm afraid to move, and I'm afraid not to.

Danger, danger, red-hot danger ...

Out of pure need and my chronic lack of self-preservation, I rotate my hips in a small circle, just to feel him a little closer, to experience an ounce of friction against him.

He lets out a low groan, almost like he's experiencing pain on the brink of pleasure.

"You're playing with fire, Dixon."

His gruff morning voice overheats my already-scorched insides.

"I'm trying to get comfortable," I lie.

"You're trying to get fucked, and you're a lot closer than you think."

"What is that supposed to mean?" I tilt my head back to look into his eyes, praying my morning breath isn't lethal.

He maintains eye contact with me as he shifts his hips under me, moving his hand from my throat and grabbing the back of my knee to lift it up, eliminating the space that was separating us. I feel the hard length of his dick, pressed right up against my pussy. All that's separating us now is his boxers and the ones I stole last night.

I gasp at the sudden contact, knowing that the wetness already seeping from me is about to soak through the thin cotton and then he'll know that I'm aroused.

His almost black eyes glint with desire as he gyrates his hips, the friction feeling so damn good that I can already feel the pleasure building.

"Just how inexperienced are you? Did you know that if I were to rip my underwear off of you, I could fuck that sweet pussy right now, in this exact position?"

I gasp at his filthy words, an involuntary whimper following the sound. The hand on my ass squeezes harder while the one under my knee shifts down, reaching for the seam on the cloth. Just two thin scraps of fabric is all that lies between us fucking, and he's about to rip them apart.

And I've never wanted anything so badly in my entire life.

The moment is shattered when a loud knock sounds on the door.

"Holden! Are you up yet?" Duke's voice is like a bucket of icy water being splashed over us.

We spring apart like we were electrocuted.

"We need to bail Cash out of jail. Warner just got here," Duke continues.

"I'm up. Two minutes," Holden grits out.

Duke's footsteps retreat from the door, causing me to exhale in relief. I know it was locked, but if anyone finds out I've been sleeping in here, all hell will break loose in this family.

Holden's dick is still tenting his boxers as he walks over to where he took off his jeans and boots last night. He pulls them on, tucking his erection inside. He looks over at me, a twist of desire and anger in his eyes.

I look away, blushing, as if he wasn't a millimeter away from entering my body thirty seconds ago.

Is he going to say anything? Are we acknowledging the dumpster-fire shitstorm we almost just started?

My legs are practically shaking from the sudden change in heated arousal to cold, angry glances. He still hates my family. My father still fucked his life up for killing my uncle. The line between what my family has done to him and who I am is far too blurry for him.

Without a word, he finishes getting dressed and walks out the door, slamming it shut behind him.

MY DAD ASKED me to get lunch with him again on Sunday. I had no idea what to expect when I agreed to it, but he seemed to be in surprisingly good spirits. He casually questioned me about the ranch as usual. I told him I was starting nursing school again next semester, to which he seemed indifferent.

He hadn't heard from my mom, which is getting stranger as time continues to go on. I tried calling her again, but there was no answer. I sent her a text, asking her to call me and saying that it's urgent. I only went to lunch in hopes that he had an update on her whereabouts.

On Monday, I send a text to my aunt, requesting a phone call. Right after it shows that it was delivered, my phone begins to ring.

"Hey, Aunt June. How are you?" I answer it while dabbing my face with a beauty blender. I'm getting ready to head to the ranch for work.

"Well, hi, deary. I haven't heard from you in ages. How's that hunky boyfriend?"

I smile, shaking my head. "I'm not with anyone right now actually. But he and I are friends. I work on his family's ranch."

"Oh! That's a shame. Hard to find a man who's tall and employed. When are you and your mother going to come see me? I'm in need of a girls' trip. We should do Miami, or—oh! A friend of mine has a house on St. Thomas. We could ..."

Her voice fades out as my anxious thoughts go into over-drive. *My mother isn't with her?*

"Hold on, Aunt June. Mom isn't staying with you?" I interrupt her vacation planning.

Her rambling pauses for a moment. "Oh, well, no. She's not here. I haven't seen her since, well ... last Thanksgiving? When did we go skiing in Breckenridge?"

My palms grow clammy. I stare at my reflection as my bottom lip begins to quiver.

Where is she?

"It's your father, isn't it?" Aunt June's voice filters through my mental breakdown.

I nod before realizing she can't see me. "He was cheating again. She was drinking a lot. I thought she was with you." The words spill out in a rush as I brace myself against the cheap Formica countertop. "She mentioned visiting you. I've been texting, calling her. She just ... she does this disappearing act sometimes, but it's been weeks this time."

"Okay, okay, deary. We'll find her. She probably met someone. I can't tell you how many times, before Clay, she would fall into the arms of some guy and be out of touch for weeks, *months* sometimes. You already know about all the disappearances since then. I'm sure she's fine!"

A tear slips down my cheek. I wipe it away forcefully. "Do you think we should file a missing person report? I mean, what if something happened?"

My father's reaction to my concerns yesterday flashes through my mind. His expression was ... guilty.

"I would say give me a few days to make contact with our mutual friends first. We don't want to panic before we've talked to who she could be staying with. If Clay did what Clay normally does, she's very likely just making her rounds until she builds up the courage to go back home."

From the sounds of it, this is a long pattern that my mother has established. Aunt June doesn't seem nearly as concerned as I am.

"Okay, let me know, please. Keep me updated on whatever you hear."

"I will, deary. Just go to work, flirt with that hunky ex of yours, and try to forget about it. I'll call you in a few days. Love you, honey."

I know she's trying to downplay it to make me feel better and not panic.

"I love you too."

The line goes dead, and I let the tears fall.

22

HOLDEN

The putrid smell of human excrement, body odor, and bleach brings on a wave of foul memories from my time spent in this prison. My throat constricts. I don't know if I can continue walking through the metal detector without vomiting.

You're not stuck here. They can't lock you up. You were freed. You served your time.

Time for the crime of protecting my sister from a rapist.

Cash goes through before me. I follow him, making eye contact with the guard who doesn't seem to recognize me. We never had any significant interactions, but I'll never forget any of their faces.

They lead us through the sterile white hallways toward the visiting room. We're surrounded by women and children, here to visit husbands and fathers. There are a few older couples who are most likely seeing their sons. This isn't a maximum-security prison, so we're able to meet with my buddy Connor face-to-face at a plastic white table.

He adjusts his glasses up on his nose, one lazy eye wandering as we speak.

"You really are a cowboy then? I'm not surprised. It's weird to see you not wearing the orange."

I nod. "It feels damn good not to be wearing orange."

The Stetson on my head isn't too out of the ordinary for Idaho, but a few of the other inmates definitely recognize me. My muscles are tense, waiting for an inevitable attack.

That can't happen here. You're not an inmate.

I tap on the table in front of Connor. "I came to ask you about something. It's a cattle hormone called M-59. They're saying it can make them gain weight rapidly without side effects. Ever heard of it?"

Connor pinches his brows together with his forefinger and thumb. "Do you know the chemical makeup?"

Cash pulls up the list of chemicals on his phone and lists them off to Connor.

After the first seven names, Connor begins to shake his head, chuckling. "They're giving this to cattle? With FDA approval? My God, what is next? They should just inject us with cancer cells now."

"It's not FDA approved. They're selling it under the table to ranchers," Cash says. "They're telling us it's on the fast track for approval."

Connor raises his brows, glancing from my face to Cash's. "Well, they're either trying to fuck you in the ass or they're about to fuck us all. Maybe both." His eyes shift to the tables around us before he lowers his voice and leans in. "It sounds like genetic engineering and expedited growth hormones.

The kind of shit that'll either kill you in your sleep or make you grow horns."

Cash and I walk out of the prison, and I inhale a deep gulp of fresh mountain air. My chest relaxes with the expanse of open earth and the lack of walls and razor-wire fence surrounding me.

"Well, this situation just got more fucked." Cash inserts the key into the ignition of our rented Ford pickup.

It roars to life, and he starts driving us toward the airport. I shut my eyes as the brightness from the sun sends shards of pain splintering through my head. I'm starting to get another debilitating migraine from only sleeping four hours over the last two days.

"We've got a bigger problem than genetically engineered cattle if that prick you beat to hell at the concert presses charges." I tap my knee, the pressure in my skull lessening the farther we get from the prison.

Cash's phone starts to ring. He answers it with one hand, keeping the other on the wheel.

"Yello?"

The guy on the other end talks for most of the call before Cash says, "Okay, well, I'll talk to my lawyer about it. But it sounds fine to me."

He ends the call, shifting in his seat.

"What?"

He shrugs. "She's paying the guy to not press assault charges."

"Who is?"

"Monroe Blue."

I chuckle. "No shit? How much?"

"Hell of a lot, I guess."

"Well, thank God you dodged that fucking bullet. Still doesn't solve the problem of that fucker Clay Dixon." I spit his name out of my mouth like the personal offense it is.

Cash's left eyebrow is split and healing, but his black eye and busted lip look like shit. He took the same beating I did when I went to jail. Mayor Dixon takes his place at the top of the food chain to the next level. I don't know if he blackmails the sheriff or if they're both just evil pricks.

He smirks. "Maybe if two of y'all could stop trying to fuck his daughter, he'd ease up a bit."

If he wasn't driving eighty miles an hour, I'd give him another black eye.

"I don't know what the fuck you're talking about."

If Cash knows, there's no telling who else does.

"Nothing, big brother, just thought we didn't shit where we slept. Or where our enemies sleep."

I grind my teeth together, attempting to slow the blood rush to my head.

"I tried to fire her. You can thank Dolly for that plan not panning out."

"Oh, I don't want her gone. Girl can cook." A few beats of silence fill the air before he continues, "Just don't know how any of us would feel about our brother screwing an ex."

My jaw tics at his words. He's not wrong. When and if Duke finds out Rosie is sleeping in my bed, he'll try busting my face on principle.

Family matters more than anything to the Redford brothers.

A sick feeling settles in my gut as we pull into the airport. I know I'm fucked with Rosie sleeping in my bed, but I'm more fucked when she's not.

It's Tuesday afternoon when I start blacking out while I'm riding my horse to check the newest batch of calves on the north side of the ranch. My hands tremble as I grip the reins. I don't think I'll make it back to the ranch house without passing out, but Queen Liz knows the way. She's been my horse for six years now, and Duke took good care of her while I was gone.

My body moves slowly as I put away my saddle and tack. I return the mare to her stable, tossing her some alfalfa hay before stumbling toward the house.

I pull out my phone to send a text to Rosie.

HOLDEN

Where are you?

She doesn't respond.

I push through the back door and into the kitchen. For a moment, I stand frozen. The ranch kitchen disappears, replaced by the prison mess hall. I'm on dishwashing duty. I look down, and instead of seeing my crocodile leather boots and jeans, I'm wearing the standard issue black tennis shoes and faded orange pants.

My heart pounds as sweat gathers on my forehead.

In the next moment, it's gone. I'm back at the ranch, and she's standing right there, staring at me with slanted eyes.

"Holden?" She's holding a gray dish rag.

I move over to her, desperate to feel her skin and make sure she's real. She's here. She's not a figment of my imagination, like she was for so long. I reach for her cheek. She's warm, and her skin is soft.

She's real.

I close my eyes, leaning down to press my forehead to hers. I breathe in her scent, the sweet vanilla mixing in with the lemon zest she must have been baking with.

"Take a break. Come with me." I don't have the energy to come up with any excuse to get her to lie beside me, but I can't fathom trying to sleep right now and waking up from a nightmare in two hours.

"Okay," she murmurs.

I reach for her hand, throwing the rag into the sink. She guides me through the hall, down to my bedroom. I'm in a daze as we go into the room. I hear her twist the lock on the knob, feeling my eyelids droop as soon as the peace of her presence settles over me.

I make it to the bed, collapsing on it. I start to remove my boots, followed by my hat.

"Stand up and take off your jeans," she says.

"Finally admitting you want in my pants?"

"Trying to keep the mud out of the sheets."

I pull them off before stripping my T-shirt off too. I sprawl out on the bed, not letting go of her hand.

"Stay here," I tell her, gripping her hand and placing it firmly against my chest.

"I'm not going anywhere," she promises.

She settles against my pillow, leaning her head back against the headboard. I let my eyes wander down the side of her face, inspecting her profile. She has long lashes, a cute little nose, and full pink lips that need to be bitten.

"Can you sleep?" I ask.

She shakes her head. "I'm not a good napper. I'll just stay awake."

I lean over, reaching for the remote on my nightstand. I turn on the TV, which immediately starts showing the last thing I watched—an old Western movie with John Wayne, *Angel and the Badman*. I place the remote on the covers between us.

"Watch something."

She grabs the remote, turning the volume down. "Have you slept since Friday?"

"A few hours."

She bites her bottom lip, and I groan. My emotions are out in the open right now as the mental exhaustion tears down my defenses. My fingers squeeze her hand tighter as I pull her body closer to mine. I don't stop until she's forced to lie right next to me, her hip bone next to my forehead and her thigh pressing against my shoulder.

"Why do you have to be so tempting all the damn time, angel?" I tilt my body toward her, my arm curling around both her legs so that I'm snuggling her lower half while she sits up.

"Just to torture you, I guess," she mumbles.

Ain't that the truth?

I close my eyes, letting sleep take me under.

23
ROSIE

"*W*hy do you have to be so tempting all the damn time, angel?"

My mind swirls with a mix of giddy excitement, anxiety, and overall confusion. Holden has never called me anything other than by my last name, Dixon, which he associates with my father and uncle.

I look down at the sleeping cowboy in my lap. His biceps and shoulder muscles are taut as he curls his arm around my legs, effectively holding me in place on his bed. There's a jagged one-inch scar between the muscles I've never noticed before. My fingers reach out to trace it softly. He doesn't stir, still passed out. My hand moves up to the scar on his jawline that I stitched up. My finger traces the pink line, where it's still healing.

Footsteps sound in the hallway, soft enough that they must belong to Dolly. I nibble my bottom lip, hoping that she's not looking for me. We generally do our own thing in the afternoons—at least until it's time to prepare for dinner.

Holden's warm body is making me feel sleepy. It's like when we're in his bed, we reach a truce. He doesn't hate me here because he needs me to sleep.

Why that is, I'm still scrambling to understand. I'm assuming it's something to do with his time in prison.

Nightmares maybe?

Him waking up and immediately holding a knife to my throat makes me think he was attacked in his sleep a lot.

But then wouldn't he want to sleep alone, with the door locked?

None of it makes any sense, and I highly doubt he's ever going to share with me why. I've already saved up enough money to start nursing school. If I keep sleeping with him at this rate and save every dime, I might be able to work less hours at the ranch and focus on school.

My phone buzzes in my back pocket. I pull it out, seeing my aunt June's name with a text icon.

AUNT JUNE

No one has heard from her. I think it's time we file a missing person report. I'm getting on a plane this afternoon. Can you meet me tonight?

My pulse quickens. Cold fear filters through me, sending tremors through my body. My fingers fly across the screen as I text her back.

ROSIE

Yes. What time? Should we bring my father in on it?

AUNT JUNE

> Yes, I'm calling him now. Let's meet at his house. Maybe she left a note he missed.

> Don't panic, deary. We will find her. She might've met someone.

ROSIE

> Okay, thank you for coming. See you soon.

Holden doesn't move for hours. I'm strangely comforted by his even breathing and the way his hold around me never loosens. I finish the old movie, and another one starts. They're actually really good films, and I love the way the cowboys drawl. I can't stop picturing Holden as one of them as I run my fingers through his hair.

I chew my fingernails down to the quick as worst-case scenarios with my mom run through my head. I text her again, telling her I love her and miss her. It's been weeks now since her last reply to me.

Around four o'clock, my aunt texts me that she landed and is getting an Uber. I know she'll be here in an hour, and I need to tell Dolly what's going on.

Holden's breathing hasn't changed, but his grip around me has loosened. Using one of the pillows, I slowly inch out of his grip and stick the pillow in his arms. He curls around it, exhaling.

I tiptoe out of the room, checking the hall for occupants before sneaking out and shutting the door behind me. Dolly's door is cracked open. I tap on it before pushing it slightly open.

"Doll?" I whisper.

She's sitting up in bed with a book in her hand. She likes all genres, but lately, she's been reading romantasy.

She looks up at me. "Hey, do you need help with dinner?"

I step farther in, wringing my hands. "Actually, I was hoping I could order y'all some pizza. My mom ... well, I haven't been able to get ahold of her. My aunt thinks it's been long enough that we should go to the sheriff."

Dolly's gray eyes widen as she closes her book. "Oh, Rosie. I'm so sorry. You really think she's ... missing? I thought she did this sometimes?"

I nod, tears threatening to spill. "She does. That's why I haven't done anything or gone to the sheriff. She disappears, goes on benders, meets people. One time, she did this with some guy on a yacht and didn't have service for ten days. This is different somehow. No one's heard from her in weeks. At the very least, I need them to look into it. Maybe pull up her phone records."

Dolly slides off the bed and walks over to me, gripping my forearm. "I'm so sorry. Is there anything I can do? Do you want me to come with you?"

I shake my head, sniffling. "No thank you. My aunt is here, and we're starting by talking to my dad and searching the house for a note or some kind of clue. She at least would've packed before leaving."

Dolly nods, message received. A Redford at my dad's house is a recipe for disaster even if it's only Dolly.

"Okay. Text me when you have an update. And of course, don't bother coming in tomorrow, however many days you need."

I smile, pulling her into a tight hug. "Thank you. You're

an amazing friend. There's a frozen lasagna and some premade chili in the freezer. Instructions are on the bag for baking if y'all don't want pizza."

"Go. We can fend for ourselves. Don't worry about us."

My eyes soften as I look at my best friend. She'd go with me if she could—I know that.

"Thank you. I'll text you."

My car barely sputters to life. I exhale a sigh of relief as I turn out of Redford Ranch's endless driveway onto the dirt road. My phone starts to ring as I come up to a Stop sign.

My father's name is on the screen. I swipe to answer it, a ball of dread forming in my stomach.

"Hello?"

"Rosie, where are you?"

I press my foot down harder on the accelerator. "I'm on my way, Dad. I have to make a quick stop at my apartment first. Aunt June told me she'd be there at five. Am I late?"

He's silent on the other end for about ten seconds.

"Dad? Can you hear me?"

"Yes, hold on."

I purse my lips and wait for him to respond. A herd of cows with the double R brand on their back end are right up against the barbed-wire fence as I speed past.

"Okay, I'm sorry, honey. I was dealing with some unimportant work stuff. So, you and your aunt are concerned for Sheri? When did you last speak to her?"

I try to remain calm while debating my response. I've been bringing up my concerns to him for weeks, but he hasn't shown any interest until now.

"It's been weeks, maybe three? Almost a month. Aunt June talked to all their mutual friends. No one has heard from her."

A twist in my gut brings a wave of nausea on. I press on the brakes, slowing as I approach a Stop sign. It's too dark outside for it not even being five o'clock in the evening. The deep gray clouds in the sky are threatening to downpour. Lightning strikes silently in the distance, but the thunder cracks a few seconds later.

"Rosie, where are you? I feel like it's not safe for you to be driving right now."

I come to a full stop, my vision blurring slightly as my mind swirls. "I'm ... I'm fine. I'll see you soon."

My fists grip the steering wheel firmly.

He sighs. "Okay, sweetheart. Be careful."

"I will." I end the call.

Raindrops begin pelting my windshield as I arrive at my apartment complex. A thousand unsavory scenarios are spinning through my mind as I mount the steps leading up to the third floor.

My mother is gone.

No one has heard from her.

Is she okay?

Does my father even care?

Yes, he's going to help.

I twist the knob to my apartment door, still deep in thought. The living room is dark as I fumble around for the light switch.

Did I lock my car?

My body twists back around as I try to remember if I was too distracted to click the Lock button on my keys. I start walking back toward the door.

Okay, I just need to grab a few things, and I'll be out of here.

I need some extra clothes for the night since I very well could end up staying over at my father's house with Aunt June. A crack of thunder sounds above my head, followed by the pitter-patter of raindrops. My skin tingles with a very palpable fear holding me in place. I reach for the switch to turn on the light, uneasiness swelling over me. My fingers finally make contact with it, and I flip it on.

My breath catches in my throat as a masked figure in all black stands directly in front of my face. A scream begins to curdle in my throat, but the figure reaches out a hand to cover my mouth as someone else comes up behind me.

"Hello, Rosie," the man whispers.

Then, I remember ... I was too distracted to realize that I never had to unlock my front door.

24
HOLDEN

I wake with a start, my fight-or-flight kicking in. I can feel the emptiness of the room, the absence of her even breathing. The coldness of solitary confinement stretches over me, paralyzing my body for a moment before sending me off the mattress and onto the floor. I finish fifty push-ups without breaking a sweat before moving into a one-armed position.

After twenty-five on the first arm, I switch to the other. My body heat seems to draw me into the present as I notice that my room is dark. The clock on my nightstand reads five thirty.

Why is it dark at five thirty? Where is Rosie?

The realization that she left my bed while I was sleeping after I told her not to hits me. However, it's been four and a half hours, so someone probably came looking for her.

Just breathe. She's probably in the kitchen, making dinner.

A cold shower is screaming my name. I'm jumpy, nerves still taut from waking up alone.

If I could just find Rosie, the panic would stop.

I decide to jump in the shower first, keeping the water temperature around the level of our deep freezer as I jump in and let it ease my aching chest and shoulder muscles. It takes over thirty minutes for me to start breathing in and out at a normal pace. I press my heated forehead against the tiles, closing my eyes.

This dependency on her is unhealthy. If I can't find another way to sleep, I'll have to fucking marry her. I can't go on like this, waking up in a panic every time she's not in my bed. The water streaming over me finally accomplishes the task of drawing me back to reality. I turn off the tap, climbing out and dressing in Wranglers and a pale green T-shirt.

I walk out into the hallway toward the kitchen. Low voices reach my ears as I approach.

"... in weeks. I don't even know what happened the last time, but apparently, this isn't so unusual for her. I could just tell she was super upset. I wish there were something I could do for her." Dolly's voice trails off as I come into view.

She shuts her mouth, standing up straight and walking over to the stove, where a pan of half-eaten lasagna is sitting.

"Hey, are you hungry? We're having lasagna," she says.

Duke and Sterling glance at each other before looking back down at their plates. The energy in the room is stifled with secrets. I know my family too well.

"What happened?" I approach the pan of lasagna, serving myself a generous portion.

My sister is tracing one of the veins in the quartzite countertop. She clears her throat before looking up at me.

"Rosie's just having some family trouble. She left early, and she probably won't be in tomorrow."

I grab a fork, taking a seat at one of the barstools at the island. I attempt a neutral expression while my mind spirals into potential explanations for what could be happening in the Dixon family that would cause Rosie to take off work so suddenly.

Does it have something to do with the ranch? Did she find out about the M-59 and our visit to Idaho?

I take a bite, chewing slowly. I can feel Duke's eyes on me. The room is silent, aside from the wind picking up outside. Charcoal-colored clouds loom outside as the trees dance.

"So, was she deep-cleaning your room or something?" Duke asks. His voice is tight.

I shove another bite in my mouth before looking over at my brother.

"No, she wasn't cleaning my room." I grab the pitcher of sweet tea and pour some into a glass, chugging the entire thing as he continues to stare at me.

"Then, why was she in there all afternoon?" His fork clatters against his plate, and he squares his shoulders back.

I know my little brother too well. This is about to get ugly if I don't play it cool.

Too bad I'm in a shit mood and it's been too long since I've been in a fight.

I lean back against the chair, stretching my legs out with a sigh. "Why are you so worried about it, little brother?" I try to hold back my smirk.

He glowers at me, his dark eyebrows lowering. He pops

his knuckles as he slowly comes to a stand. "Are you fucking my ex-girlfriend?"

I wish.

What?

I look back down at my plate, answering him before shoveling another bite in my mouth. "Now, why on earth would you think that?"

"Because I saw her go into your room and sneak out three hours later. Don't fucking lie to me."

Dolly gasps. "Oh my gosh, are you and Rosie really hooking up?"

I look up at my sister, swallowing before I answer, "Is that against the rules now or something?"

I should've just denied it, told them all it's not what it looks like.

But then I would have to tell them I can't sleep without her and that I'm paying her to stay in my room half the week. I'd also have to tell them why.

I'm the strong one, the leader of this family. I can't come back half broken and unable to function. The ranch needs me. My family needs me. I don't have the liberty of falling apart, like my father did.

And it's nobody's fucking problem, except mine, to battle these demons.

Duke lunges for me, tackling me to the ground, along with the barstool. My head smacks the wood flooring as he sends his fist into my jaw with an uppercut.

I crack a smile despite the wave of dizziness. "You've gotten stronger, little brother."

He gets one more hit in for the assumed betrayal before I

start to fight back. I roll him off of me, pinning his shoulders to the floor. He knees me in the gut, drawing a grunt from me as I try to restrain him without hitting him back.

He's pissed off and not giving up. I use one arm to pin his right wrist down, but he throws an elbow in my face, hitting me in the nose.

All right, fuck this.

I rear back, landing a punch on his jaw before stepping off of him. Blood drips down from my nose, spilling onto my shirt.

"I'm not fucking her," I tell him, wiping my nose.

He doesn't stop to listen. He stands up, trying to throw another one in my face. I block it with my forearm. I return his punch with one of my own, sending him flying into the wall of the kitchen, leaving a divot in the Sheetrock. An old family picture crashes to the floor, shattering the glass. He lunges for me again, but I can see the move before he gets to me. I duck out of the way before reaching for his head and locking his neck in the crook of my elbow in a hold he can't get out of. He claws at my arms.

"That's enough! I told you I didn't fuck her."

"Then, why was she in there with you?" he yells.

Cash has joined us in the kitchen, and he and Sterling are casually eating dinner while observing the fight. Dolly is pacing with crossed arms. She's used to brawls breaking out between us, but she's never liked it.

"Okay, Holden, he heard you. Let him go," she pleads.

I'm squeezing his neck just enough to limit his airway but not cut it off. I'm bigger and stronger than Duke, but he's always been a damn good fighter. If I hadn't been forced to work out for my sanity and fight for my own safety in prison, this would've gone on a lot longer, and he could have won.

I let him go, and he gasps for air.

"When did you get so fucking strong?" He stands up straight, red-faced and still angry.

My barstool is in a splintered heap on the floor, so I pull his over to where my plate is and sit down. I grab the napkin next to my plate and hold it up to my bloody nose.

"You think I sat around and sang 'Kumbaya' in prison after writing your pretty redhead a love letter?"

He lunges for me again. The urge to pull the knife from my pocket and slice his belly open, like I would if he were another inmate attacking me, rises. Shanks in prison aren't a myth. My barstool topples to the floor again, the crack of wood splitting the air.

"Okay! That's enough!" Dolly screams.

When I dodge his next blow, he catches me in the shoulder, jerking me sideways. I send my fist into Duke's face again, letting this one go with more force. His body jolts back. I stand up again, panting and waiting for him to get up. He jumps to his feet, eyes clearly calculating his best shot.

Sterling steps between us, pressing a hand to both our chests. "All right. Can we just agree that no one is fucking anyone's ex? Shit, the nurse isn't even here right now to stitch you up. You're getting blood on the damn floor."

We're both panting. Duke is glaring at me with a swollen eye and busted lip, and my nose is smarting while blood drips on my boots.

"Are you going to?" He spits out a bright red stream.

"On the floor? Really, Duke? You can mop it up yourself." Dolly marches off toward the cleaning closet.

He's glaring at me, demanding an answer. Sterling lowers his hands, but doesn't step out from between us. My chest is rising and falling slowly. They're all waiting for my answer, clearly curious about what my intentions are with Rosie.

"It's none of your damn business who I take to bed." I spit out the last word before walking back over to my cold plate of pasta, pulling over another barstool since Duke crushed the first two. "But if I was going to, I would've already done it."

"That's not an answer!" he roars.

Sterling holds him back by his shoulders.

I slam my fist against the counter. "She's a Dixon. Her father's the one who had Cash arrested, who sent me to jail and ultimately locked me up in solitary confinement by sending men to attack me. Warner would've gotten me off on probation if Clay Dixon hadn't funded the prosecution and convinced them I was a danger to society, self-defense or not. You think I'd really take her to bed after everything her old man put us through? The fact that you're so bent out of shape about it really is *pathetic*."

The room falls silent. I grab a piece of garlic bread, shoving a bite into my mouth and chewing.

"You were in solitary confinement?" Dolly asks quietly.

I close my eyes, exhaling. My voice is more even now. "My point is, their family has been trying to ruin ours for years, since before I killed Cain for what he did to Dolly. I know you're all in love with her, but Rosie Dixon will never be one of us. She can work here, but she's not going to be a Redford. Ever." I look over at Duke's bloodied face and clenched jawline. "And we're done spilling Redford blood over the enemy."

25
ROSIE

"Where are we?" I beg for an answer as the vehicle finally slows.

I've been blindfolded, my hands tied behind my back with some kind of rope. I came to as they shoved me into the van. Rain is pouring down outside, railing on the windows.

The water immediately streams in with the heavy, whirring drag of a van door sliding open and wets my shoulders, arms, and upper thighs. He ushers me out and forces me into a run with his hand on my back. He yanks me up three steps before banging loudly on a wooden door.

The sound of dead bolts opening and locks clicking is followed by the handle finally twisting and the door swinging open. He hauls me inside. It smells musty and old. Cold fear floods my system as my senses seem to fully return after whatever sedative they gave me. He pulls my blindfold off, and my eyes adjust to the dim light of what appears to be an old hunting cabin. The man is still wearing a mask, but it's only him and me. Before he has time to speak or tie me to a chair, I raise my foot up and stomp down on his as hard as I can.

"Ouch!" he howls.

I turn and sprint out the door. The rain pelts my face as I run off the porch, smacking into a hard chest.

This man is bigger than the other one. He latches on to me, paralyzing me with his unmoving grip.

"Going somewhere, little girl?" His voice is thick with a Southern accent.

I kick against him, fighting for my life. He's immovable as he drags me through the mud and the onslaught of raindrops. I let out a piercing scream, hoping someone can hear me through the downpour and the sound of thunder.

All my nerve endings are highly sensitive as the man shoves me through the door, his grip so tight that my shoulders feel like they're bruising. The first man steps toward me, a syringe in his hand. His eyes are dark with rage.

"I told him we needed a stronger sedative," he mumbles, louder than he's spoken before.

That voice ... why does it sound familiar?

I kick him again, this time right in the balls. He yelps in pain. The man holding my shoulders doesn't budge, patiently waiting on the other one. He finally stands back upright, eyes crazy with an unhinged anger.

"You know, you've always been a little cunt," he groans, still keeping his voice low.

Where have I heard this man speak before?

He shifts the syringe to his left hand before swinging his right elbow from the side and gouging me in the eye with it.

I scream in agony, but there's no way for me to fight

back, to shield myself from the next blow. Instead of another shot at my face, my arm stings as he sticks me with the syringe, emptying the cold liquid into my blood. Immediately, my body feels weak, and I slack against him. I try to look around the cabin for any clues about where I am, but my vision goes dark before I can take note of anything.

MY ACHING head is the first thing I'm aware of as I come to. My shoulders are tender, like maybe I fell off of a horse or did a terrible Pilates class with Dolly. My eyelids are heavy, but I force them open. My mouth feels like it's full of dry cotton balls.

I need water.

The wooden rafters of the ceiling are unfamiliar. I blink through the fogginess of my brain and turn my head to look around the room.

The cabin.

The masked men.

One had a thick accent. The other one's voice was vaguely familiar.

The memories flood back as a wave of nausea overwhelms my senses. I roll over on the springy mattress, dry-heaving. My stomach must be completely empty because nothing comes out. Before I have time to catch my breath, I hear the door opening.

I hide my face in the scratchy sheets, pretending to be

asleep again. My body shakes as I feel them drawing near, flooding my system with palpable terror. Heavy footsteps come through the door, and the frame is filled with a bald, broad-shouldered man with sharp facial features. Even with his mask off, I don't recognize him.

"Get up. I need a recording." The backwoods Southern accent of the man sends shivers down my spine.

At least he's not the one who elbowed me in the face.

I slowly turn to face him. He's standing there with no emotion in his expression as he holds out a plastic cup of water. My parched lips force me into a sitting position. My entire body aches as I reach for the cup. I drain the entire thing, not realizing how thirsty I was until it's gone, and I wish there were more.

The man sits down at the foot of the bed, pulling out his phone and a newspaper. He tosses the paper toward me.

"I need you to hold this up and tell me your name. You're asking for a twenty-million-dollar ransom."

I gape at him. *Who? Who are you asking for twenty million dollars?*

My aching shoulders and the smarting eye, which I'm sure is now black and blue, force me to keep my mouth shut. I grab the paper, holding it up in front of my chest. He holds the phone up, aiming the camera at my face.

I will not cry.

He nods.

"My name is Rosie Lou Dixon. I'm ... being held captive. They're saying they won't let me go unless you pay them twenty million dollars."

The man taps the screen, lowering the phone before he

stands up from the bed and walks back out of the room without a word, closing the door with a click. I collapse on the bed, exhaling out a sob.

I don't know what the fuck is happening. Suddenly, I find myself hoping that Holden is the one to find me. For some reason, I have no doubt that he would burst in here with guns blazing and fists swinging. He would save me from the monsters holding me captive even though he himself hates me. He might even kill them both.

Something in him needs me to survive. He can't sleep unless I'm lying beside him. I have no idea why or how he got to that place, but I'm growing accustomed to it. The feeling of being needed by someone so dark and mysterious is addictive.

"Please find me," I whisper into the gray room, hoping that wherever he is, he can sense that I need him.

I drift in and out of sleep over the next few hours. I wonder what time it is. The room I'm in only has a bed, a nightstand with a lamp on it, and a closet with an extra pillow in it.

The lone window has been boarded up with plywood. I can't see if there's any light behind it to tell me what time it is.

I feel like I'm about to piss myself before I start banging on the door. "Hey! Hello? Is anyone out there?"

Silence meets my ears. I exhale, searching around the room for any possible solution to my bodily needs. Metal scraping against metal on the exterior of the door meets my ears. I step back as someone pulls it open.

The bald man is standing there, a blank expression on his face.

"I need to pee," I mumble.

"You try to run, I'll give you another black eye," he says.

I nod. "I won't. Please just let me use the bathroom."

He reaches out and grabs my wrist, gripping it so tight that I wince. He jerks me behind him, through the dark hallway. We stop at a narrow door. He opens it, shoving me inside.

"Five minutes."

I rush toward the toilet, pulling down my leggings and relieving my aching bladder. I sigh in relief. I look up, jolting as I meet my own eyes in the mirror.

My mascara is running down my cheeks in streaks. My left eye is black and blue with a stain of dried blood in the upper-left corner. I can feel a split in the skin of my brow. My hair is a tangled mess of matted copper-red curls. My once pale pink T-shirt is stained with mud and the blood from my eye.

I've never looked worse.

The urge to cry overwhelms me. A whimper escapes my lips as a shudder runs through my entire body.

You will survive this. You're not going to die in this cabin.

I finish my business and move toward the sink to wash my hands. There's no soap or hand towel, but the thirst and hunger in my belly has me dipping my head down to fill my mouth with water. I gulp it down ravenously until the door springs open.

"That's enough. Back to your room," he grunts, grabbing my forearm with another bruising grip.

"I got it! No need to fucking bruise me every time."

He's unfazed, jerking me down the hall and shoving me so hard into the room that I stumble and fall onto the wooden floor. He slams the door before the metal clicks, latching whatever exterior lock he has on it.

I stay on the floor, my body too weak from hunger, anxiety, and the aftereffects of the sedative to move.

"You'll be okay. You'll survive this. Next time he opens the door, you'll run," I whisper to myself before dissolving into uncontrollable tears laced with hopelessness.

I'm not sure I even believe myself at this point, but the desperation inside me might be enough to drum up the courage to do it and risk another physical attack.

I have to make it out alive. I have to.

26

HOLDEN

Saturday morning dawns with delusional visions of Rosie walking toward me with the sunrise. I stare through my window into the distance, her curvaceous frame as real to me as it's ever been. I watch her sashay toward me, my mouth watering with desire. The womanly figure fades away the higher the sun climbs until I realize she was never there.

I'm alone in my room, sweating on the floor with aching shoulders. The lack of sleep is giving me mirages. I reach for my phone on the nightstand to text her again.

HOLDEN

> Just tell me you're okay. If you don't want to sleep in my room anymore, that's your choice. I just need you to respond to me.

> Dixon, please.

I stare at our text thread, each passing second more agonizing than the first. No dots appear near her name.

Finally, I get dressed before stomping out to the kitchen in search of Dolly.

My sister is sitting at the kitchen island in a pink sweatshirt. Her dark hair is braided over her shoulder. She's sipping on a mug of coffee and reading a book with a man's chest and abs plastered across the cover.

I plant my fists on the counter in front of her. "Have you heard from her?"

Her eyes scan the page for another few seconds before shifting up to meet mine. She tilts her head to the side curiously. "Rosie?"

I scoff. "Who else do you know that's been missing since Tuesday?"

Dolly scrunches up her nose. "She's not *missing*. She went to be with her family. Her mother is missing, for God's sake. I've texted her, but she has every right to some time off. I don't know what kind of twisted tasks you have her up to in your room all afternoon, but you'll *survive*."

Dolly lifts her chin defiantly before turning her eyes back to her book.

"So, you've heard from her?" I question.

My first text to Rosie was on Thursday night, politely asking her when she would be back. Friday morning, I asked her if she was getting my texts, and this morning, I'm truly beginning to think something bad happened to her. I'm sure of it.

Dolly sighs. "Yes. She texted me Friday morning that she was taking off the rest of the week."

The sting of her rejection takes me off guard. I physically

step back, realizing that not only is Rosie getting my texts, but she's also leaving me on Read.

You're the definition of pathetic.

I turn away to get myself a cup of coffee.

"What is going on with you? Are you … into her? You can tell me. I won't tell Duke."

I reach for a mug, my hand shaking. I pour the coffee, unable to lose the uneasy feeling deep inside my gut.

It's called rejection, fucker.

"It's not like that. She's been helping me sleep. Ever since prison …" It's on the tip of my tongue to tell Dolly about my time spent in solitary confinement.

She would understand. She would more than understand, probably sign me up for therapy or buy a cot to sleep on in my room, forcing everyone to take shifts as my sleeping buddy. My inability to ask for help from my family is some combination of being the oldest child and losing my mother in adolescence, then being raised by an absent alcoholic father with four younger siblings.

I don't need help.

I don't have the luxury of help.

Soft fingertips touch my forearm, jerking me back to reality. I look down at Dolly's young face.

"Holden, what did they do to you?" she whispers.

TWO AND A HALF YEARS EARLIER

Hours bleed into days, which bleed into weeks and months. Time passes on a continuum that I have no control over and no grasp of.

I stare at the white walls, praying like I've never prayed before. I don't understand who God is anymore or what my purpose on this earth could possibly be.

Twice a day, someone drops food outside of my cell before opening an eight-by-eight-inch door. The bowl sits there, filled with rice, beans, overcooked meat, along with a bruised banana occasionally. They never speak.

I grow accustomed to the bananas, looking forward to the days when they're served in the mornings. I start to notice that every three days, a brown-and-yellow banana is in the little food window. I start laughing the day I realize there's a pattern, shaking my head as I peel it.

The next time it comes, I catch myself mouthing, *Thank you.*

Thank you? What the fuck is wrong with me?

Then, the nightmares start. It's been weeks, but I don't know how many.

I'm only let out of the ten-by-ten-foot cell twice a week for thirty minutes. Two guards flank me as I'm shuffled into a small field, surrounded by a razor-wire fence. They're both armed with guns and mounted on horses. There are three additional guards stationed on the exterior of the fence.

I run the entire thirty minutes, doing sprints back and forth. The expelling of energy seems to be the only thing that gets me through the next two to three days before I'm let out again.

Every time I'm put back in with gen pop, another group attacks me within a few days. I defend myself, and I'm put back in isolation.

I ask the guards if I can get books or something to write with in my cell, but they ignore me.

I ask them if I can talk to my lawyer, but they ignore me.

It doesn't matter what I ask; they never answer.

I start fantasizing about killing them. One by one, in my dreams, I annihilate each one. First one, I have to take a rock and bash his head in. Once he falls from the horse, I grab his gun and shoot the next one.

It always ends the same. I wake up in a cold sweat in my empty cell, no sounds, except the rats in the hall scuttering about. I drop down and do one hundred push-ups. On a tiny divot in the rock wall, I can hold on long enough to get in forty-five pull-ups before I lose my grip.

I collapse onto the cold concrete, my heart rate skyrocketing. My mind races to latch on to a new fantasy to keep me occupied, to keep me grounded to reality.

Rosie Dixon's face on the night I killed her uncle flashes through my mind. Her gaping mouth as she watched another woman going down on me is my last vibrant memory before I found my sister being violated by a man twelve years older than her. Then, I shot him, and I was arrested.

Rosie Dixon is my last link to life before this nightmare.

And her father is the one who falsified the evidence that led me to this place. I also believe he must be the one who sent me to solitary confinement for an indistinguishable number of months.

Fuck Rosie Dixon.

Fuck all the Dixons.

PRESENT DAY

The bull underneath me bucks wildly. I grip the leather strap, keeping my other hand high as my body is thrown into the air and whipped back down again. The smell of cow shit, mixed with the mud from the rain over the weekend, fills the air.

"That one's a winner," Cash says from the side of the steel pipe fence.

My thighs grip the sides of the animal, clenching his back to stay on for dear life. I hear the buzzer right as my cowboy hat flies off. I reach my hand back down to hold on with the other one. One of the ranch hands rides up next to us on a horse and releases the flank strap. The bucking immediately slows, but he's still pissed that I'm riding his back.

I slide off to one side as he pivots the other way, running for the fence and easily sliding through it. The adrenaline shooting through my bloodstream is a high I spent my early twenties chasing. Now, I use it as a distraction.

I look over toward the main house and the long driveway from the county road. There's still no sign of Rosie's car.

"What time is it?" I ask Sterling.

The cowboy working the chutes runs over with my hat and hands it to me. I place it back on my head. I use the bottom of my shirt to dry the sweat on my brow.

"Eight thirty. And, no, she ain't here yet."

I throw my brother a look, but there's no use in telling him to shut up. They've all caught on that something is happening between me and Rosie even if it's just sleeping.

The sound of tires crunching gravel draws my attention toward the driveway. An unfamiliar black Lexus is coming down toward the main house. I start walking toward it, flanked by Sterling and Cash. My stomach is in knots as the car parks and a woman steps out. She's older, in her early fifties. She's classically beautiful with silver-white hair. She's dressed in creamy-white slacks and a matching button-up blouse.

"Hello. I'm here to see Rosie. Is she here?" she asks, holding out her hand to me with a tight smile. "I'm June Clancy, her aunt."

I extend my hand to shake hers. "Rosie hasn't been here since Tuesday."

June's face is stricken as she freezes in place. "What?"

The alarm bells in my head start ringing as I step toward the woman. "When did you last see her?"

She shakes her head, blinking in confusion. "I haven't seen her in years. We spoke on the phone, and we texted back and forth the last few days. She never showed up to her father's when we were supposed to meet. She said she would be here, working."

My heart beats loudly in my ears as my throat begins to

close up. The ice-cold fear that something has happened to her washes over me, surging me forward. I grab June's upper arms, jerking her toward me. She shrieks in fear.

"What happened? What was Rosie so worried about that made her leave?"

June's eyes widen and grow watery as she gapes up at me. "I—I have no idea what happened to her! We were supposed to meet at her father's house on Tuesday evening, but she texted me and said she was too tired."

I release her, spinning around and stalking up to the main house. "Then what?" I call back.

I hear her footsteps, along with Cash's and Sterling's, trying to keep up with me.

"Then, by Friday, I tried calling her, but she didn't pick up. She texted and said she was feeling sick. The last thing she texted was that she'd be here today, working, and I could come see her."

"Why was she meeting you in the first place? What happened with the Dixons?"

"Her mother is missing. She's ... been missing for weeks."

Why didn't she tell me? Did she go looking for her?

The unanswered questions shoot through my mind. I clench my fists, feeling the urge to hit someone. As soon as I reach the front door and open it, I call out for Dolly.

"Dolly! Where are you?"

I hear the mixer in the kitchen whirring.

"Kitchen!" she calls back.

I force myself to walk and not run as I approach the kitchen, where she's dumping flour into the mixing bowl.

"When was the last time you talked to Rosie, and what did she say? Talked on the phone, not a text." I plant my hands on the countertop in front of her, tensing up and trying to keep myself from driving into town and strangling Clay Dixon until he tells me when the last time was that he spoke to his daughter.

Dolly's eyes are filled with alarm as the color drains from her face. "I haven't spoken to her on the phone, only texts." Her voice is barely audible. "She was supposed to be here this morning … I thought she was running late." She visibly gulps, clapping her hand over her mouth. Tears well up in her eyes.

My body feels like it's about to burst into flames. I force myself to remain in place, to think. "Do you have her on your phone? Her location?"

Dolly sucks in a ragged sob. "Yes. I have it on Snapchat." She pulls it from the back pocket of her jeans, opening up the app.

I move around the island so I can see what she's seeing on the screen. The little cartoon Bitmoji face with red curls and aqua eyes looks exactly like Rosie. Her cartoon isn't far from the one with black hair that looks like Dolly.

"Where is that?" I peer closer at the map.

"It's her last known location. But it says … three days ago. So, it's probably not where she is anymore."

"Is it on the ranch?"

Dolly zooms in on the cartoon. "Looks like it's more on the dirt road portion if you drive toward Elmott. Why would she be going that way? She was supposed to head into La Pradera to meet her aunt."

"Her aunt is here." I reach for Dolly's phone, which she hands over.

"So, there's no way to make it update to her current location?"

Dolly shakes her head, wiping the tears from her cheek with the back of her hand. "What do you think happened? Car accident?"

I consider the possibility. Rosie could have gotten in a car accident, but wouldn't her next of kin have been notified, which means June would have heard by now? Clay Dixon wouldn't bother telling us about Rosie being hurt or hospitalized even if she was unable to communicate herself.

But why keep it from June?

Also, why all the texts? Why has she been texting and just not showing up anywhere or answering the phone?

Unless someone else has her phone.

"What should we do? Call her father?"

The possibility that Rosie was supposed to go meet her aunt at her father's house and he hasn't come looking for her is a bright red flag in my mind. This entire situation has me coiled for some kind of unhinged attack waiting in the wings.

There's nothing Clay Dixon isn't capable of when it comes to ruining my life. He made that clear after my sentencing when he came to visit me and told me exactly where I'd be sitting for the next two years—off and on in solitary confinement—followed by another thirteen in a maximum-security prison.

When I got out early, he started planning his revenge.

But what does that have to do with his wife and daughter? She was working here before I even got out.

The front door opens, and heavy footsteps approach. Cash's face is grim as he enters.

"She's calling the sheriff. I couldn't very well stop her."

I pause, debating his words and my next move.

On the one hand, Rosie is the very rich and powerful mayor's daughter. Surely, they'll do whatever they can to find her even if it is just for show.

On the other hand, she technically went missing on Redford Ranch. No one's seen her since she was here.

And I'm the first name on the mayor's shit list.

"Tell them I've been out hunting with Duke. Other than that, nobody tell the sheriff a damn thing other than that she left Tuesday afternoon. Call Warner and get him out here now."

Cash flexes his jaw, clearly catching on to what I'm thinking. I meet his eyes, and we both know that one of us is probably going to end up in jail for this.

27
ROSIE

I've lost track of the days I've been here. After seeing that my body is so weak that I can barely stand, my captor finally brought me a sandwich. It was bologna, cheese, and stale white bread. I ate it in slow bites before washing it down with the last of my cup of water. I only get one cup a day.

The purple bruise on my face has faded to an ugly greenish yellow. I tried to escape once, but he threw me up against the wall so hard that I think it cracked one of my ribs. He said if I tried it again, that was only the beginning. My side continually aches, and if I turn in the wrong direction, a sharp pain shoots through me. The cabin is cold, and all I have is one thin blanket. My teeth chatter as I lie there.

I cried for what felt like an entire day, but with no sunlight and no clock, I have no real sense of time. The only link I have to the outside world is the sound of the birds chirping outside. I've been listening to them and humming softly to myself.

Is this what happened to my mother?

Why didn't my father just pay up to get my mother back? He has plenty of money.

Will he let me die in here?

The reality that maybe he just never told me my mother was taken because he didn't want to lose twenty million dollars grips me with paralyzing fear.

What if Holden never comes for me?

In the delusional recesses of my mind, I've battled with the idea that Holden is madly in love with me. That explains why he can't sleep without me, and during his time in prison, he somehow became obsessed with me. I've always had a vivid imagination.

On the other side of my delusions, I've debated if he actually *viciously* hates me. He hates my father, and he hated my uncle enough to kill him.

I'm filled with silly girlish dreams for even imagining him coming to my rescue and saving me from this level of Hades.

I'm going to die in here. I'm going to die a virgin.

I whimper in pain and hopelessness, shifting my weight on the springy mattress to the side as I hear a commotion outside my door.

Male voices sound like they're arguing, but I can't make out either of them. I climb out of the bed, finding that my strength is depleted after having not eaten in days aside from the sandwich. I press my ear to the door, but as I do, the voices fade away. I keep my ear close up against the hollow wood for another few minutes without hearing anything. In a moment of desperation, I fear that someone came to rescue me or offer the ransom, but it went awry. Maybe a stray hunter stopped by, not knowing a girl was being held captive in the back room. I start banging my fist on the door, hoping whoever is out there isn't just another member of the group of kidnappers.

"Hey! I'm in here! Hello?" I smack my fists against the door, praying I don't pass out.

The door is jerked open, nearly causing me to fall forward. I catch myself on the doorframe, looking up into the beady eyes of the bald man.

"What the fuck are you yapping about?"

I peer around the cabin, seeing a bag of fast food from the burger place in town. My heart sinks, fresh tears forming.

"Can I use the bathroom?"

He takes a step back, opening up the door and indicating for me to enter. He knows I won't try running again. I'm too weak, and with cracked ribs, I wouldn't get far.

I stare into the mirror, my blue-green eyes bright with the fresh moisture, red-rimmed from crying. My face has bruises, a scabbed cut down the side of my eye, and I already look like I've lost some weight from lack of eating. My cheeks and eyes have sunk in.

A choked sob erupts from me as I collapse over the sink. I splash water on my face, drinking a few handfuls of it because he doesn't offer me more than a small cup a day. It tastes fresh, like spring water. It makes me think we're pretty far outside of the city limits, on someone's land. We're probably miles deep in the woods. I haven't heard any cars go by.

If I do find another opportunity to escape, I'll probably

have to run through the woods for miles before finding a public road.

And I'm too weak. I'll collapse in less than a minute.

I could hide. Maybe a hunter would find me.

I'm drying my face on the hand towel, newly resolved to take another shot at escape when I hear the sound of a loud engine, similar to the ATVs they use around the ranch. My head pops up, swiveling to the door. He usually stands behind it, but with the smell of the greasy burgers flooding the cabin, he might have decided to eat instead.

My fingers reach for the cold metal of the doorknob, twisting it slowly. It opens soundlessly. I push it back just enough so that I can see the kitchen table. He's sitting there, shoving the burger into his mouth and watching a football game on his phone, propped up against a bottle of beer.

Maybe he didn't hear the ATV.

I wait, seconds ticking by slowly. My pulse sputters as I hold my breath, growing weaker with every passing moment I remain standing. Heavy footsteps on the front porch alert the big man. His head whips up just as someone tries to open the front door. It's locked from the inside, dead-bolted with an extra metal latch that I could hear when they brought me in. Now that I see it, I'm afraid there's no way anyone can get through from the outside.

He inches over to the door, pulling a handgun out of the back of the waistband of his cargo pants.

Whoever's outside starts trying to kick the door in. I jump with the first blow to the thick wood. The kidnapper reaches for his phone on the countertop, tapping on the screen before he lifts it up to his ear.

"Someone's here. He's trying to break down the door."

Another blow rocks the frame of the door, and I squeeze my eyes shut, wondering who could possibly be out there, so dead set on getting inside.

"No, I can't see who it is through the fucking door. You want me to shoot him?"

Another kick splinters a portion of the bottom part. I frantically look around the kitchen area for any type of weapon. There's nothing in plain sight, but if I could search the drawers, maybe I'd find something. I slowly inch out of the bathroom. My bare feet don't make a sound since they took my shoes.

"Then, fucking hurry up!" the bald man roars, slamming his phone down on the countertop.

"You're not getting through this shit," he calls to whoever's outside. "And if you do, I've got a bullet with your name on it."

The kicking stops for a moment. I freeze in the hallway.

No. Come back!

I have to let them know I'm in here.

"Help me!" I scream. "Please help me!"

The bald man whips around, beady black eyes lasering in on me. I run toward the kitchen area, grabbing for the first drawer I see to search for a knife. The man snatches me before it's even half open, hauling me up to the front door like I'm weightless to him.

"She's got my pistol in her mouth, fucker! You want me to shoot or—"

Before he can finish, another kick to the door brings it crashing down. The wood splinters into the cabin, sending shards of cedar at us with force. I scream as I'm pincushioned with tiny fragments in my forearms. The man holding me down shielded himself with my body so that I took the brunt of the wood slivers.

I feel the cold barrel of the gun on my temple as I look up to see who it was that burst into the cabin after literally breaking in the door.

Holden.

Before I even have time to react to seeing his handsome, blindly enraged face, a blast sounds right next to my ear, sending ringing noises through my head as the body of the man goes limp. His arms were tightly wrapped around me, so I fall down with him.

Holden descends on us, peeling the beefy arms back from around me. His hand cups the back of my neck, the other sliding underneath the back of my knees. My heart is pounding. I can't hear anything besides the blood rushing in my ears. My gaze slowly rises to meet his as I reach to grip the collar of his shirt.

His ebony eyes are darkened with wrath, but they soften into concern as he peers down at me, inspecting my entire body from head to toe. The scar on his jawline flexes as he steps over the dead body, holding me tightly to his chest. He leans in close to my head, pressing his forehead to mine.

"Who did this to you, angel?" His voice is barely above a whisper.

I melt into him with shaking limbs, whimpering in pain and sheer relief.

I'm safe now. I'm safe with him.

28

HOLDEN

My body is vibrating with rage and horror. Rosie is cradled against me on the front of the ATV as I blaze over the heavily wooded trail.

Her arm is trickling blood and littered with splinters from when the door came down. The rest of her is covered in bruises, and dried blood is crusted on her shirt.

I should've made him suffer. A shot to the head was too merciful.

I slow the vehicle, pulling my phone from my back pocket. I hit Cash's name.

"What happened?" He knows something's wrong as soon as he answers.

"Don't let anyone on our land. I need you to get to the dirt road near the old hunting cabin. We have a body to get rid of."

"Shit."

"Yeah. Rosie is with me. Who's at the house?"

"Sheriff just pulled in. He's talking to June."

I close my eyes, trying to think through the adrenaline rush and general outrage flooding my nervous system.

"Someone kidnapped her, and from the looks of it, they're pinning it on us. Jed was holding her in the cabin."

"Motherfucker. We should've killed him."

"Well, it's done now."

Jed was one of the ranch hands from years ago. He worked for us for about six months before we caught him needlessly torturing the animals. We reported it to the authorities and fired him. Occasional instances of vandalism on the ranch always seemed suspicious, but other than upping our security, we had no recourse.

I guess he was still pissed about losing his job five years ago.

"Who was he working with?" Cash asks. "Sheriff is walking toward the house. Warner isn't here yet."

"That's what we need to find out. They'll ask to search the ranch. You have to refuse until we can get rid of the body."

"It was self-defense, right?" Cash asks.

I close my eyes, pulling Rosie closer to my chest as she whimpers in pain. "Killing Cain was self-defense too. They won't let me out this time."

Cash exhales. I look out around us at the cedar trees and overgrown brush. It's midday, but the air is chilly. Rosie is wearing the same outfit she had on when she left on Tuesday. She looks thin and sickly, like she hasn't eaten in days.

When I find out who did this to her, they're going to experience everything she did and more.

The hunting cabin hasn't been used in years because we sleep at the main house when we hunt. We stopped leasing the ranch to outside hunters years ago. It was basically aban-doned. Jed would've known about it, but he wouldn't have been behind this entire scheme. He wasn't smart enough.

"She needs medical attention and a place to sleep, and that place obviously can't be anywhere around here. I need someone to meet me with my truck."

"Duke just got back. I'll send him to the northeast corner near the old windmill with a first aid kit. How long will it take you to get over there?"

I grit my teeth. "At least an hour. She needs food and water too. Tell Dolly to pack her some clothes for a few days in an overnight bag. I need some cash from the safe."

"We'll pack the shit you need, brother. Get her out of here. Sterling and I will get rid of the body, and Warner will deal with the sheriff."

"No texts, no calls. I'll get a burner and call you when I can." I hang up the line, readjusting Rosie's head on my chest. "We got a long ride, angel. Are you gonna hold on tight to me?"

My arm goes up under hers and pulls her body tighter to me. She winces, sucking in a breath.

"My ribs ... I think they're cracked." Her fingers grip my biceps. She squeezes her eyes shut.

Are you fucking kidding me? What the fuck did he do to her?

"I'm going to get you somewhere safe, okay? You're with me now. No one is going to hurt you again."

Her eyes drift open for a split second as she nods before shutting them again.

"I knew you'd come for me," she murmurs.

My chest is tight as I press the gas. Steering with one arm

and holding her up with the other, I begin driving through the brush as fast as the ATV will go.

Duke is speeding down the highway, assaulting me with questions from the front seat about what happened.

"Slow the fuck down. The last thing we need is to get pulled over," I snap.

The tweezers are vibrating in my hand. I'm trying to remove all the wood splinters from Rosie's arm without hurting her. Everywhere I look, she has bruises in various stages of healing. I have to use self-control not to go back and slowly peel the skin off of Jed's dead body in an effort to reach retribution.

"Where are we going?" Duke asks, glancing in the rearview mirror.

"Fe Leon. You don't have your phone, do you?"

He hands it back to me. I roll the window down and toss it out.

"Stop at the next gas station and get us a couple of burners."

He nods, concern filling his eyes as he looks at Rosie. "Who would do this to her?"

She opens her eyes, meeting my gaze. "They were waiting for me in my apartment. They wore ski masks."

I get the last of the splinters out, scrunching up the napkin and tucking it into the door.

"Do you have any food?" she asks.

"Where's the food you packed?" I ask Duke.

He hands back a lunch box. I unzip it and offer her the contents. She points to the bacon, egg, and cheese breakfast sandwich Dolly must've packed from this morning's breakfast. I unwrap it for her. She takes it with trembling fingers.

"When was the last time you ate?" I ask, fearing the answer as I move my hand to gently cup the back of her thigh. I can't stop touching her, but I'm afraid I'll hurt her.

She shrugs. "I got a sandwich yesterday, I think. Maybe that was the day before. I can't remember."

I'm overcome with a new wave of rage.

I try to keep my voice steady. "They're all going to die soon."

She takes a bite, chewing slowly. "Who would've thought you'd end up killing for me?"

I'd do more than kill for you.

"What else hurts right now? Do you need a doctor?"

She shakes her head. "My ribs hurt, but they can't do anything about that. They have to heal on their own. I just need to eat ... and shower." She looks embarrassed, pulling back from me. "I know I smell bad. How long has it been?"

"Six days." I don't even need to count. Each one has been agonizing.

Her eyes grow wide. "Six days?"

"Someone texted Dolly from your phone. They told her you were with your family, looking for your mom. When you didn't show up for work this morning, your aunt came looking for you. That's when we knew you weren't with her and your father."

She blinks with uncertainty before taking another bite of the sandwich. I reach up to brush a piece of tangled red hair out of her eyes. Again, she pulls away from me.

"I'm a mess."

"You're perfection." I grip the bottom of her chin, my eyes focused on her lips.

I should've kissed her by now.

She licks her chapped lips, biting the bottom one. "Have you been sleeping enough?" she whispers.

I narrow my eyes. "You just got kidnapped, tortured, and starved while being held captive for six days, and you're asking me if I got any sleep?"

The first hint of a smile ghosts across her lips.

She leans her head back against the leather seat. "I kinda like that you can't sleep without me. Did you?"

The energy between us is charged and vibrating with need, fear, and desire. Our mutual hunger for each other is crashing down in waves, rendering me incapable of resisting my unquenchable thirst for her.

If she wasn't injured, I'd be kissing her neck.

I shake my head. "Not without some heavy sleep aids. After the third day, I started seeing things. Dolly had some leftover sleeping pills from when I was locked up, so I took those last night. I got four hours."

"So, you still can't sleep without me."

My fingers brush against the tender skin between her jawline and neck. "I still can't sleep without you," I say softly.

She licks her lips again, like she's holding back a satisfied smile. "Good."

She shifts her body so that her head is lying on my shoulder. I take the other half of the sandwich from her, hoping she finishes it when she wakes up.

I look up to see Duke's eyes watching us from the rearview mirror. He looks away, gripping the steering wheel as he drives us toward New Mexico.

Trust me, I'm not happy about needing her so much either, brother.

We make it to Fe Leon in five hours. Duke stops at the first motel off the highway. It has an extra parking lot in the back, where mostly eighteen-wheelers are parked. He finds a spot hidden between two of them before going to get us a room.

"Just one. We're not leaving her alone," I tell him.

He nods, dipping his cowboy hat as he steps out of the dual-wheeled ranch truck. Rosie is still fast asleep on my shoulder when he returns. I don't want to draw any suspicion by carrying an unconscious woman into a highway motel.

"Hey." I squeeze her hand.

She blinks at me, sitting up quickly. "Where are we?"

"Outside Fe Leon. We're going inside, and you can go back to sleep."

Duke grabs the bag Dolly packed for her, along with one he must have gotten for us, while I guide Rosie out of the truck. I grab a spare jacket from the front seat, wrapping it around her shoulders. Even if she walks in, she looks like an injured, recently starved, and kidnapped woman.

We walk by a truck driver who doesn't pay us any mind.

Duke takes us to the room, which faces the parking lot instead of the highway, using the key card to open it up.

There are two queen-size beds with cheap comforters, thin brown carpet, and Spanish-style prints of clay vases and empty deserts with cactus plants. It's clean enough with one door leading to a small bathroom. The blackout curtains and double locks on the door are the main things I'm relieved to see.

Rosie walks straight toward the bathroom, shutting the coral door behind her. All the walls and trim are the same shade of muted orange-pink.

"How many guns are in the truck?" I ask.

Duke rubs a hand over his face. "Uh, I think six. Two handguns and four rifles. What are they doing about the sheriff?"

I reach for my cowboy hat before remembering that I set it down outside of the cabin before kicking down the door. I rub the back of my neck.

"Warner is handling it. We'll call them tomorrow, check in on things."

The shower starts running inside the bathroom. I grab the purple bag Dolly packed and knock on the door.

"We got you some clothes."

"It's open," she says.

I twist the knob, opening the door just enough to push the bag inside for her. I catch a glance of her bare back in the mirror, seeing that she has a green-and-yellow bruise on her side with a red gash right below it. Pain shoots through my chest, and I ache, seeing her this way. I need to hit someone, but he's already dead.

But whoever was truly behind it is still at large.

"I'm right out here if you need me." I close the door, turning back around as my chest constricts and my fists clench.

Duke is sitting on the bed, flipping through the channels on the TV. "I know it's not the time, but I just gotta say that this is fucking weird with you and her. I don't want to talk about it. I don't wanna know when it happened and get into another fistfight when we're running from the law and she's already beat up, but, fuck, Holden ..."

He shakes his head, eyebrows pinched together as he stabs the buttons on the remote.

"Then, let's not talk about it. Let me see the keys. I'm gonna go get us some real food."

He jumps up off the bed. "I got it. I'm getting beer too."

"Find me a cowboy hat, would you?"

"I'll think about it," he grumbles.

29
ROSIE

After a long, steaming-hot shower, I step out, feeling like a brand-new woman. I scrubbed my skin and scalp until they were raw. I towel-dry the tender skin before attempting to finger-brush through my tangles. The duffel bag on the floor is Dolly's, so I send up a prayer that she thought to pack me a hairbrush and toothpaste.

After unzipping the top, I almost cry in gratitude. She sent a razor, shaving cream, mascara, a new toothbrush with toothpaste, and deodorant. I wish I could hug her. I groom myself for as long as I can remain standing, shaving every inch of myself, brushing my teeth twice before finally getting dressed in the white tank top, baby-blue zip-up sweatshirt, and light-gray leggings. Dolly's boobs aren't nearly as big as mine, but she packed me a stretchy, thin sports bra that barely covers my chest. It's better than nothing. Once I don the clean white socks and swipe some mascara on, I inspect myself in the mirror.

If only she had sent some concealer for the bruises.

My hair is still damp, cascading around my shoulders in waves and smelling like motel shampoo when I step out of the bathroom.

Holden is sitting on the end of the bed. He leans back and turns his head to face me as I walk out. His dark eyes soften instantly as he takes me in from head to toe.

"Feel better?" He clears his throat.

I nod, suddenly feeling incredibly shy. We're alone. He just rescued me from a monster, called me *angel*, and now, we're *alone*.

He looks fucking incredible. He must've changed out of the shirt he had on because the pale blue one matches the hoodie I'm wearing. His denim-clad thighs are spread apart as he leans forward again, rubbing his hands together and looking down at the carpet. The scar on his jaw is pink in the lamplight.

I sit on the other bed, afraid of what I might do if I get too close to him right now. I'm warm, almost overheated in his presence.

Damsel in distress and dark knight rescuer is a fucking addictive narrative.

He stands, walking over to the black duffel bag by the door and riffling through it. He pulls out a white box, and I recognize the first aid kit from the ranch house. He struts back over to me, his ever-confident stride hotter than ever.

Okay, remember your issues. Remember him being a dick, a murderer.

Killer. He killed a man right beside you!

The memory doesn't have the turnoff effect I was hoping for. Instead of making me wince, it sends flames of desire down to my core. I swallow over the lump in my throat as the bed pulls me toward his weight when he sits next to me.

"We should see if you need any antibiotic cream for the cuts. Where else are you hurt?"

He's going to play doctor now? Lord help me ...

"Um, there's one on my side. It might need something."

He nods, unlatching the kit. The truth is, my side is healing perfectly fine. I want him to touch me. I want to give him an excuse to touch me. Holden Redford tending to my wounds is like a deep secret, an ultimate fantasy moment come to life.

He pulls out the triple antibiotic and a Band-Aid. He sets them on the bed, turning to me. I tilt my body away, heart pounding as I slowly unzip the hoodie, sliding it off my shoulders. He inhales a sharp breath. The tank top is Dolly's, so it's skintight on my chest. My boobs are practically spilling out of it and the threadbare sports bra.

I lift the hem high enough for him to access the cut I got when I was slammed against the wall. I think a nail caught me, resulting in the cut. The bruise is from the impact, which also left my ribs cracked. When his warm fingers touch my skin, I close my eyes, holding back a moan.

My lips part, and I'm glad my face is turned away from him. He'd be able to read the unhinged desire all over my expression if he could see me. The Band-Aid is pressed into my skin gently before he tugs my shirt back into place.

"Anywhere else?" he asks, his voice hoarse.

I turn to look up into his eyes, slowly shaking my head. His eyes dip down over me, pure yearning in his gaze. I blink, my eyes trailing to his lips. I'm weak right now, too weak to hide what I want.

He wants me too. I know he does.

His callous hand never left the hem of my shirt. His fingers slowly peel it back up again, just enough to place his hand on the tender, bare skin at my waistline.

"Rosie ..." He breathes out my name like it's a desperate plea. It's the first time it's ever touched his lips, and I love the sound of it more than I thought possible.

"Hmm?" I ask, shifting closer to him on the bed so that our thighs are touching.

One moment, we're a foot apart, and in the next, he grips under my ass, lifting me effortlessly onto his lap, pulling my leg around so that I'm straddling him. My hands reach back around his neck, and our eyes meet. My hair brushes against his shoulder, leaving little damp water spots on his T-shirt. My fingers run through his black hair. His eyes roll back and close.

"You're hurt." He struggles to speak, squeezing my thighs. "I don't even know where I can touch you."

When his black-brown eyes open again, they're somehow darker than ever, the lust at war within them. The veins in his neck are popping out with his effort to resist pouncing on me.

"Where do you want to touch me?" I ask, desperate to hear his answer.

He sets his jaw, seeming to attempt to control himself. "I want to start with your lips." His voice is deep. His eyes follow the words. "I'll kiss you until you can't breathe. Then, I'll work my way down to your jawline, right here." His fingers reach up to brush the skin between my jaw and neck. "Then, I'll kiss all the way down your neck, until I get to your chest."

His eyes have made their way down to my spilling cleavage. I'm so wet; I'm afraid he can smell my arousal. He struggles to continue, his hands cupping my ass gently, like he really is afraid he'll hurt me if he touches me *anywhere*.

I'm in anguish because of his touch. I'm on the brink of begging him for it.

Kiss me. Please just fucking kiss me.

His eyes snap to mine. "I'm not taking your virginity in a motel room."

"Who said anything about sex?" I'm breathless.

"If I start with you ..." He leans closer, our lips an inch apart.

Our mouths share the same air for a few beats.

"Then what?" I whisper, trailing my fingers through the hair at his nape again.

He pulls me closer. I can feel his erection inside his jeans.

He's just as turned on as I am.

A warm satisfaction spreads through me at the realization.

"Then, I won't want to stop," he says, his voice strained.

I lick my lips in anticipation, boldly grinding my pussy against his hardness. Something about being kidnapped and thinking I might not make it out alive has made me lose what little resistance toward him I once possessed.

I want to break him. I want him to break down for me.

His right hand reaches up to cup the back of my head as he stands up, supporting my weight with one arm. He spins me around and lays me down on the bed. He hovers above me, careful not to put pressure on my ribs.

"Fuck it," he whispers right before his mouth crashes down on mine.

His lips are soft and wet, hungrily sucking on mine. I pull him closer, stretching my legs around his lower back. His hand comes down between us to cup my breast, rubbing across the top of my nipple. I want him skin on skin, flesh on flesh. The thin cotton separating us is way too much of a barrier. I've dreamed of this moment for years now, and it's surpassing all of my wildest expectations.

He's on top of me, barely pressing any weight on me, but it's just enough that I can still feel his dick, hard and long on my pussy. The rest of him is all taut muscle, barely restrained from ravishing me. His tongue pushes through my lips, tasting the inside of me. I moan into his mouth. He responds with a hungry groan of pleasure and need. I claw at his shirt, trying to pull it off of him.

"You're gonna hurt yourself, angel," he breathes out, breaking the kiss and pressing his forehead to mine.

Never stop calling me that. Ever.

"Worth it." I keep tugging, pulling up to reveal the deep V-shape of his hips and the tight, rippling abs.

I gape at his body, wondering if he'd think I was weird if I traced each of his muscles with my tongue.

He stands upright suddenly, turning to face the door. The key card is sliding in. I move to sit up quickly in a panic. A spasm in my side causes me to wince.

"Ah," I gasp in pain.

Holden turns back to me, kneeling beside the bed. "Are

you okay? Did I hurt you?" His eyes are wide with alarm. His hair is mussed from my fingers.

I shake my head, resting back against the pillow. "No. I moved too quickly."

He sets his jaw in a hard line, his eyes clouding with guilt.

"It's not your fault," I whisper.

The door finally swings open.

"Damn thing is fucked," Duke complains, kicking it shut.

I glance behind Holden to see my ex, his arms laden with shopping bags and a paper fast-food one.

"I'm not touching you again until you're better," Holden whispers, rising to stand.

I guess that means I get to do the touching.

30

HOLDEN

"So, what are the sleeping arrangements? Because if you two think I'm going to lie here and listen to my ex-girlfriend and my brother roll around in bed together all night, you've lost your damn minds." Duke kicks his boots off before leaning back against the pillows on one of the beds—the one I didn't make out with Rosie on.

I'm fresh from the shower, my lower half wrapped in a towel. I left my clean underwear in the duffel bag.

Rosie's eyes graze over me, heated and hungry. She flicks them away when I catch her.

Feeling is mutual, angel.

My dick stiffens again. It's almost to the point of being painful.

I should've made Duke get his own room.

Except she's hurt and resisting her would be ten times harder if I were alone with her.

I reach down for the bag Duke threw together for him and me. Thankfully, there are two toothbrushes and some deodorant. He also tossed in some clean shirts and under-wear. I grab what I need before returning to the bathroom.

"Are you saying you wanna cuddle with me, brother?" I leave the door cracked open while getting dressed and brushing my teeth.

"I'm saying you can sleep on the damn floor," he calls.

I chuckle, opening the door with nothing but my tight boxer briefs on. If he hadn't said that, I'd have put on a shirt. Now, I have to make him understand something.

Rosie is in my bed, and I'm nearly naked. He can take that information and file it away wherever he wants. He keeps his eyes trained on the TV as I walk between the beds before slowly crawling in next to Rosie. She's a statue beside me, not moving toward or away from me.

No doubt, this situation is awkward for her.

One of us is her first love, her high school boyfriend turned friend.

The other one of us murdered her uncle and hasn't been silent about hating her family for years.

On top of all that, he and I are brothers.

I would never coerce or force a woman to do anything physical with me, but my arms are aching to hold her. After six days apart, finding out she was taken and then injured—on top of my lack of sleep—I want nothing more than to tuck her in close tonight and sleep for ten hours straight.

I refuse to make the first move. I want her to decide if she wants to be near me, especially in Duke's presence.

Hell, maybe she wants me on the floor too.

After our kiss, that would sting.

I turn to look at her. Her eyes are focused on the hunting

show Duke is watching. I let my gaze travel down to her full rosebud lips. She blinks lazily, still looking ahead. She nibbles her bottom lip right when I feel her touch grazing my hip underneath the covers. I expect her to stop there, but she keeps going. My senses overheat when her fingers reach for my dick, grasping the half-hard length.

I jolt, my knee kicking toward the ceiling. I hold back a groan, moving my fingers to intercept her, interlacing mine with hers. Even this innocent hand-holding with her makes me feel lighter, easing the ache in my chest that I've had since she went missing.

I feel like I might explode if I don't get closer to her. She squeezes my hand, sighing contentedly. I reach around her, grabbing her waist and scooting her entire body over until it's flush with mine.

"Are you hurting?" I whisper into her hair as she leans back against my shoulder.

She shakes her head. "I'm better now."

"Did you eat any more?"

She nods. I watched her eat a chicken strip and a couple of French fries before I got into the shower.

"Who do you think would do this to me?" she whispers.

I've been racking my brain with that exact question the entire drive here. The main enemy in my life seems like an unlikely suspect, considering I don't think even Clay Dixon is corrupt enough to kidnap his own daughter and try to pin it on me.

But who else would?

The fact that she disappeared on my ranch and was being

held there is hard to justify with any other explanation other than someone trying to frame me for it.

"Maybe if you can tell me what happened—from when you left the ranch to when he took you to me finding you—it could clue me in."

Duke shifts closer. "What did Jed have to do with it?"

She turns to him. "Who's Jed?"

"The bald man who was holding you captive," I say.

She shudders, shrinking back against me.

"What did he do to you?" I hold her tighter.

Please don't say rape.

She blows out a slow exhale. "He didn't touch me … sexually."

My entire body sags in relief. I squeeze her hand tighter, encouraging her to continue.

Her bright eyes look up into mine. "He would let me out every few hours to use the bathroom. I got one cup of water a day. I only got food once—a sandwich. I think it was a few days ago. The window was boarded up so I couldn't tell what time of day or night it was. I tried to run once, and that's when my ribs … he threw me up against the wall. My eye and the other bruises had happened on the night they took me."

"How many were there?" Duke leans forward, swinging his legs over the side of his bed to face us.

"I think three? I know there was a driver and two others. One of them was the bald guy, Jed. They wore black ski masks. When I got to my apartment, they were already waiting inside. I tried to fight them off."

My body grows rigid again when I picture her being

abducted by three grown men, helpless and terrified. The days of the other two are numbered.

"How did no one hear you?" I grit out.

She shrugs. "My apartment is in a bad part of town. There are fights and screaming, even gunshots, pretty often. I only screamed once, and then they duct-taped my mouth. I was blindfolded in the car."

"Did they take you straight out to the cabin, or was the drive longer?" I ask, tracing a circle on her hand to help ease her into opening up and calm my own nerves.

She looks down at the covers, where our hands are hiding underneath. "I think it was longer. It takes me twenty minutes to get to work, but it seemed like longer. We stopped once. One or two of them got out, but the third waited in the car with me. They were gone for just a few minutes before one got back in, and he and the other one drove me out to the cabin."

"How long did it take to get to the first stop?" Duke asks.

"Um, maybe ten minutes? Not long."

"Did you hear them talking about anything, saying any names or places?" Duke continues prodding.

I'm concerned she's going to get overwhelmed and shut down, so I throw him a warning look.

"They talked about a guy, someone they were either meeting or maybe who had hired them. That's who I think we stopped to see the first time. They just said, 'Tell him we got her.' Then, Jed told them where to find the cabin. He knew it was behind some hidden gate. I think they used bolt cutters to get it open because I heard them snap."

Duke and I exchange a look. Jed could have known where

to find the cabin, but few people know it's there. We don't use it much anymore. It's just another thing to keep up with that doesn't make us any money. We spend our time and efforts on bull riding and cattle sales.

"What about—"

"That's enough for tonight." I shut Duke up.

The last thing I want to happen is for Rosie to get triggered or have trouble sleeping. She'll do better remembering and telling us things on her own time.

Duke stands up, walking toward the bathroom.

"You're safe now. You're with me, and I'm not letting you out of my sight. We'll talk more tomorrow, if you're ready for it." I adjust the covers, pulling them farther up to go over her.

You're getting soft as fuck.

She settles back against the pillows, but doesn't release my hand. I lie back on mine, looking up at the ceiling and debating how wise it is for me to lie here with her, to let myself make her promises about keeping her safe and by my side.

If there's any chance she's still in danger, I can't *not* watch out for her.

But who could have possibly done this? What do they want, if not to frame me?

"Does this mean you don't hate me anymore?" she murmurs, her eyelids growing heavy.

I roll onto my side, leaning up on my elbow to hover above her face, eyes on her mouth. "I plead the Fifth."

My lips gently press to hers. She's still for a moment. I savor her taste, caressing the side of her face with my fingers. She whimpers into me when I pull away.

I smirk. "You need to heal and sleep."

She curls her arm up around my neck. "I need to be touched more."

Fuck, she's hard to deny.

"I'll be the first to volunteer when you can sit up in bed without wincing."

I peel her arm off, lying back against my pillow. This is getting out of hand. I need to keep my distance from her before I do something I can't undo, like take her virginity.

You're not that man. You're not the one. She needs a good guy, someone clean.

"Get some sleep," I tell her.

THREE AND A HALF YEARS EARLIER

My finger is on the trigger as I approach the low crossing. We split up to look for Dolly. Her last location ping was near the grove of oak trees with the smaller tank where the cattle drink, but she wasn't there.

Cash, Sterling, Duke, and I went in four different directions. The ATV I'm on makes it hard to hear anything, so I pull on the brakes and switch off the engine.

The quiet of the night envelops me. I wait for a few minutes, listening to the sounds of nature and breathing deeply. A breeze rustles through the trees as voices rise down near the river.

One of them is Dolly's.

I throw my leg over the side of the ATV and continue on foot. My boots rustle in the overgrown grass. My spine tingles when I hear the male voice of Cain Dixon.

"The fact that you're only eighteen is fucking wild. You look older."

"Yeah, I get that a lot." Her nervous chuckle floats on the wind. "I feel like I should get to Rosie now."

"Ah, I thought you wanted some alone time with me."

I grind my teeth, debating how much of a beating I'll give him for this. I decide to wait in the bushes for a few seconds, seeing if he'll be a gentleman and leave my sister alone.

"I do ... I just thought we'd go on a real date or something."

"You need a real man. You've probably never been touched by someone who knew what they were doing. I can show you things."

I step closer, raising my weapon as Cain's smirking face comes into view. It's a full moon tonight, illuminating his expression of lust.

"I'm still a virgin, so, no, I haven't. I've never met someone I was ready to—"

He reaches for her then, hands gripping the front of her jeans. "You'll like it. I'll make you feel good."

I lunge forward, pushing aside the tree branches and brush separating me from them. It all seems to happen in slow motion. My gun is heavy in my hand as I raise it to aim for his head. I only want to scare him, to get him off my sister before I beat his face in with my fists.

Cain is so caught up in his intent to steal her virtue that

he doesn't hear me coming. Dolly screams, which seems to only fuel his resolve. I'm fifty yards away. He jerks at the button of her jeans, ripping it off. He tears off the button-up shirt she has on, scattering the buttons around as it splits open.

"Get off me!" she screams, turning panicked eyes to me.

I get within ten yards of them before speaking, pistol raised and aimed right between his wide, excited eyes. "Get the fuck away from her if you want to live to see another day."

31
ROSIE
PRESENT DAY

Rows of foundation in varying shades of creamy tan and pale white are lined up in front of me. I chew the corner of my bottom lip as I reach for one to test on my inner forearm. Holden is pacing at the end of the aisle, his flip phone pressed up against his ear. I can hear his deep baritone voice, but I can only make out his words when he's facing me.

"She's fine. She just needs some rest," he says, inspecting me carefully before turning to pace in the other direction, tipping his cowboy hat at a passing older woman.

I look back at the tube of foundation in my hand, taking a small dab and tapping it on my skin over one of the bruises on my wrist. The marbled combination of green, yellow, and purple is impossible to disguise with one color. I finally make a selection and turn over to the rows of setting powder.

"Where did they search?" he says as he shifts closer to me, serving a hard stare to a passing middle-aged man who pauses a second too long with his eyes in my direction.

The man hurries past. I think he must be on the phone with Cash. Duke is waiting in the truck for us, but Holden won't let me out of his sight. I can't decide if it's romantic or unhinged.

Who's going to kidnap me in a whole other state? How would they find me here?

Still, his presence excites and unnerves me. He seems to think whoever was behind taking me has the resources to track us. He's not taking any chances, and I feel completely protected and safe with him. At least safe from being taken again.

Emotionally? Not so much.

I select the setting powder in my shade, debating on getting a lip color and eye shadow. I decide a tinted lip balm is bare minimum, choosing a muted rose pink I know won't clash with my hair color.

The last thing I feel like I can't live without for another day is a bra that fits. I'm sure Walmart's selection won't have my size because I usually have to special order them online. Either way, a sports bra would be better than nothing. I drop the makeup into the basket he's carrying before making my way toward women's intimates. Holden trails a few steps behind me.

"There is a guy I could reach out to. He knew him, did some contract work. I might be able to get a call with him, but it'll be recorded."

My fingers reach out to trace over a pair of cheeky black underwear made of lace.

Walmart has stepped up their intimates game.

Just to see his reaction, I select a pair in my size and toss them into the basket. His eyes follow the movement before flicking back up to meet mine.

Onyx is my new favorite color.

His eyes darken to the shade I now know indicates that he's picturing me in a *compromising* position. I've seen that same look on his face so many times now, and I always thought it was a hate glare.

I've realized now that it's an eye-fucking.

The veins in his hand pop out as he grips the basket harder, following me deeper into the aisle. To my shock and delight, there's a size 32F in a plain black bra with a tiny strip of lace trim around the top of the cups. I reach for it, holding it up to my chest. It'll be a snug fit, but it'll do. I toss it into the basket.

"Warner should know how to handle it," he growls, snapping the phone shut.

I purse my lips together, trying not to smile. I brush past him, intentionally letting my shoulder touch his as I pass.

He loops his arm around my waist, hauling my body toward him and pressing his lips up to my ear. "Don't you need to try it on?"

I scrunch my toes, letting the tingles run over the surface of my skin as I curl my hand around his forearm. "Hmm, I guess I should."

He lets go, reaching down to grip my wrist and guide me toward the dressing room nearby. No one seems to be monitoring it, but one of the doors is cracked open. He pushes it all the way open, inspecting the tiny space clearly meant for just one person. I walk through, expecting him to hand me the clothes and wait.

He doesn't. Instead, he comes inside with me and locks the door behind him. I turn around in the cramped space, which is less than four by four feet.

"I don't think you're supposed to come inside with me. This is the ladies'."

"Do you want me to leave?" He reaches inside the basket, handing me the bra and panties.

I don't answer him, grabbing the items and lifting my chin with faux defiance as my cheeks heat. "Turn around."

He runs his tongue over his teeth under his lips as he sets the basket down on the ground and pivots, turning his broad back to me. He's a full foot taller than my five-foot-three frame, and it makes me feel even tinier in the cramped space. I quickly pull off the white tank top and too-small bra. My nipples pucker in the chilled air, his nearness heating my core.

If he turned around right now, he'd see me topless.

I shiver before unhooking the latch on the bra, wrapping it around my waist and fastening it around myself. I pull it up over my chest. My breasts spill out of the top a bit more than I'm comfortable with, but it'll do.

I look hot.

I never try panties on in the store, but since I plan to purchase these and I want Holden to see them on me, I do it anyway. I kick off my shoes and pull my leggings down before sliding the silky lace up over my hips. My body tilts away from him so I can survey my reflection in the mirror.

I try to imagine myself from his eyes, how he'll see me. The dip in my waist and the spill of my cleavage are sexy, but the bruise on my side is distracting. He might be even more wary of touching me after he sees it. It might bring back the rage in his eyes that I saw when he killed Jed.

I shift my feet nervously, clasping my hands in front of myself. "Okay."

His shoulders shift, the brim of his cowboy hat tilting with the movement. He exhales, eyes meeting mine before leisurely drifting over my body. I'm raw and exposed, nearly naked while he's still fully dressed.

It jerks me back to the night in the barn years ago, when he was in a compromising state, but even then, I felt like the prey.

I suck in life-giving oxygen. He starts with his eyes in the mirror, observing my front before moving to the back of me that I can't see. His jaw clenches as he steps closer, bending down and dropping to one knee so he can study the bruise on my side.

Not this man, getting on his knees for me …

Every bone in my body is liquefied. I try to remain upright in a standing position while watching this ruthless, powerful man tenderly reach out a callous hand to touch the sensitive skin over my ribs. Goose bumps prick the surface of my legs and arms.

"They'll suffer for this. All of them," he promises.

I struggle to breathe, staring at the infuriated expression on his handsome features.

He's angry, for me. He's vengeful, for me. He's protective, of me.

His focus shifts up to meet my stare in the mirror before he delicately presses his hands over each of my hips and rotates my body to face him. I'm motionless, watching him remove his cowboy hat and set it down on the bench. I gasp as he brings my hips forward, pressing his nose against my pubic bone and inhaling deeply.

Oh, fuck me ...

My legs start trembling as he pulls down my panties, tugging them slowly. My sex is exposed, the wetness already dripping from me and growing cold with the exposure to the air. The fabric pools around my legs. He lifts up my right foot, guiding them off of me before his hand cups the back of my leg and lifts it up over his shoulder. He holds it there with his right arm. My hands are at my sides because I don't know where they should go. My upper back leans up against the plastic divider wall of the dressing room.

What the fuck. What the fuck. What. The. Fuck.

His ravenous gaze collides with mine as he leans forward, leisurely swiping over the front seam of my dampened sex with his tongue.

"Ah!" I cry out, letting my head fall back against the dressing room wall. I can't help it.

He clamps his free hand over my mouth. I hold on to it, terrified I'll do it again if he pulls it away. After a few agonizing seconds, he leans in again and licks me from the labia up to my clit, like he just wanted to taste me. I'm trembling, the knee of my stationary leg nearly quivering from the effort to remain standing upright.

The sensations spreading from my pussy are foreign, something I've never experienced. The texture of his tongue, the wetness of his mouth, combined with my arousal, mixes deliciously. After less than a minute, I feel the urge to scream from the pleasure. My breathy gasps sound like someone is getting fucked in public, but I can't contain myself.

Holden grips my leg harder as my muscles tighten. The lips of my vagina are spread apart with his tongue as he feasts on me. My eyes roll back in my head. My hands move up to grip the roots of his hair, to somehow brace myself against the waves of pleasure coursing through me.

A ripple of need tears through my center, drawing a scream from the back of my throat. It's muffled by his hand, but there's no way in hell someone didn't hear it. The orgasm consumes me as he laps me up in all the right places, his mouth suctioned to my raw pink flesh. After several earth-tilting moments, I'm panting. The death grip my fingers have on his hair loosens.

Finally, he pulls back, cool air rushing in on me.

"Oh, angel, I should've guessed you'd be a screamer." He gently peppers the insides of my thighs with kisses.

I shudder, suddenly coming to my senses at the purr of his voice.

What the fuck am I doing?

Holden Redford's face is between my thighs ... in a fucking Walmart dressing room, no less.

I stand upright, leaning to the side and reaching for my clothes. My limbs feel unsteady. No one has ever ravaged me like that. No man has ever touched the skin of my vagina. My breath hitches as his dark gaze meets my eyes. He doesn't wipe my glistening wetness from his mouth as he rises to a standing position.

Instead, he uses the tip of his forefinger to wipe it away

before sticking it in his mouth and licking it, relishing one last taste. The smacking sound of his lips fills the room.

I blink, attempting to mentally and emotionally return to normal as my mouth dries at the sight. Holden grabs his cowboy hat, placing it on his head as he squares his shoulders. He patiently waits for me to get dressed, watching me in the mirror instead of turning around. Once my shoes are back on, I slowly place the bra and panties back in the basket.

He seems to be waiting for my signal to open the door. After a few moments of silence, I offer him a curt nod. He unlatches the door, and we walk out. We make our way to the checkout. He scans each of my items and pays with cash while I observe in hazy half awareness.

With the bags in one of his hands and his eyes carefully scanning the parking lot, we walk toward where Duke parked. His other hand protectively hovers above my lower back.

The sky is dark and cloudy even though it's mid-afternoon. A realization hits me when the truck comes into view. I halt in my tracks.

"Did you get the ransom message?" I blurt out.

His eyes narrow on me. "What message?"

"Jed made me record a ransom call on his phone."

I don't know how I forgot until now. My hands begin to tremble as Duke pulls closer to us.

Surely, it has to be important, some kind of clue. Who did they send the message to if not my family?

After he opens the door for me and we both climb into

the truck, Holden turns back to face me. "What did the message say?"

I twist my hands in my lap. "Just my name, that they were holding me, and to get me back, they wanted twenty million dollars."

Holden faces his brother as the truck turns onto the highway. "When did that happen? What day?"

I rack my brain, my eyes traveling out the window at the passing desert terrain. "The second one, I think."

"Well, who do you know that has twenty mil sitting around?" Duke quips, shaking his head and looking over at Holden.

He rubs his hand across the back of his neck, and my stomach drops. I know exactly what he's thinking.

My father.

"The other thing I've been wondering about is, who was sending the texts from Rosie to Dolly and her aunt? Was it Jed?" Duke asks.

My hands start shaking, so I slide them between my body and the seat to keep them still.

"Whoever took me must have grabbed my phone."

"They must have had it near the cabin because that's where the location was pinging, even though it was days old. That's how I found you," Holden says.

Who could have done this to me? Why?

32

HOLDEN

The fight to remain in the seat of a vehicle for five hours without climbing in the back seat to be closer to Rosie is overwhelming. I can't stop fantasizing about putting a bullet in her father's skull, and holding her while she sleeps seems like a fucked-up thing to do while thinking that.

I don't have any reason to be so determined that something about this scenario is amiss, but if Clay Dixon knew his daughter was missing on the second day out of six, why did her aunt come looking on our land four days after that?

If that fucker knew and simply didn't bother to share that information with anyone ...

I clench and unclench my fists, resting my head back against the leather seat and shutting my eyes.

"What has Cash said?" Duke asks.

I glance into the back seat to see Rosie's face cradled up on the seat as she lies across it, sound asleep. Her long lashes brush against her cheeks, which have finally gained some of their color back.

"Sheriff searched the ranch. He made it over to the cabin about eight hours in, after inquiring if there were any abandoned structures on the property. They'd buried the body near the ravine where the hog and cow carcasses get dragged to. The sheriff left yesterday after not finding anything."

"What about the cabin? There wasn't any trace of her being there?"

I shake my head. "Dolly cleaned it up. Told them she'd been planning a getaway there for her birthday coming up."

"Are you fucking kidding me?" Duke shifts in his seat as the entrance to the ranch comes into view. "This is fucked, Holden. Whoever did this is fucking us in the ass."

"I've got it under control, but I need you to know that when they take me into custody, you don't tell them anything, not a damn thing. You plead the Fifth and let Warner do the talking."

His silence is all the response I need.

I CRADLE Rosie closely to my chest as I walk through the double front doors to the house. Dolly gasps when she sees us, rushing toward me. Her eyes fill with tears as I nod toward the hallway leading to the bedrooms. She starts to open her door before glancing up at me with a question in her gaze. She closes it before moving down to mine. She pulls back the covers on my bed and lays a pillow down before backing away.

I try to keep the sound of my boots on the wood floor as minimal as possible as I lay Rosie down on the sheets. She miraculously doesn't stir as she sinks into the pillow. My fingers reach out to brush the hair away from her face. The delicate, pale skin of her neck and cheekbones are as pure and beautiful as ever. I pull the covers up over her and press a soft kiss to her lips before exiting the room.

Cash is pouring Warner three fingers of whiskey when I reach the den. My father is already nursing a glass, his gaze pensive and seemingly sober. Sterling is leaning back against the window frame, eyes on the dark driveway and the lit-up stone entrance we just drove through.

Warner takes his glass and claims one of the leather chairs with wooden handles. He crosses a boot over his knee before clearing his throat.

"The probability of them pinning this on you is high. The three men who kidnapped her were masked. She was held for six days on your land, and the only face she saw of her kidnappers was your former employee, who has now conveniently disappeared and can't be questioned. Her disappearance from the cabin didn't occur until law enforcement came looking for her here. Whether they found any evidence at the cabin is unclear and frankly irrelevant, as we all know Clay Dixon isn't above planting it." He speaks plainly and matter-of-factly, which I've always appreciated.

My chest tightens as I reach for the glass of whiskey Cash poured me.

"What will they set my bond at?"

At this point, all I can think about is getting out of jail once I'm arrested. Rosie clearly isn't safe. I can trust my brothers to protect her, but can I ask them to commit their lives to her safety if I'm sentenced again? For longer this time?

The thought of being locked up in a cold cell again makes my body go rigid.

What if I ran now? Would she come with me?

The thought of leaving my home, the ranch, and my family isn't an option.

Fuck that. Fuck them for making me even think it.

Warner shrugs. "Something they know will hurt to pay. Half a million probably."

It's not completely outrageous, although we will need to liquidate some assets.

"What about the money trail?" Sterling asks, turning to face me. "They had to pay Jed and the others somehow. If it didn't come from us, can't we prove we didn't do it?"

"And communication," Cash adds. "There had to be phone calls, texts, something to set it all up. We have Jed's phone."

Warner leans forward. "The calls and texts are all from one number. It's highly unlikely the number is still even active."

"What about the ransom video? Was it on the phone?" Duke walks into the room, fresh from the shower and dressed in clean jeans and a T-shirt.

"It's on there, but there's no record of who it was sent to. I contacted a buddy who's a former military hacker, but he lives on the coast of Oregon. I have to risk mailing it to him or physically take it there." Warner leans back, draining the rest of his glass.

I finish the amber liquid off before handing my glass to Cash for a refill. "Our main goal right now needs to be figuring out who took her and why they want us to go down for it. As far as the sheriff and the Dixons are concerned, she's still missing. I say we keep it that way until we have more answers. Her mother is still out there, being held, which makes me think Rosie is still in danger."

Silence fills the room. My father clears his throat after a minute of it.

"Harry and Clay and I used to be partners, back before everything went to shit and your mother and I ran off together because she got pregnant. I saw the man do unspeakable things to get ahead in every business adventure we had. It's basically why she chose me. He was always a cruel man. Harry didn't mind it as much, and he took on the dirty work Clay didn't want to mess with. Whatever has happened with the Dixon family, Harry most likely had something to do with it or hired the men who did."

Warner's brows rise. "You're not suggesting that Clay is the one who kidnapped his own wife and daughter, are you?"

My father's hand shakes as he brings the glass to his lips. He sips on it slowly before lowering it again. "Who else would want my son locked back up? Who has the resources? Who has been out to destroy Redford Ranch and take down our family?"

Cash exhales. "But to harm his own daughter?"

Dolly enters the room in a pale pink sweatshirt and matching leggings. Her eyes are red-rimmed as she cradles a glass of rosé. "I believe it. Even Rosie was worried her father, at the very least, didn't care about finding her mother. She called her aunt because he wouldn't even look for her."

I stand up, walking to the other side of the window that Sterling is at. "Then, we can't tell him she's here. I'll take her to Oregon to give the hacker the phone while y'all continue acting like nothing happened after telling the aunt and law enforcement that she's not here and you haven't heard from her."

"What if she doesn't want to go? She might want to stay and look for her mom! She isn't your prisoner!" Dolly raises her voice, emotions clearly running high.

I turn to her, blinking in surprise at the outburst.

Tears stream down her cheeks. "She might not like him very much, but she does have an influence on him. She deserves to make her own choice about it."

"What is she going to do to find her mother? Hacking the phone is our best move, and keeping her safe while taking it there is just a bonus," Duke says softly, reaching for Dolly.

She succumbs to his embrace, crying against his shoulder. "I just don't want her to lose her mom."

Duke pats her head, whispering in her ear softly. I love my sister, but she's thinking emotionally right now. Keeping Rosie safe and finding who's behind this is our best chance at finding her mother.

"You should know that we took a thirty percent profit cut at the sale yesterday. Harry approached me again about the M-59. He knew we sold for shit and offered us a case of syringes." Cash leans closer to me.

I exhale, pinching the bridge of my nose as he speaks.

"Our cattle weight was standard, but I swear every other

batch was heavier than I've ever seen, drawing our sales into the ground. He was just waiting there, knowing it would happen."

"For now, we do nothing. This crisis takes precedence, and with all the scrutiny we're under, we can't risk the Feds sniffing around our cattle business too."

Cash nods. "Agreed. What are you gonna do if she wants to go home?"

I glance up at Dolly as Duke hands her a tissue. "I guess I'll have to kidnap her myself."

33
ROSIE

My neck aches as my eyes flutter open. Strong arms lift my body up, and I see the hallway of the ranch house. The voices of Duke and Sterling reach my ears. After all the trauma from this last week, I feel exhausted. My body is craving more sleep to continue recovering and healing my many minor injuries.

The familiar scent of cedar and leather fills my nostrils, and I know Holden is taking me to his bed to sleep.

I guess the whole family knows now. What a lucky way to break the news of me sleeping in his bed. Dolly can't really be mad about it after I was kidnapped and held for ransom.

I close my eyes again, letting myself drift back into a peaceful sleep.

When I awake again, I'm immediately aware that I'm not in Holden's bed. The moving vehicle is slowing down. My eyelids flutter open, revealing the leather interior of the truck.

"Where are we?" I start to sit up, turning to face Duke.

I see Holden's ruggedly handsome face in the driver's seat. He turns to face me, not smiling. "We're nearing the border to New Mexico."

I blink in confusion. "I thought we were already at the ranch?"

Was it a dream?

I glance in the back seat for Duke, but it's empty. Holden and I are alone. My stomach clenches.

"We stopped by for a bit, but you and I have a flight to catch."

My heart hammers inside my chest. Something feels off, but I don't know what.

"A flight to where?" I ask, trying to remain calm.

"Oregon."

Oregon?!

"What's in Oregon?"

"A man who can help us figure out who did this to you and why."

I try sitting up more, but a flash of pain shoots through my side. I gasp, my hand cupping it tightly.

"What's wrong?" He reaches for me but stops right before touching me.

I blow out a slow breath, moving myself upright much slower. "I'm fine. I just don't understand what the plan is. Why do we have to fly there together to see this man?"

We pass a sign that says *Welcome to New Mexico*.

"And why are we going all the way to another state to fly there?"

"We're assuming that our closest airport is being watched for you."

"Watched by who?"

"By the authorities. You might not understand everything right now, but I'm going to need you to trust me." His deep voice is firm as he looks over at me with his depthless eyes and lowered brows.

I stare back at him for a few moments before turning my gaze toward the front windshield. My chest rises and falls slowly as I try to determine what he's not telling me.

"What about my aunt? Does she know I'm safe now?"

He grips the steering wheel tighter. "Only my family knows right now. We feel confident that your disappearance was intended to look like we were behind it. Until we have proof we didn't do it, if they know you've been found, we will be implicated. I'll probably be arrested."

A cold fear spreads over my chest and neck at the thought of Holden behind bars again.

"Why?" My voice is a whisper. "Why would anyone want to do this?"

I'm met with silence. After a few beats, he looks over at me with determination in his gaze.

"We're going to solve this, Rosie. I'm going to keep you safe, whatever it takes."

His words wrap around my bones, warming me to my core. Our proximity, his vow to protect me, the reality of our isolation, and the fact that we're inevitably bound to end up alone in a hotel room start to overwhelm my senses.

My mind flashes back to the dressing room, where he effortlessly drew an orgasm from me with his tongue. My inner thighs grow warmer with each passing mile. The erotic memory is all I can see, all I can feel as the truck seems to get smaller and smaller. My hand grips the door handle until my knuckles grow white.

Is there oxygen in here?

"Can we stop?" I blurt out.

Holden glances over at me.

"To pee. I need to pee," I explain.

"We're going to get a hotel room in the next town. It's less than ten minutes ahead."

Ten minutes crawls by at the pace of a wounded cricket. My head is swirling with possibilities.

Will he get two rooms? Two beds? Will he come on to me? Will he lap me up again and make my legs weak?

He shifts in his seat. I turn to look at him, noticing him adjusting the crotch of his jeans as the muscle in his jaw tics.

I jerk my gaze out the front window, attempting to gulp down my nerves. A hotel comes into view. This one is nicer than the one we got with Duke. The walls are white stucco with arched black window frames. It's well lit, and it has a luscious garden with a running fountain out front. Holden pulls around to the back of it and parks.

He reaches a hand toward me, causing me to inhale a sharp breath. He doesn't touch me, simply grabs the door handle from inside and opens it for me before unlatching the seat belt around my waist. He climbs out of the truck and opens the back door.

I try to get control of myself as I step out of the lifted truck and close my door behind me. He's carrying our two bags, but waits for me to be beside him before walking to the hotel entrance. A chill in the night air nips at my shoulders.

The front desk woman smiles up at us, eyes dipping over Holden appreciatively. "How can I help you this evening?"

"King-size room with a mountain view and a bottle of merlot," he says.

I gulp.

She nods, checking us in and handing him the keys and a bottle of merlot after she uses a cork opener to open it. She shoots me a knowing glance, almost as if to say, *Damn, girl, you lucky bitch.*

The decor is authentic Southwest with large plants, clay pots, and intricate hand-painted tiles. A warm fire burns in the hotel lobby hearth, crackling an invitation to stay awhile. My joints feel rubbery as we step into the elevator.

I lick my lips as the doors close. My panties are already soaked, the anticipation so great that I feel like I might collapse. He waits for me to exit once the doors open. I easily find room number 307. His fingers brush against mine, sparks shooting through me as he hands me the key card.

I refuse to look at his face, knowing the lust is written all over mine in bold black ink. Without a word, I open the door and lock myself in the bathroom before even looking at the bed.

My bright aqua eyes stare back at me in the mirror. "Tonight is the night," I whisper.

Giving myself up to him feels inevitable as I pull my hair back. He's too much for me to resist, this past week too traumatic for me to even contemplate saying no to my rescuer even if he is a killer.

Even the bathroom is decorated perfectly with muted green square tiles and a gold-framed mirror. The shower is plenty big enough for two. Holden knocks on the door as soon as I'm naked, nearly stopping my heart.

"Your bag is out here. I'm going to get us some ice," he says through the door.

Once I hear the room door close, I reach out to grab my bag, thankful for everything but especially the razor.

Every inch of me is silky-smooth, scrubbed clean, and lotioned up twenty minutes later. I dab just a tad bit of concealer to cover the remainder of the bruises on my face and side. I want him to think I'm more healed so he won't be gentle with me.

After brushing my teeth, I observe myself one more time in the mirror. I remove my hair from the bun, letting it spill around my bare shoulders before I reach for the door, still completely naked.

My limbs shake as I walk out, feigning confidence as best I can. Holden is sprawled out in an armchair in the corner. He's holding a glass of wine in one hand, the other resting on his thigh. He's changed into a plain white wife-beater and removed his cowboy hat. His eyes darken a shade, sliding over every inch of my skin at a leisurely pace. My nipples pucker under the inspection, my skin pricking with goose bumps. He takes a slow sip of the red liquid, the bulge between his legs noticeably growing.

For me.

Instead of walking over to him, I move to the dresser and grab the straw Stetson, placing it on my head. My long red tresses are spilling in big waves around my heavy breasts. He exhales, his neck veins bulging out.

The drapes on the window are open, revealing the dark mountain in the distance. The courtyard below is lit with lanterns. My bare feet meet the soft rug spread on the floor of the room as I make my way over to him.

He doesn't take his eyes off of mine as I finally stand before him, merely inches away. He hands me the glass of wine, reaching for another one beside him on the table. I drain the entire thing in one long gulp, needing every drop of liquid courage in this moment.

Every moment that has led us here has created a staggering amount of tension. He takes the empty glass from me before gripping my fingers and tugging me into his lap. I straddle him, gasping at the instant roughness of the denim on my pussy. His fingers make contact with my nipples, pinching each one softly before increasing the pressure, nearing the realm of pain.

His ebony eyes don't leave my face as he plays with my body, testing my reactions. He makes a mental note of what I like, what makes me gasp, moan, and clench my thighs together. Once my nipples are raw and my arousal has coated his jeans, he dips his head down and sucks my breast into his mouth.

"Oh fuck." I gasp and tip my head back, closing my eyes as the pleasure of his tongue marks another part of my body.

One of his hands reaches around to hold my lower back. The other begins to slowly knead my ass with strong fingers. A fire builds inside my core, the pressure between my legs growing without him even touching me there.

He switches to the other nipple right when I think I might cry from the intensity.

"Holden," I gasp, clawing at his shoulders.

I need more, more friction, more of him. I dip my head down to pepper his neck with kisses and nibbles. He growls, rising up from the chair with me wrapped around him. His mouth pops off of my breast, and his lips crash to mine. His strong arms hold me up, our tongues hungry and devouring each other with a layer of desperation we're both too exhausted to keep hiding.

He pulls away, his lips swollen and pink as he looks up at me, black-brown eyes shiny and unguarded. My arms are latched around his neck. The pressure from his dick digging into me is nearly enough to make me come with each tiny movement of his steps toward the bed.

"Are you ready for this, angel? I don't think I can be gentle with you." His tone has a desperate edge, like he's silently begging for me to either give in to him or run away screaming.

"I want it. I want you. Please ... please fuck me," I whimper in his arms, begging him with my eyes and my words.

Something snaps in him at my plea. He tosses me back on the bed, my ass meeting the covers as he pulls the shirt off and starts working on his belt. He removes the pistol tucked into his waistband and sets it on the nightstand before tugging off the Wranglers and his boxers in one movement.

I adjust the hat on my head, biting my lower lip as his dick springs out. I've never seen one before, only felt it through his jeans. I gulp, staring at it.

It's way too big to fit inside me—that's for damn sure.

He grabs my ankle, pulling me toward him. "What's the matter, Dixon? Never seen a man fully hard before?"

I shake my head, which causes him to pause, but not let go of me. I prop myself up onto my elbows, finally looking away from it and into his eyes.

"How limited ... is your experience?" He nearly chokes on the words.

My eyes widen. *Did he just ask me for details on how many bases I got to with his brother?*

"Um, I've never seen one ... only one I've touched is yours that night at the motel."

He nods. "Have you ever been fingered?" His voice is strained, almost like he's afraid of the answer.

I choose my words carefully. "By myself, yes. I've touched myself. No one else ever has ... down there."

He blinks at me, breathing slowly as he waits for me to continue.

"Um, but"—I gesture to the chair we just vacated, where he sucked on my breasts—"I've done that before, just with my pants still on." I hesitate before just ripping the Band-Aid off. "With Duke." I whisper the last word, waiting for it to land on him.

His neck veins are near bursting as he stares down at me, tracing his fingers over the skin of my ankle as he leans his face down toward my foot. He kisses the bottom of my arch on each foot before moving up to repeat it on my ankle. His eyes rise to mine.

"You think I want to hear about how my little brother

took your top off and sucked on your nipples in his pickup truck?"

I don't breathe as his warm exhales follow each kiss. He slowly makes his way up to my knees, then my quivering thighs, leaving a smoldering path in his wake. He looks up at me when he reaches my bikini line and licks his lips, like he's dying to feast on me.

"You'll be lucky if I don't kill my own kin with that fucking talk, Rosie Dixon."

34
HOLDEN

I hover my face over her lips, inhaling deeply before my tongue moves out to taste her dripping opening.

She's soaked for me, not him.

She's naked, quivering with need and desire for me. My insides are shaking with the way I want her, the unreal amount of power she has over me.

I'm relieved she never got even close to this far with him, but the fact that another man has ever seen any intimate part of her makes me want to stay in this room and claim every inch of her body until she can't even remember his fucking name.

My lips suction around the bud of her clit as her body begins to vibrate with ecstasy. My hands force her thighs farther open. She tenses up, gripping the roots of my hair hard as she cries out.

"Ah!"

I devour her pussy, savoring her salty taste. She squirms, trying to get closer to me and then farther away. Her breathy moans fill the hotel room. The muscles in her thighs tense up under my fingers.

A gush of liquid pours from her body, soaking the blanket underneath her ass. I continue lapping her up until her breathing begins to even out. My dick is as hard as steel, begging to be sheathed inside of her. She pulls me up, tugging on my hair until I'm on top of her.

The look in her eyes is vulnerable and raw. The reality of how gone for her I am slams into me as she reaches for my face, pressing a kiss to my lips and tasting herself. I kiss her back, my tongue caressing the inside of her mouth. My fingers reach for her sensitive vagina, knowing she's as primed and ready as she'll ever be.

Her fingers make contact with my cock, the soft skin making me want to cry out with carnal need. I'm hedonistic, desperate for her.

"You sure you want this tonight?"

She nods without hesitation. "I'm sure. Put it in me— *now*."

I smile at her demand. "Patience, angel."

My fingers need to stretch her out at least a little bit before I impale her with my dick and make her virgin pussy bleed. She's incredibly tight as I push my index finger inside her soft folds. Her mouth forms an O as she gasps and throws her head back. My dick pulses at the sight. I feel like I might go insane if I don't get to feel her inner walls right this *fucking* second.

I pull back before trying to slowly push two fingers inside her. She whimpers around me, her fingernails digging into my shoulders so hard that she nearly pierces the skin.

"Holden, please, please do it now. Please."

Rosie Dixon begging me to fuck her is on my list of top ten experiences in life—forever. I rise up onto the bed, where she's lying on her back, pushing between her legs.

Right as I position myself between them, a thought flashes through my brain and causes me to pause right at her entrance, dick in hand.

Is it wrong to do this if I have no intention of being with her?

Unless she tells me no, I don't think I'm physically capable of holding back as the tip of my erection nudges at her. She's still wearing my cowboy hat, looking like the personification of my version of an angel with her copper hair, flushed cheeks, and perfect, big tits. My cock is sensitive, having not entered another woman's body in almost four years.

Too late now.

Every inch I go deeper causes my brain to short-circuit. I push until I feel a barrier, looking directly into her eyes as I break through it as gently as I can. Her eyes widen, neither of us breaking visual contact.

She gasps before biting her lower lip.

I'm fully sheathed to the hilt, my brain starting to go numb with ecstasy. Her eyes roll back in her head as she lies beneath me and pants for oxygen.

I pull back, causing her to suck in and grip my arms until I feel the penetration of my skin under her nails and my blood seeping out.

I lean down, whispering in her ear, "Stay with me, angel. The pain will turn to pleasure."

She whimpers against my neck as I pull out and drive

back into her. I want nothing more than to fuck her fast and hard, coming all over her magnificent tits. Instead, I force myself to move slowly, edging myself with each sliding movement to slowly stretch her walls to fit the size of me.

Once her body seems to be taking it better, I pick up the pace and find a steady rhythm, all the while keeping my senses as alert as possible for signs of her pain and discomfort turning to satisfaction.

She starts panting and whimpering the faster I move inside her.

"Talk to me, angel. Tell me what you're feeling."

"Good. It feels *so* good."

I keep one hand on the bed to brace myself over her as I reach up, tracing her pink lips with my thumb before pushing my index finger inside her mouth. She stares at me with wide eyes, and I explore the wet insides of her mouth, going as far back as I can without choking her.

"Suck on it," I command her.

She sucks my finger in, closing her eyes and moaning around me. My hips move faster, my body nearly twitching with the intensity of how delicious her body feels around me. I watch her tits bounce before the realization of how fucking irresponsible I'm being smacks me into reality.

I jerk out of her, pressing my body down and panting, attempting to slow my heart rate.

Why the fuck did I not think about using a condom?

I stand up from the bed, moving over to my duffel bag and unzipping the side pocket and reaching inside. I was so wrapped up in the idea of getting inside her that the logical part of my brain didn't register the very real possibility that getting her pregnant would cause unnecessary complications in my life. I did, however, think about this possibility at the last gas station, where I purchased the box of little gold foil packets.

"What's wrong?" she asks.

I turn to face her as I stretch the latex over myself. "I don't think either of us has to worry about STDs, but I figure you're not on birth control since you aren't sexually active?"

She shakes her head, licking her lips as she stares down at my cock with hungry eyes again. I walk back over to her, noticing the drops of blood on the comforter as I approach. She also has some of it on her thighs.

It's been years since I slept with a virgin. It doesn't happen to all of them, considering the hymen can be broken before they even have sex through various other physical activities, even riding a horse.

I felt Rosie's hymen clearly when I first entered her, and the evidence is right before my eyes. She reaches for my hand, pulling me down on top of her.

"What?" she asks.

I look down at her, noticing that mixed in with the blood spots, there's makeup smudged on the blanket. Her side is more green and yellow than I remember it looking earlier when she first came out of the bathroom.

My nostrils flare as I realize that she covered it up so I would think they were more healed.

"Did you cover your bruises with makeup?"

She looks down at herself, seeing the smeared makeup and drops of blood. Her eyes trail back up to mine.

"I'm fine. I want this ... I want you," she murmurs.

I pull back, sitting on the edge of the bed and exhaling. My erection is still protruding, and my body is screaming for me to continue so I can feel the sweet release I need.

It's too late anyway. You already stole her innocence.

The crushing reality of what I've done to her weighs on me like an avalanche. I lean back, looking up at the ceiling. Her soft fingers trace up my thigh, and my body betrays me as it turns to her.

"I'm sick of you not listening to me when I tell you what I want." She climbs over the top of me, sitting in my lap and wrapping her arms around my neck again.

My eyes slice down to hers before resting on her lips again. My fingers tenderly reach around to grip her waist. She wraps her hand around my length, directing it to her soft entrance. I watch her mouth open in a gasp as she sits on it, sliding down until I'm fully inside her again. My hand moves up to cup the side of her cheek before meeting her eyes again.

"You don't know what you're doing. I'm insatiable," I warn her, even as she pulls me into her.

I watch her enrapturing gaze as she rides me, learning her rhythm as she goes. She braces herself on my shoulders, bouncing up and down on me, moaning and gasping until she collapses with exhaustion onto me. I spin her around, placing her on the bed facing the ceiling with my feet on the floor as I continue driving into her for a few more pumps until my dick starts to pulse.

Even though I'm wearing a condom, I pull out before my release, tearing the condom off to come on her stomach and tits. My release is a wave of pure heaven, of almost four years of celibacy finally coming to an end. Still panting, I reach a hand down, smearing my seed over one of her erect nipples with my thumb, marking her. Some deep, primal part of me groans with pleasure at the sight. I collapse onto the bed right next to her, my body buzzing with the gratification.

She sighs contentedly beside me, tracing the outline of my ear with her finger.

It's so innocent, an intimate movement between lovers. I stand up to discard the condom in the trash before dampening a clean washcloth with warm water in the bathroom. She tries sitting up, but the green-and-yellow bruise on her side looks even worse now. She collapses back against the pillows.

I clench my teeth as I spread her legs again, wiping away the blood on her inner thighs before cleaning my semen off of her chest and stomach. We don't speak again as I lie down beside her, tucking her body in close to me. I listen to her even breathing as she falls asleep, wondering what the hell I just did to her.

35
ROSIE

I spend the entire flight trying not to giggle and flirt with Holden like a teenager with a crush on her best friend's older brother. A side of him I've never seen has come out. He's pinching my waist, interlacing his fingers with mine, and not letting me get even twenty feet away from him. He's smiling more, smiling at *me*.

Sex is something I've never considered being powerful enough to make me fall so hard for someone, but last night's rendezvous, along with this morning's steamy shower, where he got on his knees for me again, has my head spinning. The orgasms, combined with this tender, protective side of him, is about to turn my uterus inside out.

"Are you hungry?" he asks as we exit our flight and start following signs for the rental cars.

"I could eat. We should find some good sushi."

His hand cups my lower back, guiding me around a group of men in jerseys. A few of them glance in my direction before seeing Holden's expression and quickly looking away.

I shall never emotionally recover from this.

I bite my lip, wondering if he'll take us straight to the hotel or to meet his contact first. My mind is already swirling with more positions to try, debating if he'll be willing to bend my body around while it's not fully healed yet. My lower half is slightly sore from last night and this morning, but it feels strangely good.

My eyes flash up to observe his profile, and I admire the stubble on his jawline he didn't shave this morning. I ache to feel it against the skin of my inner thighs again. In the background, an image catches my eye. My stomach knots as it comes into focus.

It's my face, plastered on a large TV screen in a hotel bar. Next to it is an older picture of my mother, from before she was drinking vodka around noon every day. I stop dead in my tracks, a swirl of nausea building inside me. Holden's head swivels to follow my gaze. My heart pounds, my blood turning to ice. His grip on my hand tightens as we both stare at the closed captions on the screen.

A former Texas beauty queen was found alive today, after being held against her will for nearly three weeks at an undisclosed location near the small town of La Pradera, Texas. Evidence that her twenty-one-year-old daughter, Rosie Dixon, had been held captive in the same location for some amount of time was found at the scene. The woman who was found, Sheri Dixon, says she never saw her daughter, but she heard her screams sometime during her captivity.

At this time, Rosie Dixon is still missing.

She is the daughter of the mayor of La Pradera, Clay Dixon. Mayor Dixon and local authorities have started a nationwide manhunt in search of the victim's employer. As it turns out, Holden Redford is a formerly convicted felon who was just released from prison less than three months ago. Redford was behind bars for killing a close relative of the victim, Cain Dixon, and was recently pardoned by the governor of Texas for the crime, although many believe the ruling was unlawful.

My throat constricts as Holden's mugshot fills the large screen. I've seen the photo countless times, but somehow, it looks harsher and crueler than I remember.

With his cowboy hat and facial hair, he looks considerably different from the image where his hair is cropped short and his black-brown eyes hold no remorse. Judging by the casual faces of the people around us, no one seems to recognize us. They're not paying attention to the screen. The photo they used of me is an old high school one from my senior yearbook headshots.

My body feels numb as Holden tugs on my arm, ushering me into a gift shop with racks of clothing. My vision goes blurry as I watch him grab a gray hoodie off of a rack and take it to the salesclerk, pulling me behind him and keeping his body directly in front of me. He grabs a pay-by-minute phone at the register and adds it to the purchase.

The clerk rings him up, and he pays for the items with cash. He turns to face me, ripping the tag off the hoodie as he holds it out for me to put on. I comply, my body suddenly growing weak and sluggish.

"I think I might faint." I stare down at my off-white sneakers, still stained from the dirt at Redford Ranch.

Holden pulls the hood up over my head. He leans down,

wrapping me in an embrace and directing me toward the exit.

His warm breath is on my ear, his lips brushing my skin. "You have to make it to the car, Rosie. Make it to the car, and we'll figure this out. Lean against me."

His arm cradles my shoulder, tucking me into his chest as we walk through the crowd of travelers. His cowboy hat draws attention, considering this is the northwestern United States and most of the men around here wear skinny jeans and loafers without socks. Holden's strut is confident, and the stares seem to mostly be from women who haven't seen a real cowboy their entire lives unless it was in a movie.

If they're looking at him, hopefully they're not looking at the TV right now ...

We finally get to the rental car place and check in. My head swims, my thoughts swirling in a hazy scramble before we finally get the keys. Holden's Southern drawl makes the desk clerk giggle. I'm grateful that he seems to have it all together, or I truly would collapse on the scuffed linoleum floor.

He guides me out to our car, which is a Chevy Malibu. Apparently, it's the last vehicle available that's not run on electric at Portland International Airport.

He opens my door for me before storing the bags in the trunk and climbing into the driver's side.

"Thank fuck for tinted windows." He starts the car and peels out of the parking space.

He pulls the phone out of the bag, handing it to me. "Can you put the SIM card in?"

My fingers are trembling, but I slowly attempt to complete the task.

"Why are they saying you kidnapped me? Who found my mother? What the fuck is going on?" I attempt to roll the window down to get some fresh air, but the child lock is on.

Holden does it for me from his side. Immediate relief floods through me when the clean air reaches my lungs. After a few seconds, rain starts to sprinkle in with the cold air.

"I have to get Jed's phone to the man who can go through the deleted files to prove that I had nothing to do with yours or your mother's disappearances. Once you have the SIM card in that one, we'll call Cash and see if he's heard anything."

I release a shaking breath as I power on the phone and hand it over to him. He dials the number and puts it on speakerphone.

"Hello?" Cash says.

"I just saw my mugshot on an airport bar TV in Portland." Holden glances in the rearview mirror before merging onto the highway.

"Yeah, I told you I'm not interested in selling it. That bike is one of a kind."

Judging by his casual tone and his words, Cash isn't alone. I look over at Holden, who clenches his teeth.

Who's there? The sheriff? Why can't we just tell them I was found and Holden rescued me?

"We're going to meet Warner's contact as planned. I'm gonna need you to get away and call me on this number. If you get arrested, give it to Warner and have him call me."

"Yeah, man, if I hear of anything similar for sale, I'll be sure to let you know. I gotta go. Bye." Cash hangs up.

"Fuck!" Holden slams his hand against the steering wheel.

I jump, my body tensing. "I don't understand. Why can't I just go home and tell them I'm safe? You didn't do this."

He shakes his head, jaw clenching. "You don't get it. They're framing me. They're setting me up for it, just like they did with Cain. What you say won't matter. I'll still go back to prison."

A thousand possibilities and unanswered questions fly through my mind. "But ... you did kill Cain? You were doing it in self-defense to protect Dolly, but the gun was ..." I trail off.

He waits for me to continue, only speaking after a minute of tense silence.

"The gun I used was legal. Cain raised his to shoot me. When he started to point it at Dolly was when I fired and killed him with a shot to the head. I could have gotten off because it was self-defense. The bullet that was supposedly in his skull was actually planted in the evidence room by someone. It wasn't mine. When they came to collect his body, your father had my bullet removed somehow and replaced it with one from an illegal, unregistered gun. He had someone falsify the evidence and plant a stolen weapon on my ranch, which is why the judge ruled that I had to serve time for it. I killed him with an illegal weapon, according to the evidence. False evidence."

This can't be true. Why? Why would my father ... or anyone want to do that?

Holden's voice is calm. "My killing Cain and getting away

with it wasn't on the table for your father. If I'd known how far he was going to take planting evidence, I could've prevented it. By the time we realized what he'd done, it was too late. There was no way to prove myself innocent."

Is he lying to me? Would my father really do something like this? Plant evidence?

My chin starts to quiver as I stare out the window. Dark clouds have begun gathering in the sky. Thunder rolls in the distance, and steady raindrops pelt the windshield. My window is still open, but I don't roll it up. I release a shaky exhale.

"So, you're saying my father is framing you for my and my mother's kidnapping ... to send you back to prison?"

His silence is the only answer I need as bile rises in my throat. Instead of throwing up all over the carpeted floor of the rental car, I lean my head out the window and vomit. Holden pulls the car over on the shoulder as I retch out the airport breakfast we had a few hours ago. Cold raindrops wet my hair.

By the time my stomach is emptied, I realize his hand is on my lower back. I pull myself back into the car, taking the napkin he must've found in the console.

"We don't know anything for sure yet. That's why we're playing it safe and taking Jed's phone to someone who can help. Do you believe you're safe with me?"

The tears on my cheeks have mixed in with rain as I peer up at him. I've never seen such a look of concern and fear mixed into one expression. His eyes are dark and soft at the same time.

"Whoever was behind this, we will find them out. Your

mother is safe now. You are safe now. All that matters is doing whatever it takes to keep it that way."

The determination in his gaze helps to ease the ache in my chest slightly. I slowly nod. He rolls up my window before pulling back into the traffic on the highway.

Holden calls his lawyer and updates him on the situation. I can't hear Warner's side of the conversation, but I do know Holden seems determined to keep me away from La Pradera until whoever the hacker is can break into the deleted files on the phone.

The feeling I can't seem to shake the farther we drive into the pouring rain is that I want my aunt and my mother to know I'm safe.

Surely, there's a way to notify them that I'm okay even if we don't go back home and turn ourselves in.

36
HOLDEN

Pike, the hacker, tells us he needs at least a day with the phone to do a deep dive. He wants us to come back tomorrow to pick it up.

Rosie has been solemn and barely said a word since the conversation we had in the car. Telling her that I believe her father could have been behind her kidnapping was probably a shit move, but I felt like there was no other choice. If we're being searched for by the entire nation, she has to understand why we can't go waltzing into her father's home.

"Are you hungry?"

She shrugs, looking out the window at the passing signs lit up with fast-food logos. My stomach is growling, so I know hers must be too. We haven't eaten since breakfast, and it's nearly seven p.m.

She had mentioned sushi before, which I don't like. I pull up a location on my phone for it and hit the Call button.

"What kind of sushi do you like?"

She rolls her head toward me. "Do they have a shrimp tempura roll with jalapeño and extra eel sauce?"

Eel sauce?

I repeat the order to the woman on the phone, asking her for two of them since I have no clue what else they would have.

"Add two orders of chicken fried rice and cream cheese wontons," Rosie whispers.

I add the items to the order. Once we pull into the restaurant, I ask Rosie to stay in the car in case someone might recognize us together.

When I go in, I keep my sunglasses and cowboy hat on. I have to wait another ten minutes for the food. Once I get back in the car, Rosie is sniffling and wiping at her nose. Her cheeks are flushed and damp with tears.

"What's the matter? Are you okay?"

She nods, reaching for the takeout bag. "Thanks for getting sushi."

I wish I could physically strangle her father for causing her so much distress. If he was truly behind the kidnappings, I probably will.

We don't speak as I drive us to another nice hotel. I don't expect anything from her tonight physically, but the thought of being in another room alone with her makes my heart rate quicken.

Once the front desk clerk checks us into the vintage, restored downtown hotel, we walk to the elevator. Rosie is silent, arms folded across her chest and avoiding eye contact with me.

She locks herself in the bathroom as soon as we get into

the room. I asked for two beds, thinking she might prefer it. She didn't comment on it or request a king size.

After raiding the minibar for whiskey, I collapse on the wingback chair in the corner of the room. Cash's number flashes across my phone. I swipe over the green icon to answer it.

"Finally alone?" I drawl.

"Fuck, brother. We're in some deep shit. They got a warrant to search the house. Detective tore apart your room, and they found a pair of Rosie's panties."

I close my eyes, resting my head back on the chair. "What else?"

"Her mother is in the hospital for severe malnutrition, and the aunt hasn't left her side. Dolly is a wreck. The sheriff told us that for now, he's not arresting any of us, but if they don't hear from you or her soon, that could change. They've named you as the number one suspect ... armed and dangerous. Turn on the news."

I grab the remote and flip on the TV. The first station that pops up is a national news channel. My face is plastered next to Rosie's. I turn up the volume.

I clench my fists as Mayor Dixon's voice booms over the speakers as he appears in a slick blue suit with a solemn expression.

"My daughter is strong. She's a smart girl. She is most likely still alive and potentially looking for an escape from the monster who killed my brother. If anyone sees her out in public, alone or with a companion, please don't hesitate to assist her in escaping and call the local authorities immediately. Holden Redford is a dangerous criminal who should be kept off the streets to keep all of our young women and wives safe."

My mugshot is blown up to fill the screen, as well as additional pictures of me in a cowboy hat and with and without facial hair. I think back over the interaction we had with the clerk at the front desk. He seemed indifferent to us, not paying much attention to either my or Rosie's face.

"What's Warner saying?"

Cash sighs. "He's right here. I gave him a cigar in exchange for an evening of mutual wallowing."

"You're a wanted man now, Holden," Warner says over the speaker. "At some point, you'll need to bring her in. The news just broke today, so it would be logical for any man to need time to get shit together before showing up at the police station. Pike has the phone, and right now, he's our best bet for finding out who's behind this shitstorm. Once we know that, we can make a plan for tomorrow." He hesitates, the line going silent. "Right now, there's no warrant for your arrest. You're just a suspect. The one fuckup they made with making this shit national news is that now we have a lot of witnesses. They can't arrest you without a warrant. They can only detain you for questioning."

I close my eyes, tipping the rest of the amber liquid over my lips and letting it burn down my throat.

I have two priorities right now.

The primary one is to keep Rosie Dixon safe from whatever monster actually ordered her kidnapping.

The second is to stay the fuck out of prison. I'll be useless in keeping her safe if I'm behind bars.

"I'll make contact when I have the phone tomorrow."

I hang up the call, rubbing my eyes. The door to the bathroom clicks open. I look up to see Rosie wrapped in a towel. She steps over to where I set the bags down. I stand, making my way to the bathroom and resisting the urge to touch her.

"You done in here?"

She nods as she digs through her duffel, not looking at me. I pause at the door, wishing I could pull her into my arms and whisper into her ear that I am going to get us out of this mess. I want to tell her that we will move past this, that I'll die before anyone ever hurts her, physically or emotionally, ever again.

But in this moment, the invisible barrier between us is insurmountable. She has a right to feel every drop of betrayal and resentment toward me. I'm at the center of the problem. I killed a man. I'm the one with a criminal record. I'm the one who won't let her go home to see her family.

After stepping under the warm water, I let out a moan as it spreads over my aching body. The physical stress oozing from my tense muscles nearly brings me to my knees with the small feeling of relief. I don't bother turning when I hear the door to the bathroom click open, assuming she forgot something in the room. I open my eyes when the door to the shower slides over and the air turns cold.

She's naked, fully bared to me. Her heavy breasts and smooth, perfect skin are as tempting as ever. My dick hardens as she looks up at me with those unforgettable blue-green eyes and drops down to her knees on the wet tiles. Without uttering a word, she wraps her hand around my growing erection.

I almost stop her. I almost pull her up and tuck her into my chest for a hug, murmuring sweet nothings in her ear.

But I don't because I fucking need this. I need the soft wetness of her tongue as she tastes the underside of my dick. I need the vibration of her humming mouth over me as I tighten the grip on her hair and thrust my hips forward into her.

She gargles, making a choking sound. I pull back, looking down at her. She takes a steadying breath before wrapping her lips around me again.

"You can take it, angel."

She nods as she sucks on me again. My eyes roll back in my head, a desperate, whimpering moan escaping my lips. She's inexperienced, unsure of how to please me but trying nonetheless. I have to watch her, to see her pretty pink lips around my cock.

My eyes take her in, her lashes wet from the water as she sucks on me, pulling back and moving back in again. I grab her hand, placing it on the base of my dick. She squeezes, blinking up at me.

"That's right, angel; squeeze it while you suck on me. You look so fucking angelic with my cock in your throat, baby. A fucking perfect angel."

She moans around me, the vibrations short-circuiting my brain. I slam my hand against the cold wall of the shower, bracing myself as cum shoots out of me and into her mouth. She startles, pulling back and choking. I let go of her hair, the sticky white semen dripping down over the tips of her breasts.

She spits down the drain, coughing again. I cup her cheek, tipping her chin up to meet my gaze.

"You did good, angel." I cradle her face in my hand, reaching my other one down to pull her up by her elbow.

Her eyes are rimmed red from choking. I spin her around and grab each of her wrists to place them on the tiles. She's petite, so I have to bend my knees to get in the right position to reach her soft folds. I circle the top of her clit slowly before pushing my longer middle finger into her. She gasps, bracing herself against the tiles as I finger-fuck her. She pushes her ass back against my hand, wanting more.

"You need more, baby? Tell me what you need."

She exhales, whimpering desperately, "I need all of it. Whatever you can give me."

My teeth latch on to her earlobe. "What do you need? Say it."

She pants, turning her face toward mine with hooded eyes. "I need you to fuck me."

I let out a low growl, grabbing the base of my erection and positioning myself between her cheeks from behind. She bends forward, arching her slender back. I have to squat down to find the right spot before plunging deep inside her pussy. She yelps at the motion, nearly falling.

"I've got you." I cup the front of her smooth stomach, bracing her against the front of my hips.

I thrust into her softness over and over again, relishing in her body and the way she's being molded to me, to my hard length. Before I finish, I pull out and spin her around. I reach down under her ass and thighs, lifting her easily up against the cold tiles. Her mouth drops open in ecstasy when I enter her again, thrusting hard into her.

"I want you to come on my cock."

She nods, eyes opening as she gazes into mine, pure need, desire, and a level of awe in their depths. I feel her inner walls tighten around me before she gasps, panting and moaning as the waves of her orgasm roll over her, her pale skin flushing pink.

"Good girl," I praise her.

Three more thrusts into her are all it takes for me to find my release. I pull out of her, finishing on the tiles with her limp body crushed to my wet-slicked skin. I realize with a jolt that I don't ever want another man to ever touch her like this, to ever even see her naked. A monsoon of overprotective, possessive need fills me.

She bows her head forward, resting it on my shoulder. We pant for oxygen together, my face pressed to her shoulder. I plant a kiss to her skin before slowly lowering her feet down to the mosaic.

I grab the bar of soap from the niche in the tile, lathering it up in my hands before running it over her body. I start at her shoulders before moving down to her hips, between her legs, and down to her feet. She stands still, watching me as I clean my cum from her body. I quickly lather myself with soap and rinse off. She watches with hooded eyes, still not speaking to me.

The thought that maybe she's in shock occurs to me, and I experience a brief moment of internal panic. She seems disconnected from herself, like she's not fully here mentally. I turn off the water and reach for a clean towel, drying her off completely and wrapping her up before getting another towel from the rack.

She steps out of the bathroom as I dry off. I quickly brush my teeth before joining her in the room. She took a T-shirt from my bag, the only clean one left. We desperately need to do laundry somewhere.

I slide on a pair of gym shorts I've slept in once before pouring her a glass of wine. She takes it, blinking up at the news station that's covering an earthquake that happened in Indonesia earlier today. I hand her the remote before dialing for room service. A woman answers the phone in a cheerful tone.

"Ah, yes, ma'am, I was wondering if y'all have laundry service here."

"Well, yes, sir, we do. We can pick it up now and return first thing tomorrow morning."

"Perfect. It'll be outside the door—room 618."

"You got it."

I hang up the phone before gathering up all the rest of our clothes, shoving them into a bag and setting them outside the door. Rosie sips on her wine while staring blankly at a *Friends* rerun on the TV.

"You need anything?" I ask her.

She shakes her head, leaning it down on my shoulder. I grab her hand, interlacing our fingers before drifting off into a much-needed deep sleep.

37
ROSIE

The hotel room door rattles as fists bang on it loudly. His arm is still wrapped around my waist as we both jerk awake from a peaceful sleep.

"Open up! Police!"

My heart thunders as Holden jolts upright in bed. He turns to me, his face illuminated by the dim light of the early morning pouring through a slit in the curtains. His fingers reach for mine, grasping them tightly, communicating reassurance with a tiny squeeze. His dark eyes are wide, searching mine.

His expression morphs from confused panic into calm acceptance as he realizes that I'm not as surprised by the intrusion as he is.

He slowly pulls his arm back, my fingers instantly chilled by his lack of body heat. Tears begin forming in my eyes.

I made a mistake. I made a mistake.

"You have one minute to open up, arms behind your

head!" The door rattles again, echoing the rapid pumping of blood in my chest.

"I'm sorry," I whisper. "I'll tell them you didn't take me. I'll tell them you saved me." I lean toward him.

He lifts his chin slightly, his jaw firmly set in a place of defiance, the expression of a hardened man accepting his fate. He slides from the bed, still in his gym shorts as he lies face-first on the floor, hands behind his neck.

I choke back a sob, wishing I could lift his head up to press a kiss to his lips.

"Open it," he tells me, his voice calm and cool.

I want to tell him why. I want to explain it to him. My family was worried sick, my aunt and my mother afraid for my life. They had no idea that I was completely safe, that I was cared for. I had to reach out to let them know my where-abouts. I told them where we were, reassuring my aunt that we would be home soon and see my mother. She wanted my location for her own peace of mind, but I never should've given it to her.

I stumble out of bed toward the door, tears already threatening to spill from my eyes.

"I'm coming!" I call out, sliding the lock and twisting open the door knob.

I lift my hands up, level with my face, as police officers and SWAT team members swarm the room. One of them stops to check on me as the others ascend on Holden, roughly cuffing him and lifting him up to his knees. He doesn't look at me.

They sweep the room quickly, not recovering anything. I

know he had a handgun at some point, but I don't know where he stored it.

"Are there any weapons in his possession, Miss Dixon?" one of the police officers asks me. He has a thick mustache and kind blue eyes. His uniform name tag reads Hutton.

I shake my head. "I don't think so."

He nods. "Your father is on the phone. He'd like to speak with you. You're safe now."

As strange as it is, I feel less safe now than I did when Holden said it. They lead him down the hall, and a few of the other guests poke their heads out of their room to gawk at the scene.

"He has clothes over there. Can't he get dressed first?" I ask.

They ignore my request. I'm allowed a pair of jeans to slide on in the bathroom. They turn away as I reach for a bra to put on under the T-shirt I'm wearing.

"Someone will pack up your things and bring them into the station." Officer Hutton gently guides me by my elbow down to the hotel lobby and into the parking lot.

Spectators are gathered around, clearly enjoying the early-morning entertainment. My palms sweat as I search for Holden, but they must have already driven him off.

"He didn't do anything. He saved me. I want to give my statement," I tell Officer Hutton, tears spilling down my cheeks. I wipe them away with my hands.

He turns to me, a pinch of concern in his thick brows. "You'll be able to do that at the police station. You are safe now, Miss Dixon. He can't hurt you anymore."

"He didn't hurt me! He found me being kept in this cabin

on his land by a man who used to work for them. He knows—"

He opens the door to the squad car, lights flashing, before turning to me and laying a hand on my forearm. "Ma'am, you will give your official statement at the station. You can have a phone to call whoever you need—a lawyer, your parents. They've been extremely worried about you. We will have plenty of time to go over your story."

I slowly blow out an exhale, trying to calm my breathing and heart rate before bobbing my head. He helps me into the car, then climbs into the driver's seat.

MY AUNT'S warm embrace is followed by sniffling in my ear. "Oh, my dear. You're here now; you're safe. You're safe now."

I hug her back tightly. I understand why she did it, why she thought it was the right decision. The stale air of my father's living room makes it difficult for me to breathe. The curtains are drawn, not a speck of dust in sight.

"You're going to be okay." Her eyes are red-rimmed as she pulls back to inspect me.

"Where's my mother?"

"She's asleep upstairs. The doctor has prescribed some heavy sleep aids. She ... she's had awful nightmares and traumatic flashbacks."

My inhales grow more shallow, the racing of my heart picking up speed. "I'm sorry it took me so long to get back to her." My voice is a hoarse whisper as I brush away the tear on my cheek.

Aunt June shakes her head, leading me toward the kitchen. "It's not your fault, dear, of course. That awful man will pay for his crimes against your family for the last time. You will never suffer at his hands again."

I shake my head, desperate for her to understand. "Holden didn't do this. He rescued me. He—" It's on the tip of my tongue to tell her about his shooting Jed right between the eyes at the cabin. "He's being framed. Someone set him up."

I have to speak to him.

Will he speak to me after what I did?

June's delicate features crease with concern. "Darling, I do believe you might be suffering from a case of Stockholm syndrome. Sometimes, victims can harbor feelings of ... sympathy for their captors. It's a coping mechanism to help you survive the trauma."

I shake my head more vigorously. "No! I'm telling you ... he didn't do this! The Redfords care about me. I want to speak to Dolly. I need to see her."

My aunt tilts her head to the side as she grabs an open bottle of white wine and pours two generous glasses, handing me one. "I don't see why you can't see your friend, dear. In the safety of your father's home, of course. Who knows what that girl has suffered from as well?"

She suffered from my uncle attempting to rape her—that's what.

The way none of them see what's happening is driving me out of my mind.

"Did he ... did he do anything ... to hurt you?" Her features soften as her hand closes over mine.

I know what she's asking. The answer, of course, isn't that simple. We had sex, very consensual, mind-blowing sex. I know I can't tell her that.

I shake my head. "Holden saved my life. Men in masks had come to my apartment and kidnapped me. They took me to an old cabin on Redford Ranch and held me, without food, for almost six days. All I got was one sandwich."

I pour out all the details for her the same way I did at the police station in Portland, leaving out the gritty parts about sex and murder. The last part of the story she knows because they found me when I called her from Holden's pay-by-minute phone while he was in the restaurant, getting our sushi. While he was sound asleep early this morning, I texted my aunt our location. I didn't know they'd send a SWAT team. I thought I'd have a chance to explain what happened to the police and he'd be released when I told them he was innocent.

Aunt June nods along, listening intently and sipping her wine. She seems concerned for me, shocked by the story of me being thrown around in the cabin and starved but very confused about why when Holden found me, he took me to New Mexico with his brother instead of telling the sheriff and my father immediately.

"Don't you think it's odd that he carted you off to another state when I was at their house, looking for you? Are you certain you weren't drugged and harmed in your sleep?" She says the words gently, but they feel like a blow to my stomach.

I take a long gulp of wine, the smooth liquid burning down my throat. She rubs my arms reassuringly, attempting to console me. My father enters the kitchen then, immediately coming over to me and pulling me into a stiff hug.

"That bastard will never see the light of day, you hear me? He's gone for good. You're safe now."

You're safe now. You're safe here. You're safe with us.

Why does it feel like a lie?

I tuck my face into his chest, my body trembling with all the fear and stress of the last ten days from hell.

Holden didn't do this! He's innocent!

He was right. He told me this would happen ...

I want to scream at them both, to smash the wine bottle on the floor until they fucking hear me. All they can see right now is a traumatized woman who doesn't know what she's saying. My stomach roils with an aching sickness at what I've done to him, to the man I love.

Stockholm syndrome, Aunt June said.

They think I'm suffering from some kind of trauma bond.

"You and your mother won't have to suffer like this ever again, Rosie. You and she will heal, and we'll be a family again. The Redfords will pay for this, all of them."

The skin on my neck and shoulders heats with a rash. I pull back from him, taking a step away. His eyes are creased with concern, but there are no tears. There's only anger and a hint of ... satisfaction. It's the same expression he has when he wins a hand at poker.

"The Redford family had nothing to do with this," I choke out. "They are innocent, *all* of them."

My father covers his mouth with a wrinkled hand,

shaking his head. "You need to see a doctor, a therapist. You're in shock. You've been traumatized, and you're not thinking clearly."

"Stockholm syndrome," my aunt whispers.

I howl, my scream echoing through the big, empty house. "FUCK! I am not suffering from *Stockholm syndrome!* I love him! I am *in love* with him. He saved my fucking life!"

My aunt gasps, nearly spilling her wine as her hand shoots out to clap against her chest. My father's face morphs into a reddened expression of rage. He rises to his full height, leaning toward me and jabbing his finger in my face.

"If he didn't do this, then who did? Who hates us enough to hold your mother for weeks? To starve you nearly to death, feeding you one measly sandwich? That man blames me for having to go to prison even though he murdered your uncle in cold blood, spinning some story about Cain assaulting his sister and pointing a gun at him. Your judgment has been clouded by all the time you've spent over there and your ridiculous infatuation with all the Redford boys since you were a *child.*"

He straightens himself, adjusting the front of his sports coat as he looks down on me with disdain. My bottom lip begins trembling as the fear of what he might do to Holden seeps into my bones.

Would he really send him back to prison for this ... something he is completely innocent for? Is my father that cruel?

My aunt steps toward me, shifting her body language to face my father as she wraps an arm around my waist. "How did you know she had one sandwich, Clay?"

A cold stream of ice shoots through my spine, straightening it. I stare my father down, searching his face for the truth, for an ounce of vulnerability, sorrow, *anything* to reveal the truth, to reveal that he had nothing to do with this.

But what I see instead is a trace of shame. His gaze shifts from my face to hers, a flash of fear crossing his features before he replaces it with a familiar, practiced look of stubborn pride. "I'm only assuming, with their cruelty, that she wasn't properly fed. At any rate, I need to call Ethan and arrange for you to begin seeing a psychiatrist." Ethan is my father's personal assistant. "A doctor can prescribe you some medicine that will help with this ridiculous notion that you're somehow *in love* with your captor."

Without another glance in my direction or space for discussion, he turns around and exits the room.

38

HOLDEN

Warner paces against the back wall of the holding cell they've allowed us to meet in. I forgot how cold and boring being behind bars was. Unsurprisingly, I didn't sleep a wink last night.

"Cash should be there now, and once he meets with Pike, we'll have more answers. You'll be getting out of here by end of day."

I stare up at the ceiling as I lie on the cot, my mind trailing back to yesterday morning when the police nearly busted down the door of our hotel room.

Rosie turned me in. She called her father to come arrest me.

For some reason, that knowledge makes me feel cold from the inside.

"You've been doing great. Everything you've told them is exactly what you should say. Once we have the phone, the evidence of who the real kidnapper is should be more than enough to exonerate you. Nothing else was recovered at the scene to incriminate you. Whatever Rosie Dixon has to say is the only wild card. Sheri never saw the face of her kidnappers. You have plenty of alibis for the amount of time she was missing," Warner continues.

The choice to fly to Portland and not to carry a handgun with me turned out to be incredibly vital.

"What do you think she'll say?" he finally asks.

What an excellent question.

Rosie Dixon's facial expression as she gave me head in the shower, followed by the way she clung to my shoulders while I plunged inside her during the middle of our last night together, flashes through my memory.

I chuckle, rising to a standing position. "Your guess is as good as mine."

Because right after that, while I was sleeping in her arms, she betrayed me. The ache in my chest throbs like a festering wound, one that'll need a lifetime to heal—if it doesn't kill me.

Warner's phone starts to ring, the vibration filling the cell. He looks up at me as he answers it, rubbing his hand over his beard.

"Cash."

I listen on the other side of the call, gathering that Jed's cell records indicate his communication with a man named Ethan Harlen. Harlen's texts revealed the payment method and timeline of the kidnapping plans, which dated back to the day after I was released from prison.

"Who is Ethan Harlen?" Cash says over the phone, the airport speaker in the background of the call.

I release a breath. "He's Mayor Dixon's assistant."

Warner turns to me. "They'll let you out as soon as I go

to the sheriff with the phone and tell him that it was recovered near the cabin on Redford Ranch. I'll tell him you weren't sure if it belonged to the kidnapper or not, so you sent it off to have the deleted history recovered. With the recovered data, it's clear that it did belong to the kidnapper, Jed. The ransom video Rosie had been forced to record was on it, as well as the person who it was sent to—Ethan Harlen."

THE COOL DECEMBER breeze at the ranch brings a peaceful serenity over me. Dirt clods crunch under my boots as I walk out to the barn with a glass of whiskey in my hand. The orange-and-purple hues of a West Texas sunset send rays of warmth over my skin, but they don't go deep enough to affect my heart.

I've been home for a week now. The range of emotions I've been experiencing has a touch of rage, remorse, bitterness, and desperation all mixed in.

I haven't seen or heard from Rosie. Warner has threatened me not to reach out to her. Dolly is solemn, walking around the house with a permanent frown on her lips and wet eyes. She's been interviewing housekeepers, all of them plump and nearing fifty.

I guess she's sick of her brothers sleeping with the help.

Sterling informed us tonight at dinner that he signed a four-year contract with the Marines. It didn't surprise any of us, and we drank to him serving our country. He'll ship off in the next few months for basic training.

If I wasn't needed at the ranch to figure out how the fuck to make a profit with all the other ranchers using M-59 on their cattle and sinking our profits, I might be tempted to enlist.

A group of cowboys is laughing and drinking around a firepit near the bunk room. One of them is strumming on a guitar. They all have bottled beer in their hands. Their cowboy hats have seen better days, but they get the job done. Duke is among them, animatedly telling them his latest hunting story. Cash sits back on a log with a firelit smile on his face.

"She hated when I hunted, couldn't stand the sight of it," Duke finishes.

"I heard a rumor about the mayor's daughter, that you and she never sealed the deal, Redford."

My chest tightens as I look up at my little brother's expression.

His bright blue eyes meet mine. "Nah, that was kid shit, ya know? We never got that far."

"Damn, I'd be willing to bet she's had it popped by now, but if not, I'd love to be the man who has the chance to," the one with the thick beard says. He leans forward, nearly falling out of his seat due to intoxication.

Jensen grins. "You fellas haven't forgotten the bet, have you? I say the winner also gets a hundred bucks from each of us."

I drain the rest of the amber liquid in my glass, hurling the glass into the fire, causing it to erupt in a small burst of flames. "Whoever wins that bet will answer to me, and he won't be breathing when I'm done."

My tone is casual, but the entire group stiffens and silences. I make eye contact with Duke, who stares at me for a few seconds before smirking and throwing his head back with a bark of laughter.

"Fuck, you know the world is cruel when your big brother starts saying shit like that about your ex."

The men around the fire look at each other with curious glances, studying my and Duke's faces.

He winks at me over the fire before chugging down the remainder of his beer and lifting the empty bottle in my direction. "If you can convince her to ever set foot back on this ranch, brother, she's yours."

The men around the fire roar with laughter and a couple of yee-haws.

I accept a fresh beer from one of them, tipping the contents over my lips. "How about we settle that nasty little dispute we had over her right here, right now?"

Duke's smile fades from his lips. "Why? So your psycho, prison-fighter ass can bloody my face up again? No thanks."

"She's not worth it to you," I realize with a muse.

He tilts his head to the side. "At one point, she was. Not anymore."

Cash stands up, swaying on his feet. His phone starts to buzz in his pocket. My senses heighten at the sound. He fishes it out of his jeans before swiping to answer.

"Hello?"

The person on the other end speaks for a minute. The men around the fire continue drinking and talking as Cash starts walking toward the house, phone still pressed to his ear. I follow him, ignoring Duke's eyes on me.

"Yeah, okay, I'll get back to you," Cash says.

"Who is it?" I ask.

He hangs up the phone, shaking his head with a chuckle. "You're not going to believe this."

"What?" I ask.

He exhales. "Monroe Blue wants me on her security detail."

I stare at him. We stop on the front porch while he chugs his beer.

"The country singer? The one you saved from that freak onstage?"

"That's the one."

"How much?"

He shakes his head. "Doesn't matter. I'm not taking the job. I'm not a bodyguard. I'm a rancher."

I study him for a few moments as the song of crickets fills the night.

"They're not coming for you, and you're not going back to jail. They don't have shit on us," he says.

I step into the house with him. "Once Warner files our suit against Clay Dixon, we're gonna need those cattle sales we're not getting."

We walk through the living room and into the kitchen, where Cash grabs us two more beers from the fridge in the oversize pantry.

"Mayor Dickhead has run out of options. His boys fucked up when they left Jed there alone and you found him by tracking her phone. They'd underestimated us. They made the case national news, and with the calls and connections Warner has made through it all, they can't get away with a small-town cover-up again."

Word broke two days ago that I was released from jail due to new evidence uncovering another suspect. The media frenzy surrounding the story has only circulated more and more attention, partially due to my mugshot next to Rosie's picture, which has turned into a meme online about how being kidnapped by certain felons wouldn't be all bad.

Rosie has yet to make any public statements. It's unclear if that's because her father won't let her or if she's declining to. Warner and Cash have both threatened to take my phone away if I try texting or calling her. Right now, I have to lie low while the investigation reveals my innocence.

I tip the beer back over my lips as Dolly enters the room, her phone pressed up to her ear and a small smile on her face.

"Yeah, I know. I think the whole thing is bizarre. I've never cried so much in my life." She rummages around in the fridge, pulling out some hummus and baby carrots, a block of cheese, and some salami.

Cash and I watch her curiously as she chuckles, shaking her head at something the person said on the other end of the phone. After grabbing a sleeve of crackers from the pantry, she starts making herself a snack plate. Her eyes flick up to meet mine, then Cash's before she gasps, her hand covering her mouth.

"You did *what?*"

Her wide eyes move back to mine as her mouth forms an

O. She stands, frozen in silence, as the other person continues speaking, but Dolly's eyes stay locked on to mine.

"Who is it?" I finally whisper.

She slowly forms a smile, shaking her head. "Ew, TMI! That's far enough. I don't need any more details. Holy shit."

The hair on my forearm starts to rise as I walk over to where she is, dipping my head lower toward the speaker of her phone. She swats my shoulder hard before grabbing her plate and walking out of the kitchen.

"Yeah, well, when I see you tomorrow, you and I have *much* to discuss." Her voice travels from the hallway until she shuts the door of her room.

I turn to Cash, folding my arms over my chest. "Since when does Dolly have any friends besides Rosie?"

39
ROSIE

I stare across the table into my best friend's red-rimmed gray eyes, our hands clasped together beside our coffee mugs. She sniffles, grabbing a napkin to dab at her nose. Her long black braid is resting on her shoulder. Our favorite café is decorated for Christmas with vintage ornaments and green garlands. My latte is gingerbread flavored, but Dolly opted for the Christmas-in-a-cup flavor.

"I'm so relieved, relieved for your mom's sake and yours. I know things with her aren't perfect, but, hell, it really sucks not having a mom at all. Maybe this whole thing was a wake-up call for her." She lets go of my other hand to take a sip of her steaming cup.

"She's going to be okay. I honestly do feel like it was somewhat of a wake-up call. She's finally agreed to go to rehab, and she's already looking into some up where Aunt June lives so she can visit. I just wish we could figure out who did this to us."

The gnawing words from my mother and Holden about my father claw at the back of my mind. I still can't accept it. I can't face it.

Dolly nods, exhaling. "Sometimes, bad people just do evil shit, and we can't understand why. Sometimes, it's always going to stay a mystery. I think about what Cain did all the time … how fooled I was by his attention. I've come to the conclusion that, sometimes, we just can't know what people's motives are."

I nod, bringing the rim of my mug to my lips. "Slight subject change, but I've decided that although being jobless and homeless would be even more character-building for me, it would be much more fun if I could live with my best friend."

A grin spreads wide across her face as she squeezes my hand. "Oh my gosh, I thought you'd never ask! You can have Duke's room. I've been wanting to kick him out to the bunkhouse for ages, and now that Sterling has signed with the Marines, it's the perfect—"

My eyes widen, and I cut her off. "Whoa! I'm sorry, miscommunication. I don't want to live and work on the ranch. I was thinking about a cute little two-bedroom in town somewhere. I might apply to work here actually." I look around the quaint, quiet café.

"Oh. Okay …" She trails off, an awkward silence stretching between us.

We let go of each other's hand, sip on our sweet, caffeinated drinks, and people-watch for a few minutes. We try to speak at the same time.

"Well, if—" she says.

"I guess if—" I start.

She smiles. "You first."

I exhale. "I just think, in light of the details I shared with you last night, that me living on the ranch would be a recipe for ... disaster."

She tilts her head, a mischievous grin on her lips. "Are you saying that you won't be able to keep your hands to yourself when one of my brothers is around?"

I vigorously shake my head. "I'm saying that he and I will combust if we're forced to spend time in the same room, let alone live under the same roof. He clearly still has a very low view of my family."

And considering I haven't heard from him since he was arrested because of me ... he hadn't formed the same emotional attachment that I'm suffering from.

The shame of what I did, turning him in like that, has been eating me alive. I've stared at his name in my phone, at the last texts we exchanged. I've nearly pressed the number to call him a thousand times. I can't will myself to do it, to reach out to him. If I hear his voice, I'm afraid I'll crumple in on myself, on the reality of how much I love him and how my father truly is a fucked-up, rapist-protecting, family-kidnapping psychopath.

Holden was trying to protect me from it, trying to show me that he loved me and would take care of me despite who my father was.

I shift in my seat, shoving down the steamy memories from our brief time together on the run that began seeping through my brain. Dolly traces a pattern on the tabletop, eyes staying locked on mine.

"Well, that's unfortunate because I am having a *really* hard time finding help to maintain the house. I've interviewed *so* many candidates, and ... I'm thinking I might just have to do it all on my own and hope my weak little heart doesn't give out." She lets out an exasperated sigh, pursing her lips and looking away.

I roll my eyes at her dramatic statement. "Oh, stop it. You're being ridiculous. I'm sure there's someone in town who is up to the task."

She chews her inner lip, debating my words. "Well ... now that you mention it, I bet if I asked Madi, she'd be happy to work and live there. I could give her my room so she'd be right next to Holden ..." She tilts her head, blinking at me innocently.

My stomach turns over. My breath grows ragged as I clench my fist in my lap, bending the spoon between my thumb and forefinger. I try to inhale slow, deep breaths as visions of Madi throwing herself all over Holden every second of the day *and* night tortures my imagination.

Would he offer her payment to sleep in his bed?

She'd probably do it for free ... among other things.

I suddenly feel like I might vomit.

"I don't think he'd even let me come back. I'm the one who turned him in, and the case is still ongoing ..."

"He'll do exactly as I say! He likes to think he's head honcho over the entire ranch, but I'm in charge of the house. If it makes you feel better, Duke can stay in the main house, and Holden can move to the bunkhouse."

I sigh, immediate relief flooding me. "Okay, that I might consider. If they're all okay with it and you're ... sure."

Her eyes light up as she claps her hands excitedly. "Oh, yes! They'll be fine with it. They're all sick of frozen pizza since you're not there to make their favorites. Rosie, it's going to be amazing. It's about time we lived together. Life is going to be right back to normal in no time."

I chuckle, squeezing her outstretched hand again. "You're manipulative—you know that?"

Her face contorts into a frown. "I only use my powers for good, not evil."

A wicked smile stretches across her features, and I burst out laughing.

My mother's cold fingers intertwine with mine as we walk through the rose garden. My father had it planted for her on their ten-year anniversary. She calls it his guilt garden because she found out the day after that he'd been sleeping with my nanny.

"I know I should try to remember things, but I just want to forget. I told them to stop asking me questions because I just can't relive it anymore. Your screaming was the worst part of it all."

That part of her story is a mystery to me. I cried out when my ribs were bruised, but I know I was held at the cabin the whole time. My mother was found in an abandoned trailer house ten miles outside of town, in the other direction. It was over forty minutes from the cabin.

"It must've been another poor girl who was taken," I say softly.

She shudders, shaking her head. Her auburn hair is dull and thinner than I've ever seen it. The color seems to have finally returned to her cheeks, and I haven't seen her with a drink in her hand since we've both been living under my father's roof again.

"Who do you think it was, Mother? Do you have any guesses?" I haven't asked her this yet because she's so against talking about it.

She looks around the garden and up to the back porch, where my father is sitting with his assistant, Ethan. They're out of earshot, but she still leans in to whisper in my ear, "I know this sounds crazy, but I think it was him."

Blood rushes through me, growing loud in my ears. My heart rate rises as Holden's silent suggestion flashes through my memory. He believed my father was capable of kidnapping and holding both me and my mother. That was his reasoning for not bringing me back home immediately. He didn't think it was safe.

Now, my mother is suggesting it too ...

"Why? What makes you think that?"

She pulls me to a stop, her bony fingers squeezing mine tightly as her eyes search mine. "One night, while I was being held, I thought ... I thought I heard his voice. That old trailer was drafty, so cold at night." She shivers at the memory. "It was in the middle of the night, and I awoke to a filthy rat scuttering over my foot. I freaked out, started sobbing. I thought I was going to die. Then, I heard voices … men outside. They came and went occasionally, but I only saw one man's face—that one they caught trying to cross the border into Mexico."

I nod. The sheriff told us that one of the accomplices to the kidnapping was caught crossing the Texas-Mexico border with twenty thousand dollars in cash. My mother was able to identify his photo. His was the only face she'd seen.

"I swear, I heard your father's voice that night," she whispers. "For a while, I thought I was hallucinating. But now … now, I really do believe he was there."

"What did he say?" I whisper.

She pinches the bridge of her nose and closes her eyes, like she's trying to remember. "It was something about … cattle sales? Some supplement or something. You know he's been trying to get into that underground bull riding ring to control the revenue and find a way to profit on the winnings. Nothing is ever enough for him. He never has enough power and control. And when Holden Redford was released early, I swear he lost his mind. That's when he started having another affair. I'd thought we'd finally moved past it, but when he gets that gleam in his eyes, I know I've lost him again. He gives in to this … this bloodlust. There's never enough power, never enough money, but more importantly, no one and nothing else matters when he feels wronged. He'll stop at nothing to destroy the entire Redford family, only because they took his precious brother—a *rapist*."

My father starts walking in our direction. My mother zips her lips shut, grasping my hand tighter.

"You need to get away from here, from him. We're not safe," she whispers just before he's upon us.

I form a weak smile. "Mama, I think that's enough fresh air. You don't want to overdo it. Aunt June should be back with dinner any minute now."

My father nods, reaching for her hand. She takes it with a soft, practiced smile on her lips. I marvel at how quickly she's able to cover the suspicions she just shared with me on her face. He leads her inside the house. I walk up to the porch, my stomach clenched. Ethan is tapping away on his phone without acknowledging me.

I walk in the house just in time for my aunt to arrive with takeout. She smiles at me as she lays out the bags of food.

"Where's your mother?"

"Dad just took her upstairs to lie down."

She nods, serving a plate of food up. "I'll just take this up to her."

My hand snatches her forearm, pulling her closer to me. "Do you think you and Mom could leave for Florida sooner?"

Her eyes narrow on me. "Sooner than three days from now?"

I nod, opening my mouth to speak and closing it again when I hear the back door open. Ethan's footsteps sound in the hall. I step away from her, releasing her arm.

"I'll be right back down to eat dinner with you, honey. I think we should catch up on the *Real Housewives* tonight, hmm?"

I nod. "Sure."

My father joins me in the kitchen at the large island a few moments later, where I'm buttering myself a roll.

"Ethan and I have some business to attend to. We'll be back later. Girls' night?"

I smile. "Yep. *Real Housewives* isn't going to watch itself."

He chuckles, leaning in to press a cold kiss on my forehead. My skin feels tight.

"I'm so glad you're home, sweetheart. You're safe now."

I kiss him on the cheek, patting his shoulder before taking a bite of the roll. As soon as he and Ethan leave, I run up the stairs two at a time. June and my mom stop talking as soon as I enter the room.

"They're gone," I say.

My mother reaches a trembling hand up to her temple. "You need to come with us, Rosie. You're not safe here either."

"She's right. Who knows what he'll do after your mother and I leave? You can't be here. He's clearly a sick, twisted man. We're going straight to the sheriff to share everything your mother remembers."

I shake my head. "You need to go farther away. He has too many connections here. You also need to talk to the Redfords' lawyer, Warner. He'll know what the next move should be."

"I'm not worried about any of that until we're safe!" My mother raises her voice.

Aunt June shushes her as she throws clothes in a suitcase. "This is a discussion to be had later. We don't have time now."

I steady my breathing before reaching for my mom's hand. "I want to go to the Redford Ranch. Dolly offered me my old job back and for me to live there. I love it and ..."

It's on the tip of my tongue to tell her that I'm also in love with Holden, but in light of the situation, I hold it back.

She cups my face. "You're probably safer there than you are anywhere else—at least until your father is behind bars."

My aunt comes up behind me and wraps us both in a hug. "We're getting out of this mess, ladies, and we're not looking back."

40

HOLDEN

The bull throws Jensen so high that he yelps as he comes down. He limps off out of the pens, a grimace on his face. They load another man onto the next bull. The sun is descending on the horizon, a stretch of pink spreading across the blue sky.

"We need an on-site nurse around here," Cash muses.

I spit in the dirt near my boot. "Well, don't ask me to find one."

"Trust me, I won't."

My chest aches when I think about Rosie, so I try not to. I've been drowning myself in ranch work, putting in twelve-hour days, doing whatever I can busy my hands with so I don't drive my truck into town and right up to the Dixon mansion. It's the only way I get any sleep, but I still wake up in a cold sweat most nights. It's mercifully not as bad as it used to be, but Rosie's sweet scent is beginning to fade from my pillows.

My phone buzzes with a text. I look down to see that it's in the family group chat.

DOLLY

Dinnertime! I have a surprise. :)

Cash hollers to the men that this is the last ride of the night while I make my way up to the house. The ranch hands don't live on-site, and most of them will head home soon. Warner's name flashes on my phone as I walk through the door.

"Yep." I answer it, adjusting the cowboy hat on my head. I probably smell like cow shit and sweat.

"Guess who just walked out of my office."

I close my eyes, pausing in the hallway as he continues.

More bad news. If I'm not in cuffs, I guess it could be worse.

"Sheri Dixon and June Clancy."

My stomach drops. Laughter floats out from the kitchen from two different female voices.

Rosie.

She came back?

She came back.

"What did they want?"

He chuckles. "They wanted to tell me that while Sheri Dixon was being held for ransom, she heard her husband's voice outside the trailer, talking about cattle sales and animal supplements."

Rosie's copper-red locks come into full view. My lips part as she turns, and I see her stunning profile. My eyes laser in on her lips, plump and tempting.

"She also asked me to represent her in her divorce case," Warner continues.

"So, it's locked down then?"

Rosie turns at the sound of my voice. We both still. Her eyes dip over me briefly, flashing with some emotion I want to believe is desire before she turns away.

"Oh, yeah, that fucker is going down. He's done for."

"That's good," I say.

"Yep. I'll keep you posted."

"Thanks." I hang up the phone.

Dolly is merrily stirring a pot on the stove. She grins at me. "Well, hello. Are you the only hungry one?"

I observe my sister coolly. "Guess so."

My pulse is skyrocketing. The surprise appearance of Rosie at the ranch after the last time I saw her, face down while being arrested, is unnerving.

I'm mad at her. I'm not as mad as I should be because all I can think about is kissing her ... then spreading her legs open and tying her to my bedposts.

I want to tie her up.

I blame it on my ranch-life upbringing with frequent workdays spent tying calves down for branding and cutting. I used to practice knots with rope in the barn when I was bored, and I've gotten really good at it.

Those knots would look even better around her wrists or ankles.

Except you fucked it up.

Rosie refuses to look at me as she busies herself around the kitchen, setting bowls and spoons out before washing a dish left in the sink. I take a seat at the island on one of the new barstools Dolly ordered after Duke smashed two of them.

My sister smiles widely at me again, almost freakishly so. "We made your favorite. Venison chili!"

What is she so excited about?

"Smells good," is all I offer.

My eyes roam over Rosie, the soft curve of her backside as she turns away to dry her hands. She's wearing a perfectly fitted pair of Levi jeans and a sage-green sweater that hugs her chest. My mouth waters at the tiny dip of her cleavage.

She made her choice.

I'm fucked.

She doesn't trust me to protect her, and it's something I have to live with now, apparently with her spending time under my roof.

We eat the chili in silence. Dolly makes small talk with Rosie, who still won't meet my eyes.

Cash, Sterling, and Duke join us, all greeting Rosie with confused expressions and murmuring, "Welcome back."

I'm highly aware of everywhere she moves, soaking up each giggle and smile that she bestows on all my siblings, but never me.

My father joins us for dinner, cupping her shoulder in a hug. "My girl is finally home."

She kisses him on his wrinkled cheek. He seems sober more often now than he is drunk, or maybe he's just getting better at hiding it.

I finish my bowl of chili, rising from the table to go shower.

"Thanks for dinner, Doll," I call out, rinsing my bowl to put it in the dishwasher.

"You're welcome. By the way, we need you to start moving out tomorrow so Rosie can take your room."

I freeze. Silence falls over the table. I resume my task, calmly placing my bowl and spoon in the dishwasher before pivoting to face her.

"Since when is she moving in here?"

Out of the question. I won't get a damn thing done.

Dolly pours herself another glass of iced tea and shrugs. "I offered her the position of housekeeper again, but she needs somewhere to live. I figure since Sterling is shipping out to basic training next week, it's the perfect timing."

The hard stare I pin my sister with doesn't faze her. She flashes me a sweet smile and takes another bite of chili.

"Duke, move your shit to the bunkhouse," I bark, storming toward the hallway.

"Rosie can room with me; it's no problem," he pipes up.

I pause in the doorframe, gripping it so hard that I half expect to hear a splintered crack in the wooden trim. "Move. Your shit. To the bunkhouse."

"Why don't we let Rosie decide? She can sleep wherever she wants."

Another ten seconds of silence permeates the space.

Sterling clears his throat. "Damn, this shit is good. You outdid yourself, sis."

I continue marching down the hall, sick of this bullshit competition Duke keeps trying to force me back into. Rosie made her choice, *clearly*. She doesn't want either of us. And at this point, I know he's just fucking with me to be a dick.

After pulling off my dirty work clothes, I turn on the water to let it heat. I stare at myself in the mirror.

Finally, I turn away and step into the shower.

I let the hot water spray over me, washing away the grime and filth of the day before collapsing into my bed into a restless sleep. I beg my subconscious mind to just shut the fuck up already, refusing to listen for which door Rosie might walk through down the hall.

I don't know how long she's going to keep chipping away at my heart, taking one sliver of it with her at a time, but I can't take much more of it.

I SPEND the next day outside from sunup to sundown. Sweat drips down my brow despite the mid-December chill as I mend fences and move cattle from one pasture to another. Sterling rides with me in silence, and I'm grateful for his patient, calming disposition. Duke would fuck with me and probably end up with my fist in the center of his face, and Cash would ask questions I don't feel like answering. Sterling doesn't say a word.

Once my stomach is growling with a roaring hunger, we return to the main house. Dinner was already served, and a half-eaten pan of Rosie's lasagna is sitting on the stove, covered in foil. Laughter from Rosie, Dolly, and Duke floats from the living room into the kitchen. Sterling heats up his food and walks toward the main area with his plate.

While my plate heats in the microwave, I turn around to grab a fork, smacking my head on an open cabinet door.

"Fuck," I exhale as it throbs, shutting my eyes.

Light footsteps come through the kitchen. My eyes flicker open to see Rosie, still avoiding my gaze, walk through with two empty wineglasses. On instinct, I reach out and grab her wrist.

She doesn't pull away, but her body grows still, eyes forward. She's wearing a pair of forest-green leggings with a soft, billowy, long-sleeved white shirt with a classic Santa Claus face on it. From the gentle sway of her breasts underneath, it would appear that braless Friday has begun. My hands ache to reach underneath it and feel her supple nipples under my fingertips.

"How long are you going to keep ignoring me?" I speak in a low growl.

She sighs, finally turning to face me with her big blue-green eyes. "Who said I was ignoring you?"

Her face is schooled with an expression of boredom, but the racing pulse on her neck betrays her attempt at indifference. I slide my fingers up her arm slowly.

"Where did you sleep last night?" I have to know. It'll eat me alive.

She's given you no reason to believe she wants Duke anymore. You're irrational.

She tilts her head slightly, stubborn bottom lip protruding. "Here. In a bed."

"*Whose bed?*"

My fingers have reached the top of her shoulders, just above her collarbone. I squeeze her gently, using just enough pressure to make her eyes widen before her lids grow hooded.

"Why do you care?" she whispers.

"You *know* that I care." I don't bother hiding the desire or the misery in my voice from her.

Her eyes grow darker as she folds her arms across her chest stubbornly, still holding the wineglasses. "Could've fooled me."

I release her, stepping back as if she'd slapped me. Of all the stupid, shitty things I've done in this life, not making it abundantly clear how deeply in love with her I am has to take the fucking cake.

She spins away from me, walking around the island the long way to get to the pantry. Duke bursts out laughing at something Sterling said while Dolly erupts into an animated story about something stupid one of the ranch hands did today. I turn around and stumble out of the kitchen, swiping a bottle of whiskey from the countertop as I head for my room.

I need to shower, to think, to figure out how the fuck to communicate to this woman that I am so deeply gone for her that I don't have a fucking clue how to even express it at this point. I'm mad for her. I'm losing my mind. I can't sleep without her. I can't stop obsessing about who she might be cuddling up with at night. I can't get her out of my head.

You're a fucking pussy.

I chug some of the liquid courage down as I enter my bathroom. I strip down naked, then turn on the shower. I don't bother waiting for it to heat up before stepping inside and letting the cold water shock my system. After another long draw of the liquor, the water finally warms me. I don't know how long I sit underneath it, racking my brain for some kind of gesture, some way to show her I want her, desperately.

I could buy her a horse.

Too much.

I could build her a house on the ranch for us, then ask her to move in.

Way too much.

I could just grab her face and kiss her senseless until she weakens underneath me.

Not enough.

I could invite her to a picnic, make a fancy spread for her.

Still not enough.

All of it feels trivial, too small for what we've been through and how incredibly idiotic I've been. A creaking sound draws my attention to the door of the bathroom. I look over to see a flash of red hair.

Rosie is standing in my bathroom, arms crossed. Even through the foggy glass, I can see that her eyes are watery. There's no sense in hiding it as my dick begins to swell.

I take another shot of whiskey, reaching for my growing erection. "Care to join me?"

She scoffs, grabbing the shower door and jerking it open. She doesn't bother removing her clothes before stepping into the shower with me.

Hotel-flavored memories flood my vision as the whiskey swims in my head. Her down on her knees, lips around my cock. I'm about to open my mouth with a much-needed spilling of my guts when she rears back and shoves my chest with both hands. I step back, eyes wide.

"I'm only living and working here because I'm trying to get away from my father." Her eyes are brimming with tears.

"Does that mean you finally believe me?" I bite back, expecting her to deny the allegations of him kidnapping her and her mother and framing me for it.

The water is seeping through her shirt, revealing the pebbled tips of her breasts through the white fabric. She nods, a barely perceptible motion. My throat tightens as I stare down into her eyes, searching for the truth.

"I believe you," she whispers, her wet lashes brushing against her cheeks. "And I'm so, *so* sorry, Holden." Her voice cracks.

My chest caves in. I grip the back of her neck, dipping my forehead down to hers. "I'm sorry, Rosie. I'm so fucking sorry for everything that's happened."

She sucks in a ragged inhale, choking on a sob. "I—I'm sorry ... sorry for calling them, for telling my aunt where we were. I'm so fucking sorry that they locked you up again. You'd warned me what would happen. You'd told me they'd do it, that they wouldn't give a shit about what I had to say. I should've believed you. I should've—"

She drags in a broken cry, eyes lowering in shame. I want to hold her, confess my incredible addiction to her, make love to her, beg her to move into my house and never leave it.

Instead, I reach up to wipe away a tear mixed with water. "Sleep with me tonight? I need to hold you. I need ... I just need you."

Her bottom lip quivers as she nods, relief flooding her features. I drag the soaked shirt up over her head, tossing it on the shower floor. Then, I grab the waistband of her leggings and pull them down. I get on my knees to peel them off of each foot, one by one. She braces herself on my shoulder with one hand.

With slow, gentle movements, I use my bar of soap to clean her. I spend more time than necessary on her breasts and between her legs, grazing over the surface of her skin, deliberately moving at a glacial pace. Goose bumps prick her skin despite the scorching temperature of the water.

Her breath hitches when I use the showerhead to thoroughly rinse her from head to toe. I watch her face as she gasps with the spray between her legs.

"You look so damn good when you're turned on."

"Like an angel?" she asks.

"My angel." I press a kiss to her hip bone, eyes on hers.

41
ROSIE

He still hasn't said that he loves me.

Holden is carrying me to his king-size bed, muscled shoulders stealing my focus as I try to remain grounded and not melt into his blubbering little sex doll.

He has to say it before I let him fuck me again.

He tenderly lays me on top of the covers, the dim light of the lamp illuminating the space with a romantic orange glow. He uses the towel around me to dry my long, wet hair.

"I'll sleep in here, but we are not having sex," I announce.

His dark eyes flicker up to mine as a smile ghosts across his lips. "Okay, angel. Whatever you want." He leans forward and stamps a kiss on the tip of my nose.

He stands and walks over to his chest of drawers, fishing through one for a few seconds while I admire his rounded ass cheeks.

Be strong! Don't give in. You got this!

Do I?

I swallow over a lump in my throat as dampness seeps

between my thighs. He turns around, and my eyes shift up to his face. If I see his dick, I'll give in. He pulls on my arm, lifting me up from the pillows to put one of his T-shirts over my head. He dons a pair of formfitting boxers before climbing into bed next to me. His arm wraps around my torso, pulling me up against his chest. The hard length of this erection presses into my ass cheeks. More of my arousal immediately begins to ooze out of me.

I grit my teeth. "I mean it. We're just sleeping."

He chuckles into my neck. "Holding you is more than enough for me, but I can't control my physical reaction to you. I just can't."

My chest sputters with his words. I wiggle closer to him, drawing a painful groan from him.

We lie in silence for several minutes before I break it. "Have you even missed me?"

He exhales warm air over the back of my nape as his fingers start to trace over the back of my hands. "I have not stopped thinking about you since the morning they arrested me in Portland."

I attempt to regulate my inhales so that it doesn't sound like I just ran a marathon. He waits for me, ever so patiently, to speak.

"Then, why didn't you text me?" My voice is a whisper as I attempt not to sound completely pathetic.

His fingers grasp my hip bone and squeeze hard as he sighs. "Rosie ... I've typed out a thousand messages to you. I've driven by your father's house over and over. One night, I nearly broke in, just to speak to you. I had no idea where your head was at. You called him—you called them—to arrest me for your kidnapping. I didn't know if they'd convinced you I'd done it, that I was the bad guy, or if ..." His voice grows weak as he struggles to continue.

Holy shit. He really does care ...

"You had every right to doubt me, to question who was telling the truth. Of all people, I promise I get what it means to believe that blood is thicker than water, that family comes first. I should've brought you back straightaway. Taking you with me was selfish. I just ... couldn't bear the thought of them hurting you again. I couldn't let you out of my sight. That was my fault, my wrong. I swear to God, I'll spend as much time as you'll let me proving that I'll never put any sense of—"

"No," I interrupt him, grasping his hands to my chest. "You were right. I wasn't safe with him. You were trying to prove it to me, to get the phone records. I'm sorry I ... I didn't know what to believe then. I trust you. I always have. I believe you. I feel ..." I nearly choke on my emotions as the next words leave my lips. "I feel safe with you," I whisper. "I feel safer here than I do anywhere else. I should've tried to explain to you what was going on, why I didn't come back to you. I was ... trying to come to grips with the fact that he really did this, that he was capable of it. All along, you were right. You tried to warn me. You told me that it was his doing and just ... I couldn't face it."

His grip around me tightens as he peppers kisses around my hairline, his strong legs wrapping around mine.

But he keeps his word and doesn't touch me sexually, and we both fall into a deep sleep.

I WAKE up alone the next morning. I stretch out on the bed, feeling better than I have in as long as I can remember. I inhale a deep lungful of Holden's scent from his pillow before hopping out of bed.

After showering and putting on makeup, I dress in jeans with a long-sleeved red bodysuit. Dolly and I chatter while drinking coffee, and I can tell she's internally begging me to tell her what happened last night when I didn't come to sleep in her room.

"Okay, you might as well spill it. I'm dying over here. Are you and he ... together?"

I shrug with a deep sigh. "We both kind of spilled our guts last night. Nothing happened. We just slept. I still feel like after everything, I need some kind of ... declaration from him. He's never said his exact feelings or that he wants to be exclusive or anything. I want to ... go on a date. Am I over-thinking it?"

She shakes her head vigorously. "You're not overthinking it at all. He owes you that."

I purse my lips. "I don't know if I should stop sleeping in his room until he does or ..."

She debates my question. "I think you should. He shouldn't get the goods without making the commitment."

I nod, grinning at her. "Now, do you get why I was so insistent that Duke and I were never going to happen?"

Her mouth drops open. "How long have you been crushing on Holden?"

I'm embarrassed to admit it, so I simply look away and mumble, "A while."

She laughs, shaking her head. "Damn. No wonder Duke and Holden beat the shit out of each other."

My eyes widen.

She nods, raising her brows. "Yeah, I think they worked it out in their brotherly type of way. Okay, so today, I think we should decorate for Christmas!"

I clap my hands excitedly. "Yes! I need some festivities in my life."

The holiday is merely two weeks away. I have no idea what I'm going to get everyone or when I'll even have time to go shopping.

After a few hours of decorating with Christmas music playing over the speakers, someone bursts through the back door.

"Rosie! Rosie, come quick!" Duke's eyes are wide with excitement.

My heart drops into my stomach as I jump to my feet. "What happened?"

Dolly and I race outside behind him.

"Holden's being a fucking idiot. You need to talk some sense into him," he calls over his shoulder as we race toward the barn.

Cold wind bites into my cheeks. Dolly grabs my hand, squeezing it hard as we both run. My blood is rushing loudly in my ears. Tears sting the back of my eyes as we slow to a walk and enter the barn.

"Do it," I hear Holden say.

Do what?

We finally reach the rest of the guys, right near the stacks of hay bales packed in for the winter months. Cash is holding a glowing hot branding iron. Holden is shirtless, abs and chest glistening with sweat. He's sitting on the hay bales, his teeth clenching down on a leather strap. I let out a scream when Cash moves closer to him with the branding iron.

Holden's dark eyes shift to mine before throwing an accusatory glance at Duke.

"Snitch," he grumbles. "Do it, Cash."

Cash pushes the glowing red end of the iron right onto Holden's chest. He groans, clenching down hard on the leather while the sound and smell of sizzling flesh fills the air.

Dolly shrieks, grabbing my arm and hiding behind it. My fingernails dig into my palms as I clench my fists as tight as I can.

"What the fuck are you doing?!" I scream at him, taking a step toward Cash.

Holden's muscled arms are taut, veins popping out.

After five seconds, Cash finally pulls the iron back. Holden collapses back against the hay, eyes closed and sweat dripping down the center of his chest despite the cold. He spits out the leather strap.

I look at the brand, and my breathing grows shallow. Right over his heart is the letter R, permanently burned into his flesh.

They have a Redford Ranch brand for the cattle with two

*R*s mirroring each other, and all the brothers have it on their shoulders or chest. This one is just one R.

"Do it again," Holden pants.

Cash turns and walks away with the iron. "If you insist, brother."

I slowly approach him. His black cowboy hat is tilted to the side as he lifts his head with a wry smile.

"Hey, angel. How's your day been?"

I drop to my knees beside him, grabbing his hand as a tear slides down my cheek. He smiles wider at me, lifting my hand up to plant a wet kiss on my knuckles.

"Duke ruined the surprise," he says, looking down at his chest.

My eyes follow his, seeing blood trickle down from the front point of the R.

"Why is he doing this to you?" I choke out.

He grips my hand tighter as Cash returns with the glowing iron again.

"Because I love you. And since I can't just tie a rope around your waist and take you everywhere with me, I want everyone to know you're mine. Forever."

I suck in a breath, clapping a hand over my gaping mouth. "So, the R is for ..."

"Rosie," he says, leaning back on the hay as his arm and shoulder muscles tighten.

He doesn't let go of my hand. My pulse is irregular as my mind scrambles for some kind of response to this bizarre situation and his shocking confession. I squeeze him back as Cash steps closer to him.

"Wait! Why is he doing the R again?" I panic, starting to hyperventilate.

"For Redford," Holden says, replacing the leather between his gritted teeth. "Do it."

I don't have time to process his words before Cash stamps the R on his chest, right next to the first one, burning flesh once again filling my nostrils.

RR. He is unhinged ... and so fucking hot.

I wince, watching his melted flesh spread away from the iron. Cash finally releases it. Holden collapses back again, spitting out the leather and letting out a loud sigh that's almost a roar.

"Fuck, that hurt." He chuckles, gripping my fingers tighter and once again kissing them. His lips are wet, sweat dripping down over him and making his glorious body glisten in the light.

"So, you just ... branded yourself with her initials? With *your* last name?" Dolly asks incredulously, stepping closer to inspect the double R on his chest.

Holden licks his lips, black-brown eyes meeting mine. "Yep."

"You're unhinged," I whisper.

"I am that, but I'm also just very much in love with you."

"Stop saying that!"

He tilts his head, smirking. "Why?"

"It's freaking me out." I shake my hands out, trying to bring feeling back into my fingertips.

I have no idea how to even process what he's done, branding himself with my initials, the ones he apparently wants me to have.

He laughs, rising up to stand. Shirtless Holden with fitted Wranglers, a black cowboy hat, and a gorgeous smile on his face I've rarely ever even seen is nearly enough to knock me over.

He places his hand on the wall of the barn behind me, leaning in close to me, intense gaze on my face. "Listen here, Rosie Dixon. I'm the type of man who doesn't make big decisions lightly. You burned yourself into my heart long before I did this. I just had it done to the outside now too. You're it for me."

I exhale, shaking my head as a smile finally starts to spread over my lips and butterflies flutter in my stomach. "I just ... I don't even know how to process this. You're a maniac. A big, fucking sexy *maniac*."

I reach my fingers up to his chest, careful not to touch the burned flesh, which has already stopped bleeding. I trace around the pink letters, the permanent mark of me on his body.

My chest pounds, swelling with the realization that I'm hopelessly in love with him too and that I have been for longer than I care to admit to myself.

His hand wraps around the back of my neck, pulling me closer to him as he dips his head to mine. Our lips meet in a chaste, slow kiss.

"I'm your maniac. No force on this earth will ever change that. They'd have to drag me out in cuffs to keep me away from you."

"Does this mean you want me to move in? Be your girlfriend?" I bite my lip, looking up at him.

He winks. "Yeah, we can start with girlfriend. Then I'm taking you out to dinner."

I laugh, shaking my head as happy tears roll down my cheeks. "Okay, cowboy. I guess I'll be your girlfriend."

I want to say those three little words back to him since they've been on the tip of my tongue all day, but I'm still terrified by the magnitude of what I feel. I look around the barn to see that we're alone. Everyone must have left while we were in our little love bubble. They even shut the barn doors.

He starts nuzzling my neck, pulling down the sleeve of my bodysuit. I shut my eyes, feeling the sparks of seduction shooting through the surface of my skin everywhere he touches me.

He suddenly dips his head down, arms sliding under the back of my legs and my back in a cupping motion before he sweeps me off of my feet. I yelp in surprise, going airborne. He carries me back over to the spot in the hay where they branded him, the same spot where I walked in on him getting head from another girl almost four years ago.

He sets me down on top of his discarded shirt. His fingers casually start unbuttoning my jeans, and I lift my hips to let him pull them down. He tugs off my booties, kissing the top of my feet. He drags his fingers over my exposed skin, tracing back up to my hips. The air is cold, but he heats me up with every flick of his gaze over me.

My bodysuit is buttoned up between my thighs.

"I like this." He kisses the mound of my sensitive clit through the fabric.

I groan at the slight pressure, wetness pooling there.

"I like you," I pant.

"Mmm." His lips vibrate on me, the sensitivity growing.

He scrapes over the top of me with his teeth before reaching the snap buttons. He unbuttons them with his teeth and fingers, shoving the fabric up. I don't wear underwear with bodysuits, and he seems to approve of that choice.

Before dipping down to taste me, he reaches his hands up to flip my breasts out of the V-neck, my nipples puckering in the cold. He molds my body how he wants, putting it all on display so he can enjoy me.

He moves back down to my pussy, inhaling deeply before he touches my sensitive skin with a soft kiss on my mound. I press into him, silently begging for more. He swipes one lick over me, drawing a soft gasp from my lips.

"You taste so damn good, angel," he purrs.

His hands cup my ass, lifting my hips up to his mouth as he starts to feast. His lips wrap around the ball of my clit, sucking it into his mouth and short-circuiting my brain.

"Fuck." I knock his hat off so my fingers can grip his hair.

He sucks harder, causing stars to float over my head in circles. My eyes roll back in my head, every nerve glowing hot. He doesn't stop, doesn't let up until he pushes me into a shattering orgasm. My legs shake before all my muscles tense up with the waves of pleasure washing over my skin.

He gently licks the surface of my wet pussy lips once more before his head rises, a devious smile on his glistening lips. "You did good, angel."

Fuck, I am so lucky.

"Put it in me," I demand.

He laughs, wiping the wetness from his mouth with the back of his hand before slowly buttoning me back up.

"I don't have a condom, so let's go in the house first."

I groan, debating just telling him to forget about it and put a baby in me now.

Okay, that was irrational.

"Holden," Duke's voice calls from outside the door of the barn.

His head snaps around. "Don't come in here."

"Clay Dixon is here," Duke says.

Blood rushes to my brain, making me feel lightheaded. Holden helps me stand, tucking my breasts back into my shirt before handing me my jeans. He reaches for his shirt, expression cool and grim.

He cups my face. "I'll handle this."

42

HOLDEN

I intentionally leave one button undone at the top of my shirt so I can finish it in full view of Rosie's father. His jaw clenches when he sees her walk out of the barn behind me with hay stuck in her hair. She reaches for my hand. I grip hers tightly. Ethan climbs out of the driver's side of the black SUV.

Fucker. I should just put my fist in his nose right now.

I have a strong suspicion that Ethan was the one handling the kidnapping details and Rosie's ransom video. He's Dixon's little errand boy, but the mayor was ultimately calling all the shots.

The back door opens, and Old Harry steps out of the SUV, smiling.

"Boys," he says.

Dixon motions up to the house. "Do you have a minute for a meeting, gentlemen? I think it's time we talked."

Rosie's hand is damp in mine, so I squeeze it again before leading her up to the house. Once we get inside, she goes into the kitchen with Dolly. Cash and Sterling stand up when they see Clay, frowns immediately forming on their faces.

They flank the visitors as we all walk up the stairs toward the den, where we have a card table, pool table, a bar set up with whiskey and bourbon, cognac leather chairs, and antler heads on the walls.

Cash doesn't ask before pouring each of us a glass of the amber liquid. I take a seat at the card table. Dixon and Harry follow suit. I see the bulge of a handgun on Ethan's hip as he leans back against the wall.

Cash sets the glasses in front of each of them. I lean back silently, waiting for Dixon to begin and trying to talk myself out of a violent end to this meeting.

Dixon finally clears his throat. "I don't see any reason for us to remain at odds with each other. You clearly intend to continue employing my daughter, whatever that entails. I have many contacts and connections that would benefit your cattle sales and other investments."

You've got to be shitting me.

I swirl the whiskey around in my glass, maintaining eye contact with him. After the silence continues to stretch on, he smiles uncomfortably.

"We have both done things we're not proud of. I'd be willing to let bygones be bygones, reaching a mutual agreement that would increase both of our profits and keep everyone living under their own roofs."

"Ahh, so this is about you not wanting to spend time behind bars," I muse.

He must be worried about it if he's desperate enough to come to me for help. I look to the side to see my father entering the room. He walks up to the card table, seating himself to my left.

"Clay, to what do we owe the pleasure?" he asks.

"Wyatt. I came by with a business proposition for your sons. I was under the belief that they were running things now."

Pops nods. "Holden and Cash are in charge since Holden got out."

Clay and Pops stare at each other for a few moments before Clay clears his throat and takes a sip of the whiskey. He understands that the subtle reference toward my time in prison hasn't been forgotten.

Old Harry chuckles. "Gentlemen! We all stand to benefit from a partnership like this. There are no downsides for anyone. No jail time for those who have bent the law and profits galore for all. Where's the fire? You're about to end an age-old rivalry through marriage. I say we let the past go and look toward the future."

I stand up and move over to the large gun safe in the corner of the room. "I went hunting with Duke once, when he was dating your daughter actually. We sat in this deer stand for what felt like ages. At one point, it started raining so hard that we almost called it quits. But I was starving for some venison chili."

I key the passcode into the safe, my back blocking their view. "While we sat and watched, the rain finally cleared enough for this little family of rabbits to hop out of the woods. There were three little babies and a mama. She led them to this little puddle of water to take a drink when a snake came out of the woods and snatched one of the babies.

The mama didn't know what to do, completely defenseless, so she ran off with the other two babies."

I open the safe and pull out the phone we found in the cabin that belonged to Jed and walk back over to the card table.

"The baby rabbit struggled to keep his head out of the rattler's mouth, but he started to slowly widen his mouth and swallow it. But then, just before the baby was completely inside its belly, a mountain lion came out of the woods and attacked the snake. He grabbed it up in his mouth, sinking his teeth right into the belly of the snake and swinging it around until he let go of the baby rabbit, and it hopped away, unharmed."

Clay's face has paled, and he remains motionless. I take a slow sip of my drink before tapping through the phone to get to the video of Rosie.

"After a few minutes of playing with the snake and dangling him around, the lion bit its head off and dragged it away." I press play on the video, swiveling the screen around toward Dixon.

His eyes shift down to watch his daughter, starving and terrified, asking to be rescued for ransom. I switch to the YouTube app on the phone, pulling up the search history for *screaming woman*. We're assuming it was the video they played outside of his wife's door in the trailer. The girl sounds surprisingly similar to Rosie.

"I know you've seen these clips, Clay, because it was sent to your boy there, Ethan. The funny thing is, Ethan already knew about it because he's the one who told Jed to take the video. The bizarre thing to me about this situation is that you not only ordered for your own wife and daughter to be kidnapped, starved, and held for ransom, but you also started getting this dumb fucker to sell an illegal cattle supplement to every ranch around simply to put our ranch on the downside for profits so that we'd be forced to either sell out or use the supplement, which you would then test our bulls for and get us arrested. Either way, you wanted me back behind bars for killing your piece-of-shit brother."

Clay's chair scrapes against the floor as he rises, his face growing red and the veins in his forehead popping out. "I don't need this shit from you, you fucking murderous felon. You killed him, and the state put you away for it. I have no clue why the governor would ever grant you clemency after you were clearly guilty. I pray, one day, my daughter comes to her senses and leaves this godforsaken ranch for good, but until then, I hope that she's—"

My mouth curves into a wry grin. "You wanna know why I was granted clemency? I wrote the governor a letter. I told him about the night I killed Cain Dixon and exactly why I did it.

"Six years ago, Cash, Sterling, and I were out at a bar in Elmott. We left the bar to go home with two of the bartenders who said they had another friend waiting, but when we got to their house, we heard screaming from one of the bedrooms. We had to break down the door, only to find none other than your brother, doing exactly what he tried to do to our sister the night I ended his miserable life. My brothers and I beat him to a fucking pulp that night, nearly killed him then. The girl was terrified to press charges. She knew who you were and that they'd never stick to him. He'd walk, just like he always did when big brother came running to the rescue."

The room is entrenched in silence, all eyes on me. Clay's face is ghostly white.

"You remember this, don't you? He wouldn't tell you what happened to him. You started suspecting us then, started hating our family even more. But that girl? That girl never forgot what we did. She wrote me a letter in prison after my sentencing, telling me who her uncle was. I'm sure you can guess by now, but it was the good governor of Texas, John Calhoon III. And he pardoned me for my crimes, even thanked me for ridding the world of your brother."

Clay's eyes have glassed over, like he's in shock. He's always been top dog in the political world, always used his power to hurt the innocent and further his own agenda. He's realizing he's lost for once, that he won't be able to get away with it this time because our connections are now more powerful than his. His jaw clenches tightly as he moves to stand.

Heavy steps leading up to the den interrupt us as the sheriff from the next county and two deputies enter the room, Dolly and Rosie on their heels.

"Clay Dixon, you're under arrest for ordering the kidnapping of Sheri and Rosie Dixon, as well as the illegal manufacturing and selling of supplements that are not FDA approved."

The deputy reads off his Miranda rights as he cuffs Clay and Ethan both.

Old Harry sips on his whiskey casually. My father does the same, tipping his glass toward the man.

"Rosie, honey, please listen to me. These are lies! You're safer with me," Clay begins as they lead him away.

My chest aches as she doesn't say anything to her father. Dolly pulls her closer, hugging her tightly. I stand from my chair and walk over to her, tucking her into my chest as she shudders with a teary sigh.

Old Harry rises, walking over to the bar cart to serve himself a refill.

"Ya know, you boys always were smart. I told Dixon when you refused that first dose of M-59, I knew you'd never fall for it. He had me in his clutches for a while, but I was biding my time until someone could get evidence to take that fucker down. It'll be a long road, but I think you've got what it takes."

Pops and Old Harry start bickering like always. Rosie leans against me with a heavy sigh. I lead her downstairs to the kitchen, grabbing a bottle of wine and pouring her a generous portion.

"At least it's over now. He's gone from your life. He knows that you know." Dolly rubs her arm, placing the wine I poured in her hands.

Rosie nods with a sad smile. "I'm glad it finally happened. It's just ... it's strange, I guess, for it to finally be out in the light that he actually went so far, hurting me and my mother so gravely."

I grip her shoulders, turning her to face me fully. "You have every right to take as long as you need to fully process this in whatever way you need. For now, you're here with us, no longer in danger. I'm by your side. I'm not going anywhere. No one is getting to you without going through me. You have me; you have us."

She smiles sleepily up at me. "I know you are. For now, I just want to go lie down with you. Maybe we could watch a movie together? A cheesy Hallmark one?"

I nod, gripping her hand and dragging her behind me toward my bedroom.

TWO WEEKS LATER, we're opening Christmas presents under the tree. There's a fire crackling in the hearth and the smell of a breakfast casserole filling the air.

Rosie is in silky red pajamas that I bought her. I'm dying to get her back to my room.

Our room.

I've turned into a sappy little bitch when it comes to her. I'm constantly seeking out her needs to meet them before she even has to ask. I'm worried about her.

After her father was arrested, Rosie was silent and withdrawn for a few days. I can sense that she's still grieving over the harsh reality that he ordered the kidnapping in an effort to send me back to prison, ruin our cattle sales, and ultimately force Cash and Pops to strike up a deal with him to stay afloat.

Rosie holds up the gold necklace I had made for her. There's a tiny letter *H* molded into the chain. She smiles widely and kisses my cheek.

"Baby, it's perfect. I love it."

"I don't expect you to brand yourself with it, but I need my mark on you somehow."

I've learned pretty quickly since finally admitting my feelings for her that I'm an overly possessive son of a bitch when it comes to Rosie. She doesn't seem to mind.

She turns around and hands me the ends of the chain to hook it around her neck. I fasten it, pressing a kiss to the back of her head before wrapping my arms around hers.

"There's more. That box is yours too," I whisper.

"You went way overboard," she says.

I scoff, handing her the shiny wrapped green box. "I'd better just prepare you now. I intend to spoil the fuck out of you."

She tears the paper off slowly.

"What are you doing, saving the paper? Rip that shit open!" Dolly chirps.

My siblings and Pops are all lounging around, drinking coffee and talking. We did family gifts first before Rosie and I exchanged ours to each other.

Rosie obliges, tearing it off faster to reveal the box of a brand-new MacBook. She gasps, her eyes shifting up to meet mine.

"Holden ... this is too much."

I shake my head. "Nonsense. You need a computer for your homework assignments. You're the ranch nurse."

She clutches it to her chest, grinning up at me. Her eyes are watery as she looks around the room, at all of us, her new family.

Duke clutches his leg dramatically. "Nurse! Nurse! I'm

wounded! Take me to the room and nurse me back to health!"

Dolly swats his arm. "You're an idiot."

I take the computer box from Rosie's arm and set it on the coffee table before pulling her to a stand. "Come to think of it, my leg is hurting."

She claps a hand against her chest in mock surprise. "Well, in that case, we should definitely go examine it— *privately.*"

I lean down, nuzzling the back of her neck as we walk down the hallway.

"We need our own place. I wanna make you scream," I murmur into her ear.

"There's always the barn," she muses.

I laugh into her ear, steering her toward my bedroom. "Okay, but we gotta get some kind of bed out there because I'm not interested in getting hay in uncomfortable places anymore. I'm too old for that."

"You are getting *kinda old.*" She hops up onto the bed, unbuttoning her pajama top to reveal a lacy red bra underneath.

My mouth waters. "Not too old to give you a good hard spanking, little missy."

Her eyes spark with anticipation as she licks her lips. "Bring it on, baby."

I reach for the hem of my T-shirt, peeling it off my frame before slowly approaching her up on the bed.

"By the way, now that we're alone, I have one more present for you," she says.

I dip my head between her breasts, kissing each one reverently. "What's that, baby?"

"I love you," she says softly, tracing her finger around my earlobe.

My muscles tense as I look up into her soft expression, a wave of emotion rolling over me. A smile curves across my lips as I let out a low chuckle. "Damn, that took you forever. I love you too, angel."

EPILOGUE

ROSIE

FIFTEEN MONTHS LATER

The pregnancy test stares back at me with two pink lines.

Two lines. There are two lines.

I never thought I'd be the girl who got married with a baby in her belly, but considering my wedding isn't for another two months, I guess that's the hand I've been dealt.

A slow, trembling exhale escapes my lips as someone knocks on the bathroom door.

"Rosie? Some cattle escaped from the field in the north-west corner. I'm going to see where they got out." Holden's voice comes through the door.

I quickly stash the pregnancy test box under some toilet paper in the trash can, hiding the positive one at the back of the towel cabinet.

"Okay, baby," I call back, staring at myself in the mirror as I wash my hands.

"Do you wanna ride with me?" he asks.

He'll see it on my face.

"Um, not right now, I guess. I need to start on dinner."

"Okay, babe."

His heavy footsteps retreat from the door. I grab my phone, pulling up the photo of my wedding dress. The fitting was last week, and the alterations have already begun.

Shit, I hope it fits.

The dress has a lace sweetheart neckline, with long, off-the-shoulder sleeves. The skirt spills down into an A-line shape with a short train. Our Western-themed ranch wedding has been planned out to perfection over the last six months.

"I'm going to be a mom," I whisper to myself.

My eyes water as the words wash over me. I didn't even realize my period was late until it had been two weeks. My breasts are already swollen and tender.

"There should be an online forum where we can review birth control pills. Zero out of ten stars." I fling the pack into the trash.

I walk out of the bathroom and go downstairs to start making the chicken fried steak with mashed potatoes I had planned for dinner. Holden insists on continuing to pay me to work on the ranch, even after we get married. He proposed only ten months after we started dating, and I wanted a spring wedding. Everything has been perfect—almost *too perfect.*

I wanted us to experience marriage for a while before

adding a baby to the mix. I know Holden will be an amazing dad. We want to be parents, but everything that happened with my father has given me a lot of anxiety about the prospect of starting a family.

"Hey, lovely." Dolly walks into the kitchen with a cheerful smile, holding a bouquet of wildflowers.

She pulls out a vase from the cabinet and fills it with water.

"Hi," I say with a weak smile.

"What's wrong?" she asks with a frown.

I shrug. "I'm not feeling so good today."

My stomach is queasy. When I pull the steak from the fridge to tenderize it, the smell of the raw meat causes bile to rise inside of me. I barely make it to the trash can before throwing up my lunch.

"Rosie, holy shit. Go lie down! I'll take care of this." Dolly ushers me out of the kitchen.

I heed her advice, collapsing onto my and Holden's bed. I tap on my phone screen for the office number to my doctor. After making the appointment, I close my eyes and let the tears fall.

AFTER MY MOTHER's time in rehab, my father's arrest, and their finalization of the divorce, she's been a different person. She sold their old house and bought something smaller outside of town on some acreage. She travels a lot, but we never go longer than a few days without talking.

She squeezes my hand while we wait for the doctor. "Do you need some water, honey?"

I shake my head, feeling like I might throw up again. This morning sickness has been hell for the past two weeks. After the second day, Dolly caught on to what was going on. I begged her not to tell Holden, not until I could see the doctor and confirm the pregnancy. My sickness has mostly been confined to times when he's out working the ranch, which has kept him busy every morning when I'm throwing up.

Dolly grins at me, eyeing my stomach. She can't even hide her excitement despite my physical misery. I'm warming up to the idea of motherhood, but my emotions are a complete roller coaster. I feel guilty for hiding it from Holden, but he's in such a happy love bubble that I just can't bring myself to burst it. We both agreed to wait a while for kids.

A knock sounds at the door, and a nurse walks in. "Hello, I'm the sonographer. I'm just going to get you set up and do a quick scan, and then your doctor will be in."

I nod. She squeezes cold jelly onto my lower stomach before pressing the sonogram tool up to my skin.

"If you're only about seven or eight weeks, we might not be able to see much. We'll still listen for the heartbeat," she says.

After she squishes the tool around for a few seconds, I start to get anxious. It just looks like black and gray static inside a big circle. I glance up at my mother's face as she studies the screen.

"Is that ..." she asks.

The nurse smiles. "Yes, that's the baby."

Immediately, a heartbeat sound fills the room. Dizziness overwhelms me.

That's my baby.

A sweeping sense of excitement and awe fills my chest. The invisible but palpable connection makes me catch my breath.

"That's my baby ..." I whisper.

Dolly claps excitedly, tears streaming down her face. "I'm an auntie!"

I laugh at her, wiping the moisture from my face. "Shit, I'm so ready to tell Holden now."

My mom pats my leg, handing me a tissue. Her eyes are red-rimmed too. "He's going to be thrilled, sweetheart."

Suddenly, the nurse's smile drops, right along with my heart. She stares at the monitor, squishing the tool around more.

"What is it?" I'm barely breathing.

She smiles, sending relief through me. "Um, well, I hope you're ready to hear this. You see that?" She points to the screen, where the first little circle now has two. "That's another baby. You're having twins!"

I gasp, my hand clapping over my mouth. "Shut up. You're lying."

Dolly starts jumping up and down, laughing hysterically. "Holy shit! HOLY SHIT!"

I look over at my mom's face, which is just as stunned as mine.

"Well, I guess there's just more to love."

I walk out of the office on shaky legs. The babies are both healthy, and I'm exactly eight weeks along. Dolly and I rode together, so after telling my mom goodbye, we head home.

When we walk through the front door, we can hear the guys upstairs, playing pool. Holden comes down the stairs when he hears the front door. He smiles at me, pulling me in close for a hug.

"Hey, gorgeous. Where'd you two run off to?"

Dolly pivots away from us, speed-walking down the hallway. Holden frowns, lifting my hand up to his lips to kiss the top of my knuckles.

"Is everything okay?" he asks.

The sonogram picture of the babies is in the back pocket of my jeans. My hands shake when I pull back from him and nod toward the front door.

"Can we take a walk?"

He stares me down with dark eyes, looking right into my soul. He's grown out a closely shaved beard on his face. He's wearing a straw Stetson, and the soft blue T-shirt he put on this morning with Wranglers and boots. It stretches over his broad shoulders deliciously.

"Okay," he says, walking after me.

He loops his finger through the belt loop on the back of my jeans. I lead him outside toward the patch of oak trees by the fence line. It's one of my favorite places for us to sit and talk while watching the sunset. It rained this morning, and the fields are all starting to turn bright green. The horses are grazing in the pasture beside us. The two new foals are following their mamas around as the sun starts to dip down over the horizon.

Holden leans up against the fence, resting his boot on the bottom slat. "What's wrong, Rosie Lou?"

He has every right to be shocked and to react with fear, anxiety, all the things. It took me two weeks to warm up to the idea of becoming a parent unexpectedly.

I reach into my back pocket, pulling out the sonogram pictures. He stares at my outstretched hand, blinking slowly.

"What is it?" he chokes out. "Just tell me."

I exhale, unfolding the pictures. "It's twins ... we're having twins."

His body freezes. He doesn't move for five whole seconds as anxiety crawls up my spine. I start yammering to fill the silence.

"I know we wanted to wait to start having a family. I guess my birth control just failed. I didn't miss any pills. I still think the dress will fit, so as long as I don't throw up on the way down the aisle, people won't even know I'm pregnant, not that it's any of their business anyway—"

He laughs, reaching out for my waist and lifting me up into the air. "Baby ... baby, slow down. You're telling me that you're pregnant? With twins? And everything is okay, healthy?"

He sets me up on the top slat of the fence, holding me in place. I slowly nod, studying his face as his features morph into the biggest smile I've ever seen.

"I thought you were dying from cancer. You've been acting so strange and out of it lately; I've been living in fear that you were about to tell me you had six months to live."

He chokes out the last words, emotion overwhelming him. His eyes are wet and red-rimmed.

He pulls me down off the fence, crushing me into a hug. "Having a baby, two babies, *ten babies* with you will make me so fucking unbelievably happy."

The floodgates of emotion trapped inside me break open. Sobs begin to rack my body as I cry into his chest. He holds me close, brushing his hand over my back in soothing motions until I pull back and look up at him.

"What's wrong, angel? Talk to me." His eyes are squinted with concern, still red and searching my face.

I hiccup, trying to calm down. "I'm just so relieved, so scared, overwhelmed with this happening and the wedding coming up, unprepared, excited. I have so many thoughts and emotions. I've been terrified to tell you, but also feeling so guilty for not telling you sooner."

He nods, wiping a tear from my cheek before tucking my hair behind my ear.

"And I'm just not sure how I feel about becoming a parent after everything that has happened with my family," I whisper.

He spins me around, tugging my back to his chest and wrapping his arms around my front, placing his hands on my stomach. We're facing the sunset as the sky stretches out with pink and purple clouds. The two spring foals are running around, playing with each other.

"You know, the strange thing about this whole thing is that I had a dream two nights ago that we had two kids, and they were identical twin baby girls with red hair just like yours."

I gasp, gripping the top of his hand. "You knew?"

He chuckles into my ear. "No, I didn't. I really thought you were going to tell me you were terminally ill. I've barely been able to sleep, just waiting for you to be ready to tell me. I thought the twin dream was just a cruel fantasy my subconscious created to cope."

I sag against him in relief, feeling better already that he's happy about the news. "I wasn't sure how I felt. I wanted to see the doctor before I told you. Dolly guessed. I've been throwing up every morning."

He spins me again, concern etched between his eyes now. "You should've told me. I would have stayed closer to the house, made you soup, and taken care of you."

I smile up at him, sniffling. "I'll hold you to that. I just needed time, time to accept it. I'm happy now, especially if you think we can handle it."

"Oh, baby, we can handle anything. Your past is not our future. I'm not your father. You and these babies, boys or girls, are already so loved and wanted. You're going to be an exceptional mother."

I bite my lip, pushing up onto my tiptoes to kiss the scar on his jawline. "You're gonna be a DILF."

He chuckles, reaching down to kiss the corner of my mouth. "You're already a MILF. I need to get you a bigger ring so no one misses it."

"If it's any bigger, I'll fall over. They'll see it in space."

"Fuck, I'm so in love with you," he groans, pressing his hips into me.

I turn back around to watch the last glowing light of the sunset.

"I love you more," I whisper, finally feeling an overwhelming sense of peace about the future settling over me.

He wraps his arms tighter around me before whispering in my ear, "Rosie Lou Redford, there's no one on this planet I'd rather raise a family with."

THE END

If you want more of Rosie and Holden, click here or scan the code below to read a bonus scene for Untamed.

For a sneak peak of the first chapter of book two in the Redford Ranch series, Unguarded, keep reading.

Or go ahead and dive into Cash and Monroe's story here.

Scan to read the Untamed bonus scene.

UNGUARDED CHAPTER ONE

CASH

I'm just as pathetically mesmerized by her as everyone else in the swarming crowd. Monroe Blue is onstage, her curly blonde hair and bright blue eyes blown up on the screen. Her silky white corset top and skintight, torn black jeans accentuate every delicious curve of her body. Her red lips arch into a seductive smile as the song ends, the lights fading out. Everyone around me erupts into roaring applause, pleading with her to keep going.

Pathetic.

Although, as close as I am to the stage, she is truly intoxicating. Her presence is almost otherworldly, like she's a step above the rest of humanity.

And the rest of humanity is way too fucking close to me right now.

Obsessed. The entire crowd is *obsessed* with her, along with most of the world.

A man next to me has been sweating and photographing

her since the moment she stepped onstage. I've been keeping an eye on his movements to make sure he stays away from my sister and her friend.

My sister, Dolly, and her friend Rosie insisted we get this close to the stage. I would've preferred lingering near the back, where the exits were clearly in view and I could keep at least three feet of distance between me and other people.

I glance around for the girls, wondering how long it could possibly take for them to go to the restroom and then get a refill. An uneasiness comes over me, but I can't pin down the source of it. My skin feels like it's about to spark a fire. My instincts are never wrong.

The man next to me pushes closer to the front as the band does some kind of instrument tune-up and Monroe Blue takes a sip of water. She's been performing for over an hour without a break. I look down at my phone, seeing a text from my brother about tomorrow's work schedule, and type out a response.

Someone next to me gasps, jerking my attention toward them. My gaze follows hers, up toward the stage. The man who was standing beside me has just hopped the fence and jumped up onto the stage. Time slows as he lunges for Monroe Blue and tackles her to the ground. Her piercing scream tears the night in half.

My instincts kick in, causing me to dart forward. The crowd pushes in closer to see the spectacle. I shove a man out of the way, indifferent to his protest. Monroe Blue is trying to kick her assailant off to get away. I keep expecting someone from her security detail to assist her, to get there before I do.

In the agonizingly long seconds it takes me to part the crowd and leap onto the stage, no one else comes.

The attacker tears her top, and I see the glint of a knife in his hand before I descend on him, my fist crushing his jawline. His grip on her loosens, and I take the opportunity to jerk him off of her.

I rear back and deliver another blow to his face.

In the corner of my eye, I see her crawling away. The man collapses on the stage. I straddle him, my fists landing on different parts of his face over and over again, and blood begins to decorate his features and my knuckles. All I see is red. Boiling-hot rage courses through me at the vile idea of a man laying hands on an unsuspecting woman.

Finally, someone pulls me off of him. I go willingly, thinking he might be about to pass out. He barely moves, shuddering as he coughs up blood.

Little fucker didn't even get in one shot.

The arms holding me back loosen slightly. I wipe the blood on my hands off on my jeans, surveying the area for Monroe Blue, trying to make sure there wasn't an accomplice to the attack. I sigh in relief when she steps out of the back-stage area, bright blue eyes glazed over. I step toward her, but the hands around my shoulders pull me back.

"Let him go!" she commands, her hands shaking.

They instantly obey, releasing me. I take a step closer, keeping a few feet of distance between us. Before I have time to ask her if she's okay, I notice her shirt was torn so far up that the bottom part of her breast and all of her tanned stomach are showing, and she tries to cover herself with trembling fingers in the chilly air.

I slowly unbutton the shirt I'm wearing before shrugging it off my shoulders and stretching it out to her. There's only a little bit of blood and sweat on it. The dog tags around my neck from my time in the Special Forces as a Green Beret are glinting in the stage lights.

She stares at the denim shirt with widened eyes for a few seconds before turning her back to me. At first, I think she's denying the gesture. Then, I realize she wants me to put it on her. I drape it over her slim frame, careful not to touch her skin, which, now that I'm closer to her, I see is glittery.

She turns back around to face me, clutching the shirt closely around herself. Her supple lips part as an angelic sound escapes her mouth.

"You saved my life. What's your name?"

Her raspy, iconic voice cuts me like a knife.

I tilt my cowboy hat toward her. "Cash Redford."

"Cash Redford," she repeats.

It floats off of her tongue, sounding better than anything I've ever heard in my entire life.

"Yes, ma'am."

"We need to get you to a safe place," a man with a clear-wired headset pinned to his shirt says to her, eyeing me suspiciously.

She blinks at me, clutching my shirt closer around her shoulders as a chill runs over my exposed arms and chest. "Of course. I just … I just wanted to say thank you."

I tip my hat at her again. "No thanks needed, ma'am."

Her depthless eyes don't leave mine until her team shuffles her away, toward the back of the stage.

The next thing I know, the sheriff cuffs me, reading out my Miranda rights. I roll my eyes, remaining silent.

Fucking Dixons.

Ever since my father stole his girl thirty years ago, Mayor Dixon has hated our family. The local law enforcement are pawns in his pocket, meaning, even when we're the good guys, like tonight, we go through the wringer to prove it. My older brother killing the mayor's brother didn't help the feud much.

After several hours of questioning, being shipped off to jail, and refusing to speak until my lawyer arrived, they finally let me go with a parting gift—a beating in the back of the cell block to remember the trip by. It's our local sheriff's favorite way of delivering a merciful "warning."

When I get home, I take a much-needed shower, watching the dried blood swirl around the drain. My fists are sore from the blows to the creep's face. The black eye and split lip the deputy gave me will heal in a few days.

They told me that I broke the attacker's nose in three places, along with his jaw. He'll need surgery to look even remotely close to who he used to be.

Good riddance, fucker.

I probably did the human population a favor.

The expression of awe on Monroe Blue's face when I saved her is going to haunt me. Her parted pink lips and heaving breasts were like something from a *Playboy* magazine.

Lust.

When I picture her face, I can sense the lust of a thou-sand men wishing she'd spare them a passing glance.

I collapse on my bed, trying to shove her face out of my mind so I can dream about something else, anything else.

READ BOOK TWO NOW

Read Unguarded—a bodyguard romance, book two of the Redford Ranch series.

Scan to read Unguarded.

ABOUT ARIEL & SOCIAL LINKS

Ariel is a native Texan who lives in Hawaii with her dreamy husband Justin and two kiddos.

She can't resist pairing a damaged heroine with a southern gentleman who manages to tear down her walls one brick at a time. The men in her books will open every door and carry every bag, just like Justin does.

She's eternally indebted to her writing, which rescued her from the darkest place she has ever been.

Her lifelong dream is to one day write all her books in a house by the sea, with a wine cellar that's never empty and her imaginary characters somehow becoming her real-life friends.

Previously published under the pen name Mj Hendrix.

You can keep up with Ariel and her writing/publishing journey through her amazon author profile, social media, or her website.

She's most active on TikTok as @arielhendrixauthor **and Instagram as** @arielhendrixauthor

www.arielhendrix.com

ALSO BY ARIEL HENDRIX

Before exploring the world of rough cowboys, I wrote almost exclusively about sweet, innocent, country boys.

My complete **Good Ol' Boys** interconnected standalone series can be read on kindle unlimited or on paperback.

GOOD OL' BOYS

Falling for Temptation

bad girl/good boy

Seeing Double

nerd boy/popular girl

Seducing the Saint

enemies to lovers/second chance

Kissing Friends

reverse grumpy x sunshine

BEACH READ SERIES

When Summer Ends

single mom beach romance

A NOTE FROM ARIEL

Without fail, every book I write feels like another mountain climbed. I always think it's going to be easier this time, like it's just going to happen, to feel like a walk in the park. But alas, it turns out even after writing seven full length novels it's still a tough ballgame.

I think that's why I love it.

Writing fiction feels is a world I can control. That's a depressing statement, but it's overwhelmingly true. My real life has felt very out of control for a long time now, so I cherish the time I spend in these fictional realms.

Holden, Rosie and the world of Redford Ranch has been so much fun to explore, given that I'm a Texas native and a country girl deep down in my bones. I've written a whole series of 'good' boys, and I really wanted to try my hand at the 'bad' ones. I can't wait to get to know all these wild Redford brothers with you!

I have my fiancé, Justin, to thank for much of the time I spent crafting this novel. Thank you for all the dishes you washed and macaroni noodles you boiled for the kids while I typed out 'just one more scene.'

Thank you for being my forever book boyfriend/cowboy inspiration and for the real life quotes from your lips that ended up in this book. (Example: *"I wish I could just tie a rope around your waist and take you everywhere with me. I want everyone to know you're mine. Forever.*") I love you more than words can say.

I want to thank Casey, my personal assistant, for her endless support, encouragement, and all the many things she had done to help me reach more readers. You are an incredible help to me in this difficult industry!

I want to thank Mai, my sweet best friend, who doesn't really even read romance. She's convinced I'm much better at this gig than I really am. She's my cheerleader even when I want to throw my laptop into rush-hour traffic on thirty-five, and it truly means so much, babe. I love you for it.

-Ariel